Thomas W. Hanshew

Cleek, the Master Detective

Leseklassiker

Thomas W. Hanshew

Cleek, the Master Detective

ISBN/EAN: 9783955630607

Auflage: 1

Erscheinungsjahr: 2013

Erscheinungsort: Bremen, Deutschland

CONTENTS

"OF A TRUTH YOU ARE A CHARMING FELLOW, MONSIEUR....
WHAT A PITY YOU SHOULD BE A POLICE SPY AND UPON SO
HOPELESS A CASE"

LIST OF ILLUSTRATIONS

CHAPTER I
THE AFFAIR OF THE MAN WHO CALLED HIMSELF
HAMILTON CLEEK

The thing wouldn't have happened if any other constable than Collins had been put on point duty at Blackfriars Bridge that morning. For Collins was young, good-looking, and knew it. Nature had gifted him with a susceptible heart and a fond eye for the beauties of femininity. So when he looked round and saw the woman threading her way through the maze of vehicles at "Dead Man's Corner," with her skirt held up just enough to show two twinkling little feet in French shoes, and over them a graceful, willowy figure, and over that an enchanting, if rather too highly tinted, face, with almond eyes and a fluff of shining hair under the screen of a big Parisian hat — that did for him on the spot.

He saw at a glance that she was French — exceedingly French — and he preferred English beauty, as a rule. But, French or English, beauty is beauty, and here undeniably was a perfect type, so he unhesitatingly sprang to her assistance and piloted her safely to the kerb, revelling in her voluble thanks and tingling as she clung timidly but rather firmly to him.

"Sair, I have to give you much gratitude," she said in a pretty, wistful sort of way, as they stepped on to the pavement. Then she dropped her hand from his sleeve, looked up at him, and shyly drooped her head, as if overcome with confusion and surprise at the youth and good looks of him. "Ah, it is nowhere in the world but Londres one finds these delicate attentions, these splendid sergeants de ville," she added, with a sort of sigh. "You are wonnerful, you are mos' wonnerful, you Anglais poliss. Sair, I am a stranger; I know not ze ways of this city of amazement, and if monsieur would so kindly direct me where to find the Abbey of the Ves'minster - "

Before P. C. Collins could tell her that if that were her destination, she was a good deal out of her latitude, indeed, even before she concluded what she was saying, over the rumble of the traffic there rose a thin, shrill, piping sound, which to ears trained to its call possessed a startling significance.

It was the shrilling of a police whistle far off down the Embankment.

"Hullo! That's a call to the man on point," exclaimed Collins, all alert at once. "Excuse me, mum. See you presently. Something's up. One of my mates is a-signalling me."

"Mates, monsieur? Mates? Signalling? I shall not unnerstand the vords. But yes, vat shall that mean — eh?"

"Good Lord, don't bother me now! I — I mean, wait a bit. That's the call to 'head off' some one, and - By George! there he is now, coming head on, the hound, and running like the wind!"

For of a sudden, through a break in the traffic, a scudding figure had sprung into sight. It was the figure of a man in a gray frock-coat and a shining "topper," a well-groomed, well-set-up man, with a small, turned-up moustache and hair of a peculiar reddish shade. As he swung into sight, the distant whistle shrilled again; far off in the distance voices sent up cries of "Head him off!" "Stop that man!" etcetera; then those on the pavement near to the fugitive took up the cry, joined in pursuit, and in a twinkling, what with cabmen, tram-men, draymen, and pedestrians all shouting, there was hubbub enough for Hades.

"A swell pickpocket, I'll lay my life," commented Collins, as he squared himself for an encounter and made ready to leap on the man when he came within gripping distance. "Here! get out of the way, madmazelly. Business before pleasure. And, besides, you're like to get bowled over in the rush. Here, chauffeur!" — this to the driver of a big, black motor-car which swept round the angle of the bridge at that moment, and made as though to scud down the Embankment into the thick of the chase — "pull that thing up sharp! Stop where you are! Dead still! At once, at once, do you hear? We don't want you getting in the way. Now, then" — nodding his head in the direction of the running man — "come on, you bounder; I'm ready for you!"

And, as if he really heard that invitation, and really were eager to accept it, the red-headed man did "come on" with a vengeance. And all the time, "madmazelly," unheeding Collins's advice, stood calmly and silently waiting.

Onward came the runner, with the whole roaring pack in his wake, dodging in and out among the vehicles, "flooring" people who got in his way, scudding, dodging, leaping, like a fox hard pressed by the hounds, until, all of a moment, he spied a break in the traffic, leapt through it, and — then there was mischief. For Collins sprang at him like a cat, gripped two big, strong-as-iron hands on his shoulders, and had him tight and fast.

"Got you, you ass!" snapped he, with a short, crisp, self-satisfied laugh. "None of your blessed squirming now. Keep still. You'll get out of your coffin, you bounder, as soon as out of my grip. Got you, got you! Do you understand?"

The response to this fairly took the wind out of him.

"Of course I do," said the captive gaily; "it's part of the pro-gramme that you should get me. Only, for Heaven's sake, don't spoil the film by remaining inactive, you goat! Struggle with me, handle me roughly, throw me about. Make it look real; make it look as though I actually did get away from you, not as though you let me. You chaps behind there, don't get in the way of the camera — it's in one of those cabs. Now, then, Bobby, don't be wooden! Struggle, struggle, you goat, and save the film!"

"Save the what?" gasped Collins. "Here! Good Lord! Do you mean to say – ?"

"Struggle — struggle — struggle!" cut in the man impa-tiently. "Can't you grasp the situation? It's a put-up thing: the taking of a kinematograph film, a living picture, for the Alhambra to-night! Heavens above, Marguerite, didn't you tell him?"

"Non, non! There was not ze time. You come so quick, I could not. And he — ah, le bon Dieu! — he gif me no chance. Officair, I beg, I entreat of you, make it real! Struggle, fight, keep on ze constant move. Zere!" — something tinkled on the pave-ment with the unmistakable sound of gold — "zere, monsieur, zere is de half-sovereign to pay you for ze trouble, only, for ze lof of goodness, do not pick it up while the instrument, ze camera, he is going. It is ze kinematograph, and you would spoil everything!"

The chop-fallen cry that Collins gave was lost in a roar of laughter from the pursuing crowd.

"Struggle, struggle! Don't you hear, you idiot?" broke in the red-headed man irritably. "You are being devilishly well paid for it, so for goodness' sake make it look real. That's it! Bully boy! Now, once more to the right, then loosen your grip so that I can push you away and make a feint of punching you off. All ready there, Marguerite? Keep a clear space about her, gentlemen. Ready with the motor, chauffeur? All right. Now, then, Bobby, fall back, and mind your eye when I hit out, old chap. One, two, three — here goes!"

With that he pushed the crest-fallen Collins from him, made a feint of punching his head as he reeled back, then sprang toward the spot where the Frenchwoman stood, and gave a finish to the adventure that was highly dramatic and decidedly theatrical. For "mademoiselle," seeing him approach her, struck a pose, threw out her arms, gathered him into them, to the exceeding enjoyment of the laughing throng, then both looked back and behaved as people do on the stage when "pursued," gesticulated extravagantly, and rushing to the waiting motor, jumped into it.

"Many thanks, Bobby; many thanks, everybody!" sang out the red-headed man. "Let her go, chauffeur. The camera men will pick us up again at Whitehall in a few minutes' time."

"Right you are, sir," responded the chauffeur gaily. Then "toot-toot" went the motor-horn as the gentleman in gray closed the door upon himself and his companion, and the vehicle, darting forward, sped down the Embankment in the exact direction whence the man himself had originally come, and, passing directly through that belated portion of the hurrying crowd to whom the end of the adventure was not yet known, flew on and — vanished.

And Collins, stooping to pick up the half-sovereign that had been thrown him, felt that after all it was a poor price to receive for all the jeers and gibes of the assembled onlookers.

"Smart capture, Bobby, wasn't it?" sang out a deriding voice that set the crowd jeering anew. "You'll git promoted, you will! See it in all the evenin' papers — oh, yus! "Orrible hand-to-hand struggle with a desperado. Brave constable has 'arf a quid's worth out of an infuriated ruffian!' My hat! won't your missis be proud when you take her to see that bloomin' film?'"

"Move on, now, move on!" said Collins, recovering his dignity and asserting it with a vim. "Look here, cabby, I don't take it kind of you to laugh like that; they had you just as bad as they had me. Blow that Frenchy! She might have tipped me off before I made such an ass of myself. I don't say that I'd have done it so natural if I had known, but – Hullo! What's that? Blowed if it ain't that blessed whistle again, and another crowd a-pelting this way; and — no! — yes, by Jupiter! a couple of Scotland Yard chaps with 'em. My hat! what do you suppose that means?"

He knew in the next moment. Panting and puffing, a crowd at their heels, and people from all sides stringing out from the pavement and trooping after them, the two "plain-clothes" men came racing through the grinning gathering and bore down on P. C. Collins.

"Hullo, Smathers, you in this, too?" began he, his feelings softened by the knowledge that other arms of the law would figure on that film with him at the Alhambra to-night. "Now, what are you after, you goat? That French lady, or the red-headed party in the gray suit?"

"Yes, yes, of course I am. You heard me signal you to head him off, didn't you?" replied Smathers, looking round and growing suddenly excited when he realized that Collins was empty-handed and that the red-headed man was not there. "Heavens! you never let him get away, did you? You grabbed him, didn't you — eh?"

"Of course I grabbed him. Come out of it. What are you giving me, you josser?" said Collins, with a wink and a grin. "Ain't you found out even yet, you silly? Why, it was only a faked-up thing, the taking of a kinematograph picture for the Alhambra. You and Petrie ought to have been here sooner and got your wages, you goats. I got half a quid for my share when I let him go."

Smathers and Petrie lifted up their voices in one despairing howl.

"When you what?" fairly yelled Smathers. "You fool! You don't mean to tell me that you let them take you in like that — those two? You don't mean to tell me that you had him, had him in your hands, and then let him go? You did? Oh, you seventy-seven kinds of a double-barrelled ass! Had him — think of it! — had him, and let him go! Did yourself out of a share in a reward of two hundred quid when you'd only to shut your hands and hold on to it!"

"Two hundred quid? Two hun – W — what are you talking about? Wasn't it true? Wasn't it a kinematograph picture, after all?"

"No, you fool, no!" howled Smathers, fairly dancing with despair. "Oh, you blithering idiot! You ninety-seven varieties of a fool! Do you know who you had in your hands? Do you know who you let go? It was that devil 'Forty Faces,' the 'Vanishing Cracksman,' 'The Man Who Calls Himself Hamilton Cleek'; and the woman was his pal, his confederate, his blessed stool pigeon, 'Margot, the Queen of the Apaches'; and she came over from Paris to help him in that clean scoop of Lady Dresmer's jewels last week!"

"Heavens!" gulped Collins, too far gone to say anything else, too deeply dejected to think of anything but that he had had the man for whom Scotland Yard had been groping for a year; the man over whom all England, all France, all Germany wondered, close shut in the grip of his hands and then had let him go. He was the biggest and the boldest criminal the police had ever had to cope with, the almost supernatural genius of crime, who defied all systems, laughed at all laws, mocked at all the Vidocqs, and Lupins, and Sherlock Holmeses, whether amateur or professional, French or English, German or American, that ever had or ever could be pitted against him, and who, for sheer devilry, for diabolical ingenuity, and for colossal impudence, as well as for a nature-bestowed power that was simply amazing, had not his match in all the universe.

Who or what he really was, whence he came, whether he was English, Irish, French, German, Yankee, Canadian, Italian, or Dutchman, no man knew and no man might ever hope to know unless he himself chose to reveal it. In his many encounters with the police he had assumed the speech, the characteristics, and, indeed, the facial attributes of each in turn, and assumed them with an ease and a perfection that were simply marvellous and had gained for him the sobriquet of "Forty Faces" among the police and of the "Vanishing Cracksman" among the scribes and reporters of newspaperdom. That he came in time to possess another name than these was due to his own whim and caprice, his own bald, unblushing impudence; for, of a sudden, whilst London was in a fever of excitement and all the newspapers up in arms over one of his most daring and successful coups, he chose to write boldly to both editors and police complaining that the title given him by each was both vulgar and cheap.

"You would not think of calling a great violinist like Paganini a 'fiddler,'" he wrote; "why, then, should you degrade me with the coarse term of 'cracksman'? I claim to be as much an artist in my profession as Paganini was in his, and I claim also a like courtesy from you. So, then, if in the future it becomes necessary to allude to me, and I fear it often will, I shall be obliged if you do so as 'The Man Who Calls Himself Hamilton Cleek.' In return for the courtesy, gentlemen, I promise to alter my mode of procedure, to turn over a new leaf, as it were, to give you at all times hereafter distinct information, in advance, of such places as I select for the field of my operations, and of the time when I shall pay my respects to them, and, on the morning after each such visit, to bestow some small portion of the loot upon Scotland Yard as a souvenir of the event."

And to that remarkable programme he rigidly adhered from that time forth, always giving the police twelve hours' notice, always evading their traps and snares, always carrying out his plans in spite of them, and always, on the morning after, sending some trinket or trifle to Superintendent Narkom at Scotland Yard.

7

This trifle would be in a little pink cardboard box, tied up with rose-coloured ribbon, and marked, "With the compliments of The Man Who Calls Himself Hamilton Cleek."

The detectives of the United Kingdom, the detectives of the Continent, the detectives of America — each and all had measured swords with him, tried wits with him, spread snares and laid traps for him, and each and all had retired from the field vanquished.

And this was the man that he, Police Constable Samuel James Collins, had actually had in his hands, nay, in his very arms, and then had given up for half a sovereign and let go!

"Oh, so help me! You make my head swim, Smathers, that you do!" he managed to say at last. "I had him — I had the Vanishing Cracksman in my blessed paws and then went and let that French hussy – But look here; I say, now, how do you know it was him? Nobody can go by his looks; so how do you know?"

"Know, you footler!" growled Smathers disgustedly. "Why shouldn't I know when I've been after him ever since he left Scotland Yard half an hour ago?"

"Left what? My hat! You ain't a-going to tell me that he's been there? When? Why? What for?"

"To leave one of his blessed notices, the dare-devil. What a detective he'd 'a' made, wouldn't he, if he'd only a-turned his attention that way, and been on the side of the law instead of against it? He walked in bold as brass, sat down and talked with the superintendent over some cock-and-bull yarn about a 'Black Hand' letter that he said had been sent to him, and asked if he couldn't have police protection whilst he was in town. It wasn't until after he'd left that the superintendent he sees a note on the chair where the blighter had been sitting, and when he opened it, there it was in black and white, something like this:

"The list of presents that have been sent for the wedding tomorrow of Sir Horace Wyvern's eldest daughter make interesting reading, particularly that part which describes the jewels sent — no doubt as a tribute to her father's position as the greatest brain specialist in the world – from the Austrian Court and the Continental principalities. The care of such gems is too great a responsibility for the bride. I propose, therefore, to relieve her of it tonight, and to send you the customary souvenir of the event tomorrow morning. Yours faithfully,

"The Man Who Calls Himself Hamilton Cleek.

"That's how I know, dash you! Superintendent sent me out after him, hot foot; and after a bit I picked him up in the Strand, toddling along with that French hussy as cool as you please. But, blow him! he must have eyes all round his head, for he saw me just as soon as I saw him, and he and Frenchy separated like a shot. She hopped into a taxi and flew off in one direction; he dived into the crowd and bolted in another, and before you could say Jack Robinson he was doubling and twisting, jumping into cabs and jumping out again – all to gain time, of course, for the woman to do what he'd put her up to doing – and leading me the devil's own chase through the devil's own tangles till he was ready to bunk for the Embankment. And you let him go, you blooming footler! Had him and let him go, and chucked away a third of £200 for the price of half a quid!"

And long after Smathers and Petrie had left him, the wondering crowd had dispersed, and point duty at "Dead Man's Corner" was just point duty again and nothing more, P. C. Collins stood there, chewing the cud of bitter reflection over those words and trying to reckon up just how many pounds and how much glory had been lost to him.

II

"But, damme, sir, the thing's an outrage! I don't mince my words, Mr. Narkom. I say plump and plain the thing's an outrage, a disgrace to the police, an indignity upon the community at large; and for Scotland Yard to permit itself to be defied, bamboozled, mocked at in this appalling fashion by a paltry burglar – "

"Uncle, dear, pray don't excite yourself in this manner. I am

9

quite sure that if Mr. Narkom could prevent the things – "

"Hold your tongue, Ailsa. I will not be interfered with! It's time that somebody spoke out plainly and let this establishment know what the public has a right to expect of it. What do I pay my rates and taxes for — and devilish high ones they are, too, b'gad — if it's not to maintain law and order and the proper protection of property? And to have the whole blessed country terrorized, the police defied, and people's houses invaded with impunity by a gutter-bred brute of a cracksman is nothing short of a scandal and a shame! Call this sort of tomfoolery being protected by the police? God bless my soul! one might as well be in the charge of a parcel of doddering old women and be done with it!"

It was an hour and a half after that exciting affair at "Dead Man's Corner." The scene was Superintendent Narkom's private room at headquarters, the dramatis personæ, Mr. Maverick Narkom himself, Sir Horace Wyvern, and Miss Ailsa Lorne, his niece, a slight, fair-haired, extremely attractive girl of twenty. She was the only and orphaned daughter of a much-loved sister, who, up till a year ago, had known nothing more exciting in the way of "life" than that which is to be found in a small village in Suffolk and falls to the lot of an underpaid vicar's only child. A railway accident had suddenly deprived her of both parents, throwing her wholly upon her own resources without a penny in the world. Sir Horace had gracefully come to the rescue and given her a home and a refuge, being doubly repaid for it by the affection and care she gave him and the manner in which she assumed control of a household which, hitherto, had been left wholly to the attention of servants. Lady Wyvern had long been dead, and her two daughters were of that type which devotes itself entirely to the pleasures of society and the demands of the world. A regular pepperbox of a man, testy, short-tempered, exacting, Sir Horace had flown headlong to Superintendent Narkom's office as soon as that gentleman's note, telling him of The Vanishing Cracksman's latest threat, had been delivered, and, on Miss Lorne's advice, had withheld all news of it from the members of his household, and brought her with him.

"I tell you that Scotland Yard must do something — must!

must! must!" stormed he as Narkom, resenting that stigma upon the institution, puckered up his lips and looked savage. "That fellow has always kept his word, always, in spite of your precious band of muffs, and if you let him keep it this time, when there's upward of £40,000 worth of jewels in the house, it will be nothing less than a national disgrace, and you and your wretched collection of bunglers will be covered with deserved ridicule."

Narkom swung round, smarting under these continued taunts, these "flings" at the efficiency of his prided department, his nostrils dilated, his temper strained to the breaking-point.

"Well, he won't keep it this time — I promise you that!" he rapped out sharply. "Sooner or later every criminal, no matter how clever, meets his Waterloo, and this shall be his! I'll take this affair in hand myself, Sir Horace. I'll not only send the pick of my men to guard the jewels, but I'll go with them; and if that fellow crosses the threshold of Wyvern House to-night, by the Lord, I'll have him. He will have to be the devil himself to get away from me! Miss Lorne," recollecting himself and bowing apologetically, "I ask your pardon for this strong language — my temper got the better of my manners."

"It does not matter, Mr. Narkom, so that you preserve my cousin's wedding gifts from that appalling man," she answered, with a gentle inclination of the head and with a smile that made the superintendent think she must certainly be the most beautiful creature in all the world, it so irradiated her face and added to the magic of her glorious eyes. "It does not matter what you say, what you do, so long as you accomplish that."

"And I will accomplish it, as I'm a living man, I will! You may go home feeling assured of that. Look for my men some time before dusk, Sir Horace. I will arrive later. They will come in one at a time. See that they are admitted by the area door, and that, once in, not one of them leaves the house again before I put in an appearance. I'll look them over when I arrive to be sure that there's no wolf in sheep's clothing amongst them. With a fellow like that, a diabolical rascal with a diabolical gift for impersonation, one can't be too careful. Meantime, it is just as well not to have confided this news to your daughters, who, naturally, would be nervous and upset; but I assume that you have taken some one of the servants into your confidence, in order that nobody may pass them and enter the house under any pretext whatsoever?"

"No, I have not. Miss Lorne advised against it, and, as I am always guided by her, I said nothing of the matter to anybody."

"Was that wrong, do you think, Mr. Narkom?" queried Ailsa anxiously. "I feared that if they knew they might lose their heads, and that my cousins, who are intensely nervous and highly emotional, might hear of it, and add to our difficulties by becoming hysterical and demanding our attention at a time when we ought to be giving every moment to watching for the possible arrival of that man. And as he has always lived up to the strict letter of his dreadful promises heretofore, I knew that he was not to be expected before nightfall. Besides, the jewels are locked up in the safe in Sir Horace's consulting-room, and his assistant, Mr. Merfroy, has promised not to leave the room for one instant before we return."

"Oh, well, that's all right, then. I dare say there is very little likelihood of our man getting in whilst you and Sir Horace are here, and taking such a risk as stopping in the house until nightfall to begin his operations. Still, it was hardly wise, and I should advise hurrying back as fast as possible and taking at least one servant — the one you feel least likely to lose his head — into your confidence, Sir Horace, and putting him on the watch for my men. Otherwise, keep the matter as quiet as you have done, and look for me about nine o'clock. And rely upon this as a certainty: The Vanishing Cracksman will never get away with even one of those jewels if he enters that house to-night, and never get out of it unshackled!"

PULLING THEIR HAIR — RUBBING THEIR FACES WITH A CLEAN HANDKERCHIEF IN QUEST OF ANY TRACE OF "MAKE-UP" OR DISGUISE OF ANY SORT

With that, he suavely bowed his visitors out and rang up the pick of his men without an instant's delay.

Promptly at nine o'clock he arrived, as he had promised, at Wyvern House, and was shown into Sir Horace's consulting-room, where Sir Horace himself and Miss Lorne were awaiting him and keeping close watch before the locked door of a communicating apartment in which sat the six men who had preceded him. He went in and put them all and severally through a rigid examination in quest of any trace of "make-up" or disguise of any sort, examining their badges and the marks on the handcuffs they carried with them to make sure that they bore the sign which he himself had scratched upon them in the privacy of his own room a couple of hours ago.

"No mistake about this lot," he announced, with a smile. "Has anybody else entered or attempted to enter the house?"

"Not a soul," replied Miss Lorne. "I didn't trust anybody to do the watching, Mr. Narkom. I watched myself."

"Good. Where are the jewels? In that safe?"

"No," replied Sir Horace. "They are to be exhibited in the picture gallery for the benefit of the guests at the wedding breakfast to-morrow, and as Miss Wyvern wished to superintend the arrangement of them herself, and there would be no time for that in the morning, she and her sister are in there laying them out at this moment. As I could not prevent that without telling them what we have to dread, I did not protest against it; but if you think it will be safer to return them to the safe after my daughters have gone to bed, Mr. Narkom - "

"Not at all necessary. If our man gets in, their lying there in full view like that will prove a tempting bait, and — well, he'll find there's a hook behind it. I shall be there waiting for him. Now go and join the ladies, you and Miss Lorne, and act as though nothing out of the common was in the wind. My men and I will stop here, and you had better put out the light and lock us in, so that there's no danger of anybody finding out that we are here. No doubt Miss Wyvern and her sister will go to bed earlier than usual on this particular occasion. Let them do so. Send the servants to bed, too. You and Miss Lorne go to your beds at the same time as the others — or, at least, let them think that you have done so; then come down and let us out."

To this Sir Horace assented, and, taking Miss Lorne with him, went at once to the picture gallery and joined his daughters, with whom they remained until eleven o'clock. Promptly at that hour, however, the house was locked up, the bride-elect and her sister went to bed, the servants having already gone to theirs, and stillness settled down over the darkened house. At the end of a dozen minutes, however, it was faintly disturbed by the sound of slippered feet coming along the passage outside the consulting-room, then a key slipped into the lock, the door was opened, the light switched on, and Sir Horace and Miss Lorne appeared before the eager watchers.

"Now, then, lively, my men, look sharp!" whispered Narkom. "A man to each window and each staircase, so that nobody may go up or down or in or out without dropping into the arms of one of you. Confine your attention to this particular floor, and if you hear anybody coming, lay low until he's within reach, and you can drop on him before he bolts. Is this the door of the picture gallery, Sir Horace?"

"Yes," answered Sir Horace, as he fitted a key to the lock. "But surely you will need more men than you have brought, Mr. Narkom, if it is your intention to guard every window individually, for there are four to this room — see!"

With that he swung open the door, switched on the electric light, and Narkom fairly blinked at the dazzling sight that confronted him. Three long tables, laden with crystal and silver, cut glass and jewels, and running the full length of the room, flashed and scintillated under the glare of the electric bulbs which encircled the cornice of the gallery and clustered in luminous splendour in the crystal and frosted silver of a huge central chandelier. Spread out on the middle one of these, a dazzle of splintered rainbows, a very plain of living light, lay caskets and cases, boxes and trays, containing those royal gifts of which the newspapers had made so much and the Vanishing Cracksman had sworn to make so few.

Mr. Narkom went over and stood beside the glittering mass, resting his hand against the table and feasting his eyes upon all that opulent splendour.

"God bless my soul! it's superb, it's amazing," he commented. "No wonder the fellow is willing to take risks for a prize like this. You are a splendid temptation, a gorgeous bait, you beauties; but the fish that snaps at you will find that there's a nasty hook underneath in the shape of Maverick Narkom. Never mind the many windows, Sir Horace. Let him come in by them, if that's his plan. I'll never leave these things for one instant between now and the morning. Good-night, Miss Lorne. Go to bed and to sleep. You do the same, Sir Horace. My 'lay' is here!"

With that he stooped and, lifting the long drapery which covered the table and swept down in heavy folds to the floor, crept out of sight under it, and let it drop back into place again.

"Switch off the light and go," he called to them in a low-sunk voice. "Don't worry yourselves, either of you. Go to bed, and to sleep if you can."

"As if we could," answered Miss Lorne agitatedly. "I shan't be able to close an eyelid. I'll try, of course, but I know I shall not succeed. Come, uncle, come! Oh, do be careful, Mr. Narkom; and if that horrible man does come – "

"I'll have him, so help me God!" he vowed. "Switch off the light, and shut the door as you go out. This is 'Forty Faces.' Waterloo at last."

And in another moment the light snicked out, the door closed, and he was alone in the silent room.

For ten or a dozen minutes not even the bare suggestion of a noise disturbed the absolute stillness; then, of a sudden, his trained ear caught a faint sound that made him suck in his breath and rise on his elbow, the better to listen. The sound came, not from without the house, but from within, from the dark hall where he had stationed his men. As he listened he was conscious that some living creature had approached the door, touched the handle, and by the swift, low rustle and the sound of hard breathing, that it had been pounced upon and seized. He scrambled out from beneath the table, snicked on the light, whirled open the door, and was in time to hear the irritable voice of Sir Horace say, testily, "Don't make an ass of yourself by your over-zealousness. I've only come down to have a word with Mr. Narkom," and to see him standing on the threshold, grotesque in a baggy suit of striped pyjamas, with one wrist enclosed as in a steel band by the gripped fingers of Petrie.

"Why didn't you say it was you, sir?" exclaimed that crest-fallen individual, as the flashing light made manifest his mistake. "When I heard you first, and see you come up out of that back passage, I made sure it was him; and if you'd a-struggled, I'd have bashed your head as sure as eggs."

"Thank you for nothing," he responded testily. "You might have remembered, however, that the man's first got to get into the place before he can come downstairs. Mr. Narkom," turning to the superintendent, "I was just getting into bed when I thought of something I'd neglected to tell you; and as my niece is sitting in her room with the door open, and I wasn't anxious to parade myself before her in my night clothes, I came down by the back staircase. I don't know how in the world I came to overlook it, but I think you ought to know that there's a way of getting into the picture gallery without using either the windows or the stairs, and that way ought to be both searched and guarded."

"Where is it? What is it? Why in the world didn't you tell me in the first place?" exclaimed Narkom irritably, as he glanced round the place searchingly. "Is it a panel? a secret door? or what? This is an old house, and old houses are sometimes a very nest of such things."

"Happily, this one isn't. It's a modern innovation, not an ancient relic, that offers the means of entrance in this case. A Yankee occupied this house before I bought it from him, one of those blessed shivery individuals his country breeds, who can't stand a breath of cold air indoors after the passing of the autumn. The wretched man put one of those wretched American inflictions, a hot-air furnace, in the cellar, with huge pipes running to every room in the house, great tin monstrosities bigger round than a man's body, ending in openings in the wall, with what they call 'registers' to let the heat in or shut it out as they please. I didn't have the wretched contrivance removed or those blessed 'registers' plastered up. I simply had them papered over when the rooms were done up (there's one over there near that settee), and if a man got into this house, he could get into that furnace thing and hide in one of those flues until he got ready to crawl up it as easily as not. It struck me that perhaps it would be as well for you to examine that furnace and those flues before matters go any further."

"Of course it would. Great Scott! Sir Horace, why didn't you think to tell me of this thing before?" said Narkom excitedly. "The fellow may be in it at this minute. Come, show me the wretched thing."

"It's in the cellar. We shall have to go down the kitchen stairs, and I haven't a light."

"Here's one," said Petrie, unhitching a bull's-eye from his belt and putting it into Narkom's hand. "Better go with Sir Horace at once, sir. Leave the door of the gallery open and the light on. Fish and me will stand guard over the stuff till you come back, so in case the man is in one of them flues and tries to bolt out at this end, we can nab him before he can get to the windows."

"A good idea," commented Narkom. "Come on, Sir Horace. Is this the way?"

"Yes, but you'll have to tread carefully, and mind you don't fall over anything. A good deal of my paraphernalia — bottles, retorts, and the like — is stored in the little recess at the foot of the staircase, and my assistant is careless and leaves things lying about."

Evidently the caution was necessary, for a minute or so after they had disappeared behind the door leading to the kitchen stairway, Petrie and his colleagues heard a sound as of something being overturned and smashed, and laughed softly to themselves. Evidently, too, the danger of the furnace had been grossly exaggerated by Sir Horace, for when, a few minutes later, the door opened and closed, and Narkom's men, glancing toward it, saw the figure of their chief reappear, it was plain that he was in no good temper. His features were knotted up into a scowl, and he swore audibly as he snapped the shutter over the bull's-eye and handed it back to Petrie.

"Nothing worth looking into, superintendent?"

"No, not a thing!" he replied. "The silly old josser! pulling me down there amongst the coals and rubbish for an insane idea like that! Why, the flues wouldn't admit the passage of a child; and, even then, there's a bend, an abrupt 'elbow,' that nothing but a cat could crawl up. And that's a man who's an authority on the human brain! I sent the old silly back to bed by the way he came, and if – "

There he stopped, stopped short, and sucked in his breath with a sharp, wheezing sound. For, of a sudden, a swift pattering footfall and a glimmer of moving light had sprung into being and drawn his eyes upward. There, overhead, was Miss Lorne coming down the stairs from the upper floor in a state of nervous excitement, with a bedroom candle in her shaking hand, a loose gown flung on over her nightdress, and her hair streaming over her shoulders in glorious disarray.

He stood and looked at her, with ever-quickening breath, with ever-widening eyes, as though the beauty of her had wakened some dormant sense whose existence he had never suspected, as though, until now, he had never known how fair it was possible for a woman to be, how much to be desired. And whilst he was so looking she reached the foot of the staircase and came pantingly toward him.

"Oh, Mr. Narkom, what was it – that noise I heard?" she said in a tone of deepest agitation. "It sounded like a struggle, like the noise of something breaking, and I dressed as hastily as I could and came down. Did he come? Has he been here? Have you caught him? Oh! why don't you answer me, instead of staring at me like this? Can't you see how nervous, how frightened I am? Dear Heaven! will no one tell me what has happened?"

"Nothing has happened, Miss," answered Petrie, catching her eye as she flashed round on him. "You'd better go back to bed. Nobody's been here but Sir Horace. The noise you heard was me a-grabbing of him, and he and Mr. Narkom a-tumbling over something as they went down to look at the furnace."

"Furnace? What furnace? What are you talking about?" she cried agitatedly. "What do you mean by saying that Sir Horace came down?"

"Only what the superintendent himself will tell you, Miss, if you ask him. Sir Horace came downstairs in his pyjamas a few minutes ago to say as he'd recollected about the flues of the furnace in the cellar being big enough to hold a man, and then him and Mr. Narkom went below to have a look at it."

She gave a sharp and sudden cry, and her face went as pale as a dead face.

"Sir Horace came down?" she repeated, moving back a step and leaning heavily against the banister. "Sir Horace came down to look at the furnace? We have no furnace!"

"What?"

"We have no furnace, I tell you, and Sir Horace did not come down. He is up there still. I know, because I feared for his safety, and when he went to his room I locked him in!"

"Superintendent!" The word was voiced by every man present and six pairs of eyes turned toward Narkom with a look of despairing comprehension.

"Get to the cellar. Head the man off! It's he, the Cracksman!" he shouted out. "Find him! Get him! Nab him, if you have to turn the house upside down!"

They needed no second bidding, for each man grasped the situation instantly, and in a twinkling there was a veritable pandemonium. Shouting and scrambling like a band of madmen, they lurched to the door, whirled it open, and went flying down the staircase to the kitchen and so to a discovery which none might have foreseen. For almost as they entered they saw lying on the floor a suit of striped pyjamas, and close to it, gagged, bound, helpless, trussed up like a goose that was ready for the oven, gyves on his wrists, gyves on his ankles, their chief, their superintendent, Mr. Maverick Narkom, in a state of collapse and with all his outer clothing gone!

"After him! After that devil, and a thousand pounds to the man that gets him!" he managed to gasp as they rushed to him and ripped loose the gag. "He was here when we came! He has been in the house for hours. Get him! get him! get him!"

They surged from the room and up the stairs like a pack of stampeded animals; they raced through the hall and bore down on the picture gallery in a body, and, whirling open the now closed door, went tumbling headlong in.

The light was still burning. At the far end of the room a window was wide open, and the curtains of it fluttered in the wind. A collection of empty cases and caskets lay on the middle table, but man and jewels were alike gone! Once again the Vanishing Cracksman had lived up to his promise, up to his reputation, up to the very letter of his name, and for all Mr. Maverick Narkom's care and shrewdness, "Forty Faces" had "turned the trick," and Scotland Yard was "done!"

III

Through all the night its best men sought him, its dragnets fished for him, its tentacles groped into every hole and corner of London in quest of him, but sought and fished and groped in vain. They might as well have hoped to find last summer's partridges or last winter's snow as any trace of him. He had vanished as mysteriously as he had appeared, and no royal jewels graced the display of Miss Wyvern's wedding gifts on the morrow.

But it was fruitful of other "gifts," fruitful of an even greater surprise, that "morrow." For the first time since the day he had given his promise, no "souvenir" from "The Man Who Called Himself Hamilton Cleek," no part of last night's loot came to Scotland Yard; and it was while the evening papers were making screaming "copy" and glaring headlines out of this that the surprise in question came to pass.

Miss Wyvern's wedding was over, the day and the bride had gone, and it was half-past ten at night, when Sir Horace, answering a hurry call from headquarters, drove post haste to Superintendent Narkom's private room, and, passing in under a red-and-green lamp which burned over the doorway, met that "surprise."

Maverick Narkom was there alone, standing beside his desk. The curtains of his window were drawn and pinned together, and at his elbow was an unlighted lamp of violet-coloured glass. Narkom turned as his visitor entered and made an open-handed gesture toward something which lay before him.

"Look here," he said laconically, "what do you think of this?"

Sir Horace moved forward and looked; then stopped and gave a sort of wondering cry. The electric bulbs overhead struck a glare of light on the surface of the desk, and there, spread out on the shining oak, lay a part of the royal jewels that had been stolen from Wyvern House last night.

"Narkom! You got him then, got him after all?"

"No, I did not get him. I doubt if any man could, if he chose not to be found," said Narkom bitterly. "I did not recover these jewels by any act of my own. He sent them to me; gave them up voluntarily."

"Gave them up? After he had risked so much to get them? God bless my soul, what a man! Why, there must be quite half here of what he took."

"There is half — an even half. He sent them to-night, and with them this letter. Look at it, and you will understand why I sent for you and asked you to come alone."

Sir Horace read:

There's some good in even the devil, I suppose, if one but knows how to reach it and stir it up.

I have lived a life of crime from my very boyhood because I couldn't help it, because it appealed to me, because I glory in risks and revel in dangers. I never knew, I never thought, never cared, where it would lead me, but I looked into the gateway of heaven last night, and I can't go down the path to hell any longer. Here is an even half of Miss Wyvern's jewels. If you and her father would have me hand over the other half to you, and would have The Vanishing Cracksman disappear forever, and a useless life converted into a useful one, you have only to say so to make it an accomplished thing. All I ask in return is your word of honour (to be given to me by signal) that you will send for Sir Horace Wyvern to be at your office at eleven o'clock to-night, and that you and he will grant me a private interview unknown to any other living being. A red-and-green lantern hung over the doorway leading to your office will be the signal that you agree, and a violet light in your window will be the pledge of Sir Horace Wyvern. When these two signals, these two pledges, are given, I shall come in and hand over the remainder of the jewels, and you will have looked for the first time in your life upon the real face of The Man Who Calls Himself Hamilton Cleek.

"God bless my soul! what an amazing creature, what an astounding request!" exclaimed Sir Horace, as he laid the letter down. "Willing to give up £20,000 worth of jewels for the mere sake of a private interview! What on earth can be his object? And why should he include me?"

"I don't know," said Narkom in reply. "It's worth something, at all events, to be rid of 'The Vanishing Cracksman' for good and all; and he says that it rests with us to do that. It's close to eleven now. Shall we give him the pledge he asks, Sir Horace? My signal is already hung out; shall we agree to the conditions and give him yours?"

"Yes, yes, by all means," Sir Horace made answer. And, lighting the violet lamp, Narkom flicked open the pinned curtains and set it in the window.

For ten minutes nothing came of it, and the two men, talking in whispers while they waited, began to grow nervous. Then somewhere in the distance a clock started striking eleven, and, without so much as a warning sound, the door flashed open, flashed shut again, a voice that was undeniably the voice of breeding and refinement said quietly, "Gentlemen, my compliments. Here are the diamonds and here am I!" and the figure of a man, faultlessly dressed, faultlessly mannered, and with the clear-cut features of the born aristocrat, stood in the room.

His age might lie anywhere between twenty-five and thirty-five, his eyes were straight looking and clear, his fresh, clean-shaven face was undeniably handsome, and, whatever his origin, whatever his history, there was something about him, in look, in speech, in bearing, that mutely stood sponsor for the thing called "birth."

"God bless my soul!" exclaimed Sir Horace, amazed and appalled to find the reality so widely different from the image he had drawn. "What monstrous juggle is this? Why, man alive, you're a gentleman! Who are you? What's driven you to a dog's life like this?"

"A natural bent, perhaps; a supernatural gift, certainly, Sir Horace," he made reply. "Look here. Could any man resist the temptation to use it when he was endowed by Nature with the power to do this?" His features seemed to writhe and knot and assume in as many moments a dozen different aspects. "I've had the knack of doing that since the hour I could breathe. Could any man 'go straight' with a fateful gift like that if the laws of Nature said that he should not?"

"And do they say that?"

"That's what I want you to tell me. That's why I have requested this interview. I want you to examine me, Sir Horace, to put me through those tests you use to determine the state of mind of the mentally fit and mentally unfit. I want to know if it is my fault that I am what I am, and if it is myself I have to fight in future or the devil that lives within me. I'm tired of wallowing in the mire. A woman's eyes have lit the way to heaven for me. I want to climb up to her, to win her, be worthy of her, and to stand beside her in the light."

"Her? What 'her'?"

"That's my business, Mr. Narkom, and I'll take no man into my confidence regarding that."

"Yes, my friend, but 'Margot'?"

"I'm done with her! We broke last night, when I returned, and she learned – Never mind what she learned! I'm done with her, done with the lot of them. My life is changed forever."

"In the name of Heaven, man, who and what are you?"

"Cleek – just Cleek: let it go at that," he made reply. "Whether it's my name or not is no man's business; who I am, what I am, whence I came, is no man's business, either. Cleek will do, Cleek of the Forty Faces. Never mind the past; my fight is with the future, and so – Examine me, Sir Horace, and let me know if I or Fate's to blame for what I am."

"Absolutely Fate," Sir Horace said, when, after a long examination, the man put the question to him again. "It is the criminal brain fully developed, horribly pronounced. God help you, my poor fellow; but a man simply could not be other than a thief and a criminal with an organ like that. There's no hope for you to escape your natural bent except by death. You can't be honest. You can't rise. You never will rise: it's useless to fight against it!"

"I will fight against it! I will rise! I will! I will! I will!" he cried out vehemently. "There is a way to put such craft and cunning to account; a way to fight the devil with his own weapons and crush him under the weight of his own gifts, and that way I'll take!

"Mr. Narkom" – he whirled and walked toward the superintendent, his hand outstretched, his eager face aglow – "Mr. Narkom, help me! Take me under your wing. Give me a start, give me a chance, give me a lift on the way up!"

"Good heaven, man, you – you don't mean - ?"

"I do. I do. So help me Heaven, I do. All my life I've fought against the law, now let me switch over and fight with it. I'm tired of being Cleek, the thief; Cleek, the burglar. Make me Cleek, the detective, and let us work together, hand in hand, for a common cause and for the public good. Will you, Mr. Narkom? Will you?"

"Will I? Won't I!" said Narkom, springing forward and gripping his hand. "Jove! what a detective you will make. Bully boy! Bully boy!"

"It's a compact, then?"

"It's a compact — Cleek."

"Thank you," he said in a choked voice. "You've given me my chance; now watch me live up to it. The Vanishing Cracksman has vanished forever, Mr. Narkom, and it's Cleek, the detective — Cleek of the Forty Faces from this time on. Now, give me your riddles, I'll solve them one by one."

CHAPTER II
THE PROBLEM OF THE RED CRAWL

It was half-past two o'clock in the morning of July 25, when the constable on duty at the head of Clarges Street, Piccadilly, was startled to see a red limousine swing into that quiet thoroughfare from the Curzon Street end, come to an abrupt halt, and a man who had every appearance of a sailor alight therefrom, fish a key from his pocket, and admit himself to a certain house. This house for more than a year had been known to be occupied only by one Captain Burbage, a retired seaman of advanced years, his elderly housekeeper, a deaf and dumb maid-of-all-work, and a snub-nosed, ginger-haired young chap of about nineteen — as pure a specimen of the genus Cockney as you could pick up anywhere from Bow Church to the Guildhall — who acted as a sort of body servant to the aged captain, and was known by the expressive name of "Dollops."

"Don't like the goings-on at that house at all," commented the policeman in a sort of growl. "All sorts of parties coming and going at all hours of the night. Reported it more than once, I have; and yet Superintendent Narkom says there's nothing in it and it needn't be watched. I wonder why?"

He wouldn't have wondered any longer could he have looked into the hall of the house at that moment; for the man who had just entered had no sooner closed the lower door than one above flashed open, a stream of light gushed down the stairs, and a calm, well-modulated voice said serenely: "Come right up, Mr. Narkom. I knew it would be you before your motor turned the corner. I'd know the purr of your machine among a thousand."

"Fancy that!" said Narkom, as he removed the hot wig and beard he wore, and went up the stairs two at a time. "My dear Cleek, what an abnormal animal you are! Had you" — entering the room where his now famous ally (divested of the disguise which served for the rôle of "Captain Burbage") stood leaning against the mantelpiece and calmly smoking a cigarette — "had you by any chance a fox among your forbears?"

"Oh, no. The night is very still, the back window is open, and there's a trifling irregularity in the operations of your detonator: that's all. But tell me, you've got something else for me; something important enough to bring you racing here at top speed in the middle of the night, so to speak?"

"Yes. An amazing something. It's a letter. It arrived at headquarters by the nine o'clock post to-night — or, rather, it's last night now. Merton, of course, forwarded it to my home; but I was away — did not return until after one, or I should have been here sooner. It's not an affair for 'the Yard' this time, Cleek; and I tell you frankly I do not like it."

"Why?"

"Well, it's from Paris. If you were to accept it, you — well, you know what dangers Paris would have for you above all men. There's that she-devil you broke with, that woman Margot. You know what she swore, what she wrote back when you sent her that letter telling her that you were done with her and her lot, and warning her never to set foot on English soil again? If you were to run foul of her; if she were ever to get any hint to your real identity - "

"She can't. She knows no more of my real history than you do; no more than I actually know of hers. Our knowledge of each other began when we started to 'pal' together; it ended when we split, eighteen months ago. But about this letter? What is it? Why do you say that you don't like it?"

"Well, to begin with, I'm afraid it is some trap of hers to decoy you over there, get you into some unknown place - "

"There are no 'unknown places' in Paris so far as I am concerned. I know every hole and corner of it, from the sewers on. I know it as well as I know London, as well as I know Berlin — New York — Vienna — Edinburgh — Rome. You couldn't lose me or trap me in any one of them. Is that the letter in your hand? Good — then read it, please."

Narkom, obeying the request, read:

"To the Superintendent of Police, Scotland Yard,

"Distinguished Monsieur:

"Of your grace and pity, I implore you to listen to the prayer of an unhappy man whose honour, whose reason, whose very life are in deadly peril, not alone of 'The Red Crawl,' but of things he may not even name, dare not commit to writing, lest this letter should go astray. It shall happen, monsieur, that the whole world shall hear with amazement of that most marvellous 'Cleek' — that great reader of riddles and unmasker of evildoers who, in the past year, has made the police department of England the envy of all nations; and it shall happen also that I who dare not appeal to the police of France appeal to the mercy, the humanity, of this great man, as it is my only hope. Monsieur, you have his ear, you have his confidence, you have the means at your command. Ah! ask him, pray him, implore him for the love of God, and the sake of a fellow-man, to come alone to the top floor of the house number 7 of the Rue Toison d'Or, Paris, at nine hours of the night of Friday, the 26th inst., to enter into the darkness and say but the one word 'Cleek' as a signal it is he, and I may come forward and throw myself upon his mercy. Oh, save me, Monsieur Cleek — save me! save me!"

"There, that's the lot, and there's no signature," said Narkom, laying down the letter. "What do you make of it, Cleek?"

"A very real, a very moving thing, Mr. Narkom. The cry of a human heart in deep distress; the agonized appeal of a man so wrought up by the horrors of his position that he forgets to offer a temptation in the way of reward, and speaks of outlandish things as though they must be understood of all. As witness his allusion to something which he calls 'The Red Crawl,' without attempting to explain the meaningless phrase. Whatever it is, it is so real to him that it seems as if everybody must understand."

"You think, then, that the thing is genuine?"

"So genuine that I shall answer its call, Mr. Narkom, and be alone in the dark on the top floor of No. 7, Rue Toison d'Or to-morrow night as surely as the clock strikes nine."

And that was how the few persons who happened to be in the quiet upper reaches of the Rue Bienfaisance at half-past eight o'clock the next evening came to see a fat, fussy, red-faced Englishman in a gray frock-coat, white spats, and a shining topper, followed by a liveried servant with a hat-box in one hand and a portmanteau in the other, so conspicuous, the pair of them, that they couldn't have any desire to conceal themselves, cross over the square before the Church of St. Augustine, fare forth into the darker side passages, and move in the direction of the street of the Golden Fleece.

They were, of course, Cleek and his devoted henchman Dollops — a youth he had picked up out of the streets of London and given a home, and whose especial virtues were a dog-like devotion to his employer, a facility for eating without ever seeming to get filled, and fighting without ever seeming to get tired.

"Lumme, guv'ner," whispered he, as they turned at last into the utter darkness and desertion of the narrow Rue Toison d'Or, "if this is wot yer calls Gay Paree, this precious black slit between two rows of houses, I'll take a slice of the Old Kent Road with thanks. Not even so much as a winkle-stall in sight, and me that empty my shirt-bosom's a-chafing my blessed shoulder-blades!"

"You'll see plenty of life before the game's over, I warrant you, Dollops. Now, then, my lad, here's a safe spot. Sit down on the hat-box and wait. That's No. 7, that empty house with the open door, just across the way. Keep your eye on it. I don't know how long I'll be, but if anybody comes out before I do, mind you don't let him get away."

"No fear!" said Dollops sententiously. "I'll be after him as if he was a ham sandwich, sir. Look out for my patent 'Tickle Tootsies' when you come out, guv'ner. I'll sneak over and put 'em round the door as soon as you've gone in." For Dollops, who was of an inventive turn of mind, had an especial "man-trap" of his own, which consisted of heavy brown paper, cut into squares, and thickly smeared over with a viscid, varnish-like substance that adhered to the feet of anybody incautiously stepping upon it, and so interfered with flight that it was an absolute necessity to stop and tear the papers away before running with any sort of ease and swiftness was possible. More than once this novel method of hampering for a brief period the movement of a fugitive had stood him and his master in good stead, and Dollops, who was rather proud of his achievement, never travelled without a full supply of ready-cut papers and a big collapsible tube of the viscid, ropy, varnish-like glue.

Meantime Cleek, having left the boy sitting on the hat-box in the darkness, crossed the narrow street to the open doorway of No. 7, and, without hesitation, stepped in. The place was as black as a pocket, and had that peculiar smell which belongs to houses that have long stood vacant. The house, nevertheless, was a respectable one, and, like all the others, fronted on another street. The dark Toison d'Or was merely a back passage used principally by the tradespeople for the delivery of supplies. Feeling his way to the first of the three flights of stairs which led upward into the stillness and gloom above, Cleek mounted steadily until he found himself at length in a sort of attic — quite windowless, and lit only by a skylight through which shone the ineffectual light of the stars. It was the top at last. Bracing his back against the wall, so that nobody could get behind him, and holding himself ready for any emergency, he called out in a clear, calm voice: "Cleek!"

Almost simultaneously there was a sharp metallic "snick," an electric bulb hanging from the ceiling flamed out luminously, a cupboard door flashed open, a voice cried out in joyous, perfect English: "Thank God for a man!" And, switching round with a cry of amazement, he found himself looking into the face and eyes of a woman.

And of all women in the world — Ailsa Lorne!

He sucked in his breath and his heart began to hammer.

"Miss Lorne!" he exclaimed, so carried out of himself that he scarcely knew what he did. "Good heavens above! — Miss Lorne!"

"Oh!" she ejaculated, with a little startled cry, looking up, but finding no trace of features that she knew in the round, red face of the fat gray man before her. "You know me, then? How can you? But I forget! You are English; you are that great and mysterious man Cleek; and he — ah, he must surely know everything!"

"I know you, at least," he replied, shaking with mingled embarrassment and delight at the knowledge that at last he was permitted to speak to her, to have her speak to him. "I have seen you often in London; and to find you here, like this? It fairly takes away my breath."

"The explanation is very simple, Mr. Cleek. I suppose you know that my uncle, Sir Horace Wyvern, married again last spring? The new Lady Wyvern soon let me know that I was a superfluous person in the household. I left it, of course. Sir Horace would have pensioned me off if I had let him. I couldn't bring myself to eat the bread of charity, however, and when a former schoolmate offered me a post as her companion, I gratefully accepted it. So for the past three months I have been living here in Paris with Athalie and her father, the Baron de Carjorac."

"Baron de Carjorac? Do you mean the French Minister of the Interior, the President of the Board of National Defences, Miss Lorne, that enthusiastic old patriot, that rabid old spitfire whose one dream is the wresting back of Alsace-Lorraine, the driving of the hated Germans into the sea? Do you mean that ripping old firebrand?"

"Yes. But you'd not call him that if you could see the wreck, the broken and despairing wreck, that six weeks of the Château Larouge, six weeks of that horrible 'Red Crawl' have made of him."

"'The Red Crawl'? Good heavens! then that letter, that appeal for help – "

"Came from him!" she finished excitedly. "It was he who was to have met you here to-night, Mr. Cleek. This house is one he owns; he thought he might with safety risk coming here, but — he can't! he can't! He knows now that there is danger for him everywhere; that his every step is tracked; that the snare which is about him has been about him, unsuspected, for almost a year;

that he dare not, absolutely dare not, appeal to the French police, and that if it were known he had appealed to you, he would be a dead man inside of twenty-four hours, and not only dead, but — disgraced. Oh, Mr. Cleek," she stretched out two shaking hands and laid them on his arm, lifted a white, imploring face to his, "save him! save that dear broken old man! Ah, think! think! They are our friends, our dear country's friends, these French people. Their welfare is our welfare, ours is theirs! Oh, help him, save him, Mr. Cleek — for his own sake — for mine — for France! Save him, and win my gratitude forever!"

"That is a temptation that would carry me to the ends of the earth, Miss Lorne. Tell me what the work is, and I will carry it through. What is this incomprehensible thing of which both you and Baron de Carjorac have spoken, this thing you allude to as 'The Red Crawl'?"

She gave a little shuddering cry and fell back a step, covering her face with both hands.

"Oh!" she said, with a shiver of repulsion. "It is horrible — it is necromancy beyond belief! Why, oh, why were we ever driven to that horrible Château Larouge? Why could not fate have spared the Villa de Carjorac? It could not have happened then!"

"Villa de Carjorac? That was the name of the baron's residence, I believe. I remember reading in the newspapers some five or six weeks ago that it was destroyed by fire, which originated — nobody knew how — in the apartments of the late baroness in the very dead of the night. I thought at the time it read suspiciously like the work of an incendiary, although nobody hinted at such a thing. The Château Larouge I also have a distinct memory of, as an old historic property in the neighbourhood of St. Cloud. Speaking from past experience, I know that, although it is in such a state of decay, and supposed to be uninhabitable, it has, in fact, often been occupied at a period when the police and the public believed it to be quite empty. Gentlemen of the Apache persuasion have frequently made it a place of retreat. There is also an underground passage, executed by those same individuals, which connects with the Paris sewers. That, too, the police are unaware

33

of. What can the ruined Château Larouge possibly have to do with the affairs of the Baron de Carjorac, Miss Lorne, that you connect them like this?"

"They have everything to do with them. The Château is no longer a ruin, however. It was purchased, rebuilt, refitted by the Comtesse Susanne de la Tour, Mr. Cleek, and she and her brother live there. So do we, Athalie, Baron de Carjorac, and I. So, also, does the creature — the thing — the abominable horror known as 'The Red Crawl.'"

"My dear Miss Lorne, what are you saying?"

"The truth, nothing but the truth!" she answered hysterically. "Oh, let me begin at the beginning. You'll never understand unless I do. I'll tell you in as few words as possible, as quickly as I can. It all began last winter, when Athalie and her father were at Monte Carlo. There they met Madame la Comtesse de la Tour and her brother, Monsieur Gaston Merode. The baron has position but he has not wealth, Mr. Cleek. Athalie is ambitious. She loves luxury, riches, a life of fashion, all the things that boundless money can give; and when Monsieur Merode — who is young, handsome, and said to be fabulously wealthy — showed a distinct preference for her over all the other marriageable girls he met, she was flattered out of her silly wits. Before they left Monte Carlo for Paris everybody could see that he had only to ask her hand, to have it bestowed upon him. For although the baron never has cared for the man, Athalie rules him, and her every caprice is humoured.

"But, for all he was so ardent a lover, Monsieur Merode was slow in coming to the important point. Perhaps his plans were not matured. At any rate, he did not propose to Athalie at Monte Carlo; and, although he and his sister returned to Paris at the same time as the baron and his daughter, he still deferred the proposal."

"Has he not made it yet?"

"Yes, Mr. Cleek. He made it six weeks ago, to be exact, two nights before the Villa de Carjorac was fired."

"You think it was fired, then?"

"I do now, although I had no suspicion of it at the time. Athalie received her proposal on the Saturday, the baron gave his consent on the Sunday, and on Monday night the villa was mysteriously burnt, leaving all three of us without an immediate refuge. In the meantime, Madame la Comtesse had purchased the ruin of the Château Larouge, and during the period of her brother's deferred proposal was engaged in fitting it up as an abode for herself and him. On the very day it was finished, Monsieur Merode asked for Athalie's hand."

"Oho!" said Cleek, with a strong rising inflection. "I think I begin to smell the toasting of the cheese. Of course, when the villa was burnt out, Madame la Comtesse insisted that, as the fiancée of her brother, Mademoiselle de Carjorac must make her home at the Château until the necessary repairs could be completed; and, of course, the baron had to go with her?"

"Yes," admitted Ailsa. "The baron accepted — Athalie would not have allowed him to decline had he wished to — so we all three went there and have been residing there ever since. On the night after our arrival an alarming, a horrifying, thing occurred. It was while we were at dinner that the conversation turned upon the supernatural, upon houses and places that were reputed to be haunted, and then Madame la Comtesse made a remarkable statement. She laughingly asserted that she had just learned that, in purchasing the Château Larouge, she had also become the possessor of a sort of family ghost. She said that she had only just heard, from an outside source, that there was a horrible legend connected with the place; in short, that for centuries it had been reputed to be under a sort of spell of evil and to be cursed by a dreadful visitant known as 'The Red Crawl' — a hideous and loathsome creature. It was neither spider nor octopus, but horribly resembled both and was supposed to 'appear' at intervals in the middle of the night and, like the fabled giants of fairy tales, carry off 'lovely maidens and devour them.'"

"Who is responsible for that ridiculous assertion, I wonder? I think I may say that I know as much about the Château Larouge and its history as anybody, Miss Lorne, but I never heard of this supposed 'legend' before in all my life."

"So the baron, too, declared, laughing as derisively as any of us over the story, although it is well known that he has a natural antipathy to all crawling things, an abhorrence inherited from his mother, and has been known to run like a frightened child from the appearance of a mere garden spider."

"Oho!" said Cleek again. "I see! I see! The toasted cheese smells stronger, and there's a distinct suggestion of the Rhine about it this time. There's something decidedly German about that fabulous 'monster' and that haunted Château, Miss Lorne. They are clever and careful schemers, those German Johnnies. Of course, this amazing 'Red Crawl' was proved to have an absolute foundation in fact, and equally, of course, it 'appeared' to the Baron de Carjorac?"

"Yes — that very night. After we had all gone to bed, the house was roused by his screams. Everybody rushed to his chamber, only to find him lying on the floor in a state of collapse. The thing had been in his room, he said. He had seen it, it had even touched him — a horrible, hideous red reptile, with squirming tentacles, a huge, glowing body, and eyes like flame. It had crept upon him out of the darkness, he knew not from where. It had seized him, resisted all his wild efforts to tear loose from it, and when he finally sank, overcome and fainting, upon the floor, his last conscious recollection was of the loathsome thing settling down upon his breast and running its squirming 'feelers' up and down his body."

"Of course! Of course! That was part of the game. It was after something. Something of the utmost importance to German interests. That's why the Château Larouge was refitted, why the Villa de Carjorac was burnt down, and why this Monsieur Gaston Merode became engaged to Mademoiselle Athalie."

"Oh, how could you know that, Mr. Cleek? Nobody ever suspected. The baron never confessed to any living soul until he did so to me, to-day, and then only because he had to tell somebody, in order that the appointment with you might be kept.

How, then, could you guess?"

"By putting two and two together, Miss Lorne, and discovering that they do not make five. The inference is very clear: Baron de Carjorac is President of the Board of National Defences; Germany, in spite of its public assurances to the contrary, is known by those who are 'on the inside' to harbour a very determined intention of making a secret attack, an unwarned invasion, upon England. France is the key to the situation. If, without the warning that must come through the delay of picking a quarrel and entering into an open war with the Republic, the German army can swoop down in the night, cross the frontier, and gain immediate possession of the ports of France, in five hours' time it can be across the English Channel, and its hordes pouring down upon a sleeping people. To carry out this programme, the first step would, of course, be to secure knowledge of the number, location, manner of the secret defences of France, the plans of fortification, the maps of the 'danger zone,' the documentary evidence of her strongest and weakest points. And who so likely to be the guardian of these as the Baron de Carjorac? That is how I know that 'The Red Crawl' was after something of vital importance to German interests, Miss Lorne. That he got it, I know from the fact that the baron, while hinting at disgrace and speaking of peril to his own life, dared not confide in the French authorities and ask the assistance of the French police. Moreover, if 'The Red Crawl' had failed to secure anything, the baron, with his congenital loathing of all crawling things, would have left the Château Larouge immediately."

"Oh, to think that you guessed it so easily, and it was all such a puzzle to me. I could not think, Mr. Cleek, why he did remain; why he would not be persuaded to go, although every night was adding to the horror of the thing and it seemed clear to me that he was going mad. Of course, Madame la Comtesse and her brother tried to reason him out of what he declared, tried to make him believe that it was all fancy, that he did not really see the fearful thing, it was equally in vain that I myself tried to persuade him to leave the place before his reason became unsettled. Last night" — she paused, shuddered, put both hands over her face, and drew in a deep breath — "last night, I, too, saw 'The Red Crawl,' Mr. Cleek — I, too! I, too!"

"You, Miss Lorne?"

"Yes. I made up my mind that I would — that, if it existed, I would have absolute proof of it. The countess and her brother had scoffed so frequently, had promised the baron so often that they would set a servant on guard in the corridor to watch, and then had said so often to poor, foolish, easily persuaded Athalie that it was useless doing anything so silly, as it was absolutely certain that her father only imagined the thing, that I determined to take the step myself, unknown to any of them. After everybody had gone to bed, I threw on a loose, dark gown, crept into the corridor, and hid in a niche from which I could see the door of the baron's room. I waited until after midnight — long after — and then — and then - "

"Calm yourself, Miss Lorne. Then the thing appeared, I suppose?"

"Yes; but not before something equally terrible had happened. I saw the door of the countess's room open; I saw the countess herself come out, accompanied by the man who up till then I had believed, like everybody else, was her brother."

"And who is not her brother, after all?"

"No, he is not. Theirs is a closer tie. I saw her kiss him. I saw her go with him to an angle of the corridor, lift a rug, and raise a trap in the floor."

"Hullo! Hullo!" ejaculated Cleek. "Then she, too, knows of the passage which leads to the sewers. Clearly, then, this Countess de la Tour is not what she seems, when she knows secrets that are known only to the followers of - Well, never mind. Go on, Miss Lorne, go on. You saw her lift that trap; and what then?"

"Then there came up out of it the most loathsome-looking creature I have ever seen: a huge, crawling, red shape that was like a blood-red spider, with the eyes, the hooked beak, and the writhing tentacles of an octopus. It made no sound, but it seemed to know her, to understand her, for when she waved her hand toward the open door of her own room, obeying that gesture, it dragged its huge bulk over the threshold, and passed from sight. Then the man she called her brother kissed her again, and as he descended into the darkness below the trap I heard her say quite distinctly: 'Tell Marise that I will come as soon as I can; but not to delay the revel. If I am compelled to forego it to-night, there shall be a wilder one to-morrow, when Clodoche arrives.'"

"Clodoche? By Jupiter!" Cleek almost jumped as he spoke. "Now I know the 'lay'! No; don't ask me anything yet. Go on with the story, please. What then, Miss Lorne, what then?"

"Then the man below said something which I could not hear and she answered in these words: 'No, no; there is no danger. I will guard it safely, and it shall go into no hands but Clodoche's. He and Count von Hetzler will be there about midnight to-morrow to complete the deal and pay over the money. Clodoche will want the fragment, of course, to show to the count as a proof that it is the right one, as "an earnest" of what the remainder is worth. And you must bring me that "remainder" without fail, Gaston — you hear me? — without fail! I shall be there, at the rendezvous, awaiting you, and the thing must be in our hands when Von Hetzler comes. The work must be finished to-morrow night, even if you and Serpice have to throw all caution to the winds and throttle the old fool.' Then, as if answering a further question, she laughingly added: 'Oh, get that fear out of your head. I'm not a bat, to be caught napping. I'll give it to no one but Clodoche, and not even to him until he gives the secret sign.' And then, Mr. Cleek, as she closed the trap I heard the man call back to her 'Good-night' and give her a name I had not heard before. We had always supposed that she had been christened 'Suzanne,' but as that man left he called her – "

"I know before you tell me — 'Margot'!" interjected Cleek. "I guessed the identity of this 'Countess de la Tour' from the moment you spoke of Clodoche and that secret trap. Her knowledge of those two betrayed her to me. Clodoche is a renegade Alsatian, a spy in the pay of the German Government, and an old habitué of 'The Inn of the Twisted Arm,' where the Queen of the Apaches and her pals hold their frequent revels. I can guess the remainder of your story now. You carried this news to the Baron de Carjorac, and he, breaking down, confessed to you that he had lost something."

"Yes, yes — a dreadful 'something,' Mr. Cleek: the horrible thing that has been making life an agony to him ever since. On the night when that abominable 'Red Crawl' first overcame him there was upon his person a most important document. It was a rough draft of the maps of fortification and the plan of the secret defences of France, the identical document from which was afterward transcribed the parchment now deposited in the secret archives of the Republic. When Baron de Carjorac recovered his senses after his horrifying experience – "

"That document was gone?"

"Part of it, Mr. Cleek, thank God, only a part! If it had been the parchment itself, no such merciful thing could possibly have happened. But the paper was old, much folding and handling had worn the creases through, and when, in his haste, the secret robber grabbed it, whilst that loathsome creature held the old man down, it parted directly down the middle, and he got only a vertical section of each of its many pages."

"Victoria! 'And the fool hath said in his heart There is no God,'" quoted Cleek. "So, then, the hirelings of the enemy have only got half what they are after; and, as no single sentence can be complete upon a paper torn like that, nothing can be made of it until the other half is secured, and our German friends are still 'up a gum-tree.' I know now why the baron stayed on at the Château Larouge and why 'The Red Crawl' is preparing to pay him another visit to-night: He hoped, poor chap, to find a clue to the whereabouts of the fragment he had lost; and that thing is after the fragment he still retains. Well, it will be a long, long day before either of those two fragments falls into German hands."

"Oh, Mr. Cleek, you think you can get the stolen paper back? You believe you can outwit those dreadful people and save the Baron de Carjorac's honour and his life?"

"Miss Lorne" — he took her hand in his and lifted it to his lips — "Miss Lorne, I thank you for giving me the chance! If you will do what I ask you, be where I ask you in two hours' time, so surely as we two stand here this minute, I will put back the German calendar by ten years at least. They drink 'To the day,' those German Johnnies, but by to-morrow morning the English hand you are holding will have given them reason to groan over the night!"

II

It was half-past eleven o'clock. Madame la Comtesse, answering a reputed call to the bedside of a dying friend, had departed early, and was not to be expected back, she said, until to-morrow noon. The servants — given permission by the gentleman known in the house as Monsieur Gaston Merode, and who had graciously provided a huge char-à-banc for the purpose — had gone in a body to a fair over in the neighbourhood of Sevres, and darkness and stillness filled the long, broad corridor of the Château Larouge. Of a sudden, however, a mere thread of sound wavered through the silence, and from the direction of Miss Lorne's room a figure in black, with feet muffled in thick woollen stockings, padded to an angle of the passage, lifted a trap carefully hidden beneath a huge tiger-skin rug, and almost immediately Cleek's head rose up out of the gap.

"Thank God you managed to do it. I was horribly afraid you would not," said Ailsa in a palpitating whisper.

"You need not have been," he answered. "I know a dozen places besides 'The Inn of the Twisted Arm' from which one can get into the sewers. I've screwed a bolt and socket on the inner side of this trap in case of an emergency, and I've carried a few things into the passage for 'afterward.' I suppose that fellow Merode, as he calls himself, is in his room, waiting?"

"Yes; and, although he pretends to be alone to-night, he has other men with him, hideous, ruffianly looking creatures, whom I saw him admit after the servants had gone. The countess has left

41

the house and gone I don't know where."

"I do, then. Make certain that she's at 'The Twisted Arm,' waiting, first, for the coming of Clodoche, and, second, for the arrival of this precious 'Merode' with the remaining half of the document. I've sent Dollops there to carry out his part of the programme, and when once I get the password Margot requires before she will hand over the paper, the game will be in my hands entirely. They are desperate to-night, Miss Lorne, and will stop at nothing — not even murder. There! the rug's replaced. Quick! lead me to the baron's room, there's not a minute to waste."

She took his hand and led him tiptoe through the darkness, and in another moment he was in the Baron de Carjorac's presence.

"Oh, monsieur, God forever bless you!" exclaimed the broken old man, throwing himself on his knees before Cleek.

"Out with the light — out with the light!" exclaimed he, ducking down suddenly. "Were you mad to keep it burning till I came, with that," pointing to a huge bay window opening upon a balcony, "uncurtained and the grounds, no doubt, alive with spies?"

Miss Lorne sprang to the table where the baron's reading-lamp stood, jerked the cord of the extinguisher, and darkness enveloped the room, darkness tempered only by the faint gleams of the moon streaming over the balcony and through the panes of the uncurtained window.

Cleek, on his knees beside the kneeling baron, whipped a tiny electric torch from his pocket and, shielding its flare with his scooped hands, flashed it upon the old man's face.

"Simple as rolling off a log — exactly like your pictures," he commented. "I'll 'do' you as easily as I 'do' Clodoche and I could 'do' him in the dark from memory. Quick," snicking off the light of the electric torch and rising to his feet, "into your dressing-room, baron. I want that suit of clothes; I want that ribbon, that cross — and I want them at once. You're a bit thicker set than me, but I've got my Clodoche rig on underneath this, and it will fill out your coat admirably and make us as like as two peas. Give me five minutes, Miss Lorne, and I promise you a surprise."

He flashed out of sight with the baron as he ceased speaking; and Ailsa, creeping to the window and peering cautiously out, was startled presently by a voice at her elbow saying, in a tone of extreme agitation, "Oh, mademoiselle, I fear, even yet I fear, that this Anglais monsieur attempts too moch, and that the papier he is gone forever."

"Oh, no, baron, no!" she said soothingly, as she laid a solici- tous hand upon his arm. "Do believe in him; do have faith in him. Ah, if you only knew – "

"Thanks. I reckon I shall pass muster!" interposed Cleek's voice; and it was only then she realized. "You'll find the baron in the other room, Miss Lorne, looking a little grotesque in that gray suit of mine. In with you, quickly; go with him through the other door, and get below before those fellows begin to stir. Get out of the house as quietly and as expeditiously as you can. With God's help, I'll meet you at the Hotel Louvre in the morning, and put the missing fragment in the baron's hands."

"And may God give you that help!" she answered fervently, as she moved toward the dressing-room door. "Ah, what a man! What a man!"

Then in a twinkling she was gone, and Cleek stood alone in the silent room. Giving her and the baron time to get clear of the other one, he went in on tiptoe, locked the door through which they had passed, put the key in his pocket, and returned. Going to the door which led from the main room into the corridor, he took the key from the lock of that, too, replacing it upon the outer side, and leaving the door itself slightly ajar.

"Now then for you, Mr. 'The Red Crawl,'" he said, as he walked to the baron's table, and, sinking down into a deep chair beside it, leaned back with his eyes closed as if in sleep, the faint light of the moon half-revealing his face. "I want that password, and I'll get it, if I have to choke it out of your devil's throat! And she said that she would be grateful to me all the rest of her life!

Only 'grateful,' I wonder? Is nothing else possible? What a good, good thing a real woman is!"

* * * * *

How long was it that he had been reclining there waiting before his strained ears caught the sound of something like the rustling of silk shivering through the stillness, and he knew that at last it was coming? It might have been ten minutes, it might have been twenty — he had no means of determining — when he caught that first movement, and, peering through the slit of a partly opened eye, saw the appalling thing drag its huge bulk along the balcony and, with tentacles writhing, slide over the low sill of the window, and settle down in a glowing red heap upon the floor. Fake though he knew it to be, Cleek could not repress a swift rush and prickle of "goose-flesh" at sight of it.

For a few seconds it lay dormant; then one red feeler shot out, then another, and another, and it began to edge its way across the carpet to the chair. Cleek lay still and waited, his heavy breathing sounding regularly, his head thrown back, his limp hands lying loosely, palms upward. Nearer and nearer crept the loathsome, red, glowing thing.

It crawled to his feet, and still he was quiet; it slid first one tentacle and then another over his knees and up toward his breast, and still he made no movement; then, as it rose until its hideous beaked countenance was close to his own, his hands flashed upward and clamped together like a vise — clamped on a palpitating human throat. In the twinkling of an eye the tentacles were wrapped about him, and he and "The Red Crawl" were rolling over and over on the floor and battling together.

"Serpice, you low-bred hound, I know you!" he whispered, as they struggled. "You can't utter a cry. You shan't utter a cry to bring help. I'll throttle you, you beastly renegade, that's willing to sell his own country — throttle you, do you hear? — before you shall bring any of your mates to the rescue. Oh, you've not got a weak old man to fight with this time! Do you know me? It's the 'Cracksman,' the 'Cracksman' who went over to the police. If you doubt it, now that we're in the moonlight, look up and see my face. Oho! you recognize me, I see. Well, you will die looking at me, you dog, if you deny me what I'm after. I'll loosen my grip enough for you to whisper, and no more. Now what's the password that Clodoche must give to Margot to-night at 'The Twisted Arm'? Tell me what it is; if you want your life, tell me what it is?"

"I'll see you dead first!" came in a whisper from beneath the hideous mask. Then, as Cleek's fingers clamped tight again, and the battle began anew, one long, thin arm shot out from amongst the writhing tentacles, one clutching hand gripped the leg of the table and, with a wrench and a twist, brought it crashing to the floor with a sound that a deaf man might have heard.

And in an instant there was pandemonium.

A door flew open, and, clashing heavily against the wall, sent an echo reeling along the corridor; then came a clatter of rustling feet, a voice cried out excitedly: "Come on! come on! He's had to kill the old fool to get it!" and Cleek had just time to tear loose from the shape with which he was battling, and dodge out of the way when the man Merode lurched into the room, with half a dozen Apaches tumbling in at his heels.

"Serpice!" he cried, rushing forward, as he saw the gasping red shape upon the floor; "Serpice! Mon Dieu! what is it?"

"The Cracksman!" he gulped. "Cleek! — the Cracksman who went against us! Catch him! stop him!"

"The Cracksman!" howled out Merode, twisting round in the darkness and reaching blindly for the haft of his dirk. "Nom de Dieu! Where?"

And almost before the last word was uttered a fist like a sledge-hammer shot out, caught him full in the face, and he went down with a whole smithy of sparks flashing and hissing before his eyes.

"There!" answered Cleek, as he bowled him over. "Gentlemen of the sewers, my compliments. You'll make no short cut to 'The Twisted Arm' to-night!"

Then, like something shot from a catapult, he sprang to the

door, whisked through it, banged it behind him, turned the key, and went racing down the corridor like a hare.

"It must be sheer luck now!" he panted, as he reached the angle and, kicking aside the rug, pulled up the trap. "They'll have that door down in a brace of shakes, and be after me like a pack of ravening wolves. The race is to the swift this time, gentlemen, and you'll have to take a long way round if you mean to head me off."

Then he passed down into the darkness, closed the trap-door after him, shot into its socket the bolt he had screwed there, flashed up the light of his electric torch, and, *without* the pass-word, turned toward the sewers, and ran, and ran, and ran!

III

It lacked but a minute of the stroke of twelve, and the revels at "The Twisted Arm" — wild at all times, but wilder to-night than ever — were at their noisiest and most exciting pitch. And why not? It was not often that Margot could spend a whole night with her rapscallion crew, and she had been here since early evening and was to remain here until the dawn broke gray over the housetops and the murmurs of the workaday world awoke anew in the streets of the populous city. It was not often that each man and each abandoned woman present knew to a certainty that he or she would go home through the mists of the gray morning with a fistful of gold that had been won without labour or the taking of any personal risk; and to-night the half of four hundred thousand francs was to be divided among them.

No wonder they had made a carnival of it, and tricked themselves out in gala attire; no wonder they had brought a paste tiara and crowned Margot. Margot, was in flaming red to-night, and looked a devil's daughter indeed, with her fire-like sequins and her red ankles twinkling as she threw herself into the thick of the dance and kicked, and whirled, and flung her bare arms about to the lilt of the music and the fluting of her own happy laughter.

"Per Baccho! The devil's in her to-night!" grinned old Marise, the innkeeper, from her place behind the bar, where the lid of the sewer-trap opened. "She has not been like it since the Cracksman broke with her, Toinette. But that was before your time, ma fille. Mother of the heavens! but there was a man for you! There was a king that was worthy of such a queen. Name of disaster! that she could not hold him, that the curse of virtue sapped such a splendid tree, and that she could take up with another after him!"

"Why not?" cried Toinette, as she tossed down the last half of her absinthe and twitched her flower-crowned head. "A kingdom must have a king, ma mere; and Dieu! but he is handsome, this Monsieur Gaston Merode! And if he carries out his part of the work to-night he will be worthy of the homage of all."

"'If' he carries it out — 'if'!" exclaimed Marise, with a lurch of the shoulders and a flirt of her pudgy hand. "Soul of me! that's where the difference lies. Had it been the Cracksman, there would have been no 'if.' It were done as surely as he attempted it. Name of misfortune! I had gone into a nunnery had I lost such a man. But she – "

The voice of Margot shrilled out and cut into her words.

"Absinthe, Marise, absinthe for them all and set the score down to me!" she cried. "Drink up, my bonny boys; drink up, my loyal maids. Drink — drink till your skins will hold no more. No one pays to-night but me!"

They broke into a cheer, and bearing down in a body upon Marise, threw her into a fever of haste to serve them.

"To Margot!" they shouted, catching up the glasses and lifting them high. "Vive la Reine des Apache! Vive la compagnie! To Margot! to Margot!"

She swept them a merry bow, threw them a laughing salute, and drank the toast with them.

"Messieurs, my love — mesdames et mademoiselles, my admiration," she cried, with a ripple of joy-mad laughter. "To the success of the Apaches, to the glory of four hundred thousand francs, and to the quick arrival of Serpice and Gaston." Then, her upward glance catching sight of the musicians sipping their absinthe in the little gallery above, she flung her empty glass against the wall behind them, and shook with laughter as they started in alarm and spilled the green poison when they dodged aside. "Another dance, you dawdlers!" she cried. "Does Marise pay you to sit there like mourners? Strike up, you mummies, or you pay yourselves for what you drink to-night. Soul of desires!" — as the musicians grabbed up their instruments, and a leaping, lilting, quick-beating air went rollicking out over the hubbub — "a quadrille, you angels of inspiration! Partners, gentlemen! Partners, ladies! A quadrille! A quadrille!"

They set up a many-throated cheer, flocked out with her upon the floor, and in one instant feet were flying, skirts were whirling, laughter and jest mingling with waving arms and kicking toes, and the whole place was in one mad riot of delirious joy.

And in the midst of this there rolled up suddenly a voice crying, as from the bowels of the earth, "Hola! Hola! La! la! loi!" the cry of the Apache to his kind.

"Mother of delights! It is one of us, and it comes from the sewer passage!" shrilled out Marise, as the dancers halted and Margot ran, with fleet steps, toward the bar. "Listen! listen! They come to you, Margot — Serpice and Gaston. The work is done."

"And before even Clodoche or Von Hetzler have arrived!" she replied excitedly. "Give them light, give them welcome. Be quick!"

Marise ducked down, loosened the fastenings of the trapdoor, flung it back, and, leaning over the gap with a light in her hand, called down into the darkness, "Hola! Hola! La! la! loi! Come on, comrades, come on!"

The caller obeyed instantly. A hand reached up and gripped the edge of the flooring, and out of the darkness into the light emerged the figure of a man in a leather cap and the blue blouse of a mechanic. He was a pale, fox-faced, fox-eyed fellow, with lank, fair hair, a brush of ragged yellow beard, and the look and air of the sneak and spy indelibly branded upon him.

It was Cleek.

"Clodoche!" exclaimed Marise, falling back in surprise.

"Clodoche!" echoed Margot. "Clodoche — and from the sewers?"

"Yes — why not?" he answered, his tongue thick-burred with the accent of Alsace, his shifting eyes flashing toward the huge window behind the bar, where, in the moonlight, the narrow passage leading down to the door of "The Twisted Arm" gaped evilly between double rows of scowling, thief-sheltering houses. "Name of the fiend! Is this the welcome you give the bringer of fortune, Margot?"

"But from the sewer?" she repeated. "It is incomprehensible, cher ami. You were to pilot Von Hetzler over from the Café Dupin to the square beyond there" — pointing to the window — "to leave him waiting a moment while you came on to see if it were safe for him to enter; and now you come from the sewer, from the opposite direction entirely!"

"Mother of misfortunes! You had done the same yourself — you, Lantier; you, Clopin; you Cadarousse; any of you, had you been in my boots," he made answer. "I stole a leaf from your own book, earlier in the evening. Garrotted a fellow with jewels on him, in the Rue Noir, near the Market Place, and nearly got into 'the stone bottle' for doing it. He was a decoy, set there by the police for some of you fellows, and there was a sergeant de ville after me like a whirlwind. I was not fool enough to turn the chase in this direction, so I doubled and twisted until it was safe to dive into the tavern of Fouchard, and lay in hiding there. Fouchard let his son carry a message to the count for me, and will guide him to the square. When it grew near the time to come, Fouchard let me down into the sewer passage from there. Get on with your dance, silence is always suspicious. An absinthe, Marise! Have Gaston and Serpice arrived yet with the rest of the document, Margot la reine?"

"Not yet," she answered. "But one may expect them at any minute."

"Where is the fragment we already possess?"

"Here," tapping her bodice and laughing, "tenderly shielded, mon ami; and why not? Who would not mother a thing that is to bring one four hundred thousand francs?"

"Let me see it? It must be shown to the count, remember. He will take no risks, come not one step beyond the square, until he is certain that it is the paper his Government requires. Let me have it. Let me take it to him — quick!"

She waved aside airily the hand he stretched toward her, and danced into the thick of the resumed quadrille.

"Ah, non! non! non!" she laughed, as he came after her. "The conditions were of your own making, cher ami; we break no rules even among ourselves."

"Soul of a fool! But if the count comes to the square — he is due there now, mignonne — and I am not there to show him the thing – Margot, for the love of God, let me have the paper!"

"Let me have the sign, the password!"

Cleek snapped at a desperate chance because there was nothing else to do, because he knew that at any moment now the end might come.

"'When the purse will not open, slit it!'" he hazarded, desperately — choosing, on the off-chance of its correctness, the password of the Apache.

"It is not the right one! It is by no means the right one!" she made reply, backing away from him suddenly, her absinthe-brightened eyes deriding him, her absinthe-sharpened laughter mocking him. "Your thoughts are in the Bois, cher ami. What is the password of the brotherhood to the cause of Germany, stupid? It is not right, non! non! It is not right!"

The cause of Germany! At the words the truth rushed like a flash of inspiration across Cleek's mind. The cause of Germany! what a dolt he was not to have thought of that before! There was but one phrase ever used for that among the Kaiser's people, and that phrase –

"'To the day!'" he said, with a burst of sudden laughter. "My wits are in the moon to-night, la reine. 'To the day,' of course — 'To the day'!" And even before she replied to him, he knew that he had guessed aright.

"Bravo!" she said, with a little hiccough, for the absinthe, of which she had imbibed so freely to-night, was beginning to take hold of her. "A pretty conspirator to forget how to open the door he himself locked! It is well I know thee; it is well it was our word in the beginning, or I had been suspicious, silly! Wait but a moment" — putting her hand to her breast and beginning to unfasten her bodice — "wait but a moment, Monsieur Twitching-Fingers, and the thing shall be in your hand."

The strain, the relief, were all too great for even such nerves as Cleek's, and if he had not laughed aloud, he knew that he must have cheered.

"Oho! you grin because one's fingers blunder with eagerness," hiccoughed Margot, thinking his laughter was for the trouble she had in getting the fastenings of her bodice undone. "Peste, monsieur! may not a lady well be modestly careful when – Name of the devil! what's that?"

It was the note of a whistle shrilling down the narrow passage without — the passage where Dollops, in Apache garb, had been set on watch; and, hearing it, Cleek clamped his jaws together and breathed hard. A single whistle, short and sharp, such as this, was the signal agreed upon that the real Clodoche was coming, and that he and Count von Hetzler had already appeared in the square beyond.

"Soul of a sloth! will not that hurry you, la reine?" he said excitedly, in reply to Margot's startled question. "It is the signal Fouchard's son was to give when he and Von Hetzler arrived at the place where I am to meet them. Give me the paper quick! Tear the fastenings, if they will not come undone else. One cannot keep a Von Hetzler waiting like a lackey for a scrap of ribbon and a bit of lace."

"Pardieu! they have kept better men than he waiting many an hour before this," she made reply. "But you shall have the thing in a twinkling now. There! but one more knot, and then it is in your hands."

And, had the fates not decreed otherwise, so, indeed, it would have been. But then, just then, when another second would have brought the paper into view, another moment seen it shut tight in the grip of his itching fingers, disaster came and blotted out his hopes!

Without hint or warning, without sign or sound to lessen the shock of it, the trap-door behind the bar flew up and backward with a crash that sent Marise and her assistants darting away from it in shrieking alarm; a babel of excited voices sounded, rushing feet scuffled and flashed along the shaking floor, and Merode and his followers tumbled helter-skelter into the room.

Cleek, counting on the bolt which kept them from entering the passage from the corridor of the Château Larouge and thus forcing them to take a long, roundabout journey to "The Twisted Arm," had not counted on their shortening that journey by entering the passage from Fouchard's tavern, doing, in fact, the very thing which he had declared to Margot he himself had done. And lo! here they were, howling and crowding about him, dirks in their hands and devils in their eyes and hearts — and the paper not his yet!

A clamour rose as they poured in; the dancers ceased to dance; the music ceased to play; and Margot, shutting a tight clutch on the loosened part of her half-unfastened bodice, swung away from Cleek's side, and flew in a panic to Merode.

"Gaston!" she cried, knowing from his wild look and the string of oaths and curses his followers were blurting out that something had gone amiss. "Gaston, mon cœur! Name of disaster! what is wrong?"

"Everything is wrong!" he flung back excitedly. "That devil, that renegade, that fury, Cleek, the Cracksman, is here. He came to the rescue out of the very skies and all but killed Serpice!"

"Cleek!" Fifty shrill voices joined Margot's in that screaming cry; fifty more dirks flashed into view. "Cleek in France? Cleek? Where is he? Which way did he go? Where's the narker — where — where?"

"Here, if anywhere!"

"Here?"

"Yes, unless you've been fooled, and let him get away! He knows about the paper, and is after it, Margot; and if any one has come up from the sewers within the past twenty minutes - "

They knew instantly and a roar of excited voices yelled out: "Clodoche! Clodoche! Clodoche!" as, snarling and howling like a pack of wolves, they bore down with a rush on the blue-bloused figure that was creeping toward the door.

But as they sprang it sprang also! It was neck or nothing now. Cleek realized it, and, throwing himself headlong over the bar, clutched frantically at the lever which he knew controlled the flow of gas, jammed it down with all his strength, shut off the light, and, grabbing up a chair, sent it crashing through the window.

The crowd surged on toward the wrecked bar with a yell, surged from all directions, and then abruptly stopped. For the sudden darkness within had made more prominent the moonlighted passage without; and there, scuttling away in alarm from this sudden uproar and the outward flying of that hurled chair, a figure which but a moment before had come skulking to the window could now be seen.

"There he goes — there! there!" shrilled out a chorus of excited voices, as the yellow-bearded, blue-bloused figure came into view. "After him! Catch him! Knife him!"

In an instant they were at the door, tumbling out into the darkness, pouring up the passage in hot pursuit. And it was at that moment the balance changed again. Those who were in the front rank of the pursuers were in time to see a lithe, thin figure, dressed as one of their own kind, spring up in the path of that other figure, jump on it, grip it, clap a huge square of sticky brown paper over the howling mouth of it, and bear it, struggling and kicking, to the ground.

In another second they, too, were upon it, swarming over it like rats, digging and hacking at it with their dirks. And so they were still hacking at it — although it had long since ceased to move or to make any sound — when Merode came up and called them to a halt.

"Drag it inside; let Margot have a thrust at it. It is her right. Pull off the dog's disguise, and bring me the plucky one that captured him. He shall have absinthe enough to swim in, the little king! Off with it all, Lanchere. First, the plaster, that's right. Now, the wig and beard, and after that – What's that you say? The beard is real? The hair is real? They will not come off? Name of the devil! what are you saying?"

"The truth, mon roi — the truth! Mother of disasters! It is not the Cracksman — it is the real Clodoche we have killed!"

For one moment a sort of panic held them, swayed them, and befogged their brains; then of a sudden Merode howled out "Get back! Get back! The fellow's in there still!" and led a blind race down the passage to the bar where they had seen Cleek last. It was still in darkness; but an eager hand, gripping the lever, turned on the gas again and matches everywhere were lifted to the jets.

And when the light flamed out and the room was again ablaze they knew that they might as well hope to call back yesterday as dream of finding Cleek again. For there on the floor, her limp hands turned palms upward, a chloroformed cloth folded over her mouth and nose, lay the figure of Margot, her bodice torn wide open and the paper forever gone!

* * * * *

It was five minutes later when the Count von Hetzler, crouching back in the shadow of the square and waiting for the return of Clodoche, heard a dull, whirring sound that was unmistakably the purr of a motor throb through the stillness, and, leaning forward, saw a limousine whirl up out of the darkness, cut across the square, and like a flash dash off westward. Yet in the brief instant it took to go past the place where he waited there was time for him to catch the sharp click of a lowered window, see the clear outlines of a man's face looking out, and to hear a voice from within the vehicle speak.

"Herr Count," it said in clear, incisive tones. "A positively infallible recipe for the invasion of England: Wait until the Channel freezes and then skate over. Good-night!"

CHAPTER III
THE RIDDLE OF THE SACRED SON

Had I followed my own inclination in the matter, I think I should have elected to call this particular adventure "The Riddle of the Amazing Demi-God," but as it is set down under the above title in the private note-book of Superintendent Narkom — to which volume I am under obligation for the details regarding the life and work of this most marvellous man — it follows that I must adhere closely to the recorded facts of each of his adventures, even to the most minute particular, if I am to prove myself worthy of the favour Mr. Narkom has shown me. I may freely confess, however, that I have not at all times adhered to the chronological sequence of those adventures, but have picked and chosen here and there from the record of his amazing career such cases as I have fancied most likely to appeal to the public at large, without regard to their natural order of succession or the many others that have intervened.

As Superintendent Narkom's records cover a number of years and embrace upward of three hundred adventures, obviously some must, of necessity, be omitted from these chronicles. Such omission sometimes — as in the present instance — renders it compulsory to record a few after facts connected with the adventure last detailed, in order that the reader may not be confused by the reappearance of certain persons under circumstances and in places widely separated from those in which they were left.

More than a year had passed since the affair of "The Red Crawl," when the events now to be told occurred, and while that year was fruitful of many stirring things so far as Cleek himself was concerned, but little record is obtainable of the movements of Margot and the man Merode, the two foremost figures in the Apache band with whom Cleek came to grips, for they chose to vanish suddenly from their Parisian haunts immediately after that tragical night at "The Inn of the Twisted Arm." It is certain, however, that they proceeded in due time to the East, for they were seen in both India and Ceylon several months after their disappearance from Paris. Indeed, they were obliged to fly from the latter place to escape arrest when the confession of a drunken native exposed, before its fulfilment, a plan to loot the repository of the Pearl Fisheries Company at a time when it contained several thousand pounds' worth of gems. From that point there is no record of their movements for many, many months.

Of course, after such a terrifying experience in the French capital, and not knowing when the Apache band might, knowing her part in the affair, avenge themselves upon her for the failure of the snare of "The Red Crawl," residence in France became a bugbear to Ailsa Lorne. Despite the pleadings of Athalie and the baron, whom she had served so well in giving help to Cleek, she was steadfast in her determination to leave it and to return to her native land. She therefore packed up her belongings, journeyed back to London, and set about finding some other position whereby she could earn her living.

Circumstances had so shaped themselves that Cleek had seen next to nothing of her since her return to England, much and deeply as he longed to do so. Beyond one delightful call at the modest little boarding-place where she was stopping, whilst waiting for an answer to her advertisement for a post as governess or companion, an answer which speedily came and was as speedily accepted, he had not met her at all since their parting in Paris, and, as their friendship was not sufficiently close to warrant the interchange of letters, she seemed as far away from him as ever.

Imagine, then, his surprise and delight, on returning to the house in Clarges Street late one afternoon, in company with the redoubtable Dollops, to find lying upon his table a note containing these words:

My Dear Cleek:

Kindly refrain from going out this evening. I shall call about nine o'clock, bringing with me Miss Ailsa Lorne, whom you doubtless remember, and her present patron, Angela, Countess Chepstow, the young widow of that ripping old war-horse who, as you may recall, quelled that dangerous and fanatical rising of the Cingalese at Trincomalee. These ladies wish to see you with reference to a most extraordinary case, an inexplicable mystery, which both they and I believe no man but yourself can satisfactorily probe.

Yours in haste,

Maverick Narkom.

So, then, he was to see her again, to touch her hand, hear her voice, look into the eyes that had lighted him back from the path to destruction! Cleek's heart began to hammer and his pulses to drum. Needless to say, he took extraordinary care with his toilet that evening, with the result that when the ladies arrived there was nothing even vaguely suggestive of the detective about him.

"Oh, Mr. Cleek, do help us!" implored Ailsa, after the first greetings were over. "Lady Chepstow is almost beside herself with dread and anxiety over the inexplicable thing, and I have persuaded her that if anybody on earth can solve the mystery of it, avert the new and appalling danger of it, it is you! Oh, say that you will take the case, say that you will solve it, say that you will save little Lord Chepstow and put an end to this maddening mystery!"

"Little Lord Chepstow?" repeated Cleek, glancing over at the countess, who stood, a very Niobe in her grief and despair, holding out two imploring hands in silent supplication. "That is your ladyship's son, is it not?"

"Yes," she answered, with a sort of wail; "my only son — my only child. All that I have to love, all that I have to live for in this world."

"And you think the little fellow is in peril?"

"Yes — in deadly peril."

"From what source? From whose hand?"

"I don't know! I don't know!" she answered distractedly. "Sometimes I am wild enough to suspect even Captain Hawksley, unjust and unkind as it seems."

"Captain Hawksley? Who is he?"

"My late husband's cousin; heir, after my little son, to the title and estates. He is very poor, deeply in debt, and the inheritance would put an end to all his difficulties. But he is fond of my son; they seem almost to worship each other. I, too, am fond of him. But, for all that, I have to remember that he and he alone would benefit by Cedric's death, and — and — wicked as it seems - Oh, Mr. Cleek, help me! Direct me! Sometimes I doubt him. Sometimes I doubt everybody. Sometimes I think of those other days, that other mystery, that land which reeks of them; and then — and then - Oh, that horrible Ceylon! I wish I had never set foot in it in all my life!"

Her agitation and distress were so great as to make her utterances only half coherent; and Ailsa, realizing that this sort of thing must only perplex Cleek, and leave him in the dark regarding the matter upon which they had come to consult him, gently interposed.

"Do try to calm yourself and to tell the story as briefly as possible, dear Lady Chepstow," she advised. Then, taking the initiative, added quietly, "it begins, Mr. Cleek, at a period when the little boy, whose governess I am at present, was but two years old, and at Trincomalee, where his late father was stationed with his regiment four years ago. Somebody, for some absurd reason, had set afoot a ridiculous rumour that the English had received orders from the Throne to stamp out every religion but their own. It was said if British were not exterminated, dreadful desecrations would occur, as they were determined - "

"To loot all the temples erected to Buddha, destroy the images, and make a bonfire of all the sacred relics," finished Cleek himself. "I rarely forget history, Miss Lorne, especially when it is such recent history as that memorable Buddhist rising at Trincomalee. It began upon an utterly unfounded, ridiculous rumour; it terminated, if my memory serves me correctly, in something akin to the very thing it was supposed to avert. That is to say, during the outburst of fanaticism, that most sacred of all relics — the holy tooth of Buddha — disappeared mysteriously from the temple of Dambool, and in spite of the fact that many lacs of rupees were offered for its recovery, it has never, I believe, been found, or even traced, although a huge fortune awaits the restorer, and, with it, overpowering honours from the native princes. Those must have been trying times, Lady Chepstow, for the commandant's wife, the mother of the commandant's only child?"

"Horrible! horrible!" she answered, with a shudder, forgetting for an instant the dangers of the present in the recollection of the tragical past. "For a period our lives were not safe: murder hid behind every bush, skulked in the shadow of every rock and tree, and we knew not at what minute the little garrison might be rushed under cover of the darkness and every soul slaughtered before the relief force could come to our assistance. I died a hundred deaths a day in my anxiety for husband and child. And once the very zealousness of our comrades almost brought about the horror I feared. Oh!" — with a shudder of horrified recollections she covered her eyes, as if to shut out the memory of it — "Oh! that night — that horrible night! Unknown to any of us, my baby, rising from the bed where I had left him sleeping, whilst I went outside to stand by Lord Chepstow, wandered beyond the line of defence, and, before anybody realized it, was out in the open, alone and unprotected.

"Ferralt, the cook, saw him first; saw, too, the crouching figure of a native, armed with a gun, in the shadow of the undergrowth. Without hesitation the brave fellow rushed out, fell upon the native before he could dart away, wrenched the gun from him, and brained him with the butt. A cry of the utmost horror rang out upon the air, and, uttering it, another native bounded out from a hiding-place close to where the first had been killed, and flew zig-zagging across the open where Cedric was. Evidently he had no intention of molesting the little fellow, for he fled straight on past him, still shrieking after the accident occurred; but to Ferralt it seemed as if his intention were to murder the boy, and, clapping the gun to his shoulder, in a panic of excitement, he fired. If it had been one of the soldiers, who understood marksmanship and was not likely to be in a nervous quake over the circumstances, the thing could not have happened, although the fugitive was careering along in a direct line with my precious little one. But, with Ferralt – Oh, Mr. Cleek, can you imagine my horror when I saw the flash of that shot, heard a shrill cry of pain, and saw my child drop to the ground?"

"Good heaven!" exclaimed Cleek, agitated in spite of himself. "Then the blunderer shot the child instead of the native?"

"Yes; and was so horrified by the mishap that, without waiting to learn the result, he rushed blindly to the brink of a deep ravine, and threw himself headlong to death. But the injury to Cedric was only a trifling one, after all. The bullet seemed merely to have grazed him in passing, and, beyond a ragged gash in the fleshy part of the thigh, he was not harmed at all. This I myself dressed and bandaged, and in a couple of weeks it was quite healed. But it taught me a lesson, that night of horror, and I never let my baby out of my sight for one instant from that time until the rising was entirely quelled.

"As suddenly as it had started, the trouble subsided. Native priests came under a flag of truce to Lord Chepstow, and confessed their error, acknowledged that they had never any right to suspect the British of any design upon their gods, for the loot of the temple had actually taken place in the midst of the rising, and they knew that it could not have come from the hands of the soldiers, for they had had them under surveillance all the time, and not one person of the race had ventured within a mile of the temple.

"Yet the tooth of Buddha had been taken, the sacred tooth which is more holy to Buddhists than the statue of Gautama Buddha itself. Their remorse was very real, and after that, to the day of his death from fever, eighteen months afterward, they could never show enough honour to Lord Chepstow. And even then their favour continued. They transferred to the little son the homage they had done the father, but in a far, far greater degree. If he had been a king's son they could have shown him no greater honour. Native princes showered him with rich gifts; if he walked out, his path was strewn with flowers by bowing maidens; if he went into the market-place, the people prostrated themselves before him.

"When I questioned Buddhist women of this amazing hom-

61

age to Cedric, they gave me a full explanation. My son was sacred, they said. Buddha had withdrawn his favour from his people because of the evil they had done in suspecting the father and of the innocent life — Ferralt's — which had been sacrificed, and they had been commanded of the priests to do homage to the child and thereby appease the offended god, who, doubtless, had himself spirited away the holy tooth, and would not restore it until full recompense was made to the sacred son of the sacred dead.

"When it became known that I had decided to return to England with my boy, native princes offered me fabulous sums to remain, and when they found that I could not be tempted to stay, the populace turned out in every town and village through which we passed on our way to the ship, and bowing multitudes followed us to the very last. Nor did it cease with that, for in all the years that have followed, even here in London, the homage and worship have continued. My son can go nowhere but that he is followed by Cingalese; can see no man or woman of the race but he or she prostrates herself before him and murmurs, 'Holy, most holy!' And daily, almost hourly, rich gifts are showered upon him from unknown hands, and he is watched over and guarded constantly. I tell you all this, Mr. Cleek, that you may the better understand how appalling is the horror which now assails us, how frightful is the knowledge that some one now seeks his life, and is using every means to take it."

"In other words, my dear Cleek," put in Narkom, as Lady Chepstow, overcome with emotion, broke down suddenly, "there appears to be a sudden and inexplicable change of front on the part of these fanatics, and they now seem as anxious to bring evil to the little lad as they formerly were to protect and cherish him. At any rate, some one of their order has, upon three separate occasions within the last month, endeavoured to kidnap him, and, in one instance, even attempted to murder him."

"Is that a fact?" queried Cleek sharply, glancing over at Miss Lorne. "You are certain it is not a fancy, but an absolute fact?"

"Yes; oh, yes!" she made answer agitatedly. "Twice when I

have gone into the Park with him, attempts have been made to separate us, to get him away from me; and once they did get him away, so swiftly, so adroitly, that he had vanished before I could turn round. But, although a bag had been thrown over his head to stifle his cries, he managed to make a very little one. I plunged screaming into the undergrowth from which that cry had come, and was just in time to save him. He was lying on the ground all bundled up in the bag, and his assailant, who must have heard me coming, had gone as if by magic. He, however, was able to tell me that the man was a Cingalese, and that he had 'tried to cut him with a knife.'"

"Cut him with a knife?" repeated Cleek in a reflective tone, and blew out a long, low whistle.

"Oh, but that is not the worst, Mr. Cleek," went on Ailsa. "Three days ago a woman, very beautiful and distinguished-looking, called to see Lady Chepstow regarding the reference of a former servant, one Jane Catherboys, who used to be her lady-ship's maid. After the caller left, a box of sugared violets was found lying temptingly open on a table in the main hall. Little Cedric is passionately fond of sugared violets, and, had he happened to pass that way before the box was discovered, he surely would have yielded to the temptation and eaten some. In removing the box the parlour maid accidentally upset it, and before she could gather all the violets up her ladyship's little pomeranian dog snapped up one and ate it. It was dead in six minutes' time! The sweets were simply loaded with prussic acid. When we came to inquire into the matter in the hope of tracing the mysterious caller, we found that Jane Catherboys was no longer in need of a position; that she had been married for eight months; that she knew nothing whatever of the woman, and had sent no one to inquire into her references."

"All of which shows, my dear Cleek," put in Narkom signifi-cantly, "that, whatever hand is directing these attempts, it belongs to one who knows more than a mere outsider possibly could. In short, to one who is aware of the little boy's excessive fondness for sugared violets, and is aware that Lady Chepstow once did have a maid named Jane Catherboys."

"If," said Cleek, "you mean to suggest by that that this points suspiciously in Captain Hawksley's direction, Mr. Narkom, permit me to say that it does not necessarily follow. The clever people of the under-world do nothing by halves nor without careful inquiry beforehand; that is what makes the difference between the common pickpocket and the brilliant swindler." He turned to Ailsa. "Is that all, Miss Lorne, or am I right in supposing that there is even worse to come?"

"Oh, much worse, Mr. Cleek! The knowledge that these would-be murderers, whoever they are, whatever may be their mysterious motive, have grown desperate enough to invade the house itself has driven Lady Chepstow well-nigh frantic. Of course, orders were immediately given to the servants that no stranger, no matter how well dressed, how well seeming, nor what the plea, was, from that moment, to be allowed past the threshold. We felt secure in that, knowing that no servant of the household would betray his trust, and that all would be on the constant watch for any further attempt. The unknown enemy must have found out about these precautions, for no stranger came again to the door. But last night a thing we had never counted upon happened. In the dead of the night the unknown broke into the house, into the very nursery itself, and but that Lady Chepstow, impelled she does not know by what, rose and carried the sleeping child into her own bed, he would assuredly have been murdered. The nurse, awakened by a horrible suffocating sensation, opened her eyes to find a man bending over her with a chloroform-soaked cloth, which he was about to lay over her face. She shrieked and fainted, but not before she saw the man spring to the little bed on the other side of her own, hack furiously at it with a long, murderous knife, then dart to the window and vanish. In the darkness he had not, of course, been able to see that the child's bed was empty, for its position kept it in deep shadow, and hearing the household stir at the sound of the nurse's shriek, he struck out blindly and flew to save himself from detection. The nurse states that he was undoubtedly a foreigner — a dark-skinned Asiatic — and her description of him tallies with that Cedric gave of the man who attempted to kill him that day in the Park. There, Mr. Cleek," she concluded, "that's the whole story. Can't you do something to help us; something to lift this constant state of dread and to remove this terrible danger from little Lord Chepstow's life?"

"I'll try, Miss Lorne; but it is a most extraordinary case. Where is the boy now?"

"At home, closely guarded. We appealed to Mr. Narkom, and he generously appointed two detective officers to sit with him and keep constant watch over him whilst we are away."

"And in the meantime," added Mr. Narkom, "I've issued orders for a general rounding-up of all the Cingalese who can be traced or are known to be in town. Petrie and Hammond have that part of the job in hand, and if they hit upon any Asiatic who answers to the description of this murderous rascal – "

"I don't believe they will," interposed Cleek; "or, if they do, I don't for a moment believe he will turn out to be the guilty party. In other words, I have an idea that the fellow will prove to be a European."

"But, my dear fellow, both the boy and the nurse saw the man, and, as you have heard, they both agree that he was dark-skinned and quite Oriental in appearance."

"One of the easiest possible disguises, Mr. Narkom. A wig, a stick of grease-paint, a threepenny twist of crepe hair, and there you are! No, I do not believe that the man is a Cingalese at all; and, far from his having any connection with what you were pleased to term just now a change of front on the part of the Buddhists who have so long held the little chap as something sacred, I don't believe that they know anything about him. I base that upon the fact that the child is still treated with homage whenever he goes out, according to what Miss Lorne says, and that, with the single exception of that one woman who tried to poison him, nobody but one man – this particular one man – has ever made any attempt to harm the boy. Fanatics, like those Cingalese, cleave to an idea to the end, Mr. Narkom; they don't cast it aside and go off at another tangent. You have heard what Lady Chepstow says the native women told her: the boy was sacred; their priests had commanded them to appease Buddha by doing homage to him until the tooth was found, and the tooth has not been found up to the present day! That means that nothing on earth could change their attitude toward him, that not one of the Buddhist sect would harm a solitary hair of his head for a king's ransom; so you may eliminate the Cingalese from the case entirely so far as the attempts upon the child's life are concerned. Whoever is making the attempts is doing so without their knowledge and for a purely personal reason."

"Then, in that case, this Captain Hawksley – "

"I'll have a look at that gentleman before I tumble into bed to-night, and you shall have my views upon that point to-morrow morning, Mr. Narkom. Frankly, things point rather suspiciously in the captain's direction, since he is apparently the only person likely to be benefited by the boy's death, and if a motive cannot be traced to some other person – " He stopped abruptly and held up his hand. Outside in the dim halls of the house a sudden noise had sprung into being, the noise of some one running upstairs in great haste, and, stepping quickly to the door, Cleek drew it sharply open. As he did so, Dollops came puffing up out of the lower gloom, a sheep's trotter in one hand and a letter in the other.

"Law, guv'ner!" groaned he, from midway on the staircase, "I don't believe as I'm ever goin' to be let get a square tuck-in this side of the buryin' ground! Jist finished wot was left of that there steak and kidney puddin', sir, and started on my seckint trotter, when I sees a pair o' legs nip parst the area railin's to the front door, and then nip off again like greased lightnin', and when I ups and does a flyin' leap up the kitchen stairs, there was this here envellup in the letter-box and them there blessed legs nowheres in sight. I say, sir," agitatedly, "look wot's wrote on the envellup, will yer? And us always keepin' of it so dark."

Cleek plucked the letter from his extended hand, glanced at it, and puckered up his lips; then, with a gesture, he sent Dollops back below stairs, and, returning to the room, closed the door behind him.

"The enemy evidently knows all Lady Chepstow's movements, Mr. Narkom," he said. "I expect she and Miss Lorne have been under surveillance all day and have been followed here. Look at that!" He flung the letter down on a table as he spoke, and Narkom, glancing at it, saw printed in rude, illiterate letters upon the envelope the one word "Cleek." The identity of "Captain Burbage" was known to some one, and the secret of the house in Clarges Street was a secret no longer!

"Purposely disguised, you see. No one, not even a little child, would make such a botch of copying the alphabet as that," Cleek said, as he took the letter up and opened it. The sheet it contained was lettered in the same uncouth manner and bore these words:

"Cleek, take a fool's advice and don't accept the Chepstow case. Be warned. If you interfere, somebody you care about will pay the price. You'll find it more satisfactory to buy a wedding bouquet than a funeral wreath!"

"Oh!" shuddered the two ladies in one breath. "How horrible! How cowardly!" And then, feeling that her last hope had gone, Lady Chepstow broke into a fit of violent weeping and laid her head on Ailsa's shoulder.

"Oh, my baby! My darling baby boy!" she sobbed. "And now they are threatening somebody that you, too, love. Of course, Mr. Cleek, I can't expect you to risk the sacrifice of your own dear ones for the sake of me and mine, and so — and so – Oh, take me away, Miss Lorne! Let me go back to my baby and have him while I may."

"Good-night, Mr. Cleek," said Ailsa, stretching out a shaking hand to him. "Thank you so much for what you would have done but for this. And you were our last hope, too!"

"Why give it up then, Miss Lorne?" he said, holding her hand and looking into her eyes. "Why not go on letting me be your last hope — your only hope?"

"Yes, but they — they spoke of a funeral wreath."

"And they also spoke of a wedding bouquet! I am going to

take the case, Miss Lorne — take it, and solve it, as I'm a living man. Thank you!" as her brimming eyes uplifted in deep thankfulness and her shaking hand returned the pressure of his. "Now, just give me five minutes' time in the next room — it's my laboratory, Lady Chepstow — and I'll tell you whether I shall begin with Captain Hawksley or eliminate him from the case entirely. You might go in ahead, Mr. Narkom, and get the acid bath and the powder ready for me. We'll see what the finger-prints of our gentle correspondent have to tell, and, if they are not in the records of Scotland Yard or down in my own private little book, we'll get a sample of Captain Hawksley's in the morning."

Then, excusing himself to the ladies, he passed into the inner room in company with Narkom, and carried the letter with him. When he returned it was still in his hand, but there were grayish smudges all over it.

"There's not a finger-print in the lot that is worth anything as a means of identification, Miss Lorne," he said. "But you and Lady Chepstow may accept my assurance that Captain Hawksley is not the man. The writer of this letter belongs to the criminal classes; he is on his guard against the danger of finger-prints, and he wore rubber gloves when he penned this message. When I find him, rest assured I shall find a man who has had dealings with the police before and whose finger-prints are on their records. I don't know what his game is nor what he's after yet, but I will inside of a week. I've an idea; but it's so wild a thing I'm almost afraid to trust myself to believe it possible until I stumble over something that points the same way. Now, go home with Lady Chepstow, and begin the work of helping me."

"Helping you? Oh, Mr. Cleek, can we? Is there anything we can do to help?"

"Yes. When you leave the house, act as though you are in the utmost state of dejection, and keep that up indefinitely. Make it appear, for I am certain you will be followed and spied upon, as if I had declined the case. But don't have any fear about the boy. The two constables will sleep in the room with him to-night and every night until the thing is cleared up and the danger past. To-morrow about dusk, however, you, personally, take him for a walk near the Park, and if, among the other Cingalese you may meet, you should see one dressed as an Englishman, and wearing a scarlet flower in his buttonhole, take no notice of how often you see him nor of what he may do."

"It will be you, Mr. Cleek?"

"Yes. Now go, please; and don't forget to act as if you and her ladyship were utterly broken-hearted. Also" — his voice dropped lower, his hand met her hand, and in the darkness of the hall a little silver-plated revolver was slipped into her palm — "also, take this. Keep it always with you, never be without it night or day, and if any living creature offers you violence, shoot him down as you would a mad dog. Good-night, and — remember!"

And long after she and Lady Chepstow had gone down and passed out into the night he stood there, looking the situation straight in the face and thinking his own troubled thoughts.

"A wedding bouquet! A threat against her, and the mention of a wedding bouquet!" he said, as he went back into the room and sat down to figure the puzzle out. "Only one creature in the world knows of my feelings in that direction, and only one creature in the world would be capable of that threat — Margot! But what interest could she or any of her tribe have in the death of Lady Chepstow's little son? Her game is always money. If she were after a ransom she would try to abduct the child, not to kill him, and if - " A sudden thought came and wrenched away his voice. He sat a moment twisting his fingers one through the other and frowning at the floor; then, of a sudden, he gave a cry and jumped to his feet. "Five lacs of rupees — a fortune! By George, I've got it!" he fairly shouted. "The wild guess was a correct one, I'll stake my life upon it. Now, then, to put it to the test."

II

The summer twilight was deepening into the summer dusk when Ailsa, acting upon Cleek's advice, set forth with little Lord Chepstow the following evening, and turned her steps in the direction of the Park. Although, on her way there, she observed more than once that a swarthy-skinned man in European dress, who wore a scarlet flower in his coat, and was so perfect a type of the Asiatic that he would have passed muster for one even among a gathering of Cingalese, kept appearing and disappearing at irregular intervals, it spoke well for the powers of imitation and self-effacement possessed by Dollops that she never once thought of associating that young man with the dawdling messenger boy who strolled leisurely along with a package under his arm and patronized every bun-shop, winkle stall, and pork-pie purveyor on the line of march.

For upward of an hour this sort of thing went on without any interruption and Ailsa strolled along leisurely, with the boy's hand in hers, his innocent prattle running on ceaselessly; then, of a sudden, whilst they were moving along close to the Park railings and in the shadow of the overhanging trees, the figure of an undersized man in semi-European costume, but wearing on his head the twisted turban of a Cingalese, issued from one of the gates and well-nigh collided with them.

He drew back, murmuring an apology in pidgin-English, then, seeing the child, he salaamed profoundly and murmured in a voice of deep reverence, "Holy, most holy!" and prostrated himself, with his forehead touching the ground, until Ailsa and the child had passed on. But barely had they taken five steps before Cleek appeared upon the scene, and did exactly the same thing as the Cingalese.

"All right. You may go home now. I've got my man," he whispered, as Ailsa and the boy passed by. "Look for me at Chepstow House some time to-night." Then rose, as she walked on, and went after the man who first had prostrated himself before the child.

He had risen and gone on his way, but not before witnessing Cleek's obeisance, and flashing upon him a sharp, searching look. Cleek quickened his steps and shortened the distance between them. Now or never was the time to put to the test that wild thought which last night had hammered on his brain, for it was certain that this man was in very truth a genuine Cingalese, and, as such, must know! He stretched forth his hand and touched the man, who drew back sharply, half indignantly, but changed his attitude entirely when Cleek, who knew Hindustani more than well, spoke to him in the native tongue.

"Unto thee, oh, brother!" Cleek said. "Thou, too, art of us, for thou, too, dost acknowledge the sacred shrine. These eyes have beheld thee."

All his hopes rested on the slim pillar of that one word, "shrine," and his heart almost ceased to beat as he watched to see how it was received. It broke, however, into a very tumult of disturbance in the next instant, for the man positively beamed as he gave reply.

"Sacred be the shrine!" he answered in Hindustani. "Clearly thou art of us — not of those others."

"Others? What others? I am but newly come to this country."

"Walk with me, then, to my abode, sup with me, eat of my salt, and I will tell thee then, oh, brother. But I forget: thou hast no knowledge of me. Listen, then. I am Arjeeb Noosrut, father of the High Priest Seydama, and it is among the people of my house that the gun is yet preserved. Nor has the blood of Seydama been ever washed from the wood of it! Come."

All in a moment a light seemed to break over Cleek's brain. The missing link had been supplied — the one thing that could make possible the wild thought which had come to him last night had been given into his hands. Here at last was the key to the amazing mystery! He turned without a word and went with Arjeeb Noosrut.

"What an ass!" he said to himself in the soundless words of thought. "What an ass never to have suspected it when it is all so clear!"

Meantime Ailsa and the boy, dismissed from any further need of service, walked on through the deepening dusk and turned their faces homeward. But they had not gone twenty yards from the spot where Cleek had seen them last when the little boy set up a joyful cry and pointed excitedly to a claret-coloured limousine which at that moment swung in from the middle of the roadway and slowed down as it neared the kerb.

"Oh, look, Miss Lorne; here's mummie's motor-car; and I do believe that's Bimbi peeping out of it!" exclaimed the child — "Bimbi" being his pet name for Captain Hawksley — then broke, in wild excitement, from Ailsa's detaining hand and fled to a tall, military-looking man with a fair beard and moustache who had just that moment alighted from the vehicle. "It is Bimbi — it is! — it is!" he shouted as he ran. "Oh, Bimbi, I *am* glad!"

"Ceddie, dear, you mustn't be so boisterous!" chided Ailsa, coming up with him at the kerb. "How fond he is of you to be sure, Captain Hawksley. You've come for us, I suppose? Ceddie recognized the car at once."

"Yes; jump in," he answered. "Lady Chepstow sent me after you. She's nervous, poor soul, every moment the boy's away from her. Jump in, old chap! Better take the back seat, Miss Lorne; it's more comfortable. Quite settled, both of you? That's good. All right, chauffeur — Home!"

Then he jumped in after them, closed the door, dropped into a seat, and the motor, making a wide curve out into the road, pelted away into the fast-gathering darkness.

"Bimbi says maybe he's going to be my daddy one day — didn't you, Bimbi?" said his little lordship, climbing up on to "Bimbi's" knee and snuggling close to him.

"I say, you know, you mustn't tell secrets, old chap!" was the laughing response. "Miss Lorne will hand you over to Nursie with orders to put you to bed if you do, I know. Won't you, Miss Lorne?"

"He ought to be in bed, anyhow," responded Ailsa gaily; and then, this giving the conversation a merry turn, they talked and laughed and kept up such a chatter that three-quarters of an hour went like magic and nobody seemed aware of it. But suddenly Ailsa thought, and then put her thoughts into words.

"What a long time we are in getting home," she said, and bent forward so that the light from the window might fall upon the dial of her wrist watch, then gave a little startled cry and half rose from her seat. For the darkness was now tempered by moonlight and she could see that they were no longer in the populous districts of the town, but were speeding along past woodlands and open fields in the very depths of the country. "Good gracious! Johnston must have lost his senses!" she exclaimed agitatedly. "Look where we are, Captain Hawksley! – out in the country with only a farmhouse or two in sight. Johnston! Johnston!" She bent forward and rapped wildly on the glass panel. "Johnston, stop! – turn round! – are you out of your head? Captain Hawksley, stop him – stop him, for pity's sake!"

"Sit down, Miss Lorne." He made reply in a low, level voice, a voice in which there was something that made her pluck the child to her and hold him tight to her breast. "You are not going home to-night. You are going for a ride with me; and if - Oh, that's your little game, is it?" lurching forward as she made a frantic clutch at the handle of the door. "Sit down, do you hear me? – or it will be worse for you! There!" – the cold bore of a revolver barrel touched her temple and wrung a quaking gasp of terror from her – "Do you feel that? Now you sit down and be quiet! If you make a single move, utter a single cry, I'll blow your brains out before you've half finished it! Look here, do you know who you're dealing with now? See!"

His hand reached up and twitched away the fair beard and moustache; he bent forward so that the moonlight through the glass could fall on his face. It had changed as his voice had now changed, and she saw that she was looking at the man who in those other days of stress and trial had posed as "Gaston Merode," brother to the fictitious "Countess de la Tour."

"You!" she said in a bleak voice of desolation and fright. "Dear heaven, that horrible Margot's confederate, the King of the Apaches!"

"Yes!" he rapped out. "You and that fellow Cleek came between us in one promising game, but I'm hanged if you shall do it in this one! I want this boy, and — I've got him. Now, you call off Cleek and tell him to drop this case, to make no effort to follow us or to come between us and the kid, or I'll slit your throat after I've done with his little lordship here. Lanisterre!" — to the chauffeur — "Lanisterre, do you hear?"

"*Oui, monsieur.*"

"Give her her head and get to the mill as fast as you can. Margot will be with us in another two hours' time."

III

Through the ever-deepening dusk Cleek and Arjeeb Noosrut moved onward together; and onward behind them moved, too, the same dilatory messenger boy who had loitered about in the neighbourhood of the Park, squandering his halfpence now as then, leaving a small trail of winkle shells and trotter bones to mark the record of his passage, and never seeming to lose one iota of his appetite, eat as much and as often as he would.

The walk led down into the depths of Soho, that refuge of the foreign element in London; but long before they halted at the narrow doorway of a narrow house in a narrow side street that seemed to have gone to sleep in an atmosphere of gloom and smells Cleek had adroitly "pumped" Arjeeb Noosrut dry, and the riddle of the sacred son was a riddle to him no longer. He was now only anxious to part from the man and return with the news to Lady Chepstow, and was casting round in his mind for some excuse to avoid going indoors with him to waste precious time in breaking bread and eating salt. Suddenly there lurched out of an adjoining doorway an ungainly figure in turban and sandals and the full flower of that grotesque regalia which passes muster at cheap theatres and masquerade balls for the costume of a Cingalese. The fellow had bent forward out of the deeper darkness of the house-passage into the murk and gloom of the ill-lit street, and was straining his eyes as if in search for some one long expected.

"Dog of an infidel!" exclaimed Arjeeb Noosrut, speaking in

Hundustani and spitting on the pavement as he caught sight of the man. "See, well-beloved, he is of those 'others' of which I spoke when I first met thee. There are many of them, but true believers none. They dwell in a room huddled up as unclean things in the house there; they drink and make merry far into the night, and a woman veiled and in European garb comes to them and drinks with them. Sometimes a man of her kind is with her, and they speak a tongue that is not the tongue of our people; yet have I seen them go forth into the city and do homage as we to the sacred son."

Cleek sucked in his breath and, twitching round, stared at the dim figure leaning forward in the dim light.

"By George!" he said to himself; "if I know anything, I ought to know the slouch and the low-sunk head of the Apache! And a woman comes! And a man comes! And there are five lacs of rupees! I wonder! I wonder! But no — she wouldn't come here, to a place like this, if she had ventured back into England and had called some of the band over to help. She'd go to the old spot where she and I used to lie low and laugh whilst the police were hunting for me. She'd go there, I'm sure, to the old Burnt Acre Mill, where, if you were 'stalked,' you could open the sluice gates and let the Thames and the mill stream rush in and meet, and make a hell of whirling waters that would drown a fish. She would go there if it were she. And yet — it is an Apache: I swear it is an Apache!"

He turned and looked back at Arjeeb Noosrut, then raised his hand and brushed it down the back of his head, which was always the sign "Wait!" to Dollops, and then spoke as calmly as he could.

"Brother, I will go in and break bread and eat salt with thee," he said. "But I may do no more, for to-night I am in haste."

"Come, then," the man answered; and taking him by the hand, led him in and up to a room at the back of the second storey, where, hot as the night was, the windows were closed and a woman, squatted before a lighted brasier, was dripping the contents of an oil cruse over the roasting carcase of a young kid.

"It is to shut out the sounds of the vile infidel orgies from the house adjoining," explained Arjeeb Noosrut, as Cleek walked to the tightly closed window and leant his forehead against it. "Yet, if the heat oppresses thee – "

"It does," interposed Cleek, and leant far out into the darkness as though sucking in the air when the sash was raised and the thing which had been only a dim babel of wordless sounds a moment before became now the riotous laughter and the ribald comments of men upon the verses of a comic song which one of their number was joyously singing.

"French!" said Cleek under his breath, as he caught the notes of the singer and the words of his audience, "French – I knew it!"

Then he drew in his head, and having broken of the bread and eaten of the salt which, at a word from Arjeeb Noosrut, the woman brought on a wicker tray and laid before them, he moved hastily to the door.

"Brother and son of the faithful, peace be with thee, I must go," he said. "But I come again; and it is written that thou shalt be honoured above all men when I return to thee, and that the true believers – the true sons of Holy Buddha – shall have cause to set thy name at the head of the records of those who are most blest of him!"

Then he salaamed and passed out. Closing the door behind him, he ran like a hare down the narrow stairs. At the door Dollops rose up like the imp in a pantomime and jumped toward him.

"Law, guv'ner, I'm nigh starved a-waitin' for yer!" he said in a whisper. "Wot's the lay now? A double quick change? I've got the stuff here, look!" – holding up the package he was carrying – "or a chance for me to do some fly catchin' with me bloomin' tickle tootsies?"

The man in the Cingalese costume had vanished from the doorway of the adjoining house, and, catching the boy by the arm, Cleek hurried him to it and drew him into the dark passage.

"I'm going to the back; I'm going to climb up to the windows of the second storey and see who's there and what's going on," he whispered. "Lie low and watch. I think it's Margot's gang."

"Oh, colour me blue! Them beauties? And in London? I'd give a tanner for a strong cup o' tea!"

"Shh-h! Be quiet – speak low. Don't be seen, but keep a close watch; and if anybody comes downstairs – "

"He's mine!" interjected Dollops, stripping up his sleeves. "Glue to the eyebrows and warranted to stick! Nip away, guv'ner, and leave it to the tickle tootsies and me!" Then, as Cleek moved swiftly and silently down the passage and slipped out into the sort of yard at the back of the house, he pulled out his roll of brown paper squares and his tube of adhesive, and crawling upstairs on his hands and knees, began operations at the top step. But he had barely got the first "plaster" fairly made and ready to apply when there came a rush of footsteps behind him and he was obliged to duck down and flatten himself against the floor of the landing to escape being run down by a man who dashed in through the lower door, flew at top speed up the stairs and, with a sort of blended cheer and yell, whirled open a door on the landing above and vanished. In a twinkling other cheers rang out, there was the sound of hastily moving feet and the uproar of general excitement.

"Oh, well, if you won't stop to be waited on, gents, help yourselves!" said Dollops with a chuckle. Then he began backing hastily down the stairs, squirting the contents of the tube all over the steps, and concluded the operation by scattering all the loose sheets of paper on the floor at the foot of them before slipping out into the street and composedly waiting.

Meantime Cleek, sneaking out through the rear door, found himself in a small, brick-paved yard hemmed in by a high wall thickly fringed on the top with a hedge of broken bottles. At one time in its history the house had been occupied by a catgut maker, and the rickety shed in which he had carried on his calling still clung, sagging and broken-roofed, to the building itself, its rotten slates all but vanished, and its interior piled high with mildewed bedding, mouldy old carpet, broken furniture, and refuse of every sort.

A foot or two above the roof-level of this glowed — two luminous rectangles in the blackness of darkness — the windows of the back room on the second storey; and out of these came floating still the song, the laughter, and the jabbered French he had heard in the house next door. It did not take him long to make up his mind. Gripping the swaying supports of the sagging shed, he went up it with the agility of a monkey, crawled to the nearer of the two windows, and, cautiously raising himself, peeped in. What he saw made him suck in his breath sharply and sent his heart hammering hard and fast.

A dozen men were in the room, men whose faces, despite an inartistic attempt to appear Oriental, he recognized at a glance and knew better than he knew his own. About them lay discarded portions of Cingalese attire, thrown off because of the heat, and waiting to be resumed at any moment. The air was thick with tobacco smoke and rank with spirituous odours. Sprawled figures were everywhere, and on a sort of couch against the opposite wall, a cigarette between her fingers, a glass of absinthe at her elbow, her laughter and badinage ringing out as loudly as any, lay the lissom figure of Margot!

But even as Cleek looked in upon it the picture changed. Swift, sharp, and sudden came the rattle of flying feet on the outer stairs. Margot flung aside her cigarette and jumped up, the song and the laughter came to an abrupt end, the door flew open, and with a shout and a cheer a man bounced into the room.

"Serpice! Ah, *le bon Dieu!* it is Serpice at last!" cried out Margot in joyous excitement as she and the others crowded round him. "Soul of a sluggard, don't waste time in laughing and capering like this! Speak up, speak up, you hear? Are we to fly at once to the mill and join him? Has he succeeded? Is it done?"

"Yes, yes, yes!" shouted back Serpice, throwing up his cap and capering. "It is done! It is done! Under the very nose of the Cracksman, too! Merode's got them both! The little lordship and the Mademoiselle Lorne, too! They took the bait like gudgeons;

they stepped into the automobile without a fear, and — whizz! it was off to the mill like that! La, la, la! We win, we win, we win!"

The shock of the thing was too much for Cleek. Carried out of himself by the knowledge that the woman he loved was now in peril of her life, discretion forsook him, blind rage mastered him, and he did one of the few foolish things of his life.

"You lie, you brute, you lie!" he shouted, jumping up into full view. "God help the man who lays a hand on her! Let him keep his life from me if he can!"

"The Cracksman!" yelled out Serpice. "The Cracksman! The Cracksman!" echoed Margot and the rest. Then a pistol barked and spat, the light was swept out, a bullet sang past Cleek's ear, and he realized how foolish he had been. For part of the crowd came surging to the window, part went in one blind rush for the door to head him off and hem him in, and, through the din and hubbub rang viciously the voice of Margot shrilling out: "Kill him! Kill him!" as though nothing but the sight of his blood would glut her malice.

It was neck or nothing now, and the race was to the swift. He dropped through a gap in the ragged roof, sheer down, like a shot, into the rubble and refuse below; he lurched through the shed to the door, and through that to the black passage leading to the street — the clatter on the higher staircase giving warning of the crowd coming after him — and flew like a hare hard pressed toward the outer door, and then, just then, when every little moment counted, there was a scrambling sound, a chorus of oaths, a slipping, a sliding, a bang on one step and a bump on another; and, as he darted by and sprang out into the street the hall was filled with a writhing, scuffling, swearing mass of glue-covered men struggling in a whirling waste of loose brown paper.

"This way! come quickly, for your life!" he shouted to Dollops as he came plunging out into the street. "They've got them, got the little boy! Got Miss Lorne — in spite of me. Come on! come on! come on!" He flew like an arrow from crossing to crossing and street to street with Dollops, like a shadow, at his heels.

A sudden swerve to the right brought them into a lighted and populous thoroughfare. Italian restaurants, German delicatessen shops, eating places of a dozen other nationalities lined the pavement on both sides of the street, and in front of one of these a high-power motor stood, protected by the watchful eye of an accommodating policeman while the chauffeur sampled Chianti in a wine-shop close by. With a rush and a leap Cleek was upon it, and with another rush and a leap the constable was upon him, only to be greeted with the swift flicking open of a coat and the gleam of badge that every man in the force knew.

"Cleek?"

"Yes! In the name of the Yard; in the name of the king! get out of the way! In with you, Dollops! We'll get the brutes yet!"

Then he bent over, threw in the clutch, and discarding all speed laws, sent the car humming and tearing away.

"Hold tight!" he said through his teeth. "Whatever comes, we've got to get to Burnt Acre Mill inside of an hour. If you know any prayers, Dollops, say them."

"The Lord fetch us home in time for supper!" gulped the boy obediently. "S'help me, guv'ner, the wind's goin' through my teeth like I was a mouth organ, and I'm hollow enough for a flute!"

IV

It is strange how, in moments of stress and trial, even in times of tragedy, the most commonplace thoughts will intrude themselves and the mind separate itself from the immediate events. As Merode put the cold muzzle of the revolver to Ailsa's temple and she ought, one would have supposed, to have been deaf and blind to all things but the horror of her position, one of these strange mental lapses occurred, and her mind, travelling back over the years to her early schooldays, dwelt on a punishment task set her by her preceptress — the task of copying three hundred times the phrase "Discretion is the better part of valour."

As the recollection of that time rose before her mental vision, the value of the phase itself forced its worth upon her and, huddling back in the corner of the limousine, she clutched the frightened child to her and gave implicit obedience to Merode's command to make no effort to attract attention either by word or deed. And he, fancying that he had thoroughly cowed her, withdrew the touch of the weapon from her temple, but held it ready for possible use in the grip of his thin, strong hand.

For a time the limousine kept straight on in its headlong course, then, of a sudden, it swerved to the left. The gleam of a river — all silver with moonlight — struck up through a line of trees on one side of the car, the blank, unbroken dreariness of a stretch of waste land spread out upon the other, and presently, by the slowing down of the motor, Ailsa guessed that they were nearing their destination. They reached it a few moments later, and a peep from the window, as the vehicle stopped, showed her the outlines of a ruined watermill, ghostly, crumbling, owl-haunted, looming black against the silver sky.

A crumbled wheel hung, rotten and moss-grown, over a dry water-course, where straggling willows stretched out from the bank and trailed their long, feathery ends a yard or so above the level of the weeds and grasses that carpeted the sandy bed of it, and along its edge — once built as a protection for the heedless or unwary, but now a ruin and a wreck — a moss-grown wall with a narrow, gateless archway made an irregular shadow on the moon-drenched earth. She saw that archway and that dry water-course, and a new, strong hope arose within her. Discretion had played its part; now it was time for Valour to take the stage.

"Come, get out — this is the end," said Merode, as he unlatched the door of the limousine and alighted. "You may yell here until your throat splits, for all the good it will do you. Lanisterre, show us a light; the path to the door is uncertain, and the floor of the mill is unsafe. This way, if you please, Miss Lorne. Let me have the boy, I'll look after him!"

"No, no! — not yet! Please, not yet!" said Ailsa, with a little catch in her voice as she plucked him to her and smothered his frightened cries against her breast. "Let me have him whilst I may; let me hold him to the last, Monsieur Merode. His mother trusts me. She will want to know that I — I stood by him until I could stand no longer. Please! — we are so helpless — I am so fond of him, and — he is such a very little boy. Listen! You want me to write to Mr. Cleek; you want me to ask something of him. I won't do it for myself, not if you kill me for refusing. I'll never do it for myself; but — but I will do it if you won't separate us until he has had time to say his prayers."

"Oh, all right, then," he agreed. "If it's any consolation doing a fool's trick like that, why do it! Now come along, and let's get inside the mill without any more nonsense. Lanisterre, bring that lantern here so that mademoiselle can see the path to the door. This way, if you please, Miss Lorne."

"Thank you," she said as she alighted and moved slowly in the direction of the door, soothing the child as they crept along almost within touch of the crumbling wall. "Ceddie, darling, don't cry. You are a brave little hero, I know, and heroes are never afraid to die." From the tail of her eye she watched Merode. He seemed to realize from these words to the child that she was reconciled to the inevitable, and with an air of satisfaction he put the pistol back into his pocket and walked beside her. She kept straight on with her soothing words; and, in the half shadow, neither Merode nor Lanisterre could see that one hand was lost in the folds of her skirt.

"Ceddie, darling, let Miss Lorne be able to tell mummie that her little man was a hero; that he died, as heroes always die, without a fear or a weakening to the very last. I'll stand by you, precious; I'll hold your hand; and, when the time comes - "

It came then! The gateless archway was reached at last, and the thing she had been planning all along now became possible. With one sudden push she sent the boy reeling down the incline into the dry water-course, flashed round sharply, and before Merode really knew how the thing had happened, she was standing with her back to the arch and a revolver in her levelled hand.

"Throw up your arms — throw them up at once, or, as God

hears me, I'll shoot!" she cried. "Run, Ceddie, run, baby! He shan't follow you. I'll kill him if he tries!"

"You idiot!" began Merode, and made a lurch toward her. But the pistol barked and something white-hot zig-zagged along his arm and bit like a flame into his shoulder.

"Up with your hands — up with them!" she said in a voice that shook with excitement as he howled out and made a reeling backward step. "Next time it will be the head I aim at, not the arm!" Then, lifting up her voice in one loud shriek that made the echoes bound, she called with all her strength: "Help, somebody — for God's sake help! Scream, Ceddie — scream! Help! Help!"

And lo! as she called, as if a miracle had been wrought, out of the darkness an answering voice called back to her, and the wild, swift notes of a motor horn bleated along the lonely road.

"I'm coming — I — Cleek!" that voice rang out. "Hold your own — hold it to the last, Miss Lorne, and God help the man who lays a finger on you!"

"Mr. Cleek! Mr. Cleek, oh, thank God!" she flung back with all the rapture a human voice could contain. "Come on, come on! I've got him — got that man Merode, and the boy is safe, the boy is safe! Come on! come on! come on!"

"We're a-comin', miss, you gamble on that and the lightnin's a fool to us!" shouted Dollops in reply. "Let her have it, guv'ner! Bust the bloomin' tank. Give her her head; give her her feet; give her her blessed merry-thought if she wants it! Hurrah! hurrah! hurrah!"

And then, just then, when she most needed her strength and her courage, Ailsa's evaporated. The reaction came, and, with the despairing cries of Merode and Lanisterre ringing in her ears, she sank back, weak, white, almost fainting and, leaning against the side of the archway, began to laugh and to sob hysterically. Merode seized that one moment and sprang to the breach.

Realizing that the game was all but up, that there was nothing for him now but to save his own skin if he could, he called out to Lanisterre to rip out the sparking plug of the motor and follow him, then plunged into the mill, swung over the lever which controlled the sluice gates, and, darting out by the back way, fled across the waste.

But behind him he left a scene of indescribable horror, and the shrill screaming of a little child told him when that horror began. For as the sluice gates opened a sullen roar sounded; on one side the diverted millstream, and on the other the river, rose as two solid walls of water, rushed forward and — met. In the twinkling of an eye the old water-course was one wild, leaping, roaring, gyrating whirlpool of up-flung froth and twisting waves that bore in their eddying clutch the battling figure of a drowning child.

Even before he came in sight of it the roaring waters and the fearful splash of their impact told Cleek what had been done. He could hear Ailsa's screams; he could hear the boy's feeble cries, and a moment later, when the whizzing motor panted up through the moonlight and sped by the broken wall, there was Ailsa, fairly palsied with fright, clinging weakly to the crumbling arch and uttering little sobbing, wordless, incoherent moans of fright as she stared down into the hell of waters; and below, in the foam, a little yellow head was spinning round and round and round, in dizzying circles of torn and leaping waves.

"Heavens, guv'ner!" began Dollops in a voice of appalling despair; but before he could get beyond that, Cleek's coat was off, Cleek's body had described a sort of semi-circle, and the child was no longer alone in the whirlpool!

Battling, struggling, fairly leaping, as a fish leaps in a torrent, one moment half out of the water, the next wholly submerged, Cleek struck from eddy to eddy, from circle to circle, until that little yellow head was within reach, then put forth his hand and gripped it, pulled it to him, and in another moment he was whirling round and round the whirlpool's course with the child clutched to him and its wet, white face gleaming wax-like over the angle of his shoulder.

They had not made the half of the first circle thus before Dollops had leaped to the bending willows, had scrambled up the rough trunk of the nearest of them, and, pushing his weight out upon a strong and supple bough, bent it downward until the half of its strongest withes were deep in the whirling waters.

"Grab 'em, guv'ner — grab 'em when you come by!" he sang out over the roar of the waters. "They'll hold you, sir — hold a dozen like you; and if - Well played! Got 'em the first grab! Hang on! Get a tight grip! Now, then, sir, hand over hand till you're at the bank! Good biz! Good biz! Blest if you won't be goin' in for the circus trade next! Steady does it, sir — steady, steady! Goal, by Jupiter! Now, then, hand me up the nipper — I should say the young gent — and in two minutes' time - Right! Got him! 'Ere you are, Miss Lorne — lay hold of his little lordship, will you? I've got me blessed hands full a-keepin' to me perch whilst the guv'ner's a-wobbling of the branch like this. Good biz! Now, then, sir, another 'arf a yard. That's the call! Hands on this bough and foot on the bank there. One, two, three — knew you'd do it! Safe as house, Gawd bless yer bully heart!"

And then Cleek, wet, white, panting, dragged himself out of the clutch of the whirlpool and lay breathing heavily on the ground.

"By gums, guv'ner," Dollops added as he looked down on the whirling waters, "what an egg-beater it would make, wouldn't it, sir? Ain't got such a thing as a biscuit about yer, have you? Me spine's a-rasping holes in me necktie, and I'm so flat you could slip me into a pillar box and they'd take me home for a penny stamp."

But Cleek made no reply. Wet and spent after his fierce struggle with the whirling fury he had just escaped, he lay looking up into Ailsa's eyes as she came to him with the sobbing child close pressed to her bosom and all heaven in her beaming face.

"It is not the 'funeral wreath' after all, you see, Miss Lorne," he said. "It came near to being it; but — it is not, it is not. I wonder, oh, I wonder!"

Then he laughed the foolish, vacuous laugh of a man whose

thoughts are too happy for the banality of words.

* * * * *

It was midnight and after. In the close-curtained library of Chepstow House, Cleek, with little Lord Chepstow sleeping in his arms, sat in solemn conclave with Lady Chepstow, Captain Hawksley, and Maverick Narkom. While they talked, Ailsa, like a restless spirit, wandered to and fro, now lifting the curtains to peep out into the darkness, now listening as if her whole life's hope lay in the coming of some expected sound. And in her veins there burned a fever of suspense.

"So you failed to get the rascals, did you, Mr. Narkom?" Cleek was saying. "I feared as much; but I couldn't get word to you sooner. We blew out a fuse, Dollops and I, in that mad race to the mill, and of course we had to come home at a snail's pace afterward. I'm sorry we didn't get Margot, sorrier still that that hound Merode got away. They are bound to make more trouble before the race is run. Not for her ladyship, however, and not for this dear little chap. Their troubles are at an end, and the sacred son will be a sacred son no longer."

"Oh, Mr. Cleek, do tell me what you mean," implored Lady Chepstow. "Do tell me how – "

"Doctor Fordyce at last!" struck in Ailsa excitedly, as the door-bell and the knocker clashed and the butler's swift footsteps went along the hall. "Now we shall know, Mr. Cleek, now we shall know for certain!"

"And so shall all the world," he replied as the door opened and the doctor was ushered into the room. "I don't think you were ever so welcome anywhere or at any time before, doctor," he added with a smile. "Come and look at this little chap. Bonny little specimen of a Britisher, isn't he?"

"Yes; but, my dear sir, I – I was under the impression that I was called to a scene of excitement; and you seem as peaceful as Eden here. The constable who came for me said it was something to do with Scotland Yard!"

"So it is, doctor. I had Mr. Narkom send for you to perform a very trifling but most important operation upon this little boy here."

"Upon Cedric!" exclaimed Lady Chepstow, rising in a panic of alarm. "An operation to be performed upon my baby boy? Oh, Mr. Cleek, in the name of Heaven – "

"No, your ladyship, in the name of Buddha. Don't be alarmed. It is only to be a trifling cut, a mere re-opening of that little wound in the thigh which you dressed and healed so successfully at Trincomalee. You made a mistake, all of you, that night when the boy was shot. The native poor Ferralt saw skulking along with the gun was not a mere tribesman and had not the very faintest thought of discharging that weapon at your little son, or, indeed, at anybody else in the world. He was the High Priest, Seydama, guardian of the holy tooth, the one living being who dared by right to touch it or to lay hands upon the shrine that contained it. Fearful, when the false rumour of that intended loot was circulated, that infidel eyes should look upon it, infidel hands profane the sacred relic, he determined to remove it from Dambool to the rock-hewn temple of Galwihara and to enshrine it there. For the purpose of giving no clue to his movements, he chose to abandon his priestly robes, to disguise himself as a common tribesman, and, the better to defeat the designs of those who might seek to tear it from him and hold it for ransom, he hid the holy tooth in the barrel of a gun. That gun was in his hands when Ferralt leaped out and brained him!"

"Dear heaven!" cried Lady Chepstow with a sudden burst of realization. "Then that holy relic, that fetish, the sacred tooth of Buddha – "

"Is embedded in the fleshy part of the thigh of your little son!" he finished. "Enclosed, doubtless, in a sac or cyst which protective Mother Nature has wrapped round it, the tooth is there; and, for five whole years, he has been the living shrine that held it!"

And so, in truth, it proved to be. Ten minutes later the trifling operation was over, and the long-lost relic lay in the palm of the doctor's hand.

"Take it, Captain Hawksley," said Cleek, lifting it and carrying it over to him. "There is a man in Soho, one Arjeeb Noosrut, who will know it when he sees it; and there is a vast reward. Five lacs of rupees will pay off no end of debts, and a man with that balance at his banker's can't be accused of being a fortune-hunter when he asks in marriage the hand of the woman he loves. Mr. Narkom, is your motor ready? I'm a bit fagged out, and Dollops, I know, is all but starving. Ladies and gentlemen, my best respects. The riddle is solved. Good-night!"

CHAPTER IV
THE CALIPH'S DAUGHTER

It was half-past ten on a wet September night when Superintendent Narkom's limousine pulled up in front of Cleek's house in Clarges Street, and the superintendent himself, disguised, as he always was when paying visits to his famous ally, stepped out and with infinite care assisted a companion to alight.

The figure of this second person, however, was so hidden by the folds of a long, thickly wadded cloak, the hem of which reached to within an inch or so of the pavement, that it would have been impossible for a passer-by to have decided whether it was that of a man or a woman; but the manner in which it bent, added to a shuffling uncertainty of gait — a sort of "feeling the way" movement of the feet — as Mr. Narkom guided it across the pavement to the door, suggested either great age or a state of total blindness: an affliction, by the way, of such recent date that the sufferer had not yet acquired that air of confidence and that freedom of step which is Time's kind gift to the sightless.

In a very few moments, however, all doubt as to the sex and the condition of the muffled figure was set at rest, for, upon the superintendent and his companion being admitted by Dollops to the dimly-lit hall of the house, the bent figure straightened, and it was easy to see that it was not only that of a man but of a man heavily blindfolded.

"You may take off the bandage now, Major," said Narkom, as the door closed behind them and Dollops busied himself with readjusting the fastenings. "We shall find your master in his sitting-room, I suppose, my embryo Vidocq?"

"Speaking to me, sir? Lor! You ain't never went and forgot my name after all these months, have you, Mr. Narkom?" said Dollops, not understanding the allusion. "Yes, sir; you'll find him there, sir, and frisky as a spring lamb without the peas, bless his heart! Been to the weddin' of Lady Chepstow and that there Captain Hawksley this afternoon, sir, and must have enjoyed hisself, the way he's been a-whistling and a-singing ever since he come home. What a feed they must of had with all their money! It seems almost a crime to 'a' missed it. Sent wot was left to the 'or-spittles, I hear, and me as flat as an autumn leaf after six months' pressin' in the family Bible."

"What! Hungry still, Dollops?"

"Hungry, sir? Lor, Mr. Narkom, a flute's a fool to me for hol-lowness. I'm that empty my blessed ribs is a-shaking hands with each other; and ten minutes ago, when I et a pint of winkles, the noise as they made a-gettin' by 'em, sir, you'd a thought it was somebody a-tumbling downstairs. But they say as every dog has his day, so I'm always a-livin' in hopes, sir."

"Hopes? Hopes of what?"

"That *some* time you'll come for the guv'ner to investigate a crime wot's been committed in a cookshop, sir — and *then*, wot ho! But," he added lugubriously, "they never comes to no violent end, them food-selling jossers; they always dies in their beds like a parcel of heathen!"

Narkom made no reply. By this time the man he had ad-dressed as "major" had removed the bandage from his eyes; and, beckoning him to follow, the superintendent led the way upstairs, leaving Dollops to mourn alone.

Cleek, who was sitting by a carefully shaded lamp jotting something down in his diary, closed the book and rose as the two men entered. Late as the hour was he had not yet changed the garments he had worn at Lady Chepstow's wedding in the after-noon.

"You are promptness itself, Mr. Narkom," he said gaily, as he glanced at his watch. "I am afraid that I myself overlooked the passage of time in attending to — well, other things. You will, perhaps, be interested to learn, Mr. Narkom, that Miss Lorne has decided to remain in England."

"Indeed, my dear fellow, I never heard that she contem-plated going out of it again. Did she?"

"Oh, yes; I thought you knew. Captain Hawksley has been

ordered to India with his regiment. Of course, that means that, after their honeymoon, his wife and little Lord Chepstow will accompany him. They wished Miss Lorne to continue as the boy's governess and to go with them. At the last moment, however, she decided to remain in England and to seek a new post here. But, pardon me, we are neglecting your companion, Mr. Narkom. The aftermath of previous cases cannot, I fear, be of interest to him."

"Yes, my dear chap," agreed Narkom. "Let me introduce Major Burnham-Seaforth, my dear Cleek. Major, you are at last in the presence of the one man you desire to put upon the case; if there is anything in it, be sure that he will get it out."

For just half a moment after he spoke the major's name, Narkom fancied that it seemed to have a disturbing influence upon Cleek; that there was a shadow, just a shadow of agitation suggested. But before he could put his finger upon the particular point which made this suspicion colourable, it was gone and had left no trace behind.

The major — who, by the way, was a decidedly military-looking man long past middle life — had been studying Cleek's face with a curious sort of intentness ever since he entered the room. Now he put forth his hand in acknowledgment of the introduction.

"I am delighted to have the opportunity of meeting you, Mr. Cleek," he said. "At first I thought Mr. Narkom's insistence upon my making the journey here blindfolded singularly melodramatic and absurd. I can now realize, since you are so little similar to one's preconceived idea of a police detective, that you may well wish to keep everything connected with your residence and your official capacity an inviolable secret. One does not have to be told that you are a man of birth and breeding, Mr. Cleek. Pardon me if I ask an impertinent question. Have we by any chance met before — in society or elsewhere? There is something oddly familiar in your countenance. I can't quite seem to locate it, however."

"Then I shouldn't waste my time in endeavouring to do so, Major, if I were you," responded Cleek with the utmost *sang-froid*. "It is bound to end in nothing. Points of resemblance between

91

persons who are in no way connected are of common occurrence. I have no position in society, no position of any sort but *this*. I am simply Cleek, the detective. I have a good memory, however, and if I had ever met you before I should not have forgotten it."

And with this non-committal response he dismissed the subject airily, waved the major to a seat, and the business of the interview began.

"My dear Cleek," Narkom began, opening fire without further parley, "the major has come to ask your aid in a case of singular and mystifying interest. You may or may not have heard of a music-hall artiste — a sort of conjuror and impersonator — called 'Zyco the Magician,' who was assisted in his illusions by a veiled but reputedly beautiful Turkish lady who was billed on the programmes and posters as 'Zuilika, the Caliph's Daughter.'"

"I remember the pair very well indeed. They toured the music-halls for years, and I saw their performance frequently. They were the first, I believe, to produce that afterward universal trick known as 'The Vanishing Lady.' As I have not heard anything of them nor seen their names billed for the past couple of years, I fancy they have either retired from the profession or gone to some other part of the world. The man was not only a very clever magician, but a master of mimicry. I always believed, however, that in spite of his name he was of English birth. The woman's face I never saw, of course, as she was always veiled to the eyes after the manner of Turkish ladies. But although a good many persons suspected that her birthplace was no nearer Bagdad than Peckham, I somehow felt that she was, after all, a genuine, native-born Turk."

"You are quite right in both suspicions, Mr. Cleek," put in the major agitatedly. "The man *was* an Englishman; the lady *is* a Turk."

"May I ask, Major, why you speak of the lady in the present tense and of the man in the past? Is he dead?"

"I hope so," responded the major fervently. "God knows I do, Mr. Cleek. My very hope in life depends upon that."

"May I ask why?"

"I am desirous of marrying his widow!"

"My dear Major, you cannot possibly be serious! A woman of that class?"

"Pardon me, sir, but you have, for all your cleverness, fallen a victim to the prevailing error. The lady is in every way my social equal, in her own country my superior. She *is* a caliph's daughter. The title which the playgoing public imagined was of the usual bombastic, just-on-the-programme sort, is hers by right. Her late father, Caliph Al Hamid Sulaiman, was one of the richest and most powerful Mohammedans in existence. He died five months ago, leaving an immense fortune to be conveyed to England to his exiled but forgiven child."

"Ah, I see. Then, naturally, of course – "

"The suggestion is unworthy of you, Mr. Narkom, and anything but complimentary to me. The inheritance of this money has had nothing whatever to do with my feeling for the lady. That began two years ago, when, by accident, I was permitted to look upon her face for the first, last, and only time. I should still wish to marry her if she were an absolute pauper. I know what you are saying to yourself, sir: 'There is no fool like an old fool.' Well, perhaps there isn't. But" – he turned to Cleek – "I may as well begin at the beginning and confess that even if I did not desire to marry the lady I should still have a deep interest in her husband's death, Mr. Cleek. He is – or was, if dead – the only son of my cousin, the Earl of Wynraven, who is now over ninety years of age. I am in the direct line, and if this Lord Norman Ulchester, whom you and the public know only as 'Zyco the Magician,' were in his grave there would only be that one feeble old man between me and the title."

"Ah, I see!" said Cleek in reply; then, seating himself at the table, he arranged the shade of the lamp so that the light fell full upon the major's face while leaving his own in the shadow. "Then your interest in the affair, Major, may be said to be a double one."

"More, sir, a triple one. I have a rival in the shape of my own son. He, too, wishes to marry Zuilika, is madly enamoured of her; in fact, so wildly that I have always hesitated to confess my own desires to him for fear of the consequences. He is almost a madman in his outbursts of temper; and where Zuilika is concerned – Perhaps you will understand, Mr. Cleek, when I tell you that once when he thought her husband had ill-used her he came within an ace of killing the man. There was bad blood between them always, even as boys, and, as men, it was bitterer than ever because of *her.*"

"Suppose you begin at the beginning and tell me the whole story, Major," suggested Cleek, studying the man's face narrowly. "How did the Earl of Wynraven's son come to meet this singularly fascinating lady, and where?"

"In Turkey or Arabia, I forget which. He was doing his theatrical nonsense in the East with some barn-storming show or other, having been obliged to get out of England to escape arrest for some shady transaction a year before. He was always a bad egg; always a disgrace to his name and connections. That's why his father turned him off and never would have any more to do with him. As a boy he was rather clever at conjuring tricks and impersonations of all sorts; he could mimic anything or anybody he ever saw, from the German Emperor down to a Gaiety chorus girl, and do it to absolute perfection. When his father kicked him out he turned these natural gifts to account, and, having fallen in with some professional dancing woman, joined her for a time and went on the stage with her.

"It was after he had parted from this dancer and was knocking about London and leading a disgraceful life generally that he did the thing which caused him to hurry off to the East and throw in his lot with the travelling company I have alluded to. He was always a handsome fellow and had a way with him that was wonderfully taking with women, so I suppose that that accounts as much as anything for Zuilika's infatuation and her doing the mad thing she did. I don't know when nor where nor how they first met; but the foolish girl simply went off her head over him, and he appears to have been as completely infatuated by her. Of course, in that land, the idea of a woman of her sect, of her standing, having anything to do with a Frank was looked upon as something appalling, something akin to sacrilege; and when they found that her father had got wind of it and that the fellow's life would not be safe if he remained within reach another day, they flew to the coast together, shipped for England, and were married immediately after their arrival."

"A highly satisfactory termination for the lady," commented Cleek. "One could hardly have expected that from a man so hopelessly unprincipled as you represent him to have always been. But there's a bit of good in even the devil, we are told."

"Oh, be sure that he didn't marry her from any principle of honour, my dear sir," replied the major. "If it were merely a question of that, he'd have cut loose from her as soon as the vessel touched port. Consideration of self ruled him in that as in all other things. He knew that the girl's father fairly idolized her; knew that, in time, his wrath would give way to his love, and, sooner or later the old man — who had been mad at the idea of any marriage — would be moved to settle a large sum upon her so that she might never be in want. But let me get on with my story. Having nothing when he returned to England, and being obliged to cover up his identity by assuming another name, Ulchester, after vainly appealing to his father for help on the plea that he was now honourably married and settled down, turned again to the stage, and, repugnant though such a thing was to the delicately nurtured woman he had married, compelled Zuilika to become his assistant and to go on the boards with him. That is how the afterward well-known music-hall 'team' of 'Zyco and the Caliph's Daughter' came into existence.

"The novelty of their 'turn' caught on like wildfire, and they were a success from the first, not a little of that success being due to the mystery surrounding the identity and appearance of Zuilika; for, true to the traditions of her native land, she never appeared, either in public or in private, without being closely veiled. Only her 'lord' was ever permitted to look upon her uncovered face; all that the world at large might ever hope to behold of it was the low, broad forehead and the two brilliant eyes that appeared above the close-drawn line of her yashmak. Of course

95

she shrank from the life into which she was forced, but it had its reward, for it kept her in close contact with her husband, whom she almost worshipped. So, for a time, she was proportionately happy; although, as the years passed by and her father showed no inclination to bestow the coveted 'rich allowance' upon his daughter, Ulchester's ardour began to cool. He no longer treated her with the same affectionate deference; he neglected her, in fact, and, in the end, even began to ill-use her.

"About two years ago matters assumed a worse aspect. He again met Anita Rosario, the Spanish dancer, under whose guidance he had first turned to the halls for a livelihood, and once more took up with her. He seemed to have lost all thought or care for the feelings of his wife, for, after torturing her with jealousy over his attentions to the dancer, he took a house adjoining my own — on the borders of the most unfrequented part of the common at Wimbledon — established himself and Zuilika there, and brought the woman Anita home to live with them. From that period matters went from bad to worse. Evidently having tired of the stage, both Ulchester and Anita abandoned it, and turned the house into a sort of club where gambling was carried on to a disgraceful extent. Broken hearted over the treatment she was receiving, Zuilika appealed to me and to my son to help her in her distress, to devise some plan to break the spell of Ulchester's madness and to get that woman out of the house. It was then that I first beheld her face. In her excitement she managed, somehow, to snap or loosen the fastening which held her yashmak. It fell, and let my son realize, as I realized, how wondrously beautiful it is possible for the human face to be!"

"Steady, Major, steady! I can quite understand your feelings, can realize better than most men!" said Cleek with a sort of sigh. "You looked into heaven, and — well, what then? Let's have the rest of the story."

"I think my son must have put it into her head to give Ulchester a taste of his own medicine, to attempt to excite his jealousy by pretending to find interests elsewhere. At any rate, she began to show him a great deal of attention, or, at least, so he says, although I never saw it. All I know is that she — she — well, sir, she deliberately led *me* on until I was half insane over her, and — that's all!"

"What do you mean by 'that's all'? The matter couldn't possibly have ended there, or else why this appeal to me?"

"It ended for me, so far as her affectionate treatment of me was concerned; for in the midst of it the unexpected happened. Her father died, forgiving her, as Ulchester had hoped, but doing more than his wildest dreams could have given him cause to imagine possible. In a word, sir, the caliph not only bestowed his entire earthly possessions upon her, but had them conveyed to England by trusted allies and placed in her hands. There were coffers of gold pieces, jewels of fabulous value, sufficient, when converted into English money, as they were within the week, and deposited to her credit in the Bank of England, to make her the sole possessor of nearly three million pounds."

"Phew!" whistled Cleek. "When these Orientals do it they certainly do it properly. That's what you might call 'giving with both hands,' Major, eh?"

"The gift did not end with that, sir," the major replied with a gesture of repulsion. "There was a gruesome, ghastly, appalling addition in the shape of two mummy cases — one empty, the other filled. A parchment accompanying these stated that the caliph could not sleep elsewhere but in the land of his fathers, nor sleep *there* until his beloved child rested beside him. They had been parted in life, but they should not be parted in death. An Egyptian had, therefore, been summoned to his bedside, had been given orders to embalm him after death, to send the mummy to Zuilika, and with it a case in which, when her own death should occur, *her* body should be deposited; and followers of the prophet had taken oath to see that both were carried to their native land and entombed side by side. Until death came to relieve her of the ghastly duty, Zuilika was charged to be the guardian of the mummy and daily to make the orisons of the faithful before it, keeping it always with its face toward the East."

"By George! it sounds like a page from the 'Arabian Nights,'" exclaimed Cleek. "Well, what next? Did Ulchester take kindly to this housing of the mummy of his father-in-law and the eventual coffin of his wife? Or was he willing to stand for anything so long as he got possession of the huge fortune the old man left?"

"He never did get it, Mr. Cleek. He never touched so much as one farthing of it. Zuilika took nobody into her confidence until everything had been converted into English gold and deposited in the bank to her credit. Then she went straight to him and to Anita, showed them proof of the deposit, reviled them for their treatment of her, and swore that not one farthing's benefit should accrue to Ulchester until Anita was turned out of the house in the presence of their guests and the husband took oath on his knees to join the wife in those daily prayers before the caliph's mummy. Furthermore, Ulchester was to embrace the faith of the Mohammedans that he might return with her at once to the land and the gods she had offended by marriage with a Frankish infidel."

"Which, of course, he declined to do?"

"Yes. He declined utterly. But it was a case of the crushed worm, with Zuilika. Now was *her* turn; and she would not abate one jot or tittle. There was a stormy scene, of course. It ended by Ulchester and the woman Anita leaving the house together. From that hour Zuilika never again heard his living voice, never again saw his living face! He seems to have gone wild with wrath over what he had lost and to have plunged headlong into the maddest sort of dissipation. It is known, positively known, and can be sworn to by reputable witnesses, that for the next three days he did not draw one sober breath. On the fourth, a note from him – a note which he was *seen* to write in a public house – was carried to Zuilika. In that note he cursed her with every conceivable term; told her that when she got it he would be at the bottom of the river, driven there by her conduct, and that if it was possible for the dead to come back and haunt people he'd do it. Two hours after he wrote that note he was seen getting out of the train at Tilbury and going toward the docks; but from that moment to this every trace of him is lost."

"Ah, I see!" said Cleek reflectively. "And you want to find out if he really carried out that threat and did put an end to himself, I suppose? That's why you have come to me, eh? Frankly, I don't believe that he did, Major. That sort of a man never commits suicide upon so slim a pretext as that. If he commits it at all, it's because he is at the end of his tether, and our friend 'Zyco' seems to have been a long way from the end of his. How does the lady take it? Seriously?"

"Oh, very, sir, very. Of course, to a woman of her temperament and with her Oriental ideas regarding the supernatural, etcetera, that threat to haunt her was the worst he could have done to her. At first she was absolutely beside herself with grief and horror; swore that she had killed him by her cruelty; that there was nothing left her but to die, and all that sort of thing; and for three days she was little better than a mad woman. At the end of that time, after the fashion of her people, she retired to her own room, covered herself with sackcloth and ashes, and remained hidden from all eyes for the space of a fortnight, weeping and wailing constantly and touching nothing but bread and water."

"Poor wretch! She suffers like that, then, over a rascally fellow not worth a single tear. It's marvellous, Major, what women do see in men that they can go on loving them. Has she come out of her retirement yet?"

"Yes, Mr. Cleek. She came out of it five days ago, to all appearances a thoroughly heartbroken woman. Of course, as she was all alone in the world, my son and I considered it our duty, during the time of her wildness and despair, to see that a thoroughly respectable female was called in to take charge of the house and to show respect for the proprieties, and for us to take up our abode there in order to prevent her from doing herself an injury. We are still domiciled there, but it will surprise you to learn that a most undesirable person is there also. In short, sir, that the woman Anita Rosario, the cause of all the trouble, is again an inmate of the house; and, what is more remarkable still, this time by Zuilika's own request."

"What's that? My dear Major, you amaze me! What can possibly have caused the good lady to do a thing like that?"

"She hopes, she says, to appease the dead and to avert the threatened 'haunting.' At all events, she sent for Anita some days ago. Indeed, I believe it is her intention to take the Spaniard with her when she returns to the East."

"She intends doing that, then? She is so satisfied of her husband's death that she deems no further question necessary? Intends to take no further step toward proving it?"

"It has been proved to her satisfaction. His body was recovered the day before yesterday."

"Oho! then he is dead, eh? Why didn't you say so in the beginning? When did you learn of it?"

"This very evening. That is what sent me to Superintendent Narkom with this request to be led to you. I learned from Zuilika that a body answering the description of his had been fished from the water at Tilbury and carried to the mortuary. It was horribly disfigured by contact with the piers and passing vessels, but she and Anita — and — and my son — "

"Your son, Major? Your son?"

"Yes!" replied the major in a sort of half whisper. "They — they took him with them when they went, unknown to me. He has become rather friendly with the Spanish woman of late. All three saw the body; all three identified it as being Ulchester's beyond a doubt."

"And you? Surely when you see it you will be able to satisfy any misgivings you may have?"

"I shall never see it, Mr. Cleek. It was claimed when identified and buried within twelve hours," said the major, glancing up sharply as Cleek, receiving this piece of information, blew out a soft, low whistle. "I was not told anything about it until this evening, and what I have done — in coming to you, I mean — I have done with nobody's knowledge. I — I am so horribly in the dark — I have such fearful thoughts and — and I want to be sure. I must be sure or I shall go out of my mind. That's the 'case,' Mr. Cleek. Tell me what you think of it."

"I can do that in a very few words, Major," he replied. "It is either a gigantic swindle or it is a clear case of murder. If a swindle, then Ulchester himself is at the bottom of it and it will end in murder just the same. Frankly, the swindle theory strikes me as being the more probable; in other words, that the whole thing is a put-up game between Ulchester and the woman Anita; that they played upon Zuilika's fear of the supernatural for a purpose; that a body was procured and sunk in that particular spot for the furtherance of that purpose; and if the widow attempts to put into execution this plan – no doubt instilled into her mind by Anita – of returning with her wealth to her native land, she will simply be led into some safe place and then effectually put out of the way forever. That is what I think of the case if it is to be regarded in the light of a swindle; but if Ulchester is really dead, murder, not suicide, is at the back of his taking off, and – Oh, well, we won't say anything more about it just yet awhile. I shall want to look over the ground before I jump to any conclusions. You are still stopping in the house, you and your son, I think you remarked? If you could contrive to put up an old army friend's son there for a night, Major, give me the address. I'll drop in on you there to-morrow and have a little look round."

II

When, next morning, Major Burnham-Seaforth announced the dilemma in which, through his own house being temporarily closed, he found himself owing to the proposed visit of Lieutenant Rupert St. Aubyn, son of an old army friend, Zuilika was the first to suggest the very thing he was fishing for.

"Ah, let him come here, dear friend," she said in that sad, sweetly modulated voice which so often wrung his susceptible old heart. "There is plenty of room, plenty, alas! now, and any friend of yours can only be a friend of mine. He will not annoy. Let him come here."

"Yes, let him," supplemented young Burnham-Seaforth, speaking with his eyes on Señorita Rosario, who seemed nervous and ill-pleased by the news of the expected arrival. "He won't have to be entertained by us if he only comes to see the pater; and we can easily crowd him aside if he tries to thrust himself upon us. A fellow with a name like 'Rupert St. Aubyn' is bound to be a silly ass." And when, in the late afternoon, "Lieutenant Rupert St. Aubyn," in the person of Cleek, arrived with his snub-nosed man-servant, a kitbag, several rugs, and a bundle of golf sticks, young Burnham-Seaforth saw no reason to alter that assertion. For, a "silly ass" — albeit an unusually handsome one with his fair, curling hair and his big blonde moustache — he certainly was: a lisping, "ha-ha-ing" "don't-cher-know-ing" silly ass, whom the presence of ladies seemed to cover with confusion and drive into a very panic of shy embarrassment.

"*Dios!* but he is handsome, this big, fair lieutenant!" whispered the Spaniard to young Burnham-Seaforth. "A great, handsome fool — all beauty and no brains, like a doll of wax!" Then she bent over and murmured smilingly to Zuilika: "I shall make a bigger nincompoop of this big, fair sap-head than Heaven already has done before he leaves here, just for the sake of seeing him stammer and blush!"

Only the sad expression of Zuilika's eyes told that she so much as heard, as she rose to greet the visitor. Garbed from head to foot in the deep, violet-coloured stuff which is the mourning of Turkish women, her little pointed slippers showing beneath the hem of her frock, and only her dark, mournful eyes visible between the top of the shrouding yashmak and the edge of her sequined snood, she made a pathetic picture as she stood there waiting to greet the unknown visitor.

"Sir, you are welcome," she said in a voice whose modulations were not lost upon Cleek's ears as he put forth his hand and received the tips of her little, henna-stained fingers upon his palm. "Peace be with you, who are of his people — he that I loved and mourn!" Then, as if overcome with grief at the recollection of her widowhood, she plucked away her hand, covered her eyes, and moved staggeringly out of the room. And Cleek saw no more of her that day; but he knew when she performed her orisons before the mummy case — as she did each morning and evening — by the strong, pungent odour of incense drifting through the house and filling it with a sickly scent.

Her absence seemed to make but little impression upon him, however, for, following up a well-defined plan of action, he devoted himself wholly to the Spanish woman, and both amazed her and gratified her vanity by allowing her to learn that a man may be the silliest ass imaginable and yet quite understand how to flirt and to make love to a woman. And so it fell out that instead of "Lieutenant Rupert St. Aubyn" being elbowed out by young Burnham-Seaforth, it was "Lieutenant St. Aubyn" who elbowed *him* out. Without being in the least aware of it, the flattered Anita, like an adroitly hooked trout, was being "played" in and out and round about the eddies and the deeps until the angler had her quite ready for the final dip of the net at the landing point.

All this was to accomplish exactly what it *did* accomplish, namely, the ill temper, the wrath, the angry resentment of young Burnham-Seaforth. And when the evening had passed and bedtime arrived, Cleek took his candle and retired in the direction of the rooms set apart for him, with the certainty of knowing that he had done that which would this very night prove beyond all question the guilt or innocence of one person at least who was enmeshed in this mysterious tangle. He was not surprised, therefore, at what followed his next step.

Reaching the upper landing he blew out the light of his candle, slammed the door to his own room, noisily turned the key, and shot the bolt of another, then tiptoed his way back to the staircase and looked down the well-hole into the lower hall.

Zuilika had retired to her room, the major had retired to his, and now Anita was taking up her candle to retire to hers. She had barely touched it, however, when there came a sound of swift footsteps and young Burnham-Seaforth lurched out of the drawing-room door and joined her. He was in a state of great excitement and was breathing hard.

"Anita, Miss Rosario!" he began, plucking her by the sleeve and uplifting a pale, boyish face — he was not yet twenty-two — to hers with a look of abject misery. "I want to speak to you. I simply must speak to you. I've been waiting for the chance, and now that it's come — Look here! You're not going back on me, are you?"

"Going back on you?" repeated Anita, showing her pretty white teeth in an amused smile. "What shall you mean by that 'going back on you,' eh? You are a stupid little donkey, to be sure. But then I do not care to get on the back of one, so why?"

"Oh, you know very well what I mean," he rapped out angrily. "It is not fair the way you have been treating me ever since that yellow-headed bounder came. I've had a night of misery, Zuilika never showing herself; you doing nothing, absolutely nothing, although you promised — you *know* you did! — and I heard you, I absolutely heard you persuade that St. Aubyn fool to stop at least another night."

"Yes, of course you did. But what of it? He is good company. He talks well, he sings well, he is very handsome and — well, what difference can it make to you? You are not interested in *me*, *amigo*."

"No, no; of course I'm not. You are nothing to me at all — you — oh, I beg your pardon; I didn't quite mean that. I — I mean you are nothing to me in that way. But you — you're not keeping to your word. You promised, you know, that you'd use your influence with Zuilika; that you'd get her to be more kind to me — to see me alone and — and all that sort of thing. And you've not made a single attempt. You've just sat round and flirted with that tow-headed brute and done nothing at all to help me on; and — and it's jolly unkind of you, that's what!"

Cleek heard Anita's soft rippling laughter; but he waited to hear no more. Moving swiftly away from the well-hole of the staircase he passed on tiptoe down the hall to the major's rooms, and opening the door, went in. The old soldier was standing, with arms folded, at the window looking silently out into the darkness of the night. He turned at the sound of the door's opening and moved toward Cleek with a white, agonized face and a pair of shaking, outstretched hands.

"Well?" he said with a sort of gasp.

"My dear Major," said Cleek quietly. "The wisest of men are sometimes mistaken. That is my excuse for my own shortsightedness. I said in the beginning that this was either a case of swindling or a case of murder, did I not? Well, I now amend my verdict. It is a case of swindling *and* murder; and your son has had nothing to do with either!"

"Oh, thank God! thank God!" the old man said; then sat down suddenly and dropped his face between his hands and was still for a long time. When he looked up again his eyes were red, but his lips were smiling.

"If you only knew what a relief it is," he said. "If you only knew how much I have suffered, Mr. Cleek. His friendship with that Spanish woman; his going with her to identify the body — even assisting in its hurried burial! These things all seemed so frightfully black, so utterly without any explanation other than personal guilt."

"Yet they all are easily explained, Major. His friendship for the Spanish woman is merely due to a promise to intercede for him with Zuilika. She is his one aim and object, poor little donkey! As for his identification of the body — well, if the widow herself could find points of undisputed resemblance, why not he? A nervous, excitable, impetuous boy like that and anxious, too, that the lady of his heart should be freed from the one thing, the one man, whose existence made her everlastingly unattainable, in the hands of a clever woman like Anita Rosario such a chap could be made to identify anything and to believe it as religiously as he believes. Now, go to bed and rest easy, Major. I'm going to call up Dollops and do a little night prowling. If it turns out as I hope, this little riddle will be solved to-morrow."

"But how, Mr. Cleek? It seems to me that it is as dark as ever. You put my poor old head in a whirl. You say there is swindling; you hint one moment that the body was not that of Ulchester, and in the next that murder has been done. Do, pray, tell me what it all means, what you make of this amazing case?"

"I'll do that to-morrow, Major; not to-night. The answer to the riddle — the answer that's in my mind, I mean — is at once so simple and yet so appallingly awful that I'll hazard no guess until I'm sure. Look here" — he put his hand into his pocket and pulled out a gold piece — "do you know what that is, Major?"

"It looks like a spade guinea, Mr. Cleek."

"Right; it is a spade guinea, a pocket piece I've carried for years. You've heard, no doubt, of vital things turning upon the tossing of a coin. Well, if you see me toss this coin to-morrow, something of that sort will occur. It will be tossed up in the midst of a riddle, Major; when it comes down it will be a riddle no longer."

Then he opened the door, closed it after him, and, before the Major could utter a word, was gone.

III

The promise was so vague, so mystifying, indeed, so seemingly absurd, that the Major did not allow himself to dwell upon it. As a matter of fact, it passed completely out of his mind; nor did it again find lodgment there until it was forced back upon his memory in a most unusual manner.

Whatsoever had been the result of what Cleek had called his "night prowling," he took nobody into his confidence when he and the major and the major's son and Señorita Rosario met at breakfast the next day (Zuilika, true to her training and the traditions of her people, never broke morning bread save in the seclusion of her own bedchamber, and then on her knees with her face toward the East) nor did he allude to it at any period throughout the day.

He seemed, indeed, purposely to avoid the major, and to devote himself to the Spanish woman with an ardour that was positively heartless, considering that as they two sang and flirted and went in for several sets of singles on the tennis courts, Zuilika, like a spirit of misery, kept walking, walking, walking through the halls and the rooms of the house, her woeful eyes fixed on the carpet, her henna-stained fingers constantly locking and unlocking, and moans of desolation coming now and again from behind her yashmak as her swaying body moved restlessly to and fro. For to-day was memorable. Five weeks ago this coming nightfall Ulchester had flung himself out of this house in a fury of wrath, and this time of bitter regret and ceaseless mourning had begun.

"She will go out of her mind, poor creature, if something cannot be done to keep her from dwelling on her misery like this," commented the housekeeper, coming upon that restless figure pacing the darkened hall, moaning, moaning, seeing nothing, hearing nothing, doing nothing but walk and sorrow, sorrow and walk, hour in and hour out. "It's enough to tear a body's heart to hear her, poor dear. And that good-for-nothing Spanish piece racing and shrieking round the tennis court like a she tom-cat, the heartless hussy. Her and that simpering silly that's trotting round after her had ought to be put in a bag and shaken up, that they ought. It's downright scandalous to be carrying on like that at such a time."

And so both the major and his son thought, too, and tried their best to solace the lonely mourner and to persuade her to sit down and rest.

"Zuilika, you will wear yourself out, child, if you go on walking like this," said the major solicitously. "Do rest and be at peace for a little time at least."

"I can never have peace in this land. I can never forget the day!" she answered drearily. "Oh, my beloved! Oh, my lord, it was I who sent thee to it — it was I, it was I! Give me my own country — give me the gods of my people; here there is only memory, and pain, and no rest, no rest ever!"

She could not be persuaded to sit down and rest until Anita herself took the matter into her own hands and insisted that she should. That was at tea-time. Anita, showing some little trace of feeling now that Cleek had gone to wash his hands and was no longer there to occupy her thoughts, placed a deep, soft chair near the window, and would not yield until the violet-clad figure of the mourner sank down into the depths of it and leaned back with its shrouded face drooping in silent melancholy.

And it was while she was so sitting that Cleek came into the room and did a most unusual, a most ungentlemanly thing, in the eyes of the major and his son.

Without hesitating, he walked to within a yard or two of where she was sitting, and then, in the silliest of his silly tones, blurted out suddenly: "I say, don't you know, I've had a jolly rum experience. You know that blessed room at the angle just opposite the library, the one with the locked door?"

The drooping violet figure straightened abruptly, and the major felt for the moment as if he could have kicked Cleek with pleasure. Of course they knew the room. It was there that the two mummy cases were kept, sacred from the profaning presence of any but this stricken woman. No wonder that she bent forward, full of eagerness, full of the dreadful fear that Frankish feet had crossed the threshold, Frankish eyes looked within the sacred shrine.

"Well, don't you know," went on Cleek, without taking the slightest notice of anything, "just as I was going past that door I picked up a most remarkable thing. Wonder if it's yours, madam?" glancing at Zuilika. "Just have a look at it, will you? Here, catch!" And not until he saw a piece of gold spin through the air and fall into Zuilika's lap did the major remember that promise of last night.

"Oh, come, I say, St. Aubyn, that's rather thick!" sang out young Burnham-Seaforth indignantly, as Zuilika caught the coin in her lap. "Blest if I know what you call manners, but to throw things at a lady is a new way of passing them in this part of the world, I can assure you."

"Awfully sorry, old chap, no offence, I assure you," said Cleek, more asinine than ever, as Zuilika, having picked up the piece and looked at it, disclaimed all knowledge of it, and laid it on the edge of the table without any further interest in it or him. "Just to show, you know, that I — er — couldn't have meant anything disrespectful, why — er — you all know, don't you know, how jolly much I respect Señorita Rosario, by Jove! and so – Here, señorita, you catch, too, and see if the blessed thing's yours." And, picking up the coin, tossed it into her lap just as he had done with Zuilika.

She, too, caught it and examined it, and laughingly shook her head.

"No, not mine!" she said. "I have not seen him before. To the finder shall be the keep. Come, sit here. Will you have the tea?"

"Yes, thanks," said Cleek; then dropped down on the sofa beside her, and took tea as serenely as though there were no such things in the world as murder and swindling and puzzling police riddles to solve.

And the major, staring at him, was as amazed as ever. He had said, last night, that when the coin fell the answer would be given, and yet it had fallen, and nothing had happened, and he was laughing and flirting with Señorita Rosario as composedly and as persistently as ever. More than that; after he had finished his second cup of tea, and immediately following the sound of some one just beyond the veranda rail whistling the lively, lilting measures of "There's a Girl Wanted There," "the silly ass" seemed to become a thousand times sillier than ever. He set down his cup, and, turning to Anita, said with an inane sort of giggle, "I say, you know, here's a lark. Let's have a game of 'Slap Hand,' you and I — what? Know it, don't you? You try to slap my hands, and I try to slap yours, and whichever succeeds in doing it first gets a prize. Awful fun, don't you know. Come on — start her up."

And, Anita agreeing, they fell forthwith to slapping away at the backs of each other's hands with great gusto, until, all of a sudden, the whistler outside gave one loud, shrill note, and — there was a great and mighty change.

Those who were watching saw Anita's two hands suddenly caught, heard a sharp, metallic "click," and saw them as suddenly dropped again to the accompaniment of a shrill little scream from her ashen lips, and the next moment Cleek had risen and jumped away from her side clear across to where Zuilika was; and those who were watching saw Anita jump up with a pair of steel hand-cuffs on her wrists, just as Dollops vaulted up over the veranda rail and appeared at one window, whilst Petrie appeared at an-other, Hammond poked his body through a third, and the open-ing door gave entrance to Superintendent Narkom.

"The police!" shrilled out Anita in a panic of fright. "*Madre de Dios*, the police!"

The major and his son were on their feet like a shot. Zuilika, with a faint, startled cry, bounded bolt upright, like an imp shot through a trap-door; but before the little henna-stained hands could do more than simply move, Cleek's arms went round her from behind, tight and fast as a steel clamp, there was another metallic "click," another shrill cry, and another pair of wrists were in gyves.

"Come in, Mr. Narkom; come in, constables," said Cleek, with the utmost composure. "Here are your promised prisoners — nicely trussed, you see, so that they can't get at the little pop-guns they carry — and a worse pair of rogues never went into the hands of Jack Ketch!"

"And Jack Ketch will get them, Cleek, if I know anything about it. Your hazard was right, your guess correct. I've examined the caliph's mummy-case; the mummy itself has been removed — destroyed - done away with utterly — and the poor creature's body is there!"

And here the poor, dumbfounded, utterly bewildered major found voice to speak at last.

"Mummy-case! Body! Dear God in heaven, Mr. Cleek, what are you hinting at?" he gasped. "You — you don't mean that she — that Zuilika — killed him?"

"No, Major, I don't," he made reply. "I simply mean that he killed her! The body in the mummy-case is the body of Zuilika, the caliph's daughter! This is the creature you have been wasting your pity on — see!"

With that he laid an intense grip on the concealing yashmak, tore it away, and so revealed the closely shaven, ghastly hued countenance of the cornered criminal.

"My God! Ulchester himself!" said the major in a voice of fright and surprise.

"Yes, Ulchester himself, Major. In a few more days he'd have withdrawn the money, and got out of the country, body and all, if he hadn't been nabbed, the rascal. There'd have been no tracing the crime then, and he and the Señorita here would have been in clover for the rest of their natural lives. But there's always that bright little bit of Bobby Burns's to be reckoned with. You know: 'The best laid schemes of mice and men,' etcetera — that bit. But the Yard's got them, and they'll never leave the country now. Take them, Mr. Narkom, they're yours!"

* * * * *

"How did I guess it?" said Cleek, replying to the major's query, as they sat late that night discussing the affair. "Well, I think the first faint inkling of it came when I arrived here yesterday, and smelt the overpowering odour of the incenses. There was so much of it, and it was used so frequently — twice a day — that it seemed to suggest an attempt to hide other odours of a less pleasant kind. When I left you last night, Dollops and I went down to the mummy chamber, and a skeleton key soon let us in. The unpleasant odour was rather pronounced in there. But even that didn't give me the cue, until I happened to find in the fireplace a considerable heap of fine ashes, and in the midst of them small lumps of a gummy substance, which I knew to result from the burning of myrrh. I suspected from that and from the nature of the ashes that a mummy had been burnt, and as there was only one mummy in the affair, the inference was obvious. I laid hands on the two cases and tilted them. One was quite empty. The weight of the other told me that it contained something a little heavier than any mummy ought to be. I came to the conclusion that there was a body in it, injected full of arsenic, no doubt, to prevent as much as possible the processes of decay, the odour of which the incense was concealing. I didn't attempt to open the thing; I left that until the arrival of the men from the Yard, for whom I sent Dollops this afternoon. I had a vague notion that it would not turn out to be Ulchester's body, and I had also a distinct recollection of what you said about his being able to mimic a Gaiety chorus-girl and all that sort of thing. The more I thought over it the more I realized what an excellent thing to cover a bearded face a yashmak is. Still, it was all hazard. I wasn't sure — indeed, I never was sure — until tea-time, when I caught this supposed 'Zuilika' sitting at last, and gave the spade guinea its chance to decide it."

"My dear Mr. Cleek, how could it have decided it? That's the thing that amazes me the most of all. How could the tossing of that coin have settled the sex of the wearer of those garments?"

"My dear Major, it is an infallible test. Did you never notice that if you throw anything for a man to catch in his lap, he pulls his knees together to *make* a lap, in order to catch it; whereas a woman — used to wearing skirts, and thereby having a lap already prepared — simply broadens that lap by the exactly opposite movement, knowing that whatever is thrown has no chance of slipping to the floor. That solved it at once. And now it's bedtime, Major. Good-night."

CHAPTER V
THE RIDDLE OF THE NINTH FINGER

The inn of "The Three Jolly Fishermen," which, as you may know, lies on the left bank of the Thames, within a gunshot of Richmond, was all but empty when Cleek, answering the superintendent's note, strolled into it, and discovered Narkom enjoying his tea in solitary state at a little round table in the embrasure of a bay window at the far end of the little private parlour which lies immediately behind the bar-room.

"My dear fellow, do pardon me for not waiting," said the superintendent, as his famous ally entered, looking like a college-bred athlete in his boating flannels and his brim-tilted panama, "but the fact is, you're a little behind time for once, and besides, I was absolutely famishing."

"Share the blame of my lateness with me, Mr. Narkom," said Cleek, as he tossed aside his hat and threw the fag-end of the cigarette he was smoking out through the open window. "You said in your note that there was no immediate necessity for haste, so I improved the shining hour by another spin down the river. It isn't often that duty-calls bring me to a little Eden like this. The air is like balm to-day, and as for the river — oh, the river is a sheer delight!"

Narkom rang for a fresh pot of tea and a further supply of buttered toast, and, when these were served, Cleek sat down and joined him.

"I dare say," said the superintendent, opening fire at once, "that you wonder what in the world induced me to bring you out here to meet me, my dear fellow, instead of following the usual course and calling at Clarges Street? Well, the fact is, Cleek, that the gentleman with whom I am now about to put you in touch lives in this vicinity, and is so placed that he cannot get away without running the risk of having the step he is taking discovered."

"Humph! He is closely spied upon, then?" commented Cleek. "The trouble arises from some one or something in his own household?"

"No, in his father's. The 'trouble,' so far as I can gather, seems to emanate from his stepmother, a young and very beautiful woman, who was born on the island of Java, where the father of our client met and married her some two years ago. He had gone there to probe into the truth of the amazing statement that a runic stone had been unearthed in that part of the globe."

"Ah, then you need not tell me the gentleman's name, Mr. Narkom," interposed Cleek. "I remember perfectly well the stir which that ridiculous and unfounded statement created at the time. Despite the fact that scholars of all nations scoffed at the thing and pointed out that the very term 'rune' is of Teutonic origin, one enthusiastic old gentleman — Mr. Michael Bawdrey, a retired brewer, thirsting for something more enduring than malt to carry his name down the ages — became fired with enthusiasm upon the subject, and set forth for Java 'hot foot,' as one might say. I remember that the papers made great game of him; but I heard, I fancy, that, in spite of all, he was a dear, lovable old chap, and not at all like the creature the cartoonists portrayed him."

"What a memory you have, my dear Cleek. Yes, that is the party; and he is a dear, lovable old chap at bottom. Collects old china, old weapons, old armour, curiosities of all sorts — lots of 'em bogus, no doubt, catch the charlatans among the dealers letting a chance like that slip them — and is never so happy as when showing his 'collection' to his friends and being mistaken by the ignorant for a man of deep learning."

"A very human trait, Mr. Narkom. We all are anxious that the world should set the highest possible valuation upon us. It is only when we are underrated that we object. So this dear, deluded old gentleman, having failed to secure a 'rune' in Java brought back something equally cryptic — a woman? Was the lady of his choice a native or merely an inhabitant of the island?"

"Merely an inhabitant, my dear fellow. As a matter of fact, she is English. Her father, a doctor, long since deceased, took her out there in her childhood. She was none too well off, I believe: but that did not prevent her having many suitors, among whom was Mr. Bawdrey's own son, the gentleman who is anxious to have you take up this case."

"Oho!" said Cleek, with a strong rising inflection. "So the lady was of the careful and calculating kind? She didn't care for youth and all the rest of it when she could have papa and the money-chest without waiting. A common enough occurrence. Still, this does not make up an 'affair,' and especially an 'affair' which requires the assistance of a detective, and you spoke of 'a case.' What is the case, Mr. Narkom?"

"I will leave Mr. Philip Bawdrey himself to tell you that," said Narkom, as the door opened to admit a young man of about eight and twenty, clothed in tennis flannels, and looking very much perturbed. He was a handsome, fair-haired, fair-moustached young fellow, with frank, boyish eyes and that unmistakable something which stamps the products of the 'Varsities. "Come in, Mr. Bawdrey. You said we were not to wait tea, and you see that we haven't. Let me have the pleasure of introducing Mr. – "

"Headland," put in Cleek adroitly, and with a look at Narkom as much as to say, "Don't give me away. I may not care to take the case when I hear it, so what's the use of letting everybody know who I am?" Then he switched round in his chair, rose, and held out his hand. "Mr. George Headland, of the Yard, Mr. Bawdrey. I don't trust Mr. Narkom's proverbially tricky memory for names. He introduced me as Jones once, and I lost the opportunity of handling the case because the party in question couldn't believe that anybody named Jones would be likely to ferret it out."

"Funny idea that!" commented young Bawdrey, smiling and accepting the proffered hand. "Rum lot of people you must run across in your line, Mr. Headland. Shouldn't take you for a detective myself, shouldn't even in a room full of them. College man, aren't you? Thought so. Oxon or Cantab?"

"Cantab — Emmanuel."

"Oh, Lord! Never thought I'd ever live to appeal to an Emmanuel man to do anything brilliant. I'm an Oxon chap; Brasenose is my alma mater. I say, Mr. Narkom, do give me a cup of tea, will you? I had to slip off while the others were at theirs, and I've run all the way. Thanks very much. Don't mind if I sit in that corner and draw the curtain a little, do you?" his frank, boyish face suddenly clouding. "I don't want to be seen by anybody passing. It's a horrible thing to feel that you are being spied upon at every turn, Mr. Headland, and that want of caution may mean the death of the person you love best in all the world."

"Oh, it's that kind of case, is it?" queried Cleek, making room for him to pass round the table and sit in the corner, with his back to the window and the loosened folds of the chintz curtain keeping him in the shadow.

"Yes," answered young Bawdrey, with a half-repressed shudder and a deeper clouding of his rather pale face. "Sometimes I try to make myself believe that it isn't, that it's all fancy, that she never could be so inhuman, and yet how else is it to be explained? You can't go behind the evidence; you can't make things different simply by saying that you will not believe." He stirred his tea nervously, gulped down a couple of mouthfuls of it, and then set the cup aside. "I can't enjoy anything; it takes the savour out of everything when I think of it," he added, with a note of pathos in his voice. "My dad, my dear, bully old dad, the best and dearest old boy in all the world! I suppose, Mr. Headland, that Mr. Narkom has told you something about the case?"

"A little — a very little indeed. I know that your father went to Java, and married a second wife there; and I know, too, that you yourself were rather taken with the lady at one time, and that she threw you over as soon as Mr. Bawdrey senior became a possibility."

"That's a mistake," he replied. "She never threw me over, Mr. Headland; she never had the chance. I found her out long before my father became anything like what you might call a rival, found her out as a mercenary, designing woman, and broke from her voluntarily. I only wish that I had known that he had one serious thought regarding her. I could have warned him; I could have spoken then. But I never did find out until it was too late. Trust her for that. She waited until I had gone up-country to look after some fine old porcelains and enamels that the governor had heard about; then she hurried him off and tricked him into a hasty marriage. Of course, after that I couldn't speak, I wouldn't speak. She was my father's wife, and he was so proud of her, so happy, dear old boy, that I'd have been little better than a brute to say anything against her."

"What could you have said if you had spoken?"

"Oh, lots of things; the things that made me break away from her in the beginning. She'd had other love affairs for one thing; her late father's masquerading as a doctor for another. They had only used that as a cloak. They had run a gambling-house on the sly — he as the card-sharper, she as the decoy. They had drained one poor fellow dry, and she had thrown him over after leading him on to think that she cared for him and was going to marry him. He blew out his brains in front of her, poor wretch. They say she never turned a hair. You wouldn't believe it possible, if you saw her; she is so sweet and caressing, and so young and beautiful, you'd almost believe her an angel. But there's Travers in the background — always Travers!"

"Travers! Who is he?"

"Oh, one of her old flames, the only one she ever really cared for, they say. She was supposed to have broken with him out there in Java, because they were too poor to marry; and now he's come over to England, and he's there, in the house with the dear old dad and me, and they are as thick as thieves together. I've caught them whispering and prowling about together, in the grounds and along the lanes, after she has said 'Good-night' and gone to her room and is supposed to be in bed. There's a houseful of her old friends three parts of the time. They come and they go, but Travers never goes. I know why" — waxing suddenly excited, suddenly vehement — "Yes! I know why. He's in the game with her!"

"Game! What game, Mr. Bawdrey? What is it that she is do-ing?"

"She's killing my old dad!" he answered, with a sort of sob in his excited voice. "She's murdering him by inches, that's what she's doing, and I want you to help me bring it home to her. God knows what it is she's using or how she uses it; but you know what demons they are for secret poisons, those Javanese, what means they have of killing people without a trace. And she was out there for years and years. So, too, was Travers, the brute! They know all the secrets of those beastly barbarians, and between them they're doing something to my old dad."

"How do you know that?"

"I don't know it, that's the worst of it. But I couldn't be surer of it if they took me into their secrets. But there's the evidence of his condition; there's the fact that it didn't begin until after Travers came. Look here, Mr. Headland, you don't know my dad. He's got the queerest notions sometimes. One of his fads is that it's unlucky to make a will. Well, if he dies without one, who will inherit his money, as I am an only child?"

"Undoubtedly you and his widow."

"Exactly. And if I die at pretty nearly the same time — and they'll see to that, never fear; it will be my turn the moment they are sure of him — she will inherit everything. Now, let me tell you what's happening. From being a strong, healthy man, my father has, since Travers's arrival, begun to be attacked by a mysterious malady. He has periodical fainting fits, sometimes convulsions. He'll be feeling better for a day or so; then, without a word of warning, whilst you're talking to him, he'll drop like a shot bird and go into the most horrible convulsions. The doctors can't stop it; they don't even know what it is. They only know that he's fading away — turning from a strong, virile old man into a thin, nervous, shivering wreck. But I know! I know! They're dosing him somehow with some diabolical Javanese thing, those two. And yesterday — God help me! — yesterday I, too, dropped like a shot bird; I, too, had the convulsions and the weakness and the fainting fit. My time has begun also!"

"Bless my soul! what a diabolical thing!" put in Narkom agitatedly. "No wonder you appealed to me!"

"No wonder!" Bawdrey replied. "I felt that it had gone as far as I dared let it; that it was time to call in the police and to have help before it was too late. That's the case, Mr. Headland. I want you to find some way of getting at the truth, of looking into Travers's luggage, into my stepmother's effects, and unearthing the horrible stuff with which they are doing this thing; and perhaps, when that is known, some antidote may be found to save the dear old dad and restore him to what he was. Can't you do this? For God's sake, say that you can."

"At all events, I can try, Mr. Bawdrey," responded Cleek.

"Oh, thank you, thank you!" said Bawdrey gratefully. "I don't care a hang what it costs, what your fees are, Mr. Headland. So long as you run those two to earth, and get hold of the horrible stuff, whatever it is, that they are using, I'll pay any price in the world, and count it cheap as compared with the life of my dear old dad. When can you take hold of the case? Now?"

"I'm afraid not. Mysterious things like this require a little thinking over. Suppose we say to-morrow noon? Will that do?"

"I suppose it must, although I should have liked to take you back with me. Every moment's precious at a time like this. But if it must be delayed until to-morrow — well, it must, I suppose. But I'll take jolly good care that nobody gets a chance to come within touching distance of the pater, bless him! until you do come, if I have to sit on the mat before his door until morning. Here's the address on this card, Mr. Headland. When and how shall I expect to see you again? You'll use an alias, of course?"

"Oh, certainly! Had you any old friend in your college days whom your father knew only by name and who is now too far off for the imposture to be discovered?"

"Yes. Jim Rickaby. We were as inseparable as the Siamese twins in our undergrad. days. He's in Borneo now. Haven't heard from him in a dog's age."

"Couldn't be better," said Cleek. "Then 'Jim Rickaby' let it be. You'll get a letter from him first thing in the morning saying that he's back in England, and about to run down and spend the week-end with you. At noon he will arrive, accompanied by his Borneo servant named — er — Dollops. You can put the 'blackie' up in some quarter of the house where he can move about at will without disturbing any of your own servants and can get in and out at all hours; he will be useful, you know, in prowling about the grounds at night and ascertaining if the lady really does go to bed when she retires to her room. As for 'Jim Rickaby' himself — well, you can pave the way for his operations by informing your father, when you get the letter, that he has gone daft on the subject of old china and curios and things of that sort, don't you know."

"What a ripping idea!" commented young Bawdrey. "I twig. He'll get chummy with you of course, and you can lead him on and adroitly 'pump' him regarding her, and where she keeps her keys and things like that. That's the idea, isn't it?"

"Something of that sort. I'll find out all about her, never fear," said Cleek in reply. Then they shook hands and parted, and it was not until after young Bawdrey had gone that either he or Narkom recollected that Cleek had overlooked telling the young man that Headland was not his name.

"Oh, well, it doesn't matter. Time enough to tell him that when it comes to making out the cheque," said Cleek, as the superintendent remarked upon the circumstance. Then he pushed back his chair and walked over to the window, and stood looking silently out upon the flowing river. Narkom did not disturb his reflections. He knew from past experience, as well as from the manner in which he took his lower lip between his teeth and drummed with his finger-tips upon the window ledge, that some idea relative to the working out of the case had taken shape within his mind, and so, with the utmost discretion, went on with his tea and refrained from speaking. Suddenly Cleek turned. "Mr. Narkom, do me a favour, will you? Look me up a copy of Holman's 'Diseases of the Kidneys' when you go back to town. I'll send Dollops round to the Yard to-night to get it."

"Right you are," said Narkom, taking out his pocket-book and making a note of it. "But I say, look here, my dear fellow, you can't possibly believe that it's anything of that sort, anything natural, I mean, in the face of what we've heard?"

"No, I don't. I think it's something confoundedly unnatural, and that that poor old chap is being secretly and barbarously murdered. I think that — and — I think, too - " His voice trailed off. He stood silent and preoccupied for a moment, and then, putting his thoughts into words, without addressing them to anybody: "Ayupee!" he said reflectively; "Pohon-Upas, Antjar, Galanga root, Ginger and Black Pepper — that's the Javanese method of procedure, I believe. Ayupee! — yes, assuredly, Ayupee!"

"What the dickens are you talking about, Cleek? And what does all that gibberish and that word 'Ayupee' mean?"

"Nothing — nothing. At least, just yet. I say, put on your hat and let's go for a pull on the river, Mr. Narkom. I've had enough of mysteries for to-day and am spoiling for another hour in a boat."

Then he screwed round on his heel and walked out into the brilliant summer sunshine.

II

Promptly at the hour appointed "Mr. Jim Rickaby" and his black servant arrived at Laburnam Villa and certainly the former had no cause to complain of the welcome he received at the hands of his beautiful young hostess.

He found her not only an extremely lovely woman to the eye, but one whose gentle, caressing ways, whose soft voice and simple girlish charm were altogether fascinating, and, judging from outward appearances, from the tender solicitude for her elderly husband's comfort and well-being, from the look in her eyes when she spoke to him, the gentleness of her hand when she touched him, one would have said that she really and truly loved him, and that it needed no lure of gold to draw this particular May to the arms of this one December.

He found Captain Travers a laughing, rollicking, fun-loving type of man — at least, to all outward appearances — who seemed to delight in sports and games and to have an almost childish love of card tricks and that species of entertainment which is known as parlour magic. He found the three other members of the little house-party — to wit: Mrs. Somerby-Miles, Lieutenant Forshay, and Mr. Robert Murdock — respectively, a silly, flirtatious, little gadfly of a widow; a callow, love-struck, lap-dog, young naval officer, with a budding moustache and a full-blown idea of his own importance; a dour Scotchman of middle age, with a passion for chess, a glowering scorn of frivolities, a deep abiding conviction that Scotland was the only country in the world for a self-respecting human being to dwell in, and that everything outside of the Established Church was foredoomed to flames and sulphur and the perpetual prodding of red-hot pitchforks. And last, but not least by any means, he found Mr. Michael Bawdrey just what he had been told he would find him, namely, a dear, lovable, sunny-tempered old man, who fairly idolized his young wife and absolutely adored his frank-faced, affectionate, big boy of a son, and who ought not, in the common course of things, to have an enemy or an evil wisher in all the world.

The news, which, of course, had preceded Cleek's arrival, that this whilom college chum of his son's was as great an enthusiast as he himself on the subject of old china, old porcelain, bric-a-brac, and curios of every sort, filled him with the utmost delight, and he could scarcely refrain from rushing him off at once to view his famous collection.

"Michael, dear, you mustn't overdo yourself just because you happen to have been a little stronger these past two days," said his wife, laying a gentle hand upon his arm. "Besides, we must give Mr. Rickaby time to breathe. He has had a long journey, and I am sure he will want to rest. You can take him in to see that wonderful collection after dinner, dear."

"Humph! Full of fakes, as I supposed — and she knows it," was Cleek's mental comment upon this. And he was not surprised when, finding herself alone with him a few minutes later, she said, in her pretty, pleading way:

"Mr. Rickaby, if you are an expert, don't undeceive him. I could not let you go to see the collection without first telling you. It is full of bogus things, full of frauds and shams that unscrupulous dealers have palmed off on him. But don't let him know. He takes such pride in them, and — and he's breaking down. God pity me, his health is breaking down every day, Mr. Rickaby, and I want to spare him every pang, if I can, even so little a pang as the discovery that the things he prizes are not real."

"Set your mind at rest, Mrs. Bawdrey," promised Cleek. "He will not find it out from me. He will not find anything out from me. He is just the kind of man to break his heart, to crumple up like a burnt glove, and come to the end of all things, even life, if he were to discover that any of his treasures, anything that he loved and trusted in, is a sham and a fraud."

His eyes looked straight into hers as he spoke, his hand rested lightly on her sleeve. She sucked in her breath suddenly, a brief pallor chased the roses from her cheeks, a brief confusion sat momentarily upon her. She appeared to hesitate, then looked away and laughed uneasily.

"I don't think I quite grasp what you mean, Mr. Rickaby," she said.

"Don't you?" he made answer. "Then I will tell you some time — tomorrow, perhaps. But if I were you, Mrs. Bawdrey — well, no matter. This I promise you: that dear old man shall have no ideal shattered by me."

And, living up to that promise, he enthused over everything the old man had in his collection when, after dinner that night, they went, in company with Philip, to view it. But bogus things were on every hand. Spurious porcelains, fraudulent armour, faked china were everywhere. The loaded cabinets and the glazed cases were one long procession of faked Dresden and bogus faience, of Egyptian enamels that had been manufactured in Birmingham, and of sixth-century "treasures" whose makers were still plying the trade and battening upon the ignorance of collectors.

"Now, here's a thing I am particularly proud of," said the gulled old man, reaching into one of the cases and holding out for Cleek's admiration an irregular disc of dull, hammered gold that had an iridescent beetle embedded in the flat face of it. "This scarab, Mr. Rickaby, has helped to make history, as one might say. It was once the property of Cleopatra. I was obliged to make two trips to Egypt before I could persuade the owner to part with it. I am always conscious of a certain sense of awe, Mr. Rickaby, when I touch this wonderful thing. To think, sir, to think! that this bauble once rested on the bosom of that marvellous woman; that Mark Antony must have seen it, may have touched it; that Ptolemy Auletse knew all about it, and that it is older, sir, than the Christian religion itself!"

He held it out upon the flat of his palm, the better for Cleek to see and to admire it, and signed to his son to hand the visitor a magnifying glass.

"Wonderful, most wonderful!" observed Cleek, bending over the spurious gem and focussing the glass upon it; not, however, for the purpose of studying the fraud, but to examine something he had just noticed — something round and red and angry-looking — which marked the palm itself, at the base of the middle finger. "No wonder you are proud of such a prize. I think I should go off my head with rapture if I owned an antique like that. But, pardon me, have you met with an accident, Mr. Bawdrey? That's an ugly place you have on your palm."

"That? Oh, that's nothing," he answered gaily. "It itches a great deal at times, but otherwise it isn't troublesome. I can't think how in the world I got it, to tell the truth. It came out as a sort of red blister in the beginning, and since it broke it has been spreading a great deal. But, really, it doesn't amount to anything at all."

"Oh, that's just like you, dad," put in Philip, "always making light of the wretched thing. I notice one thing, however, Rickaby, it seems to grow worse instead of better. And dad knows as well as I do when it began. It came out suddenly about a fortnight ago, after he had been holding some green worsted for my stepmother to wind into balls. Just look at it, will you, old chap?"

"Nonsense, nonsense!" chimed in the old man laughingly. "Don't mind the silly boy, Mr. Rickaby. He will have it that that green worsted is to blame, just because he happened to spy the thing the morning after."

"Let's have a look at it," said Cleek, moving nearer the light. Then, after a close examination, "I don't think it amounts to anything, after all," he added, as he laid aside the glass. "I shouldn't worry myself about it if I were you, Phil. It's just an ordinary blister, nothing more. Let's go on with the collection, Mr. Bawdrey; I'm deeply interested in it, I assure you. Never saw such a marvellous lot. Got any more amazing things, gems, I mean, like that wonderful scarab? I say!" — halting suddenly before a long, narrow case with a glass front, which stood on end in a far corner, and, being lined with black velvet, brought into ghastly prominence the suspended shape of a human skeleton contained within — "I say! What the dickens is this? Looks like a doctor's specimen, b'gad. You haven't let anybody — I mean, you haven't been buying any prehistoric bones, have you, Mr. Bawdrey?"

"Oh, that?" laughed the old man, turning round and seeing to what he was alluding. "Oh, that's a curiosity of quite a different sort, Mr. Rickaby. You are saying it looks like a doctor's specimen. It is — or, rather, it was. Mrs. Bawdrey's father was a doctor, and it once belonged to him. Properly, it ought to have no place in a collection of this sort, but — well, it's such an amazing thing I couldn't quite refuse it a place, sir. It's a freak of nature. The skeleton of a nine-fingered man."

"Of a what?"

"A nine-fingered man."

"Well, I can't say that I see anything remarkable in that. I've got nine fingers myself, nine and one over, when it comes to that."

"No, you haven't, you duffer!" put in young Bawdrey, with a laugh. "You've got eight fingers — eight fingers and two thumbs. This bony Johnny has nine fingers and two thumbs. That's what makes him a freak. I say, dad, open the beggar's box, and let Rickaby see."

His father obeyed the request. Lifting the tiny brass latch which alone secured it, he swung open the glazed door of the case, and, reaching in, drew forward the flexible left arm of the skeleton.

"There you are," he said, supporting the bony hand upon his palm, so that all its fingers were spread out and Cleek might get a clear view of the monstrosity. "What a trial he must have been to the glove trade, mustn't he?" laughing gaily. "Fancy the confusion and dismay, Mr. Rickaby, if a fellow like this walked into a Bond Street shop and asked for a pair of gloves in a hurry."

Cleek bent over and examined the thing with interest. At first glance the hand was no different from any other skeleton hand one might see any day in any place where they sold anatomical specimens for the use of members of the medical profession; but as Mr. Bawdrey, holding it on the palm of his right hand, flattened it out with the fingers of his left, the abnormality at once became apparent. Springing from the base of the fourth finger, a perfectly developed fifth appeared, curling inward toward what had once been the palm of the hand, as though, in life, it had been the owner's habit of screening it from observation by holding it in that position. It was, however, perfectly flexible, and Mr. Bawdrey had no difficulty in making it lie out flat after the manner of its mates.

The sight was not inspiring — the freaks of Mother Nature rarely are. No one but a doctor would have cared to accept the thing as a gift, and no one but a man as mad on the subject of curiosities and with as little sense of discrimination as Mr. Bawdrey would have dreamt for a moment of adding it to a collection.

"It's rather uncanny," said Cleek, who had no palate for the abnormal in Nature. "For myself, I may frankly admit that I don't like things of that sort about me."

"You are very much like my wife in that," responded the old

man. "She was of the opinion that the skeleton ought to have been destroyed or else handed over to some anatomical museum. But — well, it is a curiosity, you know, Mr. Rickaby. Besides, as I have said, it was once the property of her late father, a most learned man, sir, most learned, and as it was of sufficient interest for him to retain it — oh, well, we collectors are faddists, you know, so I easily persuaded Mrs. Bawdrey to allow me to bring it over to England with me when we took our leave of Java. And now that you have seen it, suppose we have a look at more artistic things. I have some very fine specimens of neolithic implements and weapons which I am most anxious to show you. Just step this way, please."

He let the skeleton's hand slip from his own, swing back into the case, and forthwith closed the glass door upon it; then, leading the way to the cabinet containing the specimens referred to, he unlocked it, and invited Cleek's opinion of the flint arrowheads, stone hatchets, and granite utensils within.

For a minute they lingered thus, the old man talking, laughing, exulting in his possessions, the detective examining and pretending to be deeply impressed. Then, of a sudden, without hint or warning to lessen the shock of it, the uplifted lid of the cabinet fell with a crash from the hand that upheld it, shivering the glass into fifty pieces, and Cleek, screwing round on his heel with a "jump" of all his nerves, was in time to see the figure of his host crumple up, collapse, drop like a thing shot dead, and lie writhing on the polished floor.

"Dad! Oh, heavens! Dad!" The cry was young Bawdrey's. He seemed fairly to throw himself across the intervening space and to reach his father in the instant he fell. "Now you know! Now you know!" he went on wildly, as Cleek dropped down beside him and began to loosen the old man's collar. "It's like this always; not a hint, not a sign, but just this utter collapse. My God, what are they doing it with? How are they managing it, those two? They're coming, Headland. Listen! Don't you hear them?"

The crash of the broken glass and the jar of the old man's fall had swept through all the house, and a moment later, headed by

Mrs. Bawdrey herself, all the members of the little house-party came piling excitedly into the room.

The fright and suffering of the young wife seemed very real as she threw herself down beside her husband and caught him to her with a little shuddering cry. Then her voice, uplifting in a panic, shrilled out a wild appeal for doctor, servants – help of any kind. And, almost as she spoke, Travers was beside her, Travers and Forshay and Robert Murdock – yes, and silly little Mrs. Somerby-Miles, too, forgetting in the face of such a time as this to be anything but helpful and womanly – and all of these gave such assistance as was in their power.

"Help me get him up to his own room, somebody, and send a servant post-haste for the doctor," said Captain Travers, taking the lead after the fashion of a man who is used to command. "Calm yourself as much as possible, Mrs. Bawdrey. Here, Murdock, lend a hand and help him."

"Eh, mon, there is nae help but Heaven's in sic a case as this," dolefully responded Murdock, as he came forward and solemnly stooped to obey. "The puir auld laddie! The Laird giveth and the Laird taketh awa', and the weel o' mon is as naething."

"Oh, stow your croaking, you blundering old fool!" snapped Travers, as Mrs. Bawdrey gave a heart-wrung cry and hid her face in her hands. "You and your eternal doldrums! Here, Bawdrey, lend a hand, old chap. We can get him upstairs without the assistance of this human trombone, I know."

But "this human trombone" was not minded that they should; and so it fell out that, when Lieutenant Forshay led Mrs. Somerby-Miles from the room, and young Bawdrey and Captain Travers carried the stricken man up the stairs to his own bed-chamber, his wife flying in advance to see that everything was prepared for him, Cleek, standing all alone beside the shattered cabinet, could hear Mr. Robert Murdock's dismal croakings rumbling steadily out as he mounted the staircase with the others.

For a moment after the closing door of a room overhead had shut them from his ears, he stood there, with puckered brows and pursed-up lips, drumming with his finger-tips a faint tattoo upon the framework of the shattered lid; then he walked over to the skeleton case, and silently regarded the gruesome thing within.

"Nine fingers," he muttered sententiously, "and the ninth curves inward to the palm!" He stepped round and viewed the case from all points; both sides, the front, and even the narrow space made at the back by the angle of the corner where it stood. And after this he walked to the other end of the room, took the key from the lock, slipped it in his pocket, and went out, closing the door behind him, that none might remember it had not been locked when the master of the place was carried above.

It was, perhaps, twenty minutes later that young Bawdrey came down and found him all alone in the smoking-room, bending over the table whereon the butler had set the salver containing the whisky decanter, the soda siphon, and the glasses that were always laid out there that the gentlemen might help themselves to the regulation "night-cap" before going to bed.

"I've slipped away to have a word in private with you, Headland," he said in an agitated voice, as he came in. "Oh, what consummate actors they are, those two. You'd think her heart was breaking, wouldn't you? You'd think – Hallo! I say! What on earth are you doing?" For as he came nearer he could see that Cleek had removed the glass stopper of the decanter, and was tapping with his finger-tips a little funnel of white paper, the narrow end of which he had thrust into the neck of the bottle.

"Just adding a harmless little sleeping-draught to the nightly beverage," said Cleek, in reply, as he screwed up the paper funnel and put it in his pocket. "A good sound sleep is an excellent thing, my dear fellow, and I mean to make sure that the gentlemen of this house-party have it — one gentleman in particular: Captain Travers."

"Yes; but — I say! What about me, old chap? I don't want to be drugged, and you know I have to show them the courtesy of taking a 'night-cap' with them."

"Precisely. That's where you can help me out. If any of them remark anything about the whisky having a peculiar taste, you must stoutly assert that you don't notice; and, as they've seen you drinking from the same decanter — why, there you are. Don't worry over it. It's a very, very harmless draught; you won't even have a headache from it. Listen here, Bawdrey. Somebody is poisoning your father."

"I know it. I told you so from the beginning, Headland," he answered, with a sort of wail. "But what's that got to do with drugging the whisky?"

"Everything. I'm going to find out to-night whether Captain Travers is that somebody or not. Sh-h-h! Don't get excited. Yes, that's my game. I want to get into his room whilst he is sleeping, and be free to search his effects. I want to get into every man's room here, and wherever I find poison — well, you understand?"

"Yes," he replied, brightening as he grasped the import of the matter. "What a ripping idea! And so simple."

"I think so. Once let me find the poison, and I'll know my man. Now, one other thing: the housekeeper must have a master-key that opens all the bedrooms in the place. Get it for me. It will be easier and swifter than picking the locks."

"Right you are, old chap. I'll slip up to Mrs. Jarret's room and fetch it to you at once."

"No; tuck it under the mat just outside my door. As it won't do for me to be drugged as well as the rest of you, I shan't put in an appearance when the rest come down. Say I've got a headache, and have gone to bed. As for my own 'night-cap' — well, I can send Dollops down to get the butler to pour me one out of another decanter, so that will be all right. Now, toddle off and get the key, there's a good chap. And, I say, Bawdrey, as I shan't see you again until morning — good-night."

"Good-night, old chap!" he answered in his impulsive, boyish way. "You are a friend, Headland. And you'll save my dad, God bless you! A true, true friend that's what you are. Thank God I ran across you."

Cleek smiled and nodded to him as he passed out and hurried away; then, hearing the other gentlemen coming down the stairs, he, too, made haste to get out of the room and to creep up to his own after they had assembled, and the cigar cabinet and the whisky were being passed round, and the doctor was busy above with the man who was somebody's victim.

* * * * *

The big old grandfather clock at the top of the stairs pointed ten minutes past two, and the house was hushed of every sound save that which is the evidence of deep sleep, when the door of Cleek's room swung quietly open, and Cleek himself, in dressing-gown and wadded bedroom slippers, stepped out into the dark hall, and, leaving Dollops on guard, passed like a shadow over the thick, unsounding carpet.

The rooms of all the male occupants of the house, including that of Philip Bawdrey himself, opened upon this passage. He went to each in turn, unlocked it, stepped in, closed it after him, and lit the bedroom candle.

The sleeping-draught had accomplished all that was required of it; and in each and every room he entered — Captain Travers's, Lieutenant Forshay's, Mr. Robert Murdock's — there lay the occupant thereof stretched out at full length in the grip of that deep and heavy sleep which comes of drugs.

Cleek made the round of the rooms as quietly as any shadow, even stopping as he passed young Bawdrey's on his way back to his own to peep in there. Yes; he, too, had got his share of the effective draught, for there he lay snarled up in the bed-clothes, with his arms over his head and his knees drawn up until they were on a level with his waist, and his handsome boyish face a little paler than usual.

Cleek didn't go into the room, simply looked at him from the threshold, then shut the door, and went back to Dollops.

"All serene, guv'ner?" questioned that young man in an eager whisper.

"Yes, quite," his master replied, as he turned to a writing-table whereon there lay a sealed note, and, pulling out the chair, sat down before it and took up a pen. "Wait a bit, and then you can go to bed. I'll give you still another note to deliver. While I'm writing it you may lay out my clothes."

"Slipping off, sir?"

"Yes. You will stop here, however. Now, then, hold your tongue; I'm busy."

Then he pulled a sheet of paper to him and wrote rapidly:

Dear Mr. Bawdrey — I've got my man, and am off to consult with Mr. Narkom and to have what I've found analysed. I don't know when I shall be back — probably not until the day after to-morrow. You are right. It is murder, and Java is at the bottom of it. Dollops will hand you this. Say nothing — just wait till I get back.

This he slipped, unsigned in his haste, into an envelope, handed it to Dollops, and then fairly jumped into his clothes. Ten minutes later he was out of the house, and — the end of the riddle was in sight.

III

On the morrow Mrs. Bawdrey made known the rather surprising piece of news that Mr. Rickaby had written her a note to say that he had received a communication of such vital importance that he had been obliged to leave the house that morning before anybody was up, and might not be able to return to it for several days.

"No very great hardship in that, my dear," commented Mrs. Somerby-Miles, "for a more stupid and uninteresting person I never encountered. Fancy! he never even offered to assist the gentlemen to get poor Mr. Bawdrey upstairs last night. How is the poor old dear this morning, darling? Better?"

"Yes — much," said Mrs. Bawdrey in reply. "Doctor Phillipson came to the house before four o'clock, and brought some wonderful new medicine that has simply worked wonders. Of course, he will have to stop in bed and be perfectly quiet for three or four days; but, although the attack was by far the worst he has ever had, the doctor feels quite confident that he will pull him safely through."

Now although, in the light of her apparent affection for her aged husband, she ought, one would have thought, to be exceedingly happy over this, it was distinctly noticeable that she was nervous and ill at ease, that there was a hunted look in her eyes, and that, as the day wore on, these things seemed to be accentuated. More than that, there seemed added proof of the truth of young Bawdrey's assertion that she and Captain Travers were in league with each other, for that day they were constantly together, constantly getting off into out-of-the-way places, and constantly talking in an undertone of something that seemed to worry them.

Even when dinner was over, and the whole party adjourned to the drawing-room for coffee, and the lady ought, in all conscience, to have given herself wholly up to the entertainment of her guests, it was observable that she devoted most of her time to whispered conferences with Captain Travers. They kept going to the window and looking up at the sky, as if worried and annoyed that the twilight should be so long in fading and the night in coming on. But worse than this, at ten o'clock Captain Travers made an excuse of having letters to write, and left the room, and it was scarcely six minutes later that she followed suit.

But the captain had not gone to write letters, as it had happened. Instead, he had gone straight to the morning-room, an apartment immediately behind that in which the elder Mr. Bawdrey's collection was housed, and from which a broad French window opened out upon the grounds, and it might have caused a scandal had it been known that Mrs. Bawdrey joined him there one minute after leaving the drawing-room.

"It is the time, Walter, it is the time!" she said in a breathless sort of way, as she closed the door and moved across the room to where he stood, a dimly-seen figure in the dim light. "God help and pity me! but I am so nervous I hardly know how to contain myself. The note said at ten to-night in the morning-room, and it is ten now. The hour is here, Walter, the hour is here!"

"So is the man, Mrs. Bawdrey," answered a low voice from the outer darkness; then a figure lifted itself above the screening shrubs just beyond the ledge of the open window, and Cleek stepped into the room.

She gave a little hysterical cry and reached out her hands to him.

"Oh, I am so glad to see you, even though you hint at such awful things, I am so glad, so glad!" she said. "I almost died when I read your note. To think that it is murder — murder! And but for you he might be dead even now. You will like to know that the doctor brought the stuff you sent by him and my darling is better — better."

Before Cleek could venture any reply to this, Captain Travers stalked across the room and gripped his hand.

"And so you are that great man Cleek, are you?" he said. "Bully boy! Bully boy! And to think that all the time it wasn't some mysterious natural affliction; to think that it was crime, murder, poison. What poison, man, what poison?"

"Ayupee, or, as it is variously called in the several islands of the Eastern Archipelago, Pohon-Upas, Antjar, and Ipo," said Cleek in reply. "The deadly venom which the Malays use in poisoning the heads of their arrows."

"What! that awful stuff!" said Mrs. Bawdrey, with a little shuddering cry. "And some one in this house - " Her voice broke. She plucked at Cleek's sleeve and looked up at him in an agony of entreaty. "Who?" she implored. "Who in this house could? You said you would tell to-night — you said you would. Oh, who could have the heart? Ah! who? It is true, if you have not heard it, that once upon a time there was bad blood between Mr. Murdock and him; that Mr. Murdock is a family connection; but even he, oh, even he - Tell me — tell me, Mr. Cleek?"

"Mrs. Bawdrey, I can't just yet," he made reply. "In my heart I am as certain of it as though the criminal had confessed; but I am waiting for a sign, and, until that comes, absolute proof is not possible. That it will come, and may, indeed, come at any moment now that it is quite dark, I am very certain. When it does – "

He stopped and threw up a warning hand. As he spoke a queer thudding sound struck one dull note through the stillness of the house. He stood, bent forward, listening, absolutely breathless; then, on the other side of the wall, there rippled and rolled a something that was like the sound of a struggle between two voiceless animals, and – the sign that he awaited had come!

"Follow me quickly, as noiselessly as you can. Let no one hear, let no one see!" he said in a breath of excitement. Then he sprang cat-like to the door, whirled it open, scudded round the angle of the passage to the entrance of the room where the fraudulent collection was kept, and went in with the silent fleetness of a panther. And a moment later, when Captain Travers and Mrs. Bawdrey swung in through the door and joined him, they came upon a horrifying sight.

For there, leaning against the open door of the case where the skeleton of the nine-fingered man hung, was Dollops, bleeding and faint, and with a score of toothmarks on his neck and throat. On the floor at his feet Cleek was kneeling on the writhing figure of a man who bit and tore and snarled like a cornered wolf and fought with teeth and feet and hands alike in the wild effort to get free from the grip of destiny. A locked handcuff clamped one wrist, and from it swung, at the end of the connecting chain, its unlocked mate; the marks of Dollops's fists were on his lips and cheeks, and at the foot of the case, where the hanging skeleton doddered and shook to the vibration of the floor, lay a shattered phial of deep-blue glass.

"Got you, you hound!" said Cleek through his teeth as he wrenched the man's two wrists together and snapped the other handcuff into place. "You beast of ingratitude – you Judas! Kissing and betraying like any other Iscariot! And a dear old man like that! Look here, Mrs. Bawdrey; look here, Captain Travers; what do you think of a little rat like this?"

They came forward at his word, and, looking down, saw that the figure he was bending over was the figure of Philip Bawdrey.

"Oh!" gulped Mrs. Bawdrey, and then shut her two hands over her eyes and fell away weak and shivering. "Oh, Mr. Cleek, it can't be — it can't! To do a thing like that?"

"Oh, he'd have done worse, the little reptile, if he hadn't been pulled up short," said Cleek in reply. "He'd have hanged you for it, if it had gone the way he planned. You look in your boxes; you, too, Captain Travers. I'll wager each of you finds a phial of Ayu-pee hidden among them somewhere. Came in to put more of the cursed stuff on the ninth finger of the skeleton, so that it would be ready for the next time, didn't he, Dollops?"

"Yes, guv'ner. I waited for him behind the case just as you told me to, sir, and when he ups and slips the finger of the skilli-gan into the neck of the bottle, I nips out and whacks the bracelet on him. But he was too quick for me, sir, so I only got one on; and then, the hound, he turns on me like a blessed hyena, sir, and begins a-chawin' of me windpipe. I say, guv'ner, take off his sil-ver wristlets, will you, sir, and lemme have jist ten minutes with him on my own? Five for me, sir, and five for his poor old dad!"

"Not I," said Cleek. "I wouldn't let you soil those honest hands of yours on his vile little body, Dollops. Thought you had a noodle to deal with, didn't you, Mr. Philip Bawdrey? Thought you could lead me by the nose, and push me into finding those phials just where you wanted them found, didn't you? Well, you've got a few more thoughts coming. Look here, Captain Tra-vers; what do you think of this fellow's little game? Tried to take me in about you and Mrs. Bawdrey being lovers, and trying to do away with him and his father to get the old man's money."

"Why, the contemptible little hound! Bless my soul, man, I'm engaged to Mrs. Bawdrey's cousin. And as for his stepmother, why, she threw the little worm over as soon as he began making love to her, and tried to make her take up with him by telling her how much he'd be worth when his father died."

"I guessed as much. I didn't fancy him from the first moment; and he was so blessed eager to have me begin by suspecting you two, that I smelt a rat at once. Oh, but he's been crafty enough in other things. Putting that devilish stuff on the ninth finger of the skeleton, and never losing an opportunity to get his poor old father to handle it and to show it to people. It's a strong, irritant poison — sap of the upas tree is the base of it — producing first an irritation of the skin, then a blister, and, when that broke, communicating the poison directly to the blood every time the skeleton hand touched it. A weak solution at first, so that the decline would be natural, the growth of the malady gradual. But if I'd found that phial in your room last night, as he hoped and believed I had done — well, look for yourself. The finger of the skeleton is thick with the beastly, gummy stuff to-night. Double strength, of course. The next time his father touched it he'd have died before morning. And the old chap fairly worshipping him. I suspected him, and suspected what the stuff that was being used really was from the beginning. Last night I drugged him, and then I knew."

"Knew, Mr. Cleek? Why, how could you?"

"The most virulent poisons have their remedial uses, Captain," he made reply. "You can kill a man with strychnine; you can put him in his grave with arsenic; you can also use both these powerful agents to cure and to save, in their proper proportions and in the proper way. The same rule applies to ayupee. Properly diluted and properly used, it is one of the most powerful agents for the relief, and, in some cases, the cure, of Bright's disease of the kidneys. But the Government guards this unholy drug most carefully. You can't get a drop of it in Java for love nor money, unless on the order of a recognized physician; and you can't bring it into the ports of England unless backed by that physician's sworn statement and the official stamp of the Javanese authorities. A man undeniably afflicted with Bright's disease could get these things — no other could. Well, I wanted to know who had succeeded in getting ayupee into this country and into this house. Last night I drugged every man in it, and I found out."

"But how?"

"By finding the one who could not sleep stretched out at full length. One of the strongest symptoms of Bright's disease is a tendency to draw the knees up close to the body in sleep, Captain, and to twist the arms above the head. Of all the men under this roof, this man here was the only one who slept like that last night!" He paused and looked down at the scowling, sullen creature on the floor. "You wretched little cur!" he said with a gesture of unspeakable contempt. "And all for the sake of an old man's money! If I did my duty, I'd gaol you. But if I did, it would be punishing the innocent for the crimes of the guilty. It would kill that dear old man to learn this; and so he's not going to learn it, and the law's not going to get its own." He twitched out his hand, and something tinkled on the floor. "Get up!" he said sharply. "There's the key of the handcuffs; take it and set yourself free. Do you know what's going to happen to you? To-morrow morning Dr. Phillipson is going to examine you, and to report that you'll be a dead man in a year's time if you stop another week in this country. You are going out of it, and you are going to stop out of it. Do you understand? *Stop* out of it to the end of your days. For if ever you put foot in it again I'll handle you as a terrier handles a rat! Dollops?"

"Yes, guv'ner?"

"My things packed and ready?"

"Yes, sir. And all waitin' in the arbour, sir, as you told me to have 'em."

"Good lad! Get them, and we'll catch the first train back. Mrs. Bawdrey, my best respects. Captain, all good luck to you. The riddle is solved. Good-night."

CHAPTER VI
THE WIZARD'S BELT

It was exactly three o'clock when the two-forty-seven train from Victoria set Cleek down at Wandsworth Common, and it was exactly fifteen minutes later when he was shown into the modest little drawing-room of 17 Sunnington Crescent by Mrs. Culpin herself, handed an afternoon paper, and left in sole possession of the place.

The letter that drew him to this particular house at this particular time had come from Mr. Narkom, and was couched in these words:

My Dear Cleek:

A most amazing case — probably the most amazing you have yet tackled — has just cropped up, and I am all eagerness to have you hear the astonishing details as expeditiously as possible. The client is one Captain Morrison, a retired army officer living solely on his half-pay; so the reward — if any — must of necessity be small. His daughter, Miss Mary Morrison, a young and extremely attractive girl, is involved in the amazing affair, and it is at her earnest appeal that the matter has been brought to my notice. As the captain is in such weak health that a journey of any distance is out of the question, I shall ask you to meet me at Wandsworth Common, where he lives. Will you, therefore, be at 17 Sunnington Crescent, Wandsworth, this afternoon between the hours of three and four? The house is the residence of a Mrs. Culpin, widow of one of my Yard men who was killed last autumn. I am wiring her to expect you. But, knowing your reluctance in the matter of any clue to your identity being circulated, I have given you the name you adopted in the Bawdrey affair: "George Headland." I have also taken the same precaution with regard to Captain Morrison, leaving you to disclose your identity or not, as you see fit, after you have interviewed him and the other persons connected with this extraordinary affair.

Yours, etc.,

Maverick Narkom.

Cleek did not even glance at the afternoon paper which Mrs. Culpin had so considerately left him. Instead, he walked to the open window, through which the summer sunshine was streaming, and, with his hands loosely clasped behind his back, stood looking out thoughtfully at the groups of merry children who were romping on the not far distant common and making the air melodious with their happy laughter. And so he was still standing when, some ten or a dozen minutes later, the door behind him opened and Narkom walked into the room.

"Well, here I am at last, you see, my dear fellow," said the superintendent, crossing the floor and shaking hands with him. "Ripping day, isn't it? What are you doing, admiring the view or taking stock of Mrs. Culpin's roses?"

"Neither. I was speculating in futures," replied Cleek, glancing back at the sunlit common, and then glancing away again with a faintly audible sigh. "How happy, how care-free they are, those merry little beggars, Mr. Narkom. What you said in your letter set my thoughts harking backward, and ... I was wondering what things the coming years might hold for them and for their parents. At one time, you know, that fellow Philip Bawdrey was as innocent and as guileless as any of those little shavers; and yet in the after years he proved a monster of iniquity, a beast of ingratitude, and – Oh, well, let it pass. He paid, as thankless children always do pay under God's good rule. I wonder what his thoughts were when his last hour came."

"It did come, then?"

"Yes. I had a letter from Mrs. Bawdrey the other day. News had just come of his death — from Bright's disease, of course — in Buenos Ayres. His father never knew of his guilt; never will know now, thank God! He mourned bitterly, of course, poor, dear old chap; but — well, Heaven tempers all things with its mercy. The rascal did not die an only son. There's another now, born three months ago. The longer I live the more sure I become that straight living always pays, and that Heaven never forgets to punish and to reward."

"Ten years of Scotland Yard have enabled me to endorse that

statement emphatically," replied Narkom. "'The riddle of the ninth finger' was no different in that respect from nine hundred other riddles that have come my way since I took office. Now sit down, old chap, and let us take up the present case. But I say, Cleek, speaking of rewards reminds me of what I wrote you. There's very little chance of one in this affair. All the parties connected with it are in very moderate circumstances. The sculptor fellow, Van Nant, who figures in it, was quite well to do at one time, I believe, but he ran through the greater part of his money, and a dishonest solicitor did him out of the rest. Miss Morrison herself never did have any, and, as I have told you, the captain hasn't anything in the world but his pension; and it takes every shilling of that to keep them. In the circumstances, I'd have made it a simple 'Yard' affair, chargeable to the Government, and put one of the regular staff upon it. But it's such an astounding, such an unheard-of thing, I knew you'd fairly revel in it. And besides, after all the rewards you *have* won you must be quite a well-to-do man by this time, and able to indulge in a little philanthropy."

Cleek smiled.

"I will indulge in it, of course," he said, "but not for that reason, Mr. Narkom. I wonder how much it will surprise you to learn that, at the present moment, I have just one hundred pounds in all the world?"

"My dear fellow!" Narkom exclaimed with a sort of gasp, staring at him in round-eyed amazement. "You fairly take away my breath. Why, you must have received a fortune since you took up these special cases. Fifty or sixty thousand pounds at the smallest calculation."

"More! To be precise, I have received exactly seventy-two thousand pounds, Mr. Narkom. But, as I tell you, I have to-day but one hundred pounds of that sum left. Lost in speculation? Oh, dear no! I've not invested one farthing in any scheme, company, or purchase since the night you gave me my chance and helped me to live an honest life."

"Then in the name of Heaven, Cleek, what has become of the money?"

"It has gone in the cause of my redemption, Mr. Narkom," he answered in a hushed voice. "My good friend — for you really *have* been a good friend to me, the best I ever had in all the world — my good friend, let us for only just this one minute speak of the times that lie behind. You know what redeemed me, a woman's eyes, a woman's rose-white soul. I said, did I not, that I wanted to win her, wanted to be worthy of her, wanted to climb up and stand with her in the light? You remember that, do you not, Mr. Narkom?"

"Yes, I remember. But, my dear fellow, why speak of your 'Vanishing Cracksman' days when you have so utterly put them behind you, and for five whole years have lived a life beyond reproach? Whatever you did in those times you have amply atoned for. And what can that have to do with your impoverished state?"

"It has everything to do with it. I said I would be worthy of that one dear woman, and I never can be, Mr. Narkom, until I have made restitution; until I can offer her a clean hand as well as a clean life. I can't restore the actual things that the 'Vanishing Cracksman' stole; for they are gone beyond recall, but I can, at least, restore the value of them, and that I have been secretly doing for a long time."

"Man alive! God bless my soul! Cleek, my dear fellow, do you mean to tell me that all the rewards, all the money you have earned in the past five years – "

"Have gone to the people from whom I stole things in the wretched old days that lie behind me," he finished very gently. "It goes back, in secret gifts, as fast as it is earned, Mr. Narkom. Don't you see the answers, the acknowledgments, in the 'Personal' columns of the papers now and again? Wheresoever I robbed in those old days, I am repaying in these. When the score is wiped off, when the last robbery is paid for, my hand will be clean, and I can offer it; never before."

"Cleek! My dear fellow! What a man! What a *man*! Oh, more than ever am I certain *now* that old Sir Horace Wyvern was right that night when he said that you were a gentleman. Tell me — I'll respect it — tell me, for God's sake, man, who are you? What are you, dear friend?"

"Cleek," he made reply. "Just Cleek! The rest is my secret and — God's! We've never spoken of the past since *that* night, Mr. Narkom, and, with your kind permission, we never will speak of it again. I'm Cleek, the detective, at your service once more. Now, then, let's have the new strange case on which you called me here. What's it all about?"

"Necromancy — wizardry — fairy-lore — all the stuff and nonsense that goes to the making of 'The Arabian nights'!" said Narkom, waxing excited as his thoughts were thus shoved back to the amazing affair he had in hand. "All your 'Red Crawls' and your 'Sacred Sons' and your 'Nine-fingered Skeletons' are fools to it for wonder and mystery. Talk about witchcraft! Talk about wizards and giants and enchanters and the things that witches did in the days of Macbeth! God bless my soul, they're nothing to it. Those were the days of magic, anyhow, so you can take it or leave it, as you like; but this - Look here, Cleek, you've heard of a good many queer things and run foul of a good many mysteries, I'll admit, but did you ever in this twentieth century, when witchcraft and black magic are supposed to be as dead as Queen Anne, hear of such a marvel as a man putting on a blue leather belt that was said to have the power of rendering the wearer invisible, and then forthwith melting into thin air and floating off like a cloud of pipe smoke?"

"Gammon!"

"Gammon nothing! Facts!"

"Facts? You're out of your head, man. The thing couldn't possibly happen. Somebody's having you!"

"Well, somebody had *him*, at all events. Young Carboys, I mean — the chap that's engaged, or, rather, was engaged, to Captain Morrison's daughter; and the poor girl's half out of her mind over it. He put the belt on in the presence of her and her father in their own house, mind you walked into a bedroom, and vanished like smoke. Doors locked, windows closed, room empty, belt on the floor and man gone. Not a trace of him from that moment to this; and yesterday was to have been his wedding day. There's a 'mystery' if you like. What do you make of that?"

Cleek looked at him for an instant. Then:

"My dear Mr. Narkom, for the moment I thought you were fooling," he said in a tone of deep interest. "But I see now that you are quite in earnest, although the thing sounds so preposterous, a child might be expected to scoff at it. A man to get a magic belt; to put it on, and then to melt away? Why, the 'Seven-league Boots' couldn't be a greater tax on one's credulity. Sit down and tell me all about it."

"The dickens of it is there doesn't seem to be much to tell," said Narkom, accepting the invitation. "Young Carboys, who appears to have been a decent sort of chap, had neither money, position, nor enemies, so that's an end to any idea of somebody having a reason for wishing to get rid of him; and, as he was devotedly attached to Miss Morrison, and was counting the very hours to the time of their wedding, and, in addition, had no debts, no entanglement of any sort and no possible reason for wishing to disappear, there isn't the slightest ground for suspecting that he did so voluntarily."

"Suppose you tell me the story from the beginning, and leave me to draw my own conclusions regarding that," said Cleek. "Who and what was the man? Was he living in the same house with his fiancée, then? You say the disappearance occurred there, at night, and that he went into a bedroom. Was the place his home as well as Captain Morrison's, then?"

"On the contrary. His home was a matter of three or four miles distant. He was merely stopping at the Morrisons' on that particular night; I'll tell you presently why and how he came to do that. For the present, let's take things in their proper order. Once upon a time this George Carboys occupied a fair position in the world, and his parents — long since dead — were well to do. The son, being an only child, was well looked after, sent to Eton and then to Brasenose, and all that sort of thing, and the future looked very bright for him. Before he was twenty-one, however, his father lost everything through unlucky speculations, and that forced the son to make his own living. At the 'Varsity he had fallen in with a rich young Belgian, named Maurice Van Nant, who had a taste for sculpture and the fine arts generally, and they had become the warmest and closest of friends."

"Maurice Van Nant? That's the sculptor fellow you said in the beginning had gone through his money, isn't it?"

"Yes. Well, when young Carboys was thrown on the world, so to speak, this Van Nant came to the rescue, made a place for him as private secretary and companion, and for three or four years they knocked round the world together, going to Egypt, Persia, India, etcetera, as Van Nant was mad on the subject of Oriental art, and wished to study it at the fountain head. In the meantime both Carboys' parents went over to the silent majority, and left him without a relative in the world, barring Captain Morrison, who is an uncle about seven times removed, and would, of course, naturally be heir-at-law to anything he left if he had had anything to leave, poor beggar, which he hadn't. But that's getting ahead of the story.

"Well, at the end of four years or so Van Nant came to the bottom of his purse, hadn't a stiver left; and from dabbling in art for pleasure, had to come down to it as a means of earning a livelihood. And he and Carboys returned to England, and, for purposes of economy, pooled their interests, took a small box of a house over Putney way, set up a regular 'bachelor establishment,' and started in the business of bread winning together. Carboys succeeded in getting a clerk's position in town; Van Nant set about modelling clay figures and painting mediocre pictures, and selling both whenever he could find purchasers.

"Naturally, these were slow in coming, few and far between; but with Carboys' steady two pounds a week coming in, they managed to scrape along and to keep themselves going. They were very happy, too, despite the fact that Carboys had got himself engaged to Miss Morrison, and was hoarding every penny he could possibly save in order to get enough to marry on; and this did not tend to make Van Nant overjoyed, as such a marriage would, of course, mean the end of their long association and the giving up of their bachelor quarters."

"To say nothing of leaving Van Nant to rub along as best he could without any assistance from Carboys," commented Cleek. "I think I can guess a portion of what resulted, Mr. Narkom. Van Nant did not, of course, in these circumstances have any very tender regard for Miss Morrison."

"No, he did not. In point of fact, he disliked her very much indeed, and viewed the approaching wedding with extreme disfavour."

"And yet you say that nobody had an interest in doing Carboys some sort of mischief in order to prevent that wedding from being consummated, Mr. Narkom," said Cleek with a shrug of the shoulders. "Certainly, Van Nant would have been glad to see a spoke put in that particular wheel; though I freely confess I do not see what good could come of preventing it by doing away with Carboys, as he would then be in as bad a position as if the marriage had been allowed to proceed as planned. Either way he loses Carboys' companionship and assistance; and his one wish would be to preserve both. Well, go on. What next? I'm anxious to hear about the belt. Where and how does that come in?"

"Well, it appears that Miss Morrison got hold of a humorous book called 'The Brass Bottle,' a fantastic, farcical thing, about a genie who had been sealed up in a bottle for a thousand years getting out and causing the poor devil of a hero no end of worry by heaping riches and honours upon him in the most embarrassing manner. It happened that on the night Miss Morrison got this book, and read it aloud for the amusement of her father and lover, Carboys had persuaded Van Nant to spend the evening with them. Apparently he enjoyed himself, too, for he laughed as boisterously as any of them over the farcical tale, and would not go home until he had heard the end of it. When it was finished, Miss Morrison tells me, Carboys, after laughing fit to split his sides over the predicament of the hero of the book, cried out: 'By George! I wish some old genie would take it into his head to hunt *me* up, and try the same sort of a dodge with *me*. He wouldn't find this chicken shying his gold and his gems back at his head, I can tell you. I'd accept all the Arab slaves and all the palaces he wanted to thrust on me; and then I'd make 'em all over to you, Mary, dear, so you'd never have to do another day's worrying or pinching in all your life. But never you nor anybody else depend upon an Arab's gratitude or an Arab's generosity. He'll promise you the moon, and then wriggle out of giving you so much as a star — just as Abdul ben Meerza did with me.' And upon Miss Morrison asking what he meant by that, he replied, laughingly: 'Ask Van; he knew the old codger better than I — knew his whole blessed family, blow him! — and was able to talk to the old skin-flint in his own outlandish tongue.'

"Upon Miss Morrison's acting on this suggestion, Van Nant told of an adventure Carboys had had in Persia some years previously. It appears that he saved the life of a miserly old Arab called Abdul ben Meerza at the risk of his own; that the old man was profuse in his expressions of gratitude, and, on their parting, had said: 'By the Prophet, thou shalt yet find the tree of this day's planting bear rich fruit for thee and thy feet walk upon golden stones.' But, in spite of this promise, he had walked away, and Carboys had never heard another word from nor of him from that hour until three nights ago."

"Oho!" said Cleek, with a strong, rising inflection. "And he did hear of him, then?"

"Yes," replied Narkom. "Quite unexpectedly, and while he was preparing to spend a dull evening at home with Van Nant — for the night was, as you must recollect, my dear fellow, a horribly wet and stormy one — a message came to him from Miss Morrison, asking him to come over to Wandsworth without delay, as a most amazing thing had happened. A box marked 'From Abdul ben Meerza' had been delivered there, of all astonishing places. The message concluded by saying that as it was such a horrible night the captain, her father, would not hear of his returning, so begged him to bring his effects, and come prepared to remain until morning.

"He went, of course, carrying with him a small bag containing his pyjamas, his shaving tackle, and such few accessories as would be necessary, since, if he stopped, he must start from there to business in the morning; and on his arrival was handed a small leather case addressed as he had been told. Imagining all sorts of wonders, from jewels of fabulous value to documents entitling him to endless wealth, he unfastened the case, and found within it a broad belt of blue enamelled leather secured with a circular brass clasp, on which was rudely scratched in English the words, 'The wizards of the East grew rich by being unseen. Whoso clasps this belt about his waist may become invisible for the wishing. So does ben Meerza remember.'

"Of course, Carboys treated it as the veriest rubbish — who wouldn't? Indeed, he suspected Van Nant of having played a joke upon him, and laughingly threw it aside. Then, finding that he had taken an uncomfortable journey for nothing, got some good out of it by spending a pleasant evening with the captain and his daughter. A room had been made ready for him — in fact, although he did not know it, Miss Morrison had given him hers, and had herself gone to a less attractive one — and in due time he prepared to turn in for the night. As they parted Miss Morrison, in a bantering spirit, picked up the belt and handed it to him, remarking that he had better keep it, as, after marriage, he might some time be glad to creep into the house unseen. In the same bantering spirit he had replied that he had better begin learning how the thing worked in case of necessity, and, taking the belt, clasped it round his waist, said good-night, and stepped into the room prepared for him. Miss Morrison and her father heard him close the door and pull down the blind, and that was the last that was seen or heard of him.

"In the morning the bed was found undisturbed, his locked bag on a chair, and in the middle of the floor the blue leather belt; but of the man himself there was not one trace to be found. There, that's the story, Cleek. Now what do you make of it?"

"I shall be able to tell you better after I have seen the parties concerned," said Cleek after a moment's pause. "You have brought your motor, of course? Let us step into it, then, and whizz round to Captain Morrison's house. What's that? Oh, un-

148

doubtedly a case of foul play, Mr. Narkom. But as to the motive and the matter of who is guilty, it is impossible to decide until I have looked further into the evidence. Do me a favour, will you? After you have left me at the captain's house, 'phone up the Yard, and let me have the secret cable code with the East; also, if you can, the name of the chief of the Persian police."

"My dear chap, you can't really place any credence in that absurd assertion regarding the blue belt? You can't possibly think that Abdul ben Meerza really did send the thing?"

"No, I can't," said Cleek in reply. "Because, to the best of my belief, it is impossible for a dead man to send anything; and, if my memory doesn't betray me, I fancy I read in the newspaper accounts of that big Tajik rising at Khotour a couple of months ago, that the leader one Abdul ben Meerza, a rich but exceedingly miserly merchant of the province of Elburz, was, by the Shah's command, bastinadoed within an inch of his life, and then publicly beheaded."

"By Jove! I believe you are right, my dear fellow," asserted Narkom. "I thought the name had a familiar sound as if I had, somewhere, heard it before. I suppose there is no likelihood, by any chance, that the old skinflint could have lived up to his promise and left poor Carboys something, after all, Cleek? Because, you know, if he did – "

"Captain Morrison would, as heir-at-law, inherit it," supplemented Cleek dryly. "Get out the motor, Mr. Narkom, and let's spin round and see him. I fancy I should like a few minutes' conversation with the captain. And — Mr. Narkom?"

"Yes?"

"We'll stick to the name 'George Headland' if you please. When you are out for birds it doesn't do to frighten them off beforehand."

II

It did not take more than five minutes to cover the distance between Sunnington Crescent and the modest little house where Captain Morrison and his daughter lived; so in a very brief time Cleek had the satisfaction of interviewing both.

Narkom's assertion that Miss Morrison was "half out of her mind over the distressing affair" had prepared him to encounter a weeping, red-eyed, heart-broken creature of the most excitable type. He found instead a pale, serious-faced, undemonstrative girl of somewhat uncertain age, sweet of voice, soft of step, quiet of demeanour, who was either one of those persons who repress all external evidence of internal fires, and bear their crosses in silence, or was as cold blooded as a fish and as heartless as a statue. He found the father the exact antithesis of the daughter: a nervous, fretful, irritable individual (gout had him by the heels at the time), who was as full of "yaps" and snarls as any Irish terrier, and as peevish and fussy as a fault-finding old woman. Added to this, he had a way of glancing all round the room, and avoiding the eye of the person to whom he was talking. And if Cleek had been like the generality of people, and hadn't known that some of the best and "straightest" men in the world had been afflicted in this manner, and some of the worst and "crookedest" could look you straight in the eyes without turning a hair, he might have taken this for a bad sign. Then, too, he seemed to have a great many more wrappings and swaddlings about his gouty foot than appeared to be necessary, unless it was done to make his helpless state very apparent, and to carry out his assertion that he hadn't been able to walk a foot unassisted for the past week, and could not, therefore, be in any way connected with young Carboys' mysterious disappearance. Still, even that had its contra aspect. He *might* be one of those individuals who make a mountain of agony out of a molehill of pain, and insist upon a dozen poultices where one would do.

But Cleek could not forget that, as Narkom had said, there was not the shadow of a doubt that in the event of Carboys having died possessed of means, the captain would be the heir-at-law by virtue of his kinship; and it is a great deal more satisfactory to be rich oneself than to be dependent upon the generosity of a rich son-in-law. So, after adroitly exercising the "pump" upon other matters:

"I suppose, Miss Morrison," said Cleek in a casual, off-hand sort of way, "you don't happen to know if Mr. Carboys ever made a will, do you? I am aware, from what Mr. Narkom has told me of his circumstances, that he really possessed nothing that would call for the execution of such a document; but young men have odd fancies sometimes, particularly when they become engaged, so it is just possible that he might have done such a thing. There might have been a ring or something of that sort he wanted to make sure of your getting should anything happen to him. Of course, it is an absurd suggestion, but – "

"It is not so absurd as you think, Mr. Headland," she interrupted. "As it happens, Mr. Carboys did make a will. But that was a very long time ago before he knew me, so my name did not figure in it at all. He once told me of the circumstances connected with it. It was executed when he was about three-and-twenty. It appears that there were some personal trinkets, relics of his more prosperous days: a set of jewelled waistcoat buttons, a scarf-pin, a few choice books and things like that, which he desired Mr. Van Nant to have in the event of his death (they were then going to the Orient, and times there were troublous); so he drew up a will, leaving everything he might die possessed of to Mr. Van Nant, and left the paper with the latter's solicitor when they bade good-bye to England. So far as I know, that will still exists, Mr. Headland; so" – here the faintest suggestion of a quiver got into her voice – "if anything of a tragical nature had happened to him, and – and the trinkets hadn't disappeared with him, Mr. Van Nant could claim them all, and I should not have even one poor little token to cherish in memory of him. And I am sure, I am very sure that if he had known – if he had thought - "

"Mary, for goodness' sake don't begin to snivel!" chimed in her father querulously. "It gets on my nerves. And you know very well how I am suffering! Of course, it was most inconsiderate of Carboys not to destroy that will as soon as you and he were engaged, but he knew that marriage invalidates any will a man may have made previously, and — well, you can't suppose that he ever expected things to turn out as they have done. Besides, Van Nant would have seen that you got *something* to treasure as a remembrance. He's a very decent chap, is Van Nant, Mr. Headland, although my daughter has never appeared to think so. But there's no arguing with a woman, any way."

Cleek glanced at Narkom. It was a significant glance, and said as plainly as so many words: "What do you think of it? You said there was no motive, and, provided Carboys fell heir to something of which we know nothing as yet, here are *two*! If that will was destroyed, one man would, as heir-at-law, inherit; ditto the other man if it was *not* destroyed and not invalidated by marriage. And here's the 'one' man singing the praises of the 'other' one!"

"Collusion?" queried Narkom's answering look. "Perhaps," said Cleek's in response, "one of these two men has made away with him. The question is, which? and, also, why? when? where?" Then he turned to the captain's daughter, and asked quietly: "Would you mind letting me see the room from which the young man disappeared? I confess I haven't the ghost of an idea regarding the case, captain; but if you don't mind letting your daughter show me the room – "

"Mind? Good Lord, no!" responded the captain. "All I want to know is, what became of the poor boy, and if there's any likelihood of his ever coming back alive. I'd go up with you myself, only you see how helpless I am. Mary, take Mr. Headland to the room. And please don't stop any longer than is necessary. I'm suffering agonies, and not fit to be left alone."

Miss Morrison promised to return as expeditiously as possible, and then forthwith led the way to the room in question.

"This is it, Mr. Headland," she said as she opened the door and ushered Cleek in. "Everything is just exactly as it was when George left it. I couldn't bring myself to touch a thing until after a detective had seen it. Father said it was silly and sentimental of me to go on sleeping in the little box of a hall bedroom when I could be so much more comfortable if I returned to my own. But I couldn't. I felt that I might possibly be unconsciously destroying something in the shape of a clue if I moved a solitary object; and so – Look! there is the drawn blind just as he left it; there his portmanteau on that chair by the bedside, and there – " Her voice sank to a sort of awed whisper, her shaking finger extended in the direction of a blue semicircle in the middle of the floor. "There is the belt! He had it round his waist when he crossed this threshold that night. It was lying there just as you see it when the servant brought up his tea and his shaving water the next morning, and found the room empty and the bed undisturbed."

Cleek walked forward and picked up the belt.

"Humph! Unfastened!" he said as he took it up; and Miss Morrison, closing the door, went below and left them. "Our wonderful wizard does not seem to have mastered the simple matter of making a man vanish out of the thing without first unfastening the buckle, it appears. I should have thought he could have managed that, shouldn't you, Mr. Narkom, if he could have managed the business of making him melt into thin air? Hurr-r-r!" reflectively, as he turned the belt over and examined it. "Not seen much use, apparently; the leather's quite new, and the inside quite unsoiled. British manufactured brass, too, in the buckle. Shouldn't have expected that in a Persian-made article. Inscription scratched on with the point of a knife or some other implement not employed in metal engraving. May I trouble you for a pin? Thank you. Hum-m-m! Thought so. Some dirty, clayey stuff rubbed in to make the letters appear old and of long standing. Look here, Mr. Narkom; metal quite bright underneath when you pick the stuff out. Inscription very recently added; leather, American tanned; brass, Birmingham; stitching, by the Blake shoe and harness machine; wizard, probably born in Tottenham Court Road, and his knowledge of Persia confined to Persian powder in four-penny tins."

He laid the belt aside, and walked slowly round the room, inspecting its contents before turning his attention to the portmanteau.

"Evidently the vanishing qualities of the belt did not assert themselves very rapidly, Mr. Narkom," he said, "for Mr. Carboys not only prepared to go to bed, but had time to get himself ready to hurry off to business in the morning with as little delay as possible. Look here; here are his pyjamas on the top of this chest of drawers, neatly folded, just as he left them out of his portmanteau; and as a razor has been wiped on this towel (see this slim line of dust-like particles of hair), he shaved before going to bed in order to save himself the trouble of doing so in the morning. But as there is no shaving mug visible, and he couldn't get hot water at that hour of the night, we shall probably discover a spirit lamp and its equipment when we look into the portmanteau. Now, as he had time to put these shaving articles away after using, and as no man shaves with his collar and necktie on, if we do not find those, too, in the portmanteau, we may conclude that he put them on again; and, as he wouldn't put them on again if he were going to bed, the inference is obvious: something caused him to dress and prepare to leave the house voluntarily. That 'something' must have manifested itself very abruptly, and demanded great haste — either that, or he expected to return; for you will observe that, although he replaced his shaving tackle in the portmanteau, he did not put his sleeping suit back with it. While I am poking about, do me the favour of looking in the bag, Mr. Narkom, and tell me if you find the collar and necktie there."

"Not a trace of them," announced the superintendent a moment or two later. "Here are the shaving mug, the brush, and the spirit lamp, however, just as you suggested and - Hallo! what have you stumbled upon now?" For Cleek, who had been "poking about," as he termed it, had suddenly stooped, picked up something, and was regarding it fixedly as it lay in the palm of his hand.

"A somewhat remarkable thing to discover in a lady's bedchamber, Mr. Narkom, unless - Just step downstairs, and ask Miss Morrison to come up again for a moment, will you?" And then held out his hand so that Narkom could see, in passing, that a hempseed, two grains of barley, and an oat lay upon his palm. "Miss Morrison," he inquired as Mary returned in company with the superintendent, "Miss Morrison, do you keep pigeons?"

She gave a little cry, and clasped her hands together, as if reproaching herself for some heartless act.

"Oh!" she said, moving hastily toward the window. "Poor dears! How good of you to remind me. To think that I should forget to feed them for three whole days. They may be dead by now. But at such a time I could think of nothing but this hideous mystery. My pigeons, my poor, pretty pigeons!"

"Oh, then you do keep them?"

"Yes; oh, yes. In a wire-enclosed cote attached to the house just outside this window. Homing pigeons, Mr. Headland. George bought them for me. We had an even half dozen each. We used to send messages to each other that way. He would bring his over to me, and take mine away with him at night when he went home, so we could correspond at any moment without waiting for the post. That's how I sent him the message about the arrival of the belt. Oh, do unlock the window, and let me see if the pretty dears are still alive."

"It doesn't need to be unlocked, Miss Morrison," he replied as he pulled up the blind. "See, it can be opened easily — the catch is not secured."

"Not secured? Why, how strange. I myself fastened it after I despatched the bird with the message about the belt. And nobody came into the room after that until George did so that night. Oh, do look and see if the pretty creatures are dead. They generally coo so persistently; and now I don't hear a sound from them."

Cleek threw up the sash and looked out. A huge wistaria with tendrils as thick as a man's wrist covered the side of the house, and made a veritable ladder down to the little garden; and, firmly secured to this, on a level with the window-sill and within easy reach therefrom, was the dovecote in question. He put in his hand, and slowly drew out four stiff, cold, feathered little bodies, and laid them on the dressing-table before her; then, while she was grieving over them, he groped round in all corners of the cote and drew forth still another.

"Five?" she exclaimed in surprise. "Five? Oh, but there should be only four, Mr. Headland. It is true that George brought over all six the day before; but I 'flew' one to him in the early morning, and I 'flew' a second at night, with the message about the belt; so there should be but four."

"Oh, well, possibly one was 'flown' by him to you, and it 'homed' without your knowledge."

*SWINGING THE HAMMER, HE STRUCK AT THE NYMPH WITH A
FORCE THAT SHATTERED THE MONSTROUS THING TO ATOMS*

"Yes, but it couldn't get inside the wired enclosure unassisted, Mr. Headland. See! that spring door has to be opened when it is 'returned' to the cote after it has carried its message home. You see, I trained them, by feeding them in here, to come into this room when they were flown back to me. They always flew directly in if the window was opened, or gave warning of their presence by fluttering about and beating against the panes if the sash was closed. And for a fifth pigeon to be inside the enclosure — I can't understand the thing at all. Oh, Mr. Headland, do you think it is anything in the nature of a clue?"

"It may be," he replied evasively. "Clues are funny things, Miss Morrison; you never know when you may pick one up, nor how. I shouldn't say anything to anybody about this fifth pigeon, if I were you. Let that be our secret for awhile; and if your father wants to know why I sent for you to come up here again just say I have discovered that your pigeons are dead for want of food." And for a moment or two, after she had closed the door and gone below again, he stood looking at Mr. Narkom and slowly rubbing his thumb and forefinger up and down his chin. Then, of a sudden:

"I think, Mr. Narkom, we can fairly decide, on the evidence of that fifth pigeon, that George Carboys left this room voluntarily," returned Cleek; "that the bird brought him a message of such importance it was necessary to leave this house at once, and that, not wishing to leave it unlocked while he was absent, and not — because of the captain's inability to get back upstairs afterward — having anybody to whom he could appeal to get up and lock it after him, he chose to get out of this window, and to go down by means of that wistaria. I think, too, we may decide that, as he left no note to explain his absence, he expected to return before morning, and that, as he never did return, he has met with foul play. Of course, it is no use looking for footprints in the garden in support of this hypothesis, for the storm that night was a very severe one and quite sufficient to blot out all trace of them; but - Look here, Mr. Narkom, put two and two together. If a message was sent him by a carrier pigeon, where must that pigeon have come from, since it was one of Miss Morrison's?"

"Why, from Van Nant's place, of course. It couldn't possibly come from any other."

"Exactly. And as Van Nant and Carboys lived together — kept bachelor hall — and there was never anybody but their two selves in the house at any time, why, nobody but Van Nant himself could have despatched the bird. Look at that fragment of burnt paper lying in the basin of that candlestick on the washstand. If that isn't all that's left of the paper that was tied under the pigeon's wing, and if Carboys didn't use it for the purpose of lighting the spirit lamp by which he heated his shaving water, depend upon it that, in his haste and excitement, he tucked it into his pocket, and if ever we find his body we shall find that paper on it."

"His body? My dear Cleek, you don't believe that the man has been murdered?"

"I don't know — yet. I shall, however, if this Van Nant puts anything in the way of my searching that house thoroughly or makes any pretext to follow me whilst I am doing so. I want to meet this Maurice Van Nant just as soon as I can, Mr. Narkom, just as soon as I can."

And it was barely two minutes after he had expressed this wish that Miss Morrison reappeared upon the scene accompanied by a pale, nervous, bovine-eyed man of about thirty-five years of age, and said in a tone of agitation: "Pardon me for interrupting, Mr. Headland, but this is Mr. Maurice Van Nant. He is most anxious to meet you, and father would have me bring him up at once."

Narkom screwed round on his heel, looked at the Belgian, and lost faith in Miss Morrison's powers of discrimination instantly. On the dressing-table stood Carboys' picture — heavy-jowled, sleepy-eyed, dull-looking, and on the threshold stood a man with the kindest eyes, the sweetest smile, and the handsomest and most sympathetic countenance he had seen in many a day. If the eyes are the mirror of the soul, if the face is the index of the character, then here was a man weak as water, as easily led as any lamb, and as guileless.

"You are just the man I want to see, Mr. Van Nant," said Cleek, after the first formalities were over, and assuming, as he always did at such times, the heavy, befogged expression of incompetence. "I confess this bewildering affair altogether perplexes me; but you, I understand, were Mr. Carboys' close friend and associate, and as I can find nothing in the nature of a clue here, I should like, with your permission, to look over his home quarters and see if I can find anything there."

If he had looked for any sign of reluctance or of embarrassment upon Van Nant's part when such a request should be made, he was wholly disappointed, for the man, almost on the point of tears, seized his hand, pressed it warmly, and said in a voice of eager entreaty, "Oh, do, Mr. Headland, do. Search anywhere, do anything that will serve to find my friend and to clear up this dreadful affair. I can't sleep for thinking of it; I can't get a moment's peace night or day. You didn't know him or you would understand how I am tortured and how I miss him. The best friend, the dearest and the lightest-hearted fellow that ever lived. If I had anything left in this world, I'd give it all — all, Mr. Headland, to clear up the mystery of this thing and to get him back. One man could do that, I believe, could and would, if I had the money to offer him."

"Indeed? And who may he be, Mr. Van Nant?"

"The great, the amazing, the undeceivable man, Cleek. He'd get at the truth of it. Nothing could baffle and bewilder him. But — oh, well, it's the old, old tale of the power of money. He wouldn't take the case, a high-and-mighty 'top-notcher' like that, unless the reward was a tempting one, I'm sure."

"No, I'm afraid he wouldn't," agreed Cleek, with the utmost composure. "So you must leave him out of your calculations altogether, Mr. Van Nant. And now, if you don't mind accompanying us and showing the chauffeur the way, perhaps Mr. Narkom will take us over to your house in his motor."

"Mind? No, certainly I don't mind. Anything in the world to get at a clue to this thing, Mr. Headland, anything. Do let us go, and at once."

Cleek led the way from the room. Halfway down the stairs, however, he excused himself on the plea of having forgotten his magnifying glass, and ran back to get it. Two minutes later he rejoined them in the little drawing-room, where the growling captain was still demanding the whole time and attention of his daughter, and, the motor being ready, the three men walked out, got into it, and were whisked away to the house which once had been the home of the vanished George Carboys.

It proved to be a small, isolated brick house in very bad condition, standing in an out-of-the-way road somewhere between Putney and Wimbledon. It stood, somewhat back from the road, in the midst of a little patch of ground abounding in privet and laurel bushes, and it was evident that its cheapness had been its chief attraction to the two men who had rented it, although, on entering, it was found to possess at the back a sort of extension, with top and side lights, which must have appealed to Van Nant's need of something in the nature of a studio. At all events, he had converted it into a very respectable apology for one; and Cleek was not a little surprised by what it contained.

Rich stuffs, bits of tapestry, Persian draperies, Arabian prayer-mats — relics of his other and better days and of his Oriental wanderings — hung on the walls and ornamented the floor; his rejected pictures and his unsold statues, many of them life-sized and all of clay coated with a lustreless paint to make them look like marble, were disposed about the place with an eye to artistic effect, and near to an angle where stood on a pedestal, half concealed, half revealed by artistically arranged draperies, the life-size figure of a Roman senator, in toga and sandals, there was the one untidy spot, the one utterly inartistic thing the room contained.

It was the crude, half-finished shape of a recumbent female figure, of large proportions and abominable modelling, stretched out at full length upon a long, low trestle-supported "sculptor's staging," on which also lay Van Nant's modelling tools and his clay-stained working blouse. Cleek looked at the huge, unnatural thing, out of drawing, anatomically wrong in many particulars, and felt like quoting Angelo's famous remark anent his master

Lorenzo's faun: "What a pity to have spoilt so much expensive material," and Van Nant, observing, waved his hand toward it.

"A slumbering nymph," he explained. "Only the head and shoulders finished as yet, you see. I began it the day before yesterday, but my hand seems somehow to have lost its cunning. Here are the keys of all the rooms, Mr. Headland. Carboys' was the one directly at the head of the stairs, in the front. Won't you and Mr. Narkom go up and search without me? I couldn't bear to look into the place and see the things that belonged to him and he not there. It would cut me to the heart if I did. Or, maybe you would sooner go alone, and leave Mr. Narkom to search round this room. We used to make a general sitting-room of it at nights when we were alone together, and some clue may have been dropped."

"A good suggestion, Mr. Narkom," commented Cleek, as he took the keys. "Look round and see what you can find, whilst I 'poke about' upstairs." Then he walked out of the studio. And a few moments later, Narkom going round and searching every nook and corner, whilst Van Nant, for the want of something to occupy his mind and hands worked on the nymph, could hear him moving about overhead in quest of possible clues.

For perhaps twenty minutes Cleek was away; then he came down and walked into the room looking the very picture of hopeless bewilderment.

"Mr. Narkom," he said, "this case stumps me. I believe there's magic in it, if you ask me; and as the only way to fight magic is with magic, I'm going to consult a clairvoyante, and if one of those parties can't give me a clue, I don't believe the mystery ever will be solved. I know of a ripping good one, but she is over in Ireland, and as it's a dickens of a way to go, I shan't be able to get back before the day after to-morrow at the earliest. But — look here, sir, I'll tell you what! This is Tuesday evening, isn't it? Now if you and Mr. Van Nant will be at Captain Morrison's house on Thursday evening at seven o'clock, and will wait there until I come, I'll tell you what that clairvoyante says, and whether there's any chance of this thing being solved or not. Is that agreeable, Mr.

Van Nant?"

"Quite, Mr. Headland. I'll be there promptly."

"And stop until you hear from me?"

"And stop until I hear from you."

"Right you are, sir. Now then, Mr. Narkom, if you'll let the chauffeur whisk me over to the station, I'll get back to London and on to the earliest possible train for Liverpool, so as to be on hand for the first Irish packet to-morrow. And while you're looking for your hat, sir — good evening, Mr. Van Nant — I'll step outside and tell Lennard to crank up."

With that, he passed out of the studio, walked down the hall, and went out of the house. And half a minute later, when the superintendent joined him, he found him sitting in the limousine and staring fixedly at his toes.

"My dear Cleek, did you find anything?" he queried as he took a seat beside him, and the motor swung out into the road and whizzed away. "Of course, I know you've no more idea of going to Liverpool than you have of taking a pot-shot at the moon; but there's something on your mind. I know the signs, Cleek. What is it?"

The response to this was rather startling.

"Mr. Narkom," said Cleek, answering one question with another, "what's the best thing to make powdered bismuth stick: lard, cold cream, or cocoa butter?"

III

If punctuality is a virtue, then Mr. Maurice Van Nant deserved to go on record as one of the most virtuous men in existence. For the little Dutch clock in Captain Morrison's drawing-room had barely begun to strike seven on the following Thursday evening when he put in an appearance there, and found the captain and his daughter anxiously awaiting him. But, as virtue is, on most excellent authority, its own reward, he had to be satisfied

163

with the possession of it, since neither Narkom nor Cleek was there to meet him.

But the reason for this defection was made manifest when Miss Morrison placed before him a telegram which had arrived some ten minutes earlier and read as follows: "Unavoidably delayed. Be with you at nine-thirty. Ask Mr. Van Nant to wait. Great and welcome piece of news for him, Narkom."

Van Nant smiled.

"Great and welcome news," he repeated. "Then Mr. Headland must have found something in the nature of a clue in Ireland, captain, though what he could find there I can't imagine. Frankly, I thought him a stupid sort of fellow, but if he has managed to find a clue to poor George's whereabouts over in Ireland, he must be sharper than I believed. Well, we shall know about that at half-past nine, when Mr. Narkom comes. I hope nothing will happen to make him disappoint us again."

Nothing did. Promptly at the hour appointed the red limousine whizzed up to the door, and Mr. Narkom made his appearance. But, contrary to the expectations of the three occupants of the little drawing-room, he was quite alone.

"So sorry I couldn't come earlier," he said, as he came in, looking and acting like the bearer of great good news; "but you will appreciate the delay when I tell you what caused it. What's that, Mr. Van Nant? Headland? No, he's not with me. As a matter of fact, I've dispensed with his services in this particular case. Fancy, Miss Morrison, the muff came back from Ireland this evening, said the clairvoyante he consulted went into a trance, and told him that the key to the mystery could only be discovered in Germany, and he wanted me to sanction his going over there on no better evidence than that. Of course, I wouldn't; so I took him off the case forthwith, and set out to get another and a better man to handle it. That's what delayed me. And now, Mr. Van Nant" — fairly beaming, and rubbing his palms together delightedly — "here's where the great and welcome news I spoke of comes in. I remembered how your heart is wrapped up in the solving of this great puzzle and what you said about it being a question of money alone; and so, what do you think I did? I went to that great man, Cleek. I laid the matter before him, told him there was no reward, that it was just a matter of sheer humanity — the consciousness of doing his duty and helping another fellow in distress — and, throw up your hat and cheer, my dear fellow, for you've got your heart's desire: Cleek's consented to take the case!"

A little flurry of excitement greeted this announcement. Miss Morrison grabbed his hand and burst into tears of gratitude; the captain, forgetting in his delight the state of his injured foot, rose from his chair, only to remember suddenly and sit down again, his half-uttered cheer dying on his lips; and Van Nant, as if overcome by this unexpected boon, this granting of a wish he had never dared to hope would be fulfilled, could only clap both hands over his face and sob hysterically.

"Cleek!" he said, in a voice that shook with nervous catches and the emotion of a soul deeply stirred, "Cleek to take the case? The great, the amazing, the undeceivable Cleek! Oh, Mr. Narkom, can this be true?"

"As true as that you are standing here this minute, my dear sir. Not so much of a money grabber as that muff Headland wanted you to believe, is he — eh? Waived every hope of a reward, and took the case on the spot. He'll get at the root of it, Lord, yes! Lay you a sovereign to a sixpence, Mr. Van Nant, he gets to the bottom of it and finds out what became of George Carboys in forty-eight hours after he begins on the case."

"And when will he begin, Mr. Narkom? To-morrow? The next day? Or not this week at all? When, sir — when?"

"When? Why, bless your heart, man, he's begun already or, at least, will do so in another hour and a half. He's promised to meet us at your house at eleven o'clock to-night. Chose that place because he lives at Putney, and it's nearer. Eleven was the hour he set, though, of course, he may arrive sooner; there's no counting on an erratic fellow like that chap. So we'll make it eleven, and possess our souls in patience until it's time to start."

"But, my dear Mr. Narkom, wouldn't it be better, or, at least, more hospitable if I went over to meet him, in case he does come earlier? There's no one in the house, remember, and it's locked up."

"Lord bless you, that won't bother him! Never travels without his tools, you know, skeleton keys, and all that, and he'll be in the house before you can wink an eye. Still, of course, if you'd rather be there to admit him in the regulation way - "

"It would at least be more courteous, Mr. Narkom," Miss Morrison interposed. "So great a man doing so great a favour - Oh, yes, I really think that Mr. Van Nant should."

"Oh, well, let him then, by all means," said Narkom. "Go, if you choose, Mr. Van Nant. I'd let you have my motor, only I must get over to the station and 'phone up headquarters on another affair in five minutes."

"It doesn't matter, thank you all the same. I can get a taxi at the top of the road," said Van Nant; and then, making his excuses to Miss Morrison and her father, he took up his hat and left the house. As a matter of fact, it was only courtesy that made him say that about the taxi, for there is rarely one to be found waiting about in the neighbourhood of Wandsworth Common after half-past nine o'clock at night, and nobody could have been more surprised than he when he actually did come across one, loitering about aimlessly and quite empty, before he had gone two dozen yards.

He engaged it on the spot, jumped into it, gave the chauffeur his directions, and a minute later was whizzing away to the isolated house. It was eight minutes past ten when he reached it, standing as black and lightless as when he left it four hours ago, and, after paying off the chauffeur and dismissing the vehicle, he fumbled nervously for his latchkey, found it, unlocked the door, and went hurriedly in.

"Have you come yet, Mr. Cleek?" he called out, as he shut the door and stood in the pitch-black hall. "Mr. Cleek! Mr. Cleek, are you here? It is I — Maurice Van Nant. Mr. Narkom has sent me on ahead."

Not a sound answered him, not even an echo. He sucked in his breath with a sort of wheezing sound, then groped round the hall table till he found his bedroom candle, and striking a match, lit it. The staircase leading to the upper floors gaped at him out of the partial gloom, and he fairly sprang at it. He was halfway up it when some other idea possessed him, brought him to a sudden standstill, and, facing round abruptly, he went back to the lower hall again, glimmering along it like a shadow, with the inadequate light held above him, and moving fleetly to the studio in the rear.

The door stood partly open, just as he had left it. He pushed it inward and stepped over the threshold.

"Mr. Cleek!" he called again. "Mr. Cleek! Are you here?"

And again the silence alone answered him. The studio was as he had seen it last, save for those fantastic shadows which the candle's wavering flame wreathed in the dim corners and along the pictured walls. There, on its half-draped pedestal, the Roman senator stood, dead white against the purple background, and there, close to the foot of it, the great bulk of the disproportionate nymph still sprawled, finished and whitewashed now, and looking even more of a monstrosity than ever in that waving light.

He gave one deep gulping sigh of relief, flashed across the room on tiptoe, and went down on his knees beside the monstrous thing, moving the candle this way and that along the length of it, as if searching for something, and laughing in little jerky gasps of relief when he found nothing that was not as it had been — as it should be — as he wanted it to be. And then, as he rose and patted the clay, and laughed aloud as he realized how hard it had set, then, at that instant, a white shape lurched forward and swooped downward, carrying him down with it. The candle slipped from his fingers and clattered on the floor, a pair of steel handcuffs clicked as they closed round his wrists, a voice above him said sharply: "You wanted Cleek, I believe? Well, Cleek's got you, you sneaking murderer! Gentlemen, come in! Allow me to turn over to you the murderer of George Carboys! You'll find the body inside that slumbering nymph!"

And the last thing that Mr. Maurice Van Nant saw, as he shrieked and fainted, the last thing he realized, was that lights were flashing up and men tumbling in through the opening windows; that the Roman senator's pedestal was empty, and the figure which once had stood upon it was bending over him — alive!

And just at that moment the red limousine flashed up out of the darkness, the outer door whirled open, and Narkom came pelting in.

"He took the bait, then, Cleek?" he cried, as he saw the manacled figure on the floor, with the "Roman senator" bending over and the policemen crowding in about it. "I guessed it when I saw the lights flash up. I've been on his heels ever since he snapped at that conveniently placed taxi after he left Miss Morrison and her father."

"You haven't brought them with you, I hope, Mr. Narkom? I wouldn't have that poor girl face the ordeal of what's to be revealed here to-night for words."

"No, I've not. I made a pretext of having to 'phone through to headquarters, and slipped out a moment after him. But, I say, my dear chap" — as Cleek's hands made a rapid search of the pockets of the unconscious man, and finally brought to light a folded paper — "what's that thing? What are you doing?"

"Compounding a felony in the interest of humanity," he made reply as he put the end of the paper into the flame of the candle and held it there until it was consumed. "We all do foolish things sometimes when we are young, Mr. Narkom, and George Carboys was no exception when he wrote the little thing I have just burned. Let us forget all about it. Captain Morrison is heir-at-law, and that poor girl will benefit."

"There was an estate, then?"

"Yes. My cable yesterday to the head of the Persian police set all doubt upon that point at rest. Abdul ben Meerza, parting with nothing while he lived, after the manner of misers in general, left a will bequeathing something like £12,000 to George Carboys, and his executor communicated that fact to the supposed friend of both parties, Mr. Maurice Van Nant. Exactly ten days ago, so his former solicitor informed me, Mr. Maurice Van Nant visited him unexpectedly, and withdrew from his keeping a sealed packet which had been in the firm's custody for eight years. If you want to know why he withdrew it — Dollops!"

"Right you are, guv'ner."

"Give me the sledge-hammer. Thanks! Now, Mr. Narkom, look!" And swinging the hammer, he struck at the nymph with a force that shattered the monstrous thing to atoms; and Narkom, coming forward to look when Cleek bent over the ruin he had wrought, saw in the midst of the dust and rubbish the body of a dead man, fully clothed, and with the gap of a bullet-hole in the left temple.

Again Cleek's hands began a rapid search, and again, as before, they brought to light a paper, a little crumpled ball of paper that had been thrust into the right-hand pocket of the dead man's waistcoat, as though jammed there under the stress of strong excitement and the pressure of great haste. He smoothed it out and read it carefully, then passed it over to Mr. Narkom.

"There!" he said, "that's how he lured him over to his death. That's the message the pigeon brought. Would any man have failed to fly to face the author of a foul lie like that?"

The message ran:

Beloved Mary, come to me again to-night. How sweet of you to think of such a thing as the belt to get him over and to make him stop until morning! Steal out after he goes to bed, darling. I'll leave the studio window unlocked, as usual. With a thousand kisses,

Your own devoted,

Maurice.

"The dog!" said Narkom fiercely. "And against a pure creature like Mary Morrison! Here, Smathers, Petrie, Hammond, take him away. Hanging's too good for a beastly cur like that!"

"How did I know that the body was inside the statue?" said Cleek, answering Narkom's query as they drove back in the red limousine toward London and Clarges Street. "Well, as a matter of fact, I never did know for certain until he began to examine the thing to-night. From the first I felt sure he was at the bottom of the affair, that he had lured Carboys back to the house, and murdered him; but it puzzled me to think what could possibly have been done with the body. I felt pretty certain, however, when I saw that monstrous statue."

"Yes, but why?"

"My dear Mr. Narkom, you ought not to ask that question. Did it not strike you as odd that a man who was torn with grief over the disappearance of a loved friend should think of modelling any sort of a statue on that very first day, much less such an inartistic one as that? Consider: the man has never been a first-class sculptor, it is true, but he knew the rudiments of his art, he had turned out some fairly presentable work; and that nymph was as abominably conceived and as abominably executed as if it had been the work of a raw beginner. Then there was another suspicious circumstance. Modelling clay is not exactly as cheap as dirt, Mr. Narkom. Why, then, should this man, who was confessedly as poor as the proverbial church mouse, plunge into the wild extravagance of buying half a ton of it — and at such a time? Those are the things that brought the suspicion into my mind; the certainty, however, had to be brought about beyond dispute before I could act.

"I knew that George Carboys had returned to that studio by the dry marks of muddy footprints, that were nothing like the shape of Van Nant's, which I found on the boards of the veranda and on the carpet under one of the windows; I knew, too, that it was Van Nant who had sent that pigeon. You remember when I excused myself and went back on the pretext of having forgotten my magnifying glass the other day? I did so for the purpose of looking at that fifth pigeon. I had observed something on its breast feathers which I thought, at first glance, was dry mud, as though it had fallen or brushed against something muddy in its flight. As we descended the stairs I observed that there was a similar mark on Van Nant's sleeve. I brushed against him and scraped off a fleck with my fingernails. It was the dust of dried modelling clay. That on the pigeon's breast proved to be the same substance. I knew then that the hands of the person who liberated that pigeon were the hands of some one who was engaged in modelling something or handling the clay of the modeller, and the inference was clear.

"As for the rest: when Van Nant entered that studio to-night, frightened half out of his wits at the knowledge that he would have to deal with the one detective he feared, I knew that if he approached that statue and made any attempt to examine it I should have my man, and that the hiding-place of his victim's body would be proved beyond question. When he did go to it, and did examine it – Clarges Street at last, and thank fortune for it, as I am tired and sleepy. Stop here, chauffeur. The riddle is solved, Mr. Narkom. Good-night!"

CHAPTER VII
THE RIDDLE OF THE 5.28

It was exactly thirty-two minutes past five o'clock on the evening of Friday, December 9th, when the station-master at Anerley received the following communication by wire from the signal box at Forest Hill:

5.28 down from London Bridge just passed. One first-class compartment in total darkness. Investigate.

As two stations, Sydenham and Penge, lie between Forest Hill and Anerley, in the ordinary course of events this signal-box message would have been despatched to one or the other of these; but it so happens that the 5.28 from London Bridge to Croydon is a special train, which makes no stop short of Anerley station on the way down, consequently the signalman had no choice but to act as he did.

"Wire fused, I reckon, or filament burnt out. That's the worst of electric light," commented the station-master when he received the communication. "Get a light of some sort from the lamp-room, Webb. They'll have to put up with that as far as Croydon. Move sharp. She'll be along presently." Then he took up a lantern (for, in addition to fog, a slight, sifting snow had come on about an hour previously, rendering the evening one of darkness and extreme discomfort) and crossed by way of the tunnel over to the down platform to be ready for the train's arrival, having some little difficulty in progressing easily, for it so happened that a local celebrity had been entertaining the newly elected Lord Mayor that day, and in consequence both the up and the down platforms were unusually crowded for the season and the hour.

Promptly at 5.42, the scheduled time for its arrival, the train came pelting up the snow-covered metals from Penge, and made its first stop since starting. It was packed to the point of suffocation, as it always is, and in an instant the station was in a state of congestion. Far down the uncovered portion of the platform Webb, the porter, who had now joined the station-master, spied a gap in the long line of brightly lighted windows, and the pair bore down upon it forthwith, each with a glowing lantern in his hand.

"Here she is. Now, then, let's see what's the difficulty," said the station-master, as they came abreast of the lightless compartment, where, much to his surprise, he found nobody leaning out and making a "to-do" over the matter. "Looks as if the blessed thing was empty, though that's by no means likely in a packed train like the 5.28. Hallo! Door's locked. And here's an 'Engaged' label on the window. What the dickens did I do with my key? Oh, here it is. Now, then, let's see what's amiss."

A great deal was amiss, as he saw the instant he unlocked the door and pulled it open, for the first lifting of the lantern made the cause of the darkness startlingly plain. The shallow glass globe which should have been in the centre of the ceiling had been smashed, ragged fragments of it still clinging to their fastenings, and the three electric bulbs had been removed bodily. A downward glance showed him that both these and the fragments of the broken globe lay on one seat, partly wrapped in a wet cloth, and on the other – He gave a jump and a howl, and retreated a step or two in a state of absolute panic. For there in a corner, with his face toward the engine, half sat, half leaned, the figure of a dead man, with a bullet-hole between his eyes, and a small, nickel-plated revolver loosely clasped in the bent fingers of one limp and lifeless hand.

The body was that of a man whose age could not, at the most, have exceeded eight-and-thirty, a man who must, in life, have been more than ordinarily handsome. His hair and moustache were fair, his clothing was of extreme elegance in both material and fashioning, he wore no jewellery of any description, unless one excepts a plain gold ring on the fourth finger of the left hand, his feet were shod in patent-leather boots, in the rack overhead rested a shining silk hat of the newest fashion, an orangewood walking-stick, and a pair of gray suede gloves. An evening paper lay between his feet, open, as though it had been read, and in his buttonhole there was a single mauve orchid of exquisite beauty and delicacy. The body was quite alone in the compartment, and there was not a scrap of luggage of any description.

"Suicide," gulped the startled station-master as soon as he could find strength to say anything; then he hastily slammed and relocked the door, set Webb on guard before it, and flew to notify the engine driver and to send word to the local police.

The news of the tragedy spread like wildfire, but the station-master, who had his wits about him, would allow nobody to leave the station until the authorities had arrived, and suffered no man or woman to come within a yard of the compartment where the dead man lay.

Some one has said that "nothing comes by chance," but whether that is true or not, it happened that Mr. Maverick Narkom was among those who had attended the lunch in honour of the Lord Mayor that day, and that, at the very moment when this ghastly discovery was made on the down platform at Anerley station, he was standing with the crowd on the up one, waiting for the train to Victoria. This train was to convey Cleek, whom he had promised to join at Anerley, returning from a day spent with Captain Morrison and his daughter in the beautiful home they had bought when the law decided that the captain was the legitimate heir of George Carboys and lawful successor to Abdul ben Meerza's money.

As soon as the news of the tragedy reached him Mr. Narkom crossed to the scene of action and made known his identity, and by the time the local police reached the theatre of events he was in full possession of the case, and had already taken certain steps with regard to the matter.

It was he who first thought of looking to see if any name was attached, as is often the case, to the "Engaged" label secured to the window of the compartment occupied by the dead man. There was. Written in pencil under the blue-printed "Engaged" were the three words, "For Lord Stavornell."

"By George!" he exclaimed, as he read the name which was one that half England had heard of at one time or another, and knew to belong to a man whose wild, dissipated life and violent temper had passed into proverb. "Come to the end at last, has he! Give me your lantern, porter, and open the door. Let's have a

look and see if there's any mistake or – " The whistle of the arriv-
ing train for Victoria cut in upon his words, and, putting the local
police in charge he ran for the tunnel, made for the up platform,
and caught Cleek. He remained in conversation with him for two
or three minutes after the Victoria train had gone on its way, and
was still talking with him in undertones when, a brief time later,
they appeared from the tunnel and bore down on the spot where
the local police were on guard over the dark compartment.

"Mr. George Headland, one of my best men," he explained to
the local inspector, who had just arrived. "Let us have all the light
you can, please. Mr. Headland wishes to view the body. Crowd
round, the rest of you, and keep the passengers back. Pull down
the blinds of the compartment before you turn on your bull's-
eyes. All right, porter. Tell the engine driver he'll get his orders in
a minute. Now then, Cl – Headland, decide; it rests with you."

Cleek opened the door of the compartment, stepped in, gave
one glance at the dead man, and then spoke.

"Murder!" he said. "Look how the pistol lies in his hand.
Wait a moment, however, and let me make sure." Then he took
the revolver from the yielding fingers, smelt it, smiled, then
"broke" it, and looked at the cylinder. "Just as I supposed," he
added, turning to Narkom. "One chamber has been fouled by a
shot and one cartridge has been exploded. But not to-day, not
even yesterday. That sour smell tells its own story, Mr. Narkom.
This revolver was discharged two or three days ago. The assassin
had everything prepared for this little event; but he was a fool, for
all his cleverness, for you will observe that in his haste, when he
put the revolver in the dead hand to make it appear a case of
suicide, he laid it down just as he himself took it from his pocket,
with the butt toward the victim's body and the muzzle pointing
outward between the thumb and forefinger, and with the bottom
of the cylinder, instead of the top of the trigger, touching the ball
of the thumb! It is a clear case of murder, Mr. Narkom."

"But, sir," interposed the station-master, overhearing this assertion, and looking at Cleek with eyes of blank bewilderment, "if
somebody killed him, where has that 'somebody' gone? This train

has made no stop until now since it started from London Bridge; so, even if the party was in it at the start, how in the world could he get out?"

"Maybe he chucked hisself out of the window, guv'ner," suggested Webb; "or maybe he slipped out and hung on to the footboard until the train slowed down, and then dropped off just before it come into the station here."

"Don't talk rubbish, Webb. Both doors were locked and both windows closed when we discovered the body. You saw that as plainly as I."

"Lummy, sir, so I did. Then where could he a-went to — and how?"

"Station-master," struck in Cleek, turning from examining the body, "get your men to examine all tickets, both in the train and out of it, and if there's one that's not clipped as it passed the barrier at London Bridge, look out for it, and detain the holder. I'll take the gate here, and examine all local tickets. Meantime, wire all up the road to every station from here to London Bridge, and find out if any other signalman than the one at Forest Hill noticed this dark compartment when the train went past."

Both suggestions were acted upon immediately. But every ticket, save, of course, the season ones — and the holders of these were in every case identified — was found to be properly clipped; and, in the end, every signal-box from New Cross on wired back: "All compartments lighted when train passed here."

"That narrows the search, Mr. Narkom," said Cleek, when he heard this. "The lights were put out somewhere between Honor Oak Park and Forest Hill, and it was between Honor Oak Park and Anerley the murderer made his escape. Inspector" — he turned to the officer in command of the local police — "do me a favour. Put your men in charge of this carriage, and let the train proceed. Norwood Junction is the next station, I believe, and there's a side track there. Have the carriage shunted, and keep close guard over it until Mr. Narkom and I arrive."

"Right you are, sir. Anything else?"

"Yes. Have the station-master at the junction equip a hand-car with a searchlight, and send it here as expeditiously as possible. If anybody or anything has left this train between this point and Honor Oak Park, Mr. Narkom, this thin coating of snow will betray the fact beyond the question of a doubt."

Twenty minutes later the hand-car put in an appearance, manned by a couple of linemen from the junction, and, word having been wired up the line to hold back all trains for a period of half an hour in the interests of Scotland Yard, Cleek and Narkom boarded the vehicle, and went whizzing up the metals in the direction of Honor Oak Park, the shifting searchlight sweeping the path from left to right and glaring brilliantly on the surface of the fallen snow.

Four lines of tracks gleamed steel-bright against its spotless level — the two outer ones being those employed by the local trains going to and fro between London and the suburbs, the two inner ones belonging to the main line — but not one footstep indented the thin surface of that broad expanse of snow from one end of the journey to the other.

"The murderer, whoever he is or wherever he went, never set foot upon so much as one inch of this ground, that's certain," said Narkom, as he gave the order to reverse the car and return. "You feel satisfied of that, do you not, my dear fellow?"

"Thoroughly, Mr. Narkom; there can't be two opinions upon that point. But, at the same time, he *did* leave the train, otherwise we should have found him in it."

"Granted. But the question is, *when* did he get in and *how* did he get out? We know from the evidence of the passengers that the train never stopped for one instant between London Bridge station and Anerley; that all compartments were alight up to the time it passed Honor Oak Park; that nobody abroad of it heard a sound of a pistol-shot; that the assassin could not have crept along the footboard and got into some other compartment, for *all* were so densely crowded that half a dozen people were standing in each, so he could not have entered without somebody making room for him to open the door and get in. No such thing happened, no such thing could happen, without a dozen or more people being aware of it; so the idea of a confederate may be dismissed without a thought. The unmarked surface of the snow shows that nobody alighted, was thrown out, or fell out between the two points where the tragedy must have occurred; both windows were shut and both doors of the compartment locked when the train made its first stop; yet the fellow was gone. My dear chap, are you sure, are you really *sure*, that it isn't a case of suicide after all?"

Cleek gave his shoulders a lurch and smiled indulgently.

"My dear Mr. Narkom," he said, "the position of the revolver in the dead man's hand ought, as I pointed out to you, to settle that question, even if there were no other discrepancies. In the natural order of things, a man who had just put a bullet into his own brain would, if he were sitting erect, as Lord Stavornell was, drop the revolver in the spasmodic opening and shutting of the hands in the final convulsion; but, if he retained any sort of a hold upon it, be sure his forefinger would be in the loop of the trigger. He wouldn't be holding the weapon backward, so to speak, with the cylinder against the ball of his thumb and the hammer against the base of the middle finger. If he had held it that way he simply couldn't have shot himself if he had tried. Then, if you didn't remark it, there was no scorch of powder upon the face, for another thing; and, for a third, the bullet-hole was between the eyes, a most unlikely target for a man bent upon blowing out his own brains; the temple or the roof of the mouth are the points to which natural impulse – " He stopped and laid a sharp, quick-shutting hand on the shoulder of one of the two men who were operating the car. "Turn back!" he exclaimed. "Reverse the action, and go back a dozen yards or so."

The impetus of the car would not permit of this at once, but after running on for a little time longer it answered to the brake, slowed down, stopped, and then began to back, scudding along the rail until Cleek again called it to a halt. They were within gunshot of the station at Sydenham when this occurred; the glaring searchlight was still playing on the metals and the thin layer of snow between, and Cleek's face seemed all eyes as he bent over and studied the ground over which they were gliding. Of a sudden, however, he gave a little satisfied grunt, jumped down, and picked up a shining metal object, about two and a half inches long, which lay in the space between the tracks of the main and the local lines. It was a guard's key for the locking and unlocking of compartment doors, one of the small T-shaped kind that you can buy of almost any iron-monger for sixpence or a shilling any day. It was wet from contact with the snow, but quite unrusted, showing that it had not been lying there long, and it needed but a glance to reveal the fact that it was brand new and of recent purchase.

Cleek held it out on his palm as he climbed back upon the car and rejoined Narkom.

"Wherever he got on, Mr. Narkom, here is where the murderer got off, you see, and either dropped or flung away this key when he had relocked the compartment after him," he said. "And yet, as you see, there is not a footstep, beyond those I have myself just made, to be discovered anywhere. From the position in which this key was lying, one thing is certain, however: our man got out on the opposite side from the platform toward which the train was hastening and in the middle of the right of way."

"What a mad idea! If there had been a main line express passing at the time the fellow ran the risk of being cut to pieces. None of them slow down before they prepare to make their first stop at East Croydon, and about this spot they would be going like the wind."

"Yes," said Cleek, looking fixedly at the shining bit of metal on his palm; "going like the wind. And the suction would be enormous between two speeding trains. A step outside, and he'd have been under the wheels in a wink. Yes, it would have been certain death, instant death, if there had been a main line train passing at the time; and that he was not sucked down and ground under the wheels proves that there *wasn't*." Then he puckered up his brows in that manner which Narkom had come to understand meant a thoughtfulness it was impolitic to disturb, and stood silent for a long, long time.

"Mr. Narkom," he said suddenly, "I think we have discovered all that there is to be discovered in this direction. Let us get on to Norwood Junction as speedily as possible. I want to examine that compartment and that dead body a little more closely. Besides, our half hour is about up, and the trains will be running again shortly, so we'd better get out of the way."

"Any ideas, old chap?"

"Yes, bushels of them. But they all may be exploded in another half hour. Still, these are the days of scientific marvels. Water does run uphill and men do fly, and both are in defiance of the laws of gravitation."

"Which means?"

"That I shall leave the hand-car at Sydenham, Mr. Narkom, and 'phone up to London Bridge station; there are one or two points I wish to ask some questions about. Afterward I'll hire a motor from some local garage and join you at Norwood Junction in an hour's time. Let no one see the body or enter the compartment where it lies until I come. One question, however: is my memory at fault, or was it not Lord Stavornell who was mixed up in that little affair with the French dancer, Mademoiselle Fifi de Lesparre, who was such a rage in town about a year ago?"

"Yes; that's the chap," said Narkom in reply. "And a rare bad lot he has been all his life, I can tell you. I dare say that Fifi herself was no better than she ought to have been, chucking over her country-bred husband as soon as she came into popularity, and having men of the Stavornell class tagging after her; but whether she was or was not, Stavornell broke up that home. And if that French husband had done the right thing, he would have thrashed him within an inch of his life instead of acting like a fool in a play and challenging him. Stavornell laughed at the challenge, of course; and if all that is said of him is true, he was at the bottom of the shabby trick which finally forced the poor devil to get out of the country. When his wife, Fifi, left him, the poor wretch nearly went off his head; and, as he hadn't fifty shillings in the world, he was in a dickens of a pickle when *somebody* induced a lot of milliners, dressmakers, and the like, to whom it was said that Fifi owed bills, to put their accounts into the hands of a collecting agency and to proceed against him for settlement of his wife's accounts. That was why he got out of the country posthaste. The case made a great stir at the time, and the scandal of it was so great that, although the fact never got into the papers, Stavornell's wife left him, refusing to live another hour with such a man."

"Oh, he had a wife, then?"

"Yes; one of the most beautiful women in the kingdom. They had been married only a year when the scandal of the Fifi affair arose. That was another of his dirty tricks forcing that poor creature to marry him."

"She did so against her will?"

"Yes. She was engaged to another fellow at the time, an army chap who was out in India. Her father, too, was an army man, a Colonel Something-or-other, poor as the proverbial church mouse, addicted to hard drinking, card-playing, horse-racing, and about as selfish an old brute as they make 'em. The girl took a deep dislike to Lord Stavornell the minute she saw him; knew his reputation, and refused to receive him. That's the very reason he determined to marry her, humble her pride, as it were, and repay her for her scorn of him.

"He got her father into his clutches, deliberately, of course, lent him money, took his I O U's for card debts and all that sort of thing, until the old brute was up to his ears in debt and with no prospect of paying it off. Of course, when he'd got him to that point, Stavornell demanded the money, but finally agreed to wipe the debt out entirely if the daughter married him. They went at her, poor creature, those two, with all the mercilessness of a couple of wolves. Her father would be disgraced, kicked out of the army, barred from all the clubs, reduced to beggary, and all that, if she did not yield; and in the end they so played upon her feelings, that to save him she gave in; Stavornell took out a special license, and they were married. Of course, the man never cared for her; he only wanted his revenge on her, and they say he led her a dog's life from the hour they came back to England from their honeymoon."

"Poor creature!" said Cleek sympathetically. "And what became of the other chap, the lover she wanted to marry and who
was out in India at the time all this happened?"

"Oh, they say he went on like a madman when he heard it.
Swore he'd kill Stavornell, and all that, but quieted down after a
time, and accepted the inevitable with the best grace possible.
Crawford is his name. He was a lieutenant at the time, but he's
got his captaincy since, and I believe is on leave and in England at
present — as madly and as hopelessly in love with the girl of his
heart as ever."

"Why 'hopelessly,' Mr. Narkom? Such a man as Stavornell
must have given his wife grounds for divorce a dozen times
over."

"Not a doubt of it. There isn't a judge in England who
wouldn't have set her free from the scoundrel long ago if she had
cared to bring the case into the courts. But Lady Stavornell is a
strong Church-woman, my dear fellow; she doesn't believe in
divorce, and nothing on earth could persuade her to marry Captain Crawford so long as her first husband still remained alive."

"Oho!" said Cleek. "Then Fifi's husband isn't the only man
with a grievance and a cause? There's another, eh?"

"Another? I expect there must be a dozen, if the truth were
known. There's only one creature in the world I ever heard of as
having a good word to say for the man."

"And who might that be?"

"The Hon. Mrs. Brinkworth, widow of his younger brother.
You'd think the man was an angel to hear her sing his praises.
Her husband, too, was a wild sort. Left her up to her ears in debt,
without a penny to bless herself, and with a boy of five to rear
and educate. Stavornell seems always to have liked her. At any
rate, he came to the rescue, paid off the debts, settled an annuity
upon her, and arranged to have the boy sent to Eton as soon as he
was old enough. I expect the boy is at the bottom of this good

streak in him if all is told; for, having no children of his own – I say! By George, old chap! Why, that nipper, being the heir in the direct line, is Lord Stavornell now that the uncle is dead! A lucky stroke for him, by Jupiter!"

"Yes," agreed Cleek. "Lucky for him; lucky for Lady Stavornell; lucky for Captain Crawford; and *unlucky* for the Hon. Mrs. Brinkworth and Mademoiselle Fifi de Lesparre. So, of course – Sydenham at last. Good-bye for a little time, Mr. Narkom. Join you at Norwood Junction as soon as possible, and – I say!"

"Yes, old chap?"

"Wire through to the Low Level station at Crystal Palace, will you? and inquire if anybody has mislaid an ironing-board or lost an Indian canoe. See you later. So long."

Then he stepped up on to the station platform, and went in quest of a telephone booth.

II

It was after nine o'clock when he turned up at Norwood Junction, as calm, serene, and imperturbable as ever, and found Narkom awaiting him in a small private room which the station clerk had placed at his disposal.

"My dear fellow, I never was so glad!" exclaimed the superintendent, jumping up excitedly as Cleek entered. "What kept you so long? I've been on thorns. Got bushels to tell you. First off, as Stavornell's identity is established beyond doubt, and no time has been lost in wiring the news of the murder to his relatives, both Lady Stavornell and Mrs. Brinkworth have wired back that they are coming on. I expect them at any minute now. And here's a piece of news for you. Fifi's husband is in England. The Hon. Mrs. Brinkworth has wired me to that effect. Says she has means of knowing that he came over from France the other day; and that she herself saw him in London this morning when she was up there shopping."

"Oho!" commented Cleek. "Got her wits about her, that lady,

evidently. Find anything at the Crystal Palace Low Level, Mr. Narkom?"

"Yes. My dear Cleek, I don't know whether you are a wizard or what, and I can't conceive what reason you can have for making such an inquiry, but – "

"Which was it? Canoe or ironing-board?"

"Neither, as it happens. But they've got a lady's folding cutting table; you know the sort, one of those that women use for dressmaking operations; and possible to be folded up flat, so they can be tucked away. Nobody knows who left it; but it's there awaiting an owner; and it was found – "

"Oh, I can guess that," interposed Cleek nonchalantly. "It was in a first-class compartment of the 5.18 from London Bridge, which reached the Low Level at 5.43. No, never mind questions for a few minutes, please. Let's go and have a look at the body. I want to satisfy myself regarding the point of what in the world Stavornell was doing on a suburban train at a time when he ought, properly, to be on his way home to his rooms at the Ritz, preparing to dress for dinner; and I want to find out, if possible, what means that chap with the little dark moustache used to get him to go out of town in his ordinary afternoon dress and by that particular train."

"Chap with the small dark moustache? Who do you mean by that?"

"Party that killed him. My 'phone to London Bridge station has cleared the way a bit. It seems that Lord Stavornell engaged that compartment in that particular train by telephone at three o'clock this afternoon. He arrived all alone, and was in no end of a temper because the carriage was dirty; had it swept out, and stood waiting while it was being done. After that the porter says he found him laughing and talking with a dark-moustached little man, apparently of continental origin, dressed in a Norfolk suit and carrying a brown leather portmanteau. Of course, as the platform was crowded, nobody seems to have taken any notice of the dark-moustached little man; and the porter doesn't know where he went nor when — only that he never saw him again. But I know where he went, Mr. Narkom, and I know, too, what was in that portmanteau. An air pistol, for one thing; also a mallet or hammer and that wet cloth we found, both of which were for the purpose of smashing the electric light globe without sound. And he went into that compartment with his victim!"

"Yes; but, man alive, how did he get out? Where did he go after that, and what became of the brown leather portmanteau?"

"I hope to be able to answer both questions before this night is over, Mr. Narkom. Meantime, let us go and have a look at the body, and settle one of the little points that bother me."

The superintendent led the way to the siding where the shunted carriage stood, closely guarded by the police; and, lanterns having been procured from the lamp-room, Cleek was soon deep in the business of examining the compartment and its silent occupant.

Aided by the better light, he now perceived something which, in the first hurried examination, had escaped him, or, if it had not — which is, perhaps, open to question — he had made no comment upon. It was a spot about the size of an ordinary dinner plate on the crimson carpet which covered the floor of the compartment. It was slightly darker than the rest of the surface, and was at the foot of the corner seat directly facing the dead man.

"I think we can fairly decide, Mr. Narkom, on the evidence of that," said Cleek, pointing to it, "that Lord Stavornell did have a companion in this compartment, and that it was the little dark man with the small moustache. Put your hand on the spot. Damp, you see; the effect of some one who had walked through the snow sitting down with his feet on this particular seat. Now look here." He passed his handkerchief over the stain, and held it out for Narkom's inspection. It was slightly browned by the operation. "Just the amount of dirt the soles of one's boots would be likely to collect if one came with wet feet along the muddy platform of the station."

"Yes; but, my dear chap, that might easily have happened —

particularly on such a day as this has been — before Lord Stavornell's arrival. He can't have been the only person to enter this
compartment since morning."

"Granted. But he is supposed to have been the only person
who entered it after it was swept, Mr. Narkom; and that, as I told
you, was done by his orders immediately before the train started.
We've got past the point of 'guesswork' now. We've established
the presence of the second party beyond all question. We also
know that he was a person with whom Stavornell felt at ease, and
was intimate enough with to feel no necessity for putting himself
out by entertaining with those little courtesies one is naturally
obliged to show a guest."

"How do you make that out?"

"This newspaper. He was reading at the time he was shot.
You can see for yourself where the bullet went through — this
hole here close to the top of the paper. When a man invites another man to occupy with him a compartment which he has engaged for his own exclusive use — and this Stavornell must have
done, otherwise the man couldn't have been travelling with him
— and then proceeds to read the news instead of troubling himself to treat his companion as a guest, it is pretty safe to say that
they are acquaintances of long standing, and upon such terms of
intimacy that the social amenities may be dispensed with inoffen-
sively. Now look at the position of this newspaper lying between
the dead man's feet. Curved round the ankle and the lower part
of the calf of the left leg. If we hadn't found the key we still
should have known that the murderer got out on that side of the
carriage."

"How should we have known?"

"Because a paper which has simply been dropped could not
have assumed that position without the aid of a strong current of
air. The opening of that door on the right-hand side of the body
supplied that current, and supplied it with such strength and
violence that the paper was, as one might say, absolutely sucked
round the man's leg. That is a positive proof that the train was
moving at the time it happened, for the day, as you know, has

been windless.

"Now look! No powder on the face, no smell of it in the compartment; and yet the pistol found in his hand is an ordinary American-made thirty-eight calibre revolver. We have an amateur assassin to deal with, Mr. Narkom, not a hardened criminal; and the witlessness of the fellow is enough to bring the case to an end before this night is over. Why didn't he discharge that revolver to-day, and have enough sense to bring a thimbleful of powder to burn in this compartment after the work was done? One knows in an instant that the weapon used was an air-pistol, and that the fellow's only thought was how to do the thing without sound, not how to do it with sense. I don't suppose that there are three places in all London that stock air-pistols, and I don't suppose that they sell so many as two in a whole year's time. But if one has been sold or repaired at any of the shops in the past six months — well, Dollops will know that in less than no time. I 'phoned him to make inquiries. His task's an easy one, and I've no doubt he will bring back the word I want in short order. And now, Mr. Narkom, as our friend the assassin is such a blundering, short-sighted individual, it's just possible that, forgetting so many other important things, he may have neglected to search the body of his victim. Let us do it for him."

As he spoke he bent over the dead man and commenced to search the clothing. He slid his hand into the inner pocket of the creaseless morning coat and drew out a note-book and two or three letters. All were addressed in the handwriting of women, but only one seemed to possess any interest for Cleek. It was written on pink notepaper, enclosed in a pink envelope, and was postmarked "Croydon, December 9, 2.30 P.M.," and bore those outward marks which betokened its delivery, not in course of post, but by express messenger. One instant after Cleek had looked at it he knew he need seek no further for the information he desired. It read:

Piggy! Stupid boy! The ball of the dress fancy is not for tomorrow, but to-night. I have make sudden discoverment. Come quick, by the train that shall leave London Bridge at the time of twenty-eight minute after the hour of five. You shall not fail of this, or it shall make much difficulties for me, as I come to meet it on arrival. Do not bother of the costume; I will have one ready for you. I have one large joke of the somebody else that is coming, which will make you scream of the laughter. Burn this — Fifi.

And at the bottom of the sheet:

Do burn this. I have hurt the hand, and must use the writing of my maid; and I do not want you to treasure that.

"There's the explanation, Mr. Narkom," said Cleek as he held the letter out. "That's why he came by this particular train. There's the snare. That's how he was lured."

"By Fifi!" said Narkom. "By Jove! I rather fancied from the first that we should find that she or her husband had something to do with it."

"Did you?" said Cleek with a smile. "I didn't, then; and I don't even yet!"

Narkom opened his lips to make some comment upon this, but closed them suddenly and said nothing. For at that moment one of the constables put in an appearance with news that, "Two ladies and two gentlemen have arrived, sir, and are asking permission to view the body for purposes of identification. Here are the names, sir, on this slip of paper."

"Lady Stavornell; Colonel Murchison; Hon. Mrs. Brinkworth; Captain James Crawford," Narkom read aloud; then looked up inquiringly at Cleek.

"Yes," he said. "Let them come. And — Mr. Narkom?"

"Yes?"

"Do you happen to know where they come from?"

"Yes. I learned that when I sent word of Stavornell's death to them this evening. Lady Stavornell and her father have for the past week been stopping at Cleethorp Hydro, to which they went for the purpose of remaining over the Christmas holidays; and, oddly enough, both Mrs. Brinkworth and Captain Crawford turned up at the same place for the same purpose the day before yesterday. It can't be very pleasant for them, I should imagine, for I believe the two ladies are not very friendly."

"Naturally not," said Cleek, half abstractedly. "The one loathing the man, the other loving him. I want to see those two ladies; and I particularly want to see those two men. After that – " Here his voice dropped off. Then he stood looking up at the shattered globe, and rubbing his chin between his thumb and forefinger and wrinkling up his brows after the manner of a man who is trying to solve a problem in mental arithmetic. And Narkom, unwise in that direction for once, chose to interrupt his thoughts, for no greater reason than that he had thrice heard him mutter, "Suction — displacement — resistance."

"Working out a problem, old chap?" he ventured. "Can I help you? I used to be rather good at that sort of thing."

"Were you?" said Cleek, a trifle testily. "Then tell me something. Combating a suction power of about two pounds to the square inch, how much wind does it take to make a cutting-table fly, with an unknown weight upon it, from the Sydenham switch to the Low Level station? When you've worked that out, you've got the murderer. And when you do get him he won't be any man you ever saw or ever heard of in all the days of your life! But he will be light enough to hop like a bird, heavy enough to pull up a wire rope with about three hundred pounds on the end of it, and there will be two holes of about an inch in diameter and a foot apart in one end of the table that flew."

"My dear chap!" began Narkom in tones of blank bewilderment, then stopped suddenly and screwed round on his heel. For a familiar voice had sung out suddenly a yard or two distant: "Ah! keep yer 'air on! Don't get to thinkin' you're Niagara Falls jist because yer got water on the brain!" And there, struggling in the grip of a constable, who had laid strong hands upon him, stood Dollops with a kit-bag in one hand and a half-devoured bath bun in the other.

"All right there, constable; let the boy pass. He's one of us!" rapped out Cleek; and in an instant the detaining hand fell, and Dollops' chest went out like a pouter pigeon's.

189

"Catch on to that, Suburbs?" said he, giving the constable a look of blighting scorn; and, swaggering by like a mighty conqueror, joined Cleek at the compartment door. "Nailed it at the second rap, guv'ner," he said in an undertone. "Fell down on Gamage's, picked myself up on Loader, Tottenham Court Road; 14127 A, manufactured Stockholm. Valve tightened — old customer — day before yesterday in the afternoon."

"Good boy! good boy!" said Cleek, patting him approvingly. "Keep your tongue between your teeth. Scuttle off, and find out where there's a garage, and then wait outside the station till I come."

"Right you are, sir," responded Dollops, bolting the remainder of the bun. Then he ducked down and slipped away. And Cleek, stepping back into the shadow, where his features might not be too clearly seen until he was ready that they should be, stood and narrowly watched the small procession which was being piloted to the scene of the tragedy. A moment later the four persons already announced passed under Cleek's watchful eye, and stood in the dead man's presence. Lady Stavornell, tall, graceful, beautiful, looking as one might look whose lifelong martyrdom had come at last to a glorious end; Captain Crawford, bronzed, agitated, a trifle nervous, short of stature, slight of build, with a rather cynical mouth and a small dark moustache; the Hon. Mrs. Brinkworth, a timid, dove-eyed, little wisp of a woman, with a clinging, pathetic, almost childish manner, her soft eyes red with grief, her mobile mouth a-quiver with pain, the marks of tears on her lovely little face; and, last of all, Colonel Murchison, heavy, bull-necked, ponderous of body, and purple of visage a living, breathing monument of Self.

"Hum-m-m!" muttered Cleek to himself, as this unattractive person passed by. "Not he — not by his hand. He never struck the blow — too cowardly, too careful. And yet - Poor little woman! poor little woman!" And his sympathetic eyes went past the others — past Mrs. Brinkworth, sobbing and wringing her hands and calling piteously on the dead to speak — and dwelt long and tenderly upon Lady Stavornell.

A moment he stood there silent, watching, listening, making neither movement nor sound; then of a sudden he put forth his hand and tapped Narkom's arm.

"Detain this party, every member of it, by any means, on any pretext, for another forty-five minutes," he whispered. "I said the assassin was a fool; I said the blunders made it possible for the case to be concluded to-night, did I not? Wait for me. In three-quarters of an hour the murderer will be here on this spot with me!" Then he screwed round on his heel, and before Narkom could speak was gone, soundlessly and completely gone, just as he used to go in his Vanishing Cracksman's days, leaving just that promise behind him.

III

It wanted but thirteen minutes of being midnight when the gathering about the siding where the shunted carriage containing the body of the murdered man still stood received something in the nature of a shock when, on glancing round as a sharp whistle shrilled a warning note, they saw an engine, attached to one solitary carriage, backing along the metals and bearing down upon them.

"I say, Mr. Knockem, or Narkhim, or whatever your name is," blurted out Colonel Murchison, as he hastily caught the Hon. Mrs. Brinkworth by the arm and whisked her back from the metals, leaving his daughter to be looked after by Captain Crawford, "look out for your blessed bobbies. Somebody's shunting another coach in on top of us; and if the ass doesn't look what he's doing – There! I told you!" as the coach in question settled with a slight jar against that containing the body of Lord Stavornell. "Of all the blundering, pig-headed fools! Might have killed some of us. What next, I wonder?"

What next, as a matter of fact, gave him cause for even greater wonder; for as the two carriages met, the door of the last compartment in the one which had just arrived opened briskly, and out of it stepped first a couple of uniformed policemen, next a ginger-haired youth with a kit-bag in one hand and a saveloy in the other, then the trim figure of the lady who had so long and popularly been known in the music-hall world as Mademoiselle Fifi de Lesparre, and last of all – "Cleek!" blurted out Narkom, overcome with amazement, as he saw the serenely alighting figure. And "Cleek!" went in a little rippling murmur throughout the entire gathering, civilians and local police alike.

"All right, Mr. Narkom," said Cleek himself, with a slight shrug of the shoulders. "Even the best of us slip up sometimes; and since everybody knows now, we'll have to make the best of it. Gentlemen, ladies, you, too, my colleagues, my best respects. Now to business." Then he stepped out of the shadow in which he had alighted into the full glow of the lanterns and the flare which had been lit close to the door of the dead man's carriage, conscious that every eye was fixed upon his face and that the members of the local force were silently and breathlessly "spotting" him. But in that moment the weird birth-gift had been put into practice, and Narkom fetched a sort of sigh of relief as he saw that a sagging eyelid, a twisted lip, a queer, blurred *something* about all the features, had set upon that face a living mask that hid effectually the face he knew so well.

"To business?" he repeated. "Ah, yes, quite so, my dear Cleek. Shall I tell the ladies and gentlemen of your promise? Well, listen. Mr. Cleek is more than a quarter of an hour beyond the time he set, but he gave me his word that this riddle would be solved to-night, to-night, ladies and gentlemen, and that when I saw him here the murderer would be with him."

"Oh, bless him! bless him!" burst forth Mrs. Brinkworth impulsively. "And he brings her! That wicked woman! Oh, I knew that she had something to do with it."

"Your pardon, Mrs. Brinkworth, but for once your woman's intuition is at fault," said Cleek quietly. "Mademoiselle Fifi is not here as a prisoner, but as a witness for the Crown. She has had nothing even in the remotest to do with the crime. Her name was used to trap Lord Stavornell to his death. But the lady is here to prove that she never heard of the note which was found on Lord

Stavornell's body; to prove also that, although it is true she did expect to go to a fancy-dress ball with his lordship, that fancy-dress ball does not occur until next Friday, the sixteenth inst., not the ninth, and that she never even heard of any alteration in the date."

"Ah, non! non! non! nevaire! I do swear!" chimed in Fifi herself, almost hysterical with fright. "I know nossing — nossing!"

"That is true," said Cleek quietly. "There is not any question of Mademoiselle Fifi's complete innocence of any connection with this murder."

"Then her husband?" ventured Captain Crawford agitatedly. "Surely you have heard what Mrs. Brinkworth has said about seeing him in town to-day?"

"Yes, I have heard, Captain. But it so happens that I know for a certainty M. Philippe de Lesparre had no more to do with it than had his wife."

"But, my dear sir," interposed the colonel; "the — er — foreign person at the station, the little slim man in the Norfolk suit, the fellow with the little dark moustache? What of him?"

"A great deal of him. But there are other men who are slight, other men who have little dark moustaches, Colonel. That description would answer for Captain Crawford here; and if he, too, were in town to-day - "

"I was in town!" blurted out the captain, a sudden tremor in his voice, a sudden pallor showing through his tan. "But, good God, man! you — you can't possibly insinuate - "

"No, I do not," interposed Cleek. "Set your mind at rest upon that point, Captain; for the simple reason that the little dark man is a little dark fiction; in other words, he does not and never did exist!"

"What's that?" fairly gasped Narkom. "Never existed? But, my dear Cleek, you told me that the porter at London Bridge saw him and - "

"I told you what the porter told me; what the porter thought he saw, and what we shall, no doubt, find out in time at least fifty other people thought they saw, and what was, doubtless, the 'good joke' alluded to in the forged note. The only man against whom we need direct our attention, the only man who had any hand in this murder, is a big, burly, strong-armed one like Colonel Murchison here."

"What's that?" roared out the colonel furiously. "By the Lord Harry, do you dare to assert that I — I sir — killed the man?"

"No, I do not. And for the best of reasons. The assassin was shut up in that compartment with Lord Stavornell from the moment he left London Bridge; and I happen to know, Colonel, that although you were in town to-day, you never put foot aboard the 5.28 from the moment it started to the one in which it stopped. And at that final moment, Colonel," he reached round, took something from his pocket, and then held it out on the palm of his hand, "at that final moment, Colonel, you were passing the barrier at the Crystal Palace Low Level with a lady, whose ticket from London Bridge had never been clipped, and with this air-pistol, which she had restored to you, in your coat pocket!"

"W-w-what crazy nonsense is this, sir? I never saw the blessed thing in all my life."

"Oh, yes, Colonel. Loader, of Tottenham Court Road, repaired the valve for you the day before yesterday, and I found it in your room just - Quick! nab him, Petrie! Well played! After the king, the trump; after the confederate, the assassin! And so - " He sprang suddenly, like a jumping cat, and there was a click of steel, a shrill, despairing cry, then the rustle of something falling. When Captain Crawford and Lady Stavornell turned and looked, he was standing with both hands on his hips, looking frowningly down on the spot where the Hon. Mrs. Brinkworth lay, curled up in a limp, unconscious heap, with a pair of handcuffs locked on her folded wrists.

"I said that when the murderer was found, Mr. Narkom," he said as the superintendent moved toward him, "it would be no man you ever saw or ever heard of in all your life. I knew it was a woman from the bungling, unmanlike way that pistol was laid in the dead hand; the only question I had to answer was *which* woman — Fifi, Lady Stavornell, or this wretched little hypocrite. Here's your 'little dark man,' here's the assassin. The Norfolk suit and the false moustache are in her room at the hydro. She made Stavornell think that she, too, was going to the fancy ball, and that the surprise Fifi had planned was for her to meet him as she did and travel with him. When the train was under way she shot him. Why? Easily explained, my dear chap. His death made her little son heir to the estates. During his minority she would have the handling of the funds; with them she and her precious husband would have a gay life of it in their own selfish little way!"

"Her what? Lord, man, do you mean to say that she and the colonel – "

"Were privately married seven weeks ago, Mr. Narkom. The certificate of their union was tucked away in Colonel Murchison's private effects, where it was found this evening."

* * * * *

"How was the escape from the compartment managed after the murder was accomplished?" said Cleek, answering Narkom's query, as they whizzed home through the darkness together by the last up train that night. "Simplest thing in the world. As you know, the 5.28 from London Bridge runs without stop to Anerley. Well, the 5.18 from the same starting-point runs to the Crystal Palace Low Level, taking the main line tracks as far as Sydenham, where it branches off at the switch and curves away in an opposite direction. That is to say, for a considerable distance they run parallel, but eventually diverge.

"Now, as the 5.18 is a train with several stops, the 5.28, being a through one, overtakes her, and several times between Brockley and Sydenham they run side by side, at so steady a pace and on such narrow gauge that the footboard running along the side of the one train is not more than two and a half feet separated from the other. Their pace is so regular, their progress so even, that one could with ease step from the footboard of the one to the footboard of the other but for the horrible suction which would inevitably draw the person attempting it down under the wheels.

"Well, something had to be devised to overcome the danger of that suction. But what? I asked myself, for I guessed from the first how the escape had occurred, and I knew that such a thing absolutely required the assistance of a confederate. That meant that the confederate would have to do, on the 5.18, exactly what they had trapped Stavornell into doing on the other train: that is, secure a private compartment, so that when the time came for the escape to be accomplished he could remove the electric bulbs from the roof of his compartment, open the door, and, when the two came abreast, the assassin could do the same on the other train, and presto! the dead man would be alone. But what to use to overcome the danger of that horrible suction?"

"Ah, I see now what you were driving at when you inquired about the ironing-board or the Indian canoe. The necessary sections to construct a sort of bridge could be packed in either?"

"Yes. But they chose a simple plan, the cutting-table. A good move that. Its breadth minimised the peril of the suction; only, of course, it would have to be pulled up afterward, to leave no clue, and the added space would call for enormous strength to overcome the power of that suction; and enormous strength meant a powerful man. The rest you can put together without being told, Mr. Narkom. When that little vixen finished her man, she put out the lights, opened the door (deliberately locking it after her to make the thing more baffling), crossed over on that table, was helped into the other compartment by Murchison, and then as expeditiously as possible slipped on the loose feminine outer garments she carried with her in the brown portmanteau, the table was hauled up and taken in — nothing but wire rope for that, sir — and the thing was done.

"Murchison, of course, purchased two tickets, so that they might pass the barrier at the Low Level unquestioned when they left, but he wasn't able to get the extra ticket clipped at London Bridge because there was no passenger for it. That's how I got on to the little game! For the rest, they planned well. Those two trains being always packed, nobody could see the escape from the one to the other, because people would be standing up in every compartment, and the windows completely blocked. But if – Hullo! Victoria at last, thank goodness, 'and so to bed,' as Pepys says. The riddle's solved, Mr. Narkom. Good-night!"

CHAPTER VIII
THE LION'S SMILE

It was on the very stroke of five when Cleek, answering an urgent message from headquarters, strolled into the bar parlour of "The Fiddle and Horseshoe," which, as you may possibly know, stands near to the Green in a somewhat picturesque by-path between Shepherd's Bush and Acton, and found Narkom in the very act of hanging up his hat and withdrawing his gloves preparatory to ordering tea.

"My dear Cleek, what a model of punctuality you are," said the superintendent, as he came forward and shook hands with him. "You would put Father Time himself to the blush with your abnormal promptness. Do make yourself comfortable for a moment or two while I go and order tea. I've only just arrived. Shan't be long, old chap."

"Pray don't hurry yourself upon my account, Mr. Narkom," replied Cleek, as he tossed his hat and gloves upon a convenient table and strolled leisurely to the window and looked out on the quaint, old-fashioned arbour-bordered bowling green, all steeped in sunshine and zoned with the froth of pear and apple blooms, thick-piled above the time-stained brick of the enclosing wall. "These quaint old inns, which the march of what we are pleased to call 'progress' is steadily crowding off the face of the land, are always deeply interesting to me; I love them. What a day! What a picture! What a sky! As blue as what Dollops calls the 'Merry Geranium Sea.' I'd give a Jew's eye for a handful of those apple blossoms, they are divine!"

Narkom hastened from the room without replying. The strain of poetry underlying the character of this strange, inscrutable man, his amazing love of Nature, his moments of almost womanish weakness and sentiment, astonished and mystified him. It was as if a hawk had acquired the utterly useless trick of fluting like a nightingale, and being himself wholly without imagination, he could not comprehend it in the smallest degree.

When he returned a few minutes later, however, the idealist

seemed to have simmered down into the materialist, the extraordinary to have become merged in the ordinary, for he found his famous ally no longer studying the beauties of Nature, but giving his whole attention to the sordid commonplaces of man. He was standing before a glaringly printed bill, one of many that were tacked upon the walls, which set forth in amazing pictures and double-leaded type the wonders that were to be seen daily and nightly at Olympia, where, for a month past, "Van Zant's Royal Belgian Circus and World-famed Menagerie" had been holding forth to "Crowded and delighted audiences." Much was made of two "star turns" upon this lurid bill: "Mademoiselle Marie de Zanoni, the beautiful and peerless bare-back equestrienne, the most daring lady rider in the universe," for the one; and, for the other, "Chevalier Adrian di Roma, king of the animal world, with his great aggregation of savage and ferocious wild beasts, including the famous man-eating African lion, Nero, the largest and most ferocious animal of its species in captivity." And under this latter announcement there was a picture of a young and handsome man, literally smothered with medals, lying at full length, with his arms crossed and his head in the wide-open jaws of a snarling, wild-eyed lion.

"My dear chap, you really do make me believe that there actually is such a thing as instinct," said Narkom, as he came in. "Fancy your selecting that particular bill out of all the others in the room! What an abnormal individual you are!"

"Why? Has it anything to do with the case you have in hand?"

"Anything to do with it? My dear fellow, it *is* 'the case.' I can't imagine what drew your attention to it."

"Can't you?" said Cleek, with a half smile. Then he stretched forth his hand and touched the word "Nero" with the tip of his forefinger. "That did. Things awaken a man's memory occasionally, Mr. Narkom, and – Tell me, isn't that the beast there was such a stir about in the newspapers a fortnight or so ago, the lion that crushed the head of a man in full view of the audience?"

"Yes," replied Narkom, with a slight shudder. "Awful thing,

wasn't it? Gave me the creeps to read about it. The chap who was killed, poor beggar, was a mere boy, not twenty, son of the Chevalier di Roma himself. There was a great stir about it. Talk of the authorities forbidding the performance, and all that sort of thing. They never did, however, for on investigation – Ah, the tea at last, thank fortune. Come, sit down, my dear fellow, and we'll talk whilst we refresh ourselves. Landlady, see that we are not disturbed, will you, and that nobody is admitted but the parties I mentioned?"

"Clients?" queried Cleek, as the door closed and they were alone together.

"Yes. One, Mdlle. Zelie, the 'chevalier's' only daughter, a slack-wire artist; the other, Signor Scarmelli, a trapeze performer, who is the lady's fiance."

"Ah, then our friend the chevalier is not so young as the picture on the bill would have us believe he is."

"No, he is not. As a matter of fact, he is considerably past forty, and is, or rather, was, up to six months ago, a widower, with three children, two sons and a daughter."

"I suppose," said Cleek, helping himself to a buttered scone, "I am to infer from what you say that at the period mentioned, six months ago, the intrepid gentleman showed his courage yet more forcibly by taking a second wife? Young or old?"

"Young," said Narkom in reply. "Very young, not yet four-and-twenty, in fact, and very, very beautiful. That is she who is 'featured' on the bill as the star of the equestrian part of the program: 'Mdlle. Marie de Zanoni.' So far as I have been able to gather, the affair was a love match. The lady, it appears, had no end of suitors, both in and out of the profession; it has even been hinted that she could, had she been so minded, have married an impressionable young Austrian nobleman of independent means who was madly in love with her; but she appears to have considered it preferable to become 'an old man's darling,' so to speak, and to have selected the middle-aged chevalier rather than some one whose age is nearer her own."

"Nothing new in that, Mr. Narkom. Young women before Mdlle. Marie de Zanoni's day have been known to love elderly men sincerely: young Mrs. Bawdrey, in the case of 'The Nine-fingered Skeleton,' is an example of that. Still, such marriages are not common, I admit, so when they occur one naturally looks to see if there may not be 'other considerations' at the bottom of the attachment. Is the chevalier well-to-do? Has he expectations of any kind?"

"To the contrary; he has nothing but the salary he earns, which is by no means so large as the public imagines; and as he comes of a long line of circus performers, all of whom died early and poor, 'expectations,' as you put it, do not enter into the affair at all. Apparently the lady did marry him for love of him, as she professes and as he imagines; although, if what I hear is true, it would appear that she has lately outgrown that love. It seems that a Romeo more suitable to her age has recently joined the show in the person of a rider called Signor Antonio Martinelli; that he has fallen desperately in love with her, and that – "

He bit off his words short and rose to his feet. The door had opened suddenly to admit a young man and a young woman, who entered in a state of nervous excitement. "Ah, my dear Mr. Scarmelli, you and Miss Zelie are most welcome," continued the superintendent. "My friend and I were this moment talking about you."

Cleek glanced across the room, and, as was customary with him, made up his mind instantly. The girl, despite her association with the arena, was a modest, unaffected little thing of about eighteen; the man was a straight-looking, clear-eyed, boyish-faced young fellow of about eight-and-twenty, well, but by no means flashily, dressed, and carrying himself with the air of one who respects himself and demands the respect of others. He was evidently an Englishman, despite his Italian *nom de théâtre*, and Cleek decided out of hand that he liked him.

"We can shelve 'George Headland' in this instance, Mr. Narkom," he said, as the superintendent led forward the pair for the purpose of introducing them, and suffered himself to be presented in the name of Cleek.

The effect of this was electrical; would, in fact, had he been a vain man, have been sufficiently to gratify him to the fullest, for the girl, with a little "Oh!" of amazement, drew back and stood looking at him with a sort of awe that rounded her eyes and parted her lips, while the man leaned heavily upon the back of a convenient chair and looked and acted as one utterly overcome.

"Cleek!" he repeated, after a moment's despairful silence. "You, sir, are that great man? This is a misfortune indeed."

"A misfortune, my friend? Why a 'misfortune,' pray? Do you think the riddle you have brought is beyond my powers?"

"Oh, no; not that — never that!" he made reply. "If there is any one man in the world who could get at the bottom of it, could solve the mystery of the lion's change, the lion's smile, you are that man, sir, you. That is the misfortune: that you could do it, and yet I cannot expect it, cannot avail myself of this great oppor- tunity. Look! I am doing it all on my own initiative, sir, for the sake of Zelie and that dear, lovable old chap, her father. I have saved fifty-eight pounds, Mr. Cleek. I had hoped that that might tempt a clever detective to take up the case; but what is such a sum to such a man as you?"

"If that is all that stands in the way, don't let it worry you, my good fellow," said Cleek, with a smile. "Put your fifty-eight pounds in your pocket against your wedding-day, and good luck to you. I'll take the case for nothing. Now then, what is it? What the dickens did you mean just now when you spoke about 'the lion's change' and 'the lion's smile'? What lion — Nero? Here, sit down and tell me all about it."

"There is little enough to tell, Heavens knows," said young Scarmelli, with a sigh, accepting the invitation after he had grate- fully wrung Cleek's hand, and his fiancée, with a burst of happy tears, had caught it up as it slipped from his and had covered it with thankful kisses. "That, Mr. Cleek, is where the greatest diffi- culty lies, there is so little to explain that has any bearing upon the matter at all. It is only that the lion, Nero, that is, the chevalier's special pride and special pet, seems to have undergone some great and inexplicable change, as though he is at times under some evil spell, which lasts but a moment and yet makes that moment a tragical one. It began, no one knows why nor how, two weeks ago, when, without hint or warning, he killed the person he loved best in all the world, the chevalier's eldest son. Doubtless you have heard of that?"

"Yes," said Cleek. "But what you are now telling me sheds a new light upon the matter. Am I to understand, then, that all that talk, on the bills and in the newspapers, about the lion being a savage and a dangerous one is not true, and that he really is attached to his owner and his owner's family?"

"Yes," said Scarmelli. "He is indeed the gentlest, most docile, most intelligent beast of his kind living. In short, sir, there's not a 'bite' in him; and, added to that, he is over thirty years old. Zelie, Miss di Roma, will tell you that he was born in captivity; that from his earliest moment he has been the pet of her family; that he was, so to speak, raised with her and her brothers; that, as children, they often slept with him; that he will follow those he loves like any dog, fight for them, protect them, let them tweak his ears and pull his tail without showing the slightest resentment, even though they may actually hurt him. Indeed, he is so general a favourite, Mr. Cleek, that there isn't an attendant connected with the show who would not, and, indeed, has not at some time, put his head in the beast's mouth, just as the chevalier does in public, certain that no harm could possibly come of the act.

"You may judge, then, sir, what a shock, what a horrible surprise it was when the tragedy of two weeks ago occurred. Often, to add zest to the performance, the chevalier varies it by allowing his children to put their heads into Nero's mouth instead of doing so himself, merely making a fake of it that he has the lion under such control that he will respect any command given by him. That is what happened on that night. Young Henri was chosen to put his head into Nero's mouth, and did so without fear or hesitation. He took the beast's jaws and pulled them apart, and laid his head within them, as he had done a hundred times before; but of a sudden an appalling, an uncanny, thing happened. It was as though some supernatural power laid hold of the beast and made a thing of horror of what a moment before had been a noble-looking animal. Suddenly a strange hissing noise issued from its jaws, its lips curled upward until it smiled — smiled, Mr. Cleek! — oh, the ghastliest, most awful, most blood-curdling smile imaginable and then, with a sort of mingled snarl and bark, it clamped its jaws together and crushed the boy's head as though it were an egg-shell!"

He put up his hands and covered his eyes as if to shut out some appalling vision, and for a moment or two nothing was heard but the low sobbing of the victim's sister.

"As suddenly as that change had come over the beast, Mr. Cleek," Scarmelli went on presently, "just so suddenly it passed, and it was the docile, affectionate animal it had been for years. It seemed to understand that some harm had befallen its favourite — for Henri was its favourite — and, curling itself up beside his body, it licked his hands and moaned disconsolately in a manner almost human. That's all there is to tell, sir, save that at times the horrid change, the appalling smile, repeat themselves when either the chevalier or his son bend to put a head within its jaws, and but for their watchfulness and quickness the tragedy of that other awful night would surely be repeated. Sir, it is not natural; I know now, as surely as if the lion itself has spoken, that some one is at the bottom of this ghastly thing, that some human agency is at work, some unknown enemy of the chevalier's is doing some-thing, God alone knows what or why, to bring about his death as his son's was brought about."

And here, for the first time, the chevalier's daughter spoke.

"Ah, tell him all, Jim, tell him all!" she said, in her pretty bro-ken English. "Monsieur, may the good God in heaven forgive me if I wrong her; but — but – Ah, Monsieur Cleek, sometimes I feel that she, my stepmother, and that man, that 'rider' who knows not how to ride as the artist should, monsieur, I cannot help it, but I feel that they are at the bottom of it."

"Yes, but why?" queried Cleek. "I have heard of your father's second marriage, mademoiselle, and of this Signor Antonio Martinelli, to whom you allude. Mr. Narkom has told me. But why should you connect these two persons with this inexplicable thing. Does your father do so, too?"

"Oh, no! oh, no!" she answered excitedly. "He does not even know that we suspect, Jim and I. He loves her, monsieur. It would kill him to doubt her."

"Then why should you?"

"Because I cannot help it, monsieur. God knows, I would if I could, for I care for her dearly, I am grateful to her for making my father happy. My brothers, too, cared for her. We believed she loved him; we believed it was because of that that she married him. And yet — and yet – Ah, monsieur, how can I fail to feel as I do when this change in the lion came with that man's coming? And she — ah, monsieur, why is she always with him? Why does she curry favour of him and his rich friend?"

"He has a rich friend, then?"

"Yes, monsieur. The company was in difficulties; Monsieur van Zant, the proprietor, could not make it pay, and it was upon the point of disbanding. But suddenly this indifferent performer, this rider who is, after all, but a poor amateur and not fit to appear with a company of trained artists, suddenly this Signor Martinelli comes to Monsieur van Zant to say that, if he will engage him, he has a rich friend, one Señor Sperati, a Brazilian coffee planter, who will 'back' the show with his money and buy a partnership in it. Of course M. van Zant accepted; and since then this Señor Sperati has travelled everywhere with us, has had the entrée like one of us, and his friend, the bad rider, has fairly bewitched my stepmother, for she is ever with him, ever with them both, and — and – Ah, mon Dieu! the lion smiles, and my people die! Why does it 'smile' for no others? Why is it only they, my father, my brother, they alone?"

"Is that a fact?" said Cleek, turning to young Scarmelli. "You say that all connected with the circus have so little fear of the beast that even attendants sometimes do this foolhardy trick?

Does the lion never 'smile' for any of those?"

"Never, Mr. Cleek, never under any circumstances. Nor does it always smile for the chevalier and his son. That is the mystery of it. One never knows when it is going to happen; one never knows why it does happen. But if you could see that uncanny smile – "

"I should like to," interposed Cleek. "That is, if it might happen without any tragical result. Hum-m-m! Nobody but the chevalier and the chevalier's son! And when does it happen in their case, during the course of the show, or when there is nobody about but those connected with it?"

"Oh, always during the course of the entertainment, sir. Indeed, it has never happened at any other time – never at all."

"Oho!" said Cleek. "Then it is only when they are dressed and made up for the performance, eh? Hum-m-m! I see." Then he lapsed into silence for a moment, and sat tracing circles on the floor with the toe of his boot. But, of a sudden: "You came here directly after the matinee, I suppose?" he queried, glancing up at young Scarmelli.

"Yes; in fact, before it was wholly over."

"I see. Then it is just possible that all the performers have not yet got into their civilian clothes. Couldn't manage to take me round behind the scenes, so to speak, if Mr. Narkom will lend us his motor to hurry us there? Could, eh? That's good. I think I'd like to have a look at that lion and, if you don't mind, an introduction to the parties concerned. No! don't fear; we won't startle anybody by revealing my identity or the cause of the visit. Let us say that I'm a vet. to whom you have appealed for an opinion regarding Nero's queer conduct. All ready, Mr. Narkom? Then let's be off."

Two minutes later the red limousine was at the door, and, stepping into it with his two companions, he was whizzed away to Olympia and the first step toward the solution of the riddle.

II

As it is the custom of those connected with the world of the circus to eat, sleep, have their whole being, as it were, within the environment of the show, to the total exclusion of hotels, boarding-houses, or outside lodgings of any sort, he found on his arrival at his destination the entire company assembled in what was known as the "living-tent," chatting, laughing, reading, playing games and killing time generally whilst waiting for the call to the "dining-tent," and this gave him an opportunity to meet all the persons connected with the "case," from the "chevalier" himself to the Brazilian coffee planter who was "backing" the show.

He found this latter individual a somewhat sullen and taciturn man of middle age, who had more the appearance of an Austrian than a Brazilian, and with a swinging gait and an uprightness of bearing which were not to be misunderstood.

"Humph! Known military training," was Cleek's mental comment as soon as he saw the man walk. "Got it in Germany, too; I know that peculiar 'swing.' What's his little game, I wonder? And what's a Brazilian doing in the army of the Kaiser? And, having been in it, what's he doing dropping into this line; backing a circus, and travelling with it like a Bohemian?"

But although these thoughts interested him, he did not put them into words nor take anybody into his confidence regarding them.

As for the other members of the company, he found "the indifferent rider," known as Signor Antonio Martinelli, an undoubted Irishman of about thirty years of age, extremely handsome, but with a certain "shiftiness" of the eye which was far from inspiring confidence, and with a trick of the tongue which suggested that his baptismal certificate probably bore the name of Anthony Martin. He found, too, that all he had heard regarding the youth and beauty of the chevalier's second wife was quite correct, and although she devoted herself a great deal to the Brazilian coffee planter and the Irish-Italian "Martinelli," she had a way of looking over at her middle-aged spouse, without his knowledge, that left no doubt in Cleek's mind regarding the real state of her feelings toward the man. And last, but not least by any means, he found the chevalier himself a frank, open-minded, open-hearted, lovable man, who ought not, in the natural order of things, to have an enemy in the world. Despite his high-falutin *nom de théâtre*, he was Belgian, a big, soft-hearted, easy-going, unsuspicious fellow, who worshipped his wife, adored his children, and loved every creature of the animal world.

How well that love was returned, Cleek saw when he went with him to that part of the building where his animals were kept, and watched them "nose" his hand or lick his cheek whenever the opportunity offered. But Nero, the lion, was perhaps the greatest surprise of all, for so tame, so docile, so little feared was the animal, that its cage door was open, and they found one of the attendants squatting cross-legged inside and playing with it as though it were a kitten.

"There he is, doctor," said the chevalier, waving his hand toward the beast. "Ah, I will not believe that it was anything but an accident, sir. He loved my boy. He would hurt no one that is kind to him. Fetch him out, Tom, and let the doctor see him at close quarters."

Despite all these assurances of the animal's docility Cleek could not but remember what the creature had done, and, in consequence, did not feel quite at ease when it came lumbering out of the cage with the attendant and ranged up alongside of him, rubbing its huge head against the chevalier's arm after the manner of an affectionate cat.

"Don't be frightened, sir," said Tom, noticing this. "Nothing more'n a big dog, sir. Had the care of him for eight years, I have — haven't I, chevalier? — and never a growl or scratch out of him. No 'smile' for your old Tom, is there, Nero, boy, eh? No fear! Ain't a thing as anybody does with him, sir, that I wouldn't do off-hand and feel quite safe."

"Even to putting your head in his mouth?" queried Cleek.

"Lor', yes!" returned the man, with a laugh. "That's nothing.

Done it many a day. Look here!" With that he pulled the massive jaws apart, and, bending down, laid his head within them. The lion stood perfectly passive, and did not offer to close his mouth until it was again empty. It was then that Cleek remembered, and glanced round at young Scarmelli.

"He never 'smiles' for any but the chevalier and his son, I believe you said," he remarked. "I wonder if the chevalier himself would be as safe if he were to make a feint of doing that?" For the chevalier, like most of the other performers, had not changed his dress after the matinee, since the evening performance was so soon to begin; and if, as Cleek had an idea, that the matter of costume and make-up had anything to do with the mystery of the thing, here, surely, was a chance to learn.

"Make a feint of it? Certainly I will, doctor," the chevalier replied. "But why a feint? Why not the actual thing?"

"No, please — at least, not until I have seen how the beast is likely to take it. Just put your head down close to his muzzle, chevalier. Go slow, please, and keep your head at a safe distance."

The chevalier obeyed. Bringing his head down until it was on a level with the animal's own, he opened the ponderous jaws. The beast was as passive as before; and, finding no trace of the coming of the mysterious and dreaded "smile," he laid his face between the double row of gleaming teeth, held it there a moment, and then withdrew it uninjured. Cleek took his chin between his thumb and forefinger and pinched it hard. What he had just witnessed would seem to refute the idea of either costume or make-up having any bearing upon the case.

"Did you do that to-day at the matinee performance, chevalier?" he hazarded, after a moment's thoughtfulness.

"Oh, yes," he replied. "It was not my plan to do so, however. I alter my performance constantly to give variety. To-day I had arranged for my little son to do the trick; but somehow – Ah! I am a foolish man, monsieur; I have odd fancies, odd whims, sometimes odd fears, since — since that awful night. Something came over me at the last moment, and just as my boy came into the cage to perform the trick I changed my mind. I would not let him do it. I thrust him aside and did the trick myself."

"Oho!" said Cleek. "Will the boy do it to-night, then, chevalier?"

"Perhaps," he made reply. "He is still dressed for it. Look, here he comes now, monsieur, and my wife, and some of our good friends with him. Ah, they are so interested, they are anxious to hear what report you make upon Nero's condition."

Cleek glanced round. Several members of the company were advancing toward them from the "living-tent." In the lead was the boy, a little fellow of about twelve years of age, fancifully dressed in tights and tunic. By his side was his stepmother, looking pale and anxious. But although both Signor Martinelli and the Brazilian coffee planter came to the edge of the tent and looked out, it was observable that they immediately withdrew, and allowed the rest of the party to proceed without them.

"Dearest, I have just heard from Tom that you and the doctor are experimenting with Nero," said the chevalier's wife, as she came up with the others and joined him. "Oh, do be careful, do! Much as I like the animal, doctor, I shall never feel safe until my husband parts with it or gives up that ghastly 'trick.'"

"My dearest, my dearest, how absurdly you talk!" interrupted her husband. "You know well that without that my act would be commonplace, that no manager would want either it or me. And how, pray, should we live if that were to happen?"

"There would always be my salary; we could make that do."

"As if I would consent to live upon your earnings and add nothing myself! No, no! I shall never do that, never. It is not as though that foolish dream of long ago had come true, and I might hope one day to retire. I am of the circus, and of it I shall always remain."

"I wish you might not; I wish the dream might come true, even yet," she made reply. "Why shouldn't it? Wilder ones have come true for other people; why should they not for you?"

Before her husband could make any response to this, the whole trend of the conversation was altered by the boy.

"Father," he said, "am I to do the trick to-night? Señor Sperati says it is silly of me to sit about all dressed and ready if I am to do nothing, like a little super, instead of a performer and an artist."

"Oh, but that is not kind of the señor to say that," his father replied, soothing his ruffled feelings. "You are an artist, of course; never super — no, never. But if you shall do the trick or not, I cannot say. It will depend, as it did at the matinee. If I feel it is right, you shall do it; but if I feel it is wrong, then it must be no. You see, doctor," catching Cleek's eye, "what a little enthusiast he is, and with how little fear."

"Yes, I do see, chevalier; but I wonder if he would be willing to humour me in something? As he is not afraid, I've an odd fancy to see how he'd go about the thing. Would you mind letting him make the feint you yourself made a few minutes ago? Only, I must insist that in this instance it be nothing more than a feint, chevalier. Don't let him go too near at the time of doing it. Don't let him open the lion's jaws with his own hands. You do that. Do you mind?"

"Of a certainty not, monsieur. Gustave, show the good doctor how you go about it when papa lets you do the trick. But you are not really to do it just yet, only to bend the head near to Nero's mouth. Now then, come see."

As he spoke he divided the lion's jaws and signalled the child to bend. He obeyed. Very slowly the little head drooped nearer to the gaping, full-fanged mouth, very slowly and very carefully, for Cleek's hand was on the boy's shoulder, Cleek's eyes were on the lion's face. The huge brute was as meek and as undisturbed as before, and there was actual kindness in its fixed eyes. But of a sudden, when the child's head was on a level with those gaping jaws, the lips curled backward in a ghastly parody of a smile, a weird, uncanny sound whizzed through the bared teeth, the passive body bulked as with a shock, and Cleek had just time to snatch the boy back when the great jaws struck together with a snap that would have splintered a skull of iron had they closed upon it.

The hideous and mysterious "smile" had come again, and, brief though it was, its passing found the boy's sister lying on the ground in a dead faint, the boy's stepmother cowering back, with covered eyes and shrill, affrighted screams, and the boy's father leaning, shaken and white, against the empty cage and nursing a bleeding hand.

In an instant the whole place was in an uproar. "It smiled again! It smiled again!" ran in broken gasps from lip to lip; but through it all Cleek stood there, clutching the frightened child close to him, but not saying one word, not making one sound. Across the dark arena came a rush of running footsteps, and presently Señor Sperati came panting up, breathless and pale with excitement.

"What's the matter? What's wrong?" he cried. "Is it the lion again? Is the boy killed? Speak up!"

"No," said Cleek very quietly, "nor will he be. The father will do the trick to-night, not the son. We've had a fright and a lesson, that's all." And, putting the sobbing child from him, he caught young Scarmelli's arm and hurried him away. "Take me somewhere that we can talk in safety," he said. "We are on the threshold of the end, Scarmelli, and I want your help."

"Oh, Mr. Cleek, have you any idea, any clue?"

"Yes, more than a clue. I know how, but I have not yet discovered why. Now, if you know, tell me what did the chevalier mean, what did his wife mean, when they spoke of a dream that might have come true but didn't? Do you know? Have you any idea? Or, if you have not, do you think your fiancée has?"

"Why, yes," he made reply. "Zelie has told me about it often. It is of a fortune that was promised and never materialised. Oh, such a long time ago, when he was quite a young man, the chevalier saved the life of a very great man, a Prussian nobleman of great wealth. He was profuse in his thanks and his promises, that nobleman; swore that he would make him independent for life, and all that sort of thing."

"And didn't?"

"No, he didn't. After a dozen letters promising the chevalier things that almost turned his head, the man dropped him entirely. In the midst of his dreams of wealth a letter came from the old skinflint's steward enclosing him the sum of six hundred marks, and telling him that as his master had come to the conclusion that wealth would be more of a curse than a blessing to a man of his class and station, he had thought better of his rash promise. He begged to tender the enclosed as a proper and sufficient reward for the service rendered, and 'should not trouble the young man any further.' Of course, the chevalier didn't reply. Who would, after having been promised wealth, education, everything one had confessed that one most desired? Being young, high-spirited, and bitterly, bitterly disappointed, the chevalier bundled the six hundred marks back without a single word, and that was the last he ever heard of the Baron von Steinheid from that day to this."

"The Baron von Steinheid?" repeated Cleek, pulling himself up as though he had trodden upon something.

"Do you mean to say that the man whose life he saved – Scarmelli, tell me something: Does it happen by any chance that the 'Chevalier di Roma's' real name is Peter Janssen Pullaine?"

"Yes," said Scarmelli, in reply. "That is his name. Why?"

"Nothing, but that it solves the riddle, and the lion has smiled for the last time! No, don't ask me any questions; there isn't time to explain. Get me as quickly as you can to the place where we left Mr. Narkom's motor. Will this way lead me out? Thanks! Get back to the others, and look for me again in two hours' time; and Scarmelli?"

"Yes, sir?"

"One last word: don't let that boy get out of your sight for one instant, and don't, no matter at what cost, let the chevalier do his turn to-night before I get back. Good-bye for a time. I'm off."

Then he moved like a fleetly passing shadow round the angle of the building, and two minutes later was with Narkom in the red limousine.

"To the German embassy as fast as we can fly," he said as he scrambled in. "I've something to tell you about that lion's smile, Mr. Narkom, and I'll tell it while we're on the wing."

III

It was nine o'clock and after. The great show at Olympia was at its height; the packed house was roaring with delight over the daring equestrianship of "Mademoiselle Marie de Zanoni," and the sound of the cheers rolled in to the huge dressing-tent, where the artists awaited their several turns, and the chevalier, in spangled trunks and tights, all ready for his call, sat hugging his child and shivering like a man with the ague.

"Come, come, buck up, man, and don't funk it like this," said Señor Sperati, who had graciously consented to assist him with his dressing because of the injury to his hand. "The idea of you losing your nerve, you of all men, and because of a little affair like that. You know very well that Nero is as safe as a kitten to-night, that he never has two smiling turns in the same week, much less the same day. Your act's the next on the programme. Buck up and go at it like a man."

"I can't, señor, I can't!" almost wailed the chevalier. "My nerve is gone. Never, if I live to be a thousand, shall I forget that awful moment, that appalling 'smile.' I tell you there is wizardry in the thing; the beast is bewitched. My work in the arena is done, done forever, señor. I shall never have courage to look into the beast's jaws again."

"Rot! You're not going to ruin the show, are you, and after all the money I've put into it? If you have no care for yourself, it's your duty to think about me. You can at least try. I tell you you must try! Here, take a sip of brandy, and see if that won't put a bit of courage into you. Hallo!" as a burst of applause and the thud of a horse's hoofs down the passage to the stables came rolling in, "there's your wife's turn over at last; and there — listen! the ringmaster is announcing yours. Get up, man; get up and go out."

"I can't, señor, I can't! I can't!"

"But I tell you you must."

And just here an interruption came.

"Bad advice, my dear captain," said a voice, Cleek's voice, from the other end of the tent; and with a twist and a snarl the "señor" screwed round on his heel in time to see that other intruders were putting in an appearance as well as this unwelcome one.

"Who the deuce asked you for your opinion?" rapped out the "señor" savagely. "And what are you doing in here, anyhow? If we want the service of a vet., we're quite capable of getting one for ourselves without having him shove his presence upon us unasked."

"You are quite capable of doing a great many things, my dear captain, even making lions smile!" said Cleek serenely. "It would appear that the gallant Captain von Gossler, nephew, and, in the absence of one who has a better claim, heir to the late Baron von Steinheid — That's it, nab the beggar. Played, sir, played! Hustle him out and into the cab, with his precious confederate, the Irish-Italian 'signor,' and make a clean sweep of the pair of them. You'll find it a neck-stretching game, captain, I'm afraid, when the jury comes to hear of that poor boy's death and your beastly part in it."

By this time the tent was in an uproar, for the chevalier's wife had come hurrying in, the chevalier's daughter was on the verge of hysterics, and the chevalier's prospective son-in-law was alternately hugging the great beast-tamer and then shaking his hand and generally deporting himself like a respectable young man who had suddenly gone daft.

"Governor!" he cried, half laughing, half sobbing. "Bully old governor. It's over — it's over. Never any more danger, never any more hard times, never any more lion's smiles."

"No, never," said Cleek. "Come here, Madame Pullaine, and

hear the good news with the rest. You married for love, and you've proved a brick. The dream's come true, and the life of ease and of luxury is yours at last, Mr. Pullaine."

"But, sir, I — I do not understand," stammered the chevalier. "What has happened? Why have you arrested the Señor Sperati? What has he done? I cannot comprehend."

"Can't you? Well, it so happens, chevalier, that the Baron von Steinheid died something like two months ago, leaving the sum of sixty thousand pounds sterling to one Peter Janssen Pullaine and the heirs of his body, and that a certain Captain von Gossler, son of the baron's only sister, meant to make sure that there was no Peter Janssen Pullaine and no heirs of his body to inherit one farthing of it."

"Sir! Dear God, can this be true?"

"Perfectly true, chevalier. The late baron's solicitors have been advertising for some time for news regarding the whereabouts of Peter Janssen Pullaine, and if you had not so successfully hidden your real name under that of your professional one, no doubt some of your colleagues would have put you in the way of finding it out long ago. The baron did not go back on his word and did not act ungratefully. His will, dated twenty-nine years ago, was never altered in a single particular. I rather suspect that that letter and that gift of money which came to you in the name of his steward, and was supposed to close the affair entirely, was the work of his nephew, the gentleman whose exit has just been made. A crafty individual that, chevalier, and he laid his plans cleverly and well. Who would be likely to connect him with the death of a beast-tamer in a circus, who had perished in what would appear an accident of his calling? Ah, yes, the lion's smile was a clever idea. He was a sharp rascal to think of it."

"Sir! You — you do not mean to tell me that he caused that? He never went near the beast — never — even once."

"Not necessary, chevalier. He kept near you and your children; that was all that he needed to do to carry out his plan. The lion was as much his victim as anybody else. What it did it could not help doing. The very simplicity of the plan was its passport to success. All that was required was the unsuspected sifting of snuff on the hair of the person whose head was to be put in the beast's mouth. The lion's smile was not, properly speaking, a smile at all, chevalier; it was the torture which came of snuff getting into its nostrils, and when the beast made that uncanny noise and snapped its jaws together, it was simply the outcome of a sneeze. The thing would be farcical if it were not that tragedy hangs on the thread of it, and that a life, a useful human life, was destroyed by means of it. Yes, it was clever, it was diabolically clever; but you know what Bobby Burns says about the best-laid schemes of mice and men. There's always a Power higher up that works the ruin of them."

With that he walked by and, going to young Scarmelli, put out his hand.

"You're a good chap and you've got a good girl, so I expect you will be happy," he said; and then lowered his voice so that the rest might not reach the chevalier's ears. "You were wrong to suspect the little stepmother," he added. "She's true blue, Scarmelli. She was only playing up to those fellows because she was afraid the 'señor' would drop out and close the show if she didn't, and that she and her husband and the children would be thrown out of work. She loves her husband — that's certain — and she's a good little woman; and, Scarmelli?"

"Yes, Mr. Cleek?"

"There's nothing better than a good woman on this earth, my lad. Always remember that. I think you, too, have got one. I hope you have. I hope you will be happy. What's that? Owe me? Not a rap, my boy. Or, if you feel that you must give me something, give me your prayers for equal luck when my time comes, and send me a slice of the wedding cake. The riddle's solved, old chap. Good-night!"

CHAPTER IX
THE MYSTERY OF THE STEEL ROOM

"Oh, blow!" said Dollops disgustedly, as the telephone bell jingled. "A body never gets a square meal in this house now that that blessed thing's been put in!" Then he laid down his knife and fork, scuttled upstairs to the instrument, and unhooked the receiver. "'Ullo! Wot's the rumpus?" he shouted into it. "Yus, this is Captain Burbage's. Wot? No, he ain't in. Dunno when he will be. Dunno where he is. Who is it as wants him? If there's any message – "

The sound of some one whistling softly the opening bars of the national anthem at the other end of the wire cut in upon his words and filled him with a sudden deep and startled interest.

"Oh, s'help me!" he said, with a sort of gasp. "The Yard!" Then, lowering his voice to a shrill whisper, "That you, Mr. Narkom? Beg yer pardon, sir. Yus, it's me – Dollops. Wot? No, sir. Went out two hours ago. Gone to Kensington Palace Gardens. Tulips is out, and you couldn't hold him indoors with a chain at tulip time. Yus, sir – top hat, gray spats; same's the captain always wears, sir."

Narkom, at the other end of the line, called back: "If I miss him, if he comes in without seeing me, tell him to wait; I'll be round before three. Good-bye!" then hung up the receiver and turned to the gentleman who stood by the window on the other side of the private office agitatedly twirling the end of his thick gray-threaded moustache with one hand, while with the other he drummed a nervous tattoo upon the broad oaken sill. "Not at home, Sir Henry; but fortunately I know where to find him with but little loss of time," he said, and pressed twice upon an electric button beside his desk. "My motor will be at the door in a couple of minutes, and with ordinary luck we ought to be able to pick him up inside of the next half hour."

Sir Henry – Sir Henry Wilding, Bart., to give him his full name and title – a handsome, well-set-up man of about forty years of age, well groomed, and with the upright bearing which comes of military training, twisted round on his heel at this and gave the superintendent an almost grateful look.

"I hope so, God knows, I hope so, Mr. Narkom," he said agitatedly. "Time is the one important thing at present. The suspense and uncertainty are getting on my nerves so horribly that the very minutes seem endless. Remember, there are only three days before the race, and if those rascals, whoever they are, get at Black Riot before then, God help me, that's all! And if this man Cleek can't probe the diabolical mystery, they *will* get at her, too, and put Logan where they put Tolliver, the brutes!"

"You may trust Cleek to see that they don't, Sir Henry. It is just the kind of case he will glory in; and if Black Riot is all that you believe her, you'll carry off the Derby plate in spite of these enterprising gentry who – Hallo! here's the motor. Clap on your hat, Sir Henry, and come along. Mind the step! Kensington Palace Gardens, Lennard – and as fast as you can streak it."

The chauffeur proved that he could "streak it" as close to the margin of the speed limits as the law dared wink at, even in the case of the well-known red limousine, and in a little over twenty minutes pulled up before the park gates. Narkom jumped out, beckoned Sir Henry to follow him, and together they hurried into the grounds in quest of Cleek.

Where the famous tulip beds made splotches of brilliant colour against the clear emerald of the closely clipped grass they came upon him, a solitary figure in the garb of the elderly seaman, "Captain Burbage, of Clarges Street," seated on one of the garden benches, his hands folded over the knob of his thick walking-stick and his chin resting upon them, staring fixedly at the gorgeous flowers and apparently deaf and blind to all else.

He was not, however, for as the superintendent approached without altering his gaze or his attitude in the slightest particle, he said with the utmost calmness: "Superb, are they not, my friend? What a pity they should be scentless. It is as though Heaven had created a butterfly and deprived it of the secret of flight. Walk on, please, without addressing me. I am quite friendly with that policeman yonder, and I do not wish him to suspect that the elderly gentleman he is so kind to is in any way connected with the Yard. Examine the tulips. That's right. You came in your limousine, of course? Where is it?"

"Just outside the gates, at the end of the path on the right," replied Narkom, halting with Sir Henry and appearing to be wholly absorbed in pointing out the different varieties of tulips.

"Good," replied Cleek, apparently taking not the slightest notice. "I'll toddle on presently, and when you return from inspecting the flowers you will find me inside the motor awaiting you."

"Do, old chap, and please hurry; time is everything in this case. Let me introduce you to your client. (Keep looking at the flowers, please, Sir Henry.) I have the honour to make you acquainted with Sir Henry Wilding, Cleek; he needs you, my dear fellow."

"Delighted – in both instances. My compliments, Sir Henry. By any chance that Sir Henry Wilding whose mare, Black Riot, is the favourite for next Wednesday's Derby?"

"Yes, that very man, Mr. Cleek; and if – "

"Don't get excited and don't turn, please; our friend the policeman is looking this way. What's the case? One of 'nobbling'? Somebody trying to get at the mare?"

"Yes. A desperate 'somebody,' who doesn't stop even at murder. A very devil incarnate who seems to possess the power of invisibility and who strikes in the dark. Save me, Mr. Cleek! All I've got in the world is at stake, and if anything happens to Black Riot, I'm a ruined man."

"Yar-r-r!" yawned the elderly sea captain, rising and stretching. "I do believe, constable, I've been asleep. Warm weather this for May. A glorious week for Epsom. Shan't see you to-morrow, I'm afraid. Perhaps shan't see you until Thursday. Here, take that, my lad, and have half-a-crown's worth on Black Riot for the Derby; she'll win it, sure."

"Thanky, sir. Good luck to you, sir."

"Same to you, my lad. Good day." Then the old gentleman in the top hat and gray spats moved slowly away, passed down the tree-shaded walk, passed the romping children, passed the Princess Louise's statue of Queen Victoria, and, after a moment, vanished. Ten minutes later, when Narkom and Sir Henry returned to the waiting motor, they found him seated within it awaiting them, as he had promised. Giving Lennard orders to drive about slowly in the least frequented quarters, while they talked, the superintendent got in with Sir Henry, and opened fire on the "case" without further delay.

"My dear Cleek," he said, "as you appear to know all about Sir Henry and his famous mare, there's no need to go into that part of the subject, so I may as well begin by telling you at once that Sir Henry has come up to town for the express purpose of getting you to go down to his place in Suffolk to-night in company with him. You are his only hope of outwitting a diabolical agency which has set out to get at the horse and put it out of commission before Derby Day, and in the most mysterious, the most inscrutable manner ever heard of, my dear chap. Already one groom who sat up to watch with her has been killed, another hopelessly paralysed, and to-night Logan, the mare's trainer, is to sit up with her in the effort to baulk the almost superhuman rascal who is at the bottom of it all. Conceive, if you can, my dear fellow, a power so crafty, so diabolical, that it gets into a locked and guarded stable, gets in, my dear Cleek, despite four men constantly pacing back and forth before each and every window and door that leads into the place and with a groom on guard inside, and then gets out again in the same mysterious manner without having been seen or heard by a living soul. In addition to all the windows being small and covered with a grille of iron, a fact which would make it impossible for any one to get in or out once the doors were closed and guarded, Sir Henry himself will tell you that the stable has been ransacked from top to bottom, every hole and every corner probed into, and not a living creature of any sort discovered. Yet only last night the groom, Tolliver, was set upon inside the place and killed outright in his efforts to protect the horse; killed, Cleek, with four men patrolling outside, and willing to swear, each and every one of them, that nothing and no one, either man, woman, child, or beast, passed them going in or getting out from sunset until dawn."

"Hum-m-m!" said Cleek, sucking in his lower lip. "Mysterious, to say the least. Was there no struggle? Did the men on guard hear no cry?"

"In the case of the first groom, Murple, the one that was paralysed — no," said Sir Henry, as the question was addressed to him. "But in the case of Tolliver — yes. The men heard him cry out, heard him call out 'help!' but by the time they could get the doors open it was all over. He was lying doubled up before the entrance to Black Riot's stall, with his face to the floor, as dead as Julius Cæsar, poor fellow, and not a sign of anybody anywhere."

"And the horse? Did anybody get at that?"

"No; for the best of reasons. As soon as these attacks began, Mr. Cleek, I sent up to London. A gang of twenty-four men came down, with steel plates, steel joists, steel posts, and in seven hours' time Black Riot's box was converted into a sort of safe, to which I alone hold the key the instant it is locked up for the night. A steel grille about half a foot deep, and so tightly meshed that nothing bigger than a mouse could pass through, runs all round the enclosure close to the top of the walls, and this supplies ventilation. When the door is closed at night, it automatically connects itself with an electric gong in my own bedroom, so that the slightest attempt to open it, or even to touch it, would hammer out an alarm close to my head."

"Has it ever done so?"

"Yes, last night, when Tolliver was killed."

"How killed, Sir Henry? Stabbed or shot?"

"Neither. He appeared to have been strangled, poor fellow, and to have died in most awful agony."

"Strangled! But, my dear sir, that would hardly have been possible in so short a time. You say your men heard him call out for help. Granted that it took them a full minute — and it probably did not take them half one — to open the doors and come to his assistance, he would not be stone dead in so short a time; and he was stone dead when they got in, I believe you said?"

"Yes. God knows what killed him, the coroner will find that out, no doubt, but there was no blood shed and no mark upon him that I could see."

"Hum-m-m! Was there any mark on the door of the steel stall?"

"Yes. A long scratch, somewhat semi-circular, and sweeping downward at the lower extremity. It began close to the lock and ended about a foot and a half lower."

"Undoubtedly, you see, Cleek," put in Narkom, "some one tried to force an entrance to the steel room and get at the mare, but the prompt arrival of the men on guard outside the stable prevented his doing so."

Cleek made no response. Just at that moment the limousine was gliding past a building whose courtyard was one blaze of parrot tulips, and, his eye caught by the flaming colours, he was staring at them and reflectively rubbing his thumb and forefinger up and down his chin. After a moment, however:

"Tell me something, Sir Henry," he said abruptly. "Is anybody interested in your not putting Black Riot into the field on Derby Day? Anybody with whom you have a personal acquaintance, I mean, for of course I know there are other owners who would be glad enough to see him scratched. But is there anybody who would have a particular interest in your failure?"

"Yes — one: Major Lambson-Bowles, owner of Minnow. Minnow's second favourite, as perhaps you know. It would delight Lambson-Bowles to see me 'go under'; and, as I'm so certain of Black Riot that I've mortgaged every stick and stone I have in the world to back her, I should go under if anything happed to the mare. That would suit Lambson-Bowles down to the ground."

"Bad blood between you, then?"

"Yes, very. The fellow's a brute, and — I thrashed him once, as he deserved, the bounder. It may interest you to know that my only sister was his first wife. He led her a dog's life, poor girl, and death was a merciful release to her. Twelve months ago he married a rich American woman, widow of a man who made millions in hides and leather. That's when Lambson-Bowles took up racing and how he got the money to keep a stud. Had the beastly bad taste, too, to come down to Suffolk — within a gunshot of Wilding Hall — take Elmslie Manor, the biggest place in the neighbourhood, and cut a dash under my very nose, as it were."

"Oho!" said Cleek; "then the major is a neighbour as well as a rival for the Derby plate. I see! I see!"

"No, you don't — altogether," said Sir Henry quickly. "Lambson-Bowles is a brute and a bounder in many ways, but — well, I don't believe he is low-down enough to do this sort of thing, and with murder attached to it, too, although he did try to bribe poor Tolliver to leave me. Offered my trainer double wages, too, to chuck me and take up his horses."

"Oh, he did that, did he? Sure of it, Sir Henry?"

"Absolutely. Saw the letter he wrote to Logan."

"Hum-m-m! Feel that you can rely on Logan, do you?"

"To the last grasp. He's as true to me as my own shadow. If you want proof of it, Mr. Cleek, he's going to sit in the stable and keep guard himself to-night, in the face of what happened to Murple and Tolliver."

"Murple is the groom who was paralysed, is he not?" said Cleek, after a moment. "Singular thing that. What paralysed him, do you think?"

"Heavens knows. He might just as well have been killed as poor Tolliver was, for he'll never be any use again, the doctors say. Some injury to the spinal column, and with it a curious affection of the throat and tongue. He can neither swallow nor speak. Nourishment has to be administered by tube, and the tongue is horribly swollen."

"I am of the opinion, Cleek," put in Narkom, "that strangulation is merely part of the procedure of the rascal who makes these diabolical nocturnal visits. In other words, that he is armed with some quick-acting infernal poison, which he forces into the mouths of his victims. That paralysis of the muscles of the throat is one of the symptoms of prussic acid poisoning, you must remember."

"I do remember, Mr. Narkom," replied Cleek enigmatically. "My memory is much stimulated by these details, I assure you. I gather from them that, whatever is administered, Murple did not get quite so much of it as Tolliver, or he, too, would be dead. Sir Henry" — he turned again to the baronet — "do you trust everybody else connected with your establishment as much as you trust Logan?"

"Yes. There's not a servant connected with the hall that hasn't been in my service for years, and all are loyal to me."

"May I ask who else is in the house besides the servants?"

"My wife, Lady Wilding, for one; her cousin, Mr. Sharpless, who is on a visit to us, for another; and for a third, my uncle, the Rev. Ambrose Smeer, the famous revivalist."

"Mr. Smeer does not approve of the race track, of course?"

"No, he does not. He is absurdly 'narrow' on some subjects, and 'sport' of all sorts is one of them. But, beyond that, he is a dear, lovable, old fellow, of whom I am amazingly fond."

"Hum-m-m! And Lady Wilding and Mr. Sharpless, do they, too, disapprove of racing?"

"Quite to the contrary. Both are enthusiastic upon the subject and both have the utmost faith in Black Riot's certainty of winning. Lady Wilding is something more than attached to the mare; and as for Mr. Sharpless, he is so upset over these rascally attempts that every morning when the steel room is opened and the animal taken out, although nothing ever happens in the daylight, he won't let her get out of his sight for a single instant until she is groomed and locked up for the night. He is so incensed, so worked up over this diabolical business, that I verily believe if he caught any stranger coming near the mare he'd shoot him in his tracks."

"Hum-m-m!" said Cleek abstractedly, and then sat silent for a long time staring at his spats and moving one thumb slowly round the breadth of the other, his fingers interlaced and his lower lip pushed upward over the one above.

"There, that's the case, Cleek," said Narkom, after a time. "Do you make anything out of it?"

"Yes," he replied; "I make a good deal out of it, Mr. Narkom, but, like the language of the man who stepped on the banana skin, it isn't fit for publication. One question more, Sir Henry. Heaven forbid it, of course, but if anything should happen to Logan to-night, who would you put on guard over the horse to-morrow?"

"Do you think I could persuade anybody if a third man perished?" said the baronet, answering one question with another. "I don't believe there's a groom in England who'd take the risk for love or money. There would be nothing for it but to do the watching myself. What's that? Do it? Certainly, I'd do it! Everybody that knows me knows that."

"Ah, I see!" said Cleek, and lapsed into silence again.

"But you'll come, won't you?" exclaimed Sir Henry agitatedly. "It won't happen if you take up the case; Mr. Narkom tells me he is sure of that. Come with me, Mr. Cleek. My motor is waiting at the garage. Come back with me, for God's sake, for humanity's sake, and get at the bottom of the thing."

"Yes," said Cleek in reply. "Give Lennard the address of the garage, please; and — Mr. Narkom?"

"Yes, old chap?"

"Pull up at the first grocer's shop you see, will you, and buy me a couple of pounds of the best white flour that's milled; and if you can't manage to get me either a sieve or a flour dredger, a tin pepper-pot will do!"

II

It was two o'clock when Sir Henry Wilding's motor turned its back upon the outskirts of London, and it was a quarter past seven when it whirled up to the stables of Wilding Hall, and the baronet and his gray-headed, bespectacled and gray-spatted companion alighted, having taken five hours and a quarter to make a journey which the trains which run daily between Liverpool Street and Darsham make in four.

As a matter of fact, however, they really had outstripped the train, but it had been Cleek's pleasure to make two calls on the way, one at Saxmundham, where the paralysed Murple lay in the infirmary of the local practitioner, the other at the mortuary where the body of Tolliver was retained, awaiting the sitting of the coroner. Both the dead and the still living man Cleek had subjected to a critical personal examination, but whether either furnished him with any suggested clue he did not say. The only remark he made upon the subject was when Sir Henry, on hearing from Murple's wife that the doctor had said he would probably not last the week out, had inquired if the woman knew where to "put her hand on the receipt for the payment of the last premium, so that her claim could be sent in to the life assurance company without delay when the end came."

"Tell me something, Sir Henry," said Cleek, when he heard that, and noticed how gratefully the woman looked at the baronet when she replied, "Yes, Sir Henry, God bless you, sir!" "Tell me, if it is not an impertinent question, did you take out an insurance policy on Murple's life and pay the premium on it yourself? I gathered the idea that you did from the manner in which the woman spoke to you."

"Yes, I did," replied Sir Henry. "As a matter of fact, I take out a similar policy, payable to the widow, for every married man I employ in connection with my racing stud."

"May I ask why?"

"Well, for one thing, they usually are too poor and have too many children to support to be able to take it out for themselves, and exercising racers has a good many risks. Then, for another thing, I'm a firm believer in the policy of life assurance. It's just so much money laid up in safety, and one never knows what may happen."

"Then it is fair," said Cleek, "to suppose, in that case, that you have taken out one on your own life?"

"Yes — rather! And a whacking big one, too."

"And Lady Wilding is, of course, the beneficiary?"

"Certainly. There are no children, you know. As a matter of fact, we have been married only seven months. Before the date of my wedding the policy was in my Uncle Ambrose's, the Rev. Mr. Smeer's, favour."

"Ah, I see!" said Cleek reflectively. Then fell to thinking deeply over the subject, and was still thinking of it when the motor whizzed into the stableyard at Wilding Hall and brought him into contact for the first time with the trainer, Logan. He didn't much fancy Logan at first blush, and Logan didn't fancy him at all at any time.

"Hur!" he said disgustedly, in a stage aside to his master as Cleek stood on the threshold of the stable, with his head thrown back and his chin at an angle, sniffing the air somewhat after the manner of a bird-dog. "Hur! If un's the best Scotland Yard could let out to ye, sir, a half-baked old softy like that, the rest of 'em must be a blessed poor lot, Ah'm thinkin'. What's un doin' now, the noodle? — snuffin' the air like he did not understand the smell of it! He'd not be expectin' a stable to be scented with eau de cologne, would he? What's un name, sir?"

"Cleek."

"Hur! Sounds like a golf-stick an' Ah've no doubt he's got a head like one: main thick and with a twist in un. I dunna like 'tecs, Sir Henry, and I dunna like this one especial. Who's to tell as he aren't in with they devils as is after Black Riot? Naw! I dunna like him at all."

Meantime, serenely unconscious of the displeasure he had

excited in Logan's breast, Cleek went on sniffing the air and "poking about," as he phrased it, in all corners of the stable; and when, a moment later, Sir Henry went in and joined him, he was standing before the door of the steel room examining the curving scratch of which the baronet had spoken.

"What do you make of it, Mr. Cleek?"

"Not much in the way of a clue, Sir Henry, a clue to any possible intruder, I mean. If your artistic soul hadn't rebelled against bare steel, which would, of course, have soon rusted in this ammonia-impregnated atmosphere, and led you to put a coat of paint over the metal, there would have been no mark at all, the thing is so slight. I am of the opinion that Tolliver himself caused it. In short, that it was made by either a pin or a cuff button in his wristband when he was attacked and fell. But enlighten me upon a puzzling point, Sir Henry: What do you use coriander and oil of sassafras for in a stable?"

"Coriander? Oil of sassafras? I don't know what the dickens they are. Have you found such things here?"

"No; simply smelt them. The combination is not usual – indeed, I know of but one race in the world who make any use of it, and they merely for a purpose which, of course, could not possibly exist here, unless – "

He allowed the rest of the sentence to go by default, and, turning, looked all round the place. For the first time he seemed to notice something unusual for the equipment of a stable, and regarded it with silent interest. It was nothing more nor less than a box, covered with sheets of virgin cork, and standing on the floor just under one of the windows, where the light and air could get to a weird-looking, rubbery-leaved, orchid-like plant, covered with ligulated scarlet blossoms which grew within it.

"Sir Henry," he said, after a moment, "may I ask how long it is since you were in South America?"

"I? Never was there in my life, Mr. Cleek – never."

"Ah! Then who connected with the hall has been?"

"Oh, I see what you are driving at," said Sir Henry, following the direction of his gaze. "That Patagonian plant, eh? That belonged to poor Tolliver. He had a strange fancy for ferns and rock plants and things of that description, and as that particular specimen happens to be one that does better in the atmosphere of a stable than elsewhere, he kept it in here."

"Who told him that it does better in the atmosphere of a stable?"

"Lady Wilding's cousin, Mr. Sharpless. It was he who gave Tolliver the plant."

"Oho! Then Mr. Sharpless has been to South America, has he?"

"Why, yes. As a matter of fact, he comes from there; so also does Lady Wilding. I should have thought you would have remembered that, Mr. Cleek, when – But perhaps you have never heard? She – they – that is," stammering confusedly and colouring to the temples, "up to seven months ago, Mr. Cleek, Lady Wilding was on the – er – music-hall stage. She and Mr. Sharpless were known as 'Signor Morando and La Belle Creole' and they did a living statue turn together. It was highly artistic; people raved; I – er – fell in love with the lady and – that's all!"

But it wasn't; for Cleek, reading between the lines, saw that the mad infatuation which had brought the lady a title and an over-generous husband had simmered down as such things always do sooner or later and that the marriage was very far from being a happy one. As a matter of fact, he learned later that the county, to a woman, had refused to accept Lady Wilding; that her ladyship, chafing under this ostracism, was for having a number of her old professional friends come down to visit her and make a time of it, and that, on Sir Henry's objecting, a violent quarrel had ensued, and the Rev. Ambrose Smeer had come down to the hall in the effort to make peace. And he learned something else that night which gave him food for deep reflection: the Rev. Ambrose Smeer, too, had been to South America. When he met that gentleman, in spite of the fact that Sir Henry thought so highly of him, and it was known that his revival meetings had done a world of good, Cleek did not fancy the Rev. Ambrose Smeer any more than he fancied the trainer, Logan.

But to return to the present. By this time the late-falling twilight of May had begun to close in, and presently — as the day was now done and the night approaching — Logan led in Black Riot from the paddock, followed by a slim, sallow-featured, small-moustached man, bearing a shotgun, and dressed in gray tweeds. Sir Henry, who, it was plain to see, had a liking for the man, introduced this newcomer to Cleek as the South American, Mr. Andrew Sharpless.

"That's the English of it, Mr. Cleek," said the latter jovially, but with an undoubted Spanish twist to the tongue. "I wouldn't have you risk breaking your jaw with the Brazilian original. Delighted to meet you, sir. I hope to Heaven you will get at the bottom of this diabolical thing. What do you think, Henry? Lambson-Bowles's jockey was over in this neighbourhood this afternoon. Trying to see how Black Riot shapes, of course, the bounder! Fortunately, I saw him skulking along on the other side of the hedge, and gave him two minutes in which to make himself scarce. If he hadn't, if he had come a step nearer to the mare, I'd have shot him down like a dog. That's right, Logan, put her up for the night, old chap, and I'll get out your bedding."

"Aye," said Logan, through his clamped teeth, "and God help man or devil that comes a-nigh her this night. God help him, Lunnon Mister, that's all Ah say!" Then he passed into the steel room with the mare, attended her for the night, and, coming out a minute or two later, locked her up and gave Sir Henry the key.

"Broke her and trained her, Ah did; and willin' to die for her, Ah am, if Ah can't pull un through no other way," he said, pausing before Cleek and giving him a black look. "A Derby winner her's cut out for, Lunnon Mister, and a Derby winner her's goin' to be, in spite of all the Lambson-Bowleses and the low-down horse-nobblers in Christendom!" Then he switched round and walked over to Sharpless, who had taken a pillow and a bundle of blankets from the convenient cupboard, and was making a bed of them on the floor at the foot of the locked steel door.

"Thanky, sir, 'bliged to un, sir," said Logan, as Sharpless hung up the shotgun and, with a word to the baronet, excused himself and went in to dress for dinner. Then he faced round again on Cleek, who was once more sniffing the air, and pointed to the rude bed: "There's where Ted Logan sleeps this night — there!" he went on suddenly; "and them as tries to get at Black Riot comes to grips with me first, me and the shotgun Mr. Sharpless has left Ah. And if Ah shoot, Lunnon Mister, Ah shoot to kill!"

Cleek turned to the baronet.

"Do me a favour, Sir Henry," he said. "For reasons of my own, I want to be in this stable alone for the next ten minutes, and after that let no one come into it until morning. I won't be accountable for this man's life if he stops in here to-night, and for his sake, as well as for your own, I want you to forbid him to do so."

Logan seemed to go nearly mad with rage at this.

"Ah won't listen to it! Ah will stop here, Ah will! Ah will!" he cried out in a passion. "Who comes ull find Ah here waitin' to come to grips with un. Ah won't stop out — Ah won't! Don't un listen to Lunnon Mister, Sir Henry, for God's sake, don't!"

"I am afraid I must, in this instance, Logan. You are far too suspicious, my good fellow. Mr. Cleek doesn't want to 'get at' the mare; he wants to protect her; to keep anybody else from getting at her, so join the guard outside if you are so eager. You must let him have his way." And, in spite of all Logan's pleading, Cleek did have his way.

Protesting, swearing, almost weeping, the trainer was turned out and the doors closed, leaving Cleek alone in the stable; and the last Logan and Sir Henry saw of him until he came out and rejoined them he was standing in the middle of the floor, with his hands on both hips, staring fixedly at the impromptu bed in front of the steel-room door.

"Put on the guard now and see that nobody goes into the place until morning, Sir Henry," he said, when he came out and rejoined them some minutes later. "Logan, you silly fellow, you'll do no good fighting against Fate. Make the best of it and stop where you are."

That night Cleek met Lady Wilding for the first time. He found her what he afterward termed "a splendid animal," beautiful, statuesque, more of Juno than of Venus, and freely endowed with the languorous temperament and the splendid earthy loveliness which grows nowhere but under tropical skies and in the shadow of palm groves and the flame of cactus flowers. She showed him but scant courtesy, however, for she was but a poor hostess, and after dinner carried her cousin away to the billiard-room, and left her husband to entertain the Rev. Ambrose and the detective as best he could. Cleek needed but little entertaining, however, for in spite of his serenity he was full of the case on hand, and kept wandering in and out of the house and upstairs and down until eleven o'clock came and bed claimed him with the rest.

His last wakeful recollection was of the clock in the lower corridor striking the first quarter after eleven; then sleep claimed him, and he knew no more until all the stillness was suddenly shattered by a loud-voiced gong hammering out an alarm and the sound of people tumbling out of bed and scurrying about in a panic of fright. He jumped out of bed, pulled on his clothing, and rushed out into the hall, only to find it alive with startled people, and at their head Sir Henry, with a dressing-gown thrown on over his pyjamas and a bedroom candle in his shaking hand.

"The stable!" he cried out excitedly. "Come on, come on, for God's sake. Some one has touched the door of the steel room; and yet the place was left empty, empty!"

But it was no longer empty, as they found out when they reached it, for the doors had been flung open, the men who had been left on guard outside the stables were now inside it, the electric lights were in full blaze, the shotgun still hanging where Sharpless had left it, the impromptu bed was tumbled and tossed in a man's death agony, and at the foot of the steel door Logan lay, curled up in a heap and stone dead!

"He would get in, Sir Henry; he'd have shot one or the other of us if we hadn't let him," said one of the outer guards, as Sir Henry and Cleek appeared. "He would lie before the door and watch, sir, he simply would; and God have mercy on him, poor chap; he was faithful to the last!"

"And the last might not have come for years, the fool, if he had only obeyed," said Cleek; then lapsed into silence and stood staring at a dust of white flour on the red-tiled floor and at a thin wavering line that broke the even surface of it.

III

It was perhaps two minutes later when the entire household, mistress, guests, and servants alike, came trooping across the open space between the hall and the stables in a state of semi-deshabille, but in that brief space of time friendly hands had reverently lifted the body of the dead man from its place before the steel door, and Sir Henry was nervously fitting the key to the lock in a frantic effort to get in and see if Black Riot was safe.

"*Dios!* what is it? What has happened?" cried Lady Wilding, as she came hurrying in, followed closely by Sharpless and the Rev. Ambrose Smeer. Then, catching sight of Logan's body, she gave a little scream and covered her eyes. "The trainer, Andrew, the trainer now!" she went on half hysterically. "Another death — another! Surely they have got the wretch at last?"

"The mare! The mare, Henry! Is she safe?" exclaimed Sharpless excitedly, as he whirled away from his cousin's side and bore down upon the baronet. "Give me the key, you're too nervous." And, taking it from him, unlocked the steel room and passed swiftly into it.

In another instant Black Riot was led out, uninjured, untouched, in the very pink of condition and, in spite of the tragedy and the dead man's presence, one or two of the guards were so carried away that they essayed a cheer.

"Stop that! Stop it instantly!" rapped out Sir Henry, facing round upon them. "What's a horse, even the best, beside the loss of an honest life like that?" and flung out a shaking hand in the direction of dead Logan. "It will be the story of last night over again, of course? You heard his scream, heard his fall, but he was dead when you got to him – dead – and you found no one here?"

"Not a soul, Sir Henry. The doors were all locked; no grille is missing from any window; no one is in the loft; no one in any of the stalls; no one in any crook or corner of the place."

"Send for the constable, the justice of the peace, anybody!" chimed in the Rev. Ambrose Smeer at this. "Henry, will you never be warned; never take these awful lessons to heart? This sinful practice of racing horses for money – "

"Oh, hush, hush! Don't preach me a sermon now, uncle," interposed Sir Henry. "My heart's torn, my mind crazed by this abominable thing. Poor old Logan! Poor, faithful old chap! Oh!" He whirled and looked over at Cleek, who still stood inactive, staring at the flour-dusted floor. "And they said that no mystery was too great for you to get at the bottom of it, no riddle too complex for you to find the answer? Can't you do something? Can't you suggest something? Can't you see any glimmer of light at all?"

Cleek looked up, and that curious smile which Narkom knew so well, and would have known had he been there was the "danger signal," looped up one corner of his mouth.

"I fancy it is *all* 'light,' Sir Henry," he said. "I may be wrong, but I fancy it is merely a question of comparative height. Do I puzzle you by that? Well, let me explain. Lady Wilding there is one height, Mr. Sharpless is another, and I am a third; and if they two were to place themselves side by side, and, say, about four inches apart, and I were to stand immediately behind them, the difference would be most apparent. There you are. Do you grasp it?"

"Not in the least."

"Bothered if I do either," supplemented Sharpless. "It all

sounds like tommy rot to me."

"Does it?" said Cleek. "Then let me explain it by illustration," and he walked quietly toward them. "Lady Wilding, will you oblige me by standing here? Thank you very much. Now, if you please, Mr. Sharpless, will you stand beside her ladyship while I take up my place here immediately behind you both? That's it exactly. A little nearer, please — just a little, so that your left elbow touches her ladyship's right. Now then," his two hands moved briskly, there was a click-click; and then: "There you are; that explains it, my good Mr. and Mrs. Filippo Bucarelli; explains it completely!"

And as he stepped aside on saying this, those who were watching, those who heard Lady Wilding's scream and Mr. Sharpless's snarling oath and saw them vainly try to spring apart and dart away, saw also that a steel handcuff was on the woman's right wrist, its mate on the man's left one, and that they were firmly chained together.

"In the name of heaven, man," began Sir Henry, appalled by this, and growing red and white by rapid turns.

"I fancy that heaven has very little to do with this precious pair, Sir Henry," interposed Cleek. "You want the two people who are accountable for these diabolical crimes, and there they stand."

"What! Do you mean to tell me that Sharpless, that my wife – "

"Don't give the lady a title to which she has not and never had any legal right, Sir Henry. If it had ever occurred to you to emulate my example to-night and search the lady's effects, you would have found that she was christened Enriqua Dolores Torjada, and that she was married to Señor Filippo Bucarelli here, at Valparaiso in Chili, three years ago, and that her marriage to you was merely a clever little scheme to get hold of a pot of money and share it with her rascally husband."

"It's a lie!" snarled out the male prisoner. "It's an infernal policeman's lie! You never found any such thing!"

"Pardon me, but I did," replied Cleek serenely. "And what's more, I found the little phial of coriander and oil of sassafras in your room, señor, and I shall finish off the Mynga Worm in another ten minutes!"

Bucarelli and his wife gave a mingled cry, and, chained together though they were, made a wild bolt for the door; only, however, to be met on the threshold by the local constable to whom Cleek had dispatched a note some hours previously.

"Thank you, Mr. Philpotts; you are very prompt," he said. "There are your prisoners nicely trussed and waiting for you. Take them away, we are quite done with them here. Sir Henry" — he turned to the baronet — "if Black Riot is fitted to win the Derby she will win it and you need have no more fear for her safety. No one has ever for one moment tried to get at her. You yourself were the one that precious pair were after, and the bait was your life assurance. By killing off the watchers over Black Riot one by one they knew that there would come a time, when, being able to get no one else to take the risk of guarding the horse and sleeping on that bed before the steel-room door, you would do it yourself; and when that time came they would have had you."

"But how? By what means?"

"By one of the most diabolical imaginable. Among the reptiles of Patagonia, Sir Henry, there is one, a species of black adder, known in the country as the Mynga Worm whose bite is more deadly than that of the rattler or the copperhead, and as rapid in its action as prussic acid itself. It has, too, a great velocity of movement and a peculiar power of springing and hurling itself upon its prey. The Patagonians are a barbarous people in the main and, like all barbarous people, are vengeful, cunning, and subtle. A favourite revenge of theirs upon unsuspecting enemies is to get within touch of them and secretly to smear a mixture of coriander and oil of sassafras upon some part of their bodies, and then either to lure or drive them into the forest. By a peculiar arrangement of Mother Nature this mixture has a fascination, a maddening effect upon the Mynga Worm, just as a red rag has on a bull, and, enraged by the scent, it finds the spot smeared with it and delivers its deadly bite."

"Good heaven! How horrible! And you mean to tell me – "

"That they employed one of those deadly reptiles in this case? Yes, Sir Henry. I suspected it the very moment I smelt the odour of the coriander and sassafras, but I suspected that an animal or a reptile of some kind was at the bottom of the mystery at a prior period. That is why I wanted the flour. Look! Do you see where I sifted it over this spot near the Patagonian plant? And do you see those serpentine tracks through the middle of it? The Mynga Worm is there in that box, at the roots of that plant. Now see!"

He caught up a horse blanket, spread it on the floor, lifted the box and plant, set them down in the middle of it and, with a quick gathering up of the ends of the blanket, converted it into a bag and tied it round with a hitching strap.

"Get spades, forks, anything, and dig a hole outside in the paddock," he went on. "Make a deep hole, a yard deep at the least – then get some straw, some paraffin, turpentine, anything that will burn furiously and quickly, and we will soon finish the little beast."

The servants flew to obey, and when the hole was dug, he carried the bag out and lowered it carefully into it, covered it with straw, drenched this with a gallon or more of lamp oil, and rapidly applied a match to it and sprang back.

A moment later those who were watching saw a small black snake make an ineffectual effort to leap out of the blazing mass, fall back into the flames, and disappear forever.

* * * * *

"The method of procedure?" said Cleek, answering the baronet's query as the latter was pouring out what he called "a nerve settler" prior to following the Rev. Ambrose's example and going to bed. "Very cunning, and yet very, very simple, Sir Henry. Bucarelli made a practice, as I saw this evening, of helping the chosen watcher to make his bed on the floor in front of the door to the steel room, but during the time he was removing the blankets from the cupboard his plan was to smear them with the coriander and sassafras and so arrange the top blanket that when the watcher lay down, the stuff touched his neck or throat and made that the point of attack for the snake, whose fang makes a small round spot not bigger than the end of a knitting needle, which is easily passed over by those not used to looking for such a thing. There was such a spot on Tolliver's throat; such another at the base of Murple's skull, and there is a third in poor Logan's left temple. No, no more, please; this is quite enough. Success to Black Riot and the Derby! The riddle is solved, Sir Henry. Good-night!"

CHAPTER X
THE RIDDLE OF THE SIVA STONES

Cleek threw aside his newspaper as the telephone jingled, and walking to the instrument, unhooked the receiver.

"Hallo!" he said; then, a second later, "Yes. This is Captain Burbage speaking," he added, and stood silent, waiting. Not for long, however. Almost instantly the connecting line hummed with the sound of some one at the other end whistling the opening bars of "God Save the King," and that settled it.

"You, is it, Mr. Narkom?" Cleek said, as the anthem broke off at an agreed point, which point, by the way, was altered every twenty-four hours. "No, nothing in particular. I was only reading the account of Black Riot's Derby. Ripping, wasn't it? Half a yard ahead of the nearest competitor, and Minnow nowhere. What? Yes, certainly, if you want me. A great hurry, eh? Yes, start this minute if that will do. What's that? Yes; I know the place well. All right. I'll be there almost as soon as you are. Good-bye," and he switched off the line instantly.

Five minutes later, accompanied by Dollops bearing the inevitable brown leather kit-bag, in case a change of attire should be found necessary, he emerged from the house in Clarges Street, walked down Piccadilly as far as Duke Street, turned from that into Jermyn Street, and strolled leisurely along in the direction of the Geological Museum, keeping a sharp look-out, however, for the red limousine.

Of a sudden it came pelting round the corner of Regent Street, whizzed along until Lennard, the chauffeur, caught sight of the well-known figure, then swung to the kerb close to the corner of York Street and came to an abrupt halt. In another moment Cleek had taken the brown kit-bag from Dollops, stepped with it into the vehicle, and was by Narkom's side.

"Well," he said, gripping the superintendent's welcoming hand and settling himself comfortably as the motor swung out into the roadway again and continued on its way. "Here I am, you see, Mr. Narkom, and," nodding toward the kit-bag, "pre-

240

pared for any emergency, as they say in the melodramas. It isn't often you give me a 'hurry call' like this, so it's fair to suppose that you have something of unusual importance on hand."

"If you said I had something positively amazing on hand you'd come a deal nearer the mark, my dear fellow," returned the superintendent. "The steel-room case was a fool to it for mystery, although it is not entirely unlike it in some respects; for the thing happened behind locked doors, and there's no clue to when, where, or how the assassin got in nor the ghost of an explanation to be given as to how he got out again. That is where the two cases are alike; but where they differ, is the most amazing point; for the dickens of it is that whereas the steel room was a stable and there were a few people on guard, this crime was committed in a house filled with company. A reception was in progress, yet not only was one of the best-known figures in London society done to death under the very noses, so to speak, of her friends and acquaintances, but jewels of immense value, jewels of historical interest, in fact, were carried off in the most unaccountable manner. In brief, my dear Cleek, the victim was the aged Duchess of Heatherlands; the jewels that have vanished are those two marvellous blush-pink diamonds known to the world of gem collectors as 'The Siva Stones.' Surely, you whose knowledge seems unlimited" – noting the blank look on Cleek's face – "must have heard of those divine gems?"

"Indeed, yes," replied Cleek. "I have good reason to know of them, as I shall prove to you presently. My knowledge of the diamonds is so complete that I can tell you at once that they weigh twenty-four and one sixty-fifth carats each; that, apart from their marvellous and most unusual colour, a delicate azalea pink, like the first flush of the morning, they are, perhaps, the most perfectly cut and most perfectly matched pair of diamonds in the world. What may be their earliest history it is impossible to state. All that is positively known of them is that they once formed two of the three eyes of the god Siva, and that they were abstracted from the head of the idol during the loot of the Hindu temples after Clive's defeat of Suraja Dowlah, in 1757. They were subsequently brought to England, where, in course of time, they passed into the possession of the fifth Duke of Heatherlands, who bestowed them upon his wife as a personal gift, so that they were never at any time included in the entail."

"My dear Cleek," said Narkom, looking at him with positive bewilderment, "is there anything you do not know? It is positively marvellous that you should be in possession of all these details regarding the Siva stones."

Cleek looked down at his toes and a faint flush reddened his drooping face.

"Not so marvellous as you may think, Mr. Narkom, when I tell you the genesis of it," he said with a slight show of embarrassment. "The S'aivas, or worshippers of Siva, have never relaxed their efforts to regain possession of the stones and return them to their place in the head of their desecrated idol. They have, in fact, offered immense sums to the successive holders of them, and an immense reward to anybody who shall be instrumental in restoring them. In the old times, in my vanishing cracksman days, I once planned to get that reward by stealing the gems, and if I had lived that life another month — if the eyes of a woman had not dimmed the splendid opulence of these cold eyes of a god - " His voice sank and dropped off into silence, and Narkom had the good sense and the good taste to look out of the window and say nothing.

"And so these remarkable diamonds have been stolen after all, have they?" said Cleek, breaking silence suddenly. "And that vulgar and overbearing old shrew, the Dowager Duchess of Heatherlands, has paid for the possession of them with her life! Ah, my dear Mr. Narkom, what a disastrous thing lust of power and craving for position is! The lady would better have stuck to her father's beer vats and the glory of Hobson and Simkin's entire, and Heatherlands might better have left her there instead of selling her the right to wear his ducal coronet. They both would have lived and died a deal happier, I am sure."

"Yes," agreed Narkom. "They lived a veritable cat-and-dog life, I believe, although it was years before my time, or yours either, for the matter of that, so I can only speak from hearsay. His

242

Grace didn't find Miss Simkins, the brewer's daughter, so enviable a possession after marriage as she had appeared before; and, as she held the purse-strings — and held them closely, too — he got precious little but abuse and unhappiness out of the bargain. The lady, feeling herself miles above her former connections when she became duchess, cut her own people completely; and as her husband's family would have none of her at any price, she simply made enemies for herself on both sides. It was perhaps just as well for all concerned that there were no children."

"And at the duke's death some ten or a dozen years ago, the title passed, I believe, to his younger brother, who in his turn died about eighteen months ago and passed it on to a cousin, a young fellow of about two-and-twenty, who had recently married a girl as little blest with this world's goods as was he himself."

"Yes," replied Narkom. "And as his grandmother was one of the ladies who had been bitterest in cutting the ex-Miss Simkins, the old girl never let any of her sympathies or her sovereigns go his way. Of course he tried to make up to her, talked about 'upholding the dignity of the name,' and all that, but it was no go; old money-bags wouldn't part with a stiver. So the interview wound up with some pretty plain speaking on both sides, and the young duke flung himself out of the house in a towering passion and with no good will toward her, which was a bad thing all round, and particularly bad for him."

"Why?"

"Because that happened only the day before yesterday. Last night the old duchess was murdered, and, so far as can be ascertained with certainty, he was the last person with her and the last to see her alive."

"Hum-m-m!" said Cleek, pulling down his lower lip and frowning at his toes. "Not nice that, for the duke, I must admit."

"Not at all nice," agreed Narkom. "As a matter of fact, I should not be at all surprised if a warrant for his arrest were issued before morning. Still, of course, there is the Hindu to be taken into consideration. As you yourself said, those beggars have always been after the stones."

"Oho! So there's a Hindu in the affair, is there?"

"Yes. Been hanging about the place for weeks and weeks, trying to make friends with the servants. Peddles embroidered table covers, silk scarves, crêpe shawls, lucky charms, and things of that sort. Hasn't missed coming, the housekeeper tells me, one solitary day for the past month until the present one. Of course, he may turn up before night, although it's hours and hours past his regular time for calling; but, at the same time, it must be admitted that it has a queer look.

"Then, too, there's a third party, or, indeed, I might as well say a third and a fourth, for they are brother and sister, a Miss Lucretia Spender and her brother Tom. They're relations of the late duchess on the Simkins's side. Mother was an aunt of hers. Not particularly prepossessing, either of them. Run a second-hand clothing shop over in Camden Town; down on their luck and expected the brokers in. Came to see the duchess in the effort to borrow money. She bundled them out neck and crop, and the brokers did come in and they went out into the streets, poor wretches. That was ten days ago. But both were seen hanging about the house last night as late as eleven o'clock. The murder was committed and the jewels stolen somewhere between midnight and three o'clock in the morning."

Cleek looked up.

"Suppose you begin the thing at the beginning instead of giving me the case piecemeal in this fashion, Mr. Narkom," he said. "How did it all start? Was the duchess giving an entertainment last night?"

"No; but Captain and Mrs. Harvey Glossop were, and the thing happened at their house, within a stone's throw of Hyde Park Corner."

"Captain Harvey Glossop," repeated Cleek. "Happen by any chance that he's related to Glossop, the big company promoter who floated 'Sapavo' and made 'Oxine' a household word three years ago?"

"Same man. Worth a million sterling if he's worth a penny. Isn't really a military man, you know. Was 'captain' in the volunteers up to the time of their disbanding. Topping fine fellow, popular everywhere. Makes money hand over fist, and gives the best dinners in town, they say."

"Two very excellent passports to Society under modern conditions," commented Cleek. "Well, go on. Captain and Mrs. Glossop were giving a reception, and Her Grace of Heatherlands was there?"

"Yes — as their guest. As a matter of fact she had been their guest for the past eight months. She and Mrs. Glossop took a great fancy to each other when they met at Nice last October, and the duchess, being entirely alone and getting too old to care much for social affairs, rented her house in Park Lane to an American family, and took up her abode with the Glossops. A suite of rooms was placed at her disposal, and, since, unlike most feminine friendships, this one grew warmer and closer every day, she appears to have been perfectly comfortable and happy for the first time in many years."

"Good. Let us have the story of last night now, please. How did the duchess come to have the Siva stones in her personal possession at that time? Surely she was not insane enough to keep the gems in the house with her?"

"No; she never did that. They were always in the strong room at her banker's. She hadn't even seen them, much less worn them, for years until, on her order, they were brought to her from the bank yesterday morning so that she might appear in them last night, for last night was an exceptional occasion."

"In what particular way?"

"It was to be Mrs. Glossop's last 'at home' for a long, long time. Her health not being very good of late, the doctors had ordered a voyage to the Cape, and everything has long been in readiness for her departure next Wednesday fortnight. As last night's affair was in the nature of a sort of leave-taking, the duchess resolved to come out of her recent retirement and to wear the famous Siva stones. She did so. I hear from Captain Glossop that she made her appearance so covered with jewels that she appeared like a jeweller's window, in the midst of which shone the two amazing diamonds, suspended by a slender chain about her neck, and putting every other jewel she wore to shame by their gorgeous magnificence."

"I can well imagine that they would, Mr. Narkom. They produced a sensation, of course?"

"Rather! The captain tells me that they fairly took away his breath. It was the first time either he or his wife had ever seen them; indeed, it appears that it was the first time the young Duke of Heatherlands himself, who, with his bride, was present, had set eyes upon the appallingly magnificent things. He was heard to say to his young duchess that it was 'not only beastly vulgar, but beastly rough — Heatherland Court with a ton weight of mortgages upon it, you without so much as a decent bracelet, and all that money locked up and useless, when a tenth of it would put baby and us in clover!'"

"He was right there, Mr. Narkom; it was rough. He, with a wife and a little son, and loaded down with debts and cares at three-and-twenty, and the duchess with millions lying idle and unheeded at eighty-three! Well, go on, please; what followed?"

"After remaining 'on exhibition' until half-past eleven," resumed the superintendent, "the duchess took leave of the other guests, kissed Mrs. Glossop good-night, and retired to her own rooms with the avowed intention of going to bed. About twelve minutes later the young Duke of Heatherlands, too, left the room, and went up after her."

"Hum-m-m! What for?"

"He says for the purpose of making one final appeal to her, to what womanhood was in her, by showing her the miniature his wife wore of their little son and heir. The old duchess's maid says that she met him on the stairs as she was coming down, and told him that her mistress was sitting in her tea-gown taking her regular glass of hot whisky-and-water before getting into bed; so he would have to be quick if he wished to speak to her for, as soon as she had finished that, she would lock and bolt the door and go to bed forthwith.

"He says, however, that when he got to the room the door was already locked, that in answer to his knocking and appealing the old duchess had merely told him to go about his business. She said she paid her rates and taxes to support unions and work-houses for paupers, and that she wasn't going to support any on the outside.

"After that, he says, he came away, knowing that it was hopeless, went down and rejoined his wife, and in five or ten minutes' time they said good-night to their host and hostess and went home. That was the very last interview, so far as anybody has been able to discover, that any one had with the Dowager Duchess of Heatherlands. On account of the weak state of Mrs. Glossop's health, the entertainment broke up early. At half-past twelve the final guest took his departure; at one, Captain Glossop's man helped his master to undress and get into his bed. At the same moment Mrs. Glossop's maid performed a like office for her mistress, saw her in hers, put out the light, and in another ten minutes every soul in the house was between sheets and asleep.

"At three o'clock, however, a startling thing occurred. Godwin, the cook, waking thirsty and finding her water-bottle empty, rose and went downstairs to fill it. She returned in a panic to rouse the housekeeper, Mrs. Condiment, and tell her that there was a light burning in the old duchess's room, its reflection being clearly visible under the door and through the keyhole. She, the cook, had knocked on the door to inquire if anything was wanted, as she knew the duchess's maid was asleep in another part of the house. But she had been unable to get any sort of a response.

"Well, to make a long story short, my dear Cleek," went on Narkom, "the household was roused, the door of the duchess's room was found to be both locked and bolted on the inside — so securely that, all other efforts to open it proving unavailing, an axe had to be procured and the barrier hacked down. When the last fragment fell and the captain and his servants could get into the room, a horrible sight awaited them. On the duchess's dressing-table her two bedroom candles were still burning, just as the maid says she left them when she went out and met the young duke coming up the stairs; on the bed lay the duchess herself, stone dead, a noosed rope drawn tightly round her neck, used, no doubt, to keep her from calling out, and the bedding was literally saturated with the blood which flowed from several stab wounds in the breast, the side, and the fleshy upper part of both arms."

"Hum-m-m!" commented Cleek. "That looks as if she had struggled very desperately, and one would hardly expect that from a woman of her advanced years and choked into breathlessness at that. Still, her arms could not have been cut otherwise; arms are not vital parts, and the maddest of assassins would know that. So, of course, they were either slashed unavoidably in a desperate death struggle or, else – " His brows knotted, his voice slipped off into reflective silence. He took his chin between his thumb and forefinger and squeezed it hard. After a moment, however: "Mr. Narkom," he inquired, "were the Siva stones found to have been stolen at the same time that the body was discovered, or was their loss learned of later?"

"Oh, at the very instant the body was discovered, my dear chap. It could hardly have been overlooked for so much as an instant, for the slender chain upon which they had formerly hung was lying across the body, the setting of the gems had been prised open and the diamond removed."

"Singular circumstances, both."

"In what way, Cleek?"

"Well, for one thing, it shows that the assassin must have had plenty of time and a very good reason for taking the stones without their setting. If he hadn't, he'd have grabbed the thing and done that elsewhere. Must have taken them to the light for the purpose and laid them down upon some firm, hard surface; you can't pick a diamond out of a good setting without some little difficulty, Mr. Narkom, and certainly not in the palm of your hand. Why, then, should the assassin have brought the chain back after that operation and laid it upon the body of the victim?

Rather looks as if he wanted the fact that the stones had disappeared to be apparent at first glance. Any other jewels stolen at the same time?"

"No; only the Siva stones."

"Hum-m-m! And the noosed rope that was about the neck of the murdered woman; what was that like? Something that had been brought from outside the house or something that could be picked up within it?"

"As a matter of fact, my dear fellow, it was part of the bell-rope that belonged to that very room. It had been cut off and converted into a noose."

"Oho!" said Cleek. "I see — I see!" Then, after a moment: "Pull down the blinds of the limousine, will you, Mr. Narkom?" he added as he bent and picked up the kit-bag. "I want to do a little bit in the way of a change; and, if you are proceeding directly to the scene of the murder – "

"I am, dear chap. Any idea, Cleek?"

"Bushels. Tell you if they're worth anything after I've seen the body. If they are – Well, I shall either have the Siva stones in my hand before eight o'clock to-night, or – "

"Yes, old chap? Or what?"

"Or the Hindu's got 'em and they're already out of the country for good and all. And — Mr. Narkom, 'George Headland' will do, if you please."

II

Lennard having slackened the speed of the motor considerably, and in addition taken two or three wide curves out of the direct line, it was quite half-past four when the limousine stopped in front of the Glossop residence, about which a curious collection of morbid-minded people had gathered. There alighted therefrom, first the superintendent, and then the over-dressed figure with the lank, fair hair and the fresh-coloured, insipid countenance of as perfect a specimen of the genus sap-head as you could pick up anywhere between John o' Groat's and Land's End. A flower was in his buttonhole, a monocle in his eye, and the gold head of his jointed walking-stick was sucked into the red eyelet of his puckered-up lips.

"Oh, yez! Oh, yez!" sang out derisively a bedraggled female on the edge of the crowd as this utterly unrecognizable edition of Cleek stepped out upon the pavement. "Oh, yez! Oh, yez! 'Ere's to give notice! Them's the bright sparks wot rides in motor-cars, them is, and my poor 'usband a hoofin' of it all the dies of 'is blessed life!"

"Move on, now — move on!" cautioned the constable on guard, waving her aside and making a clear passage for the superintendent and his companion across the pavement and up the steps. And a moment later Cleek was in the house, in the morning-room, in the presence of Captain Harvey Glossop, his wife, and the young Duke of Heatherlands.

The lady was a pale, fragile-looking woman of about three-and-twenty, very beautiful, very well bred, low-voiced, and altogether charming. Her husband was some five or six years her senior, a genial, kindly man with a winning smile, an engaging personality, and the manners of one used to the good things of life and, like all people who really are used to them, making no boast of it and putting on no "side" whatsoever. As for the young duke — well, he was just an impetuous, hot-headed, hot-tongued, lovable boy, the kind of chap who, in a moment of temper, would swear to have your heart's blood, but, if you stumbled and fell the next moment, would risk breaking his neck to get to you and help you and offer you his last shilling to cab it home.

"Well, here I am, you see, Mr. Narkom," blurted out his impulsive Grace as the superintendent and Cleek came in. "If any of your lot want me they won't have to hunt me up and they won't find me funking it, no matter how black it looks for me. I didn't kill her, I didn't even get to see her; and anybody that says I did, lies — that's all!"

"My dear Heatherlands," protested the captain, "don't work

yourself up into such a pitch of excitement. I don't suppose Mr. Narkom has come here to arrest you. It is just as black with regard to that mysterious Hindu fellow, remember. Perhaps a little blacker when you come to recall how suddenly and mysteriously he has disappeared. And, certainly, his motive looks quite as strong as yours."

"I haven't any motive — I never did have one, and I take it beastly unkind of you to say that, Glossop!" blurted out the young duke impetuously. "Just because I'm hard up is no reason why I should commit murder and robbery. What could I want with the Siva stones? I couldn't sell them, could I, marked things that every diamond dealer in the world knows? Oh, yes, I know what people say: I could have turned them over to the Hindu and claimed the reward; that perhaps I did and that that's why this particular Hindu has disappeared. But it's not true. I didn't have anything to do with it. I didn't get into the room at all last night. And even if I had I couldn't have bolted it on the inside after I'd left it, could I? If you and your lot want me, Mr. Narkom, I'm here, and I'll face every charge they can bring against me."

"Pardon me, your Grace, but I'm not here for the purpose of apprehending anybody," replied Narkom suavely. "My errand is of a totally different sort, I assure you. Captain Glossop, allow me to make you acquainted with a great friend of mine, Mr. George Headland. Mr. Headland is an amateur investigator of criminal matters, and he has taken a fancy to look into the details of this one. It may be that he will stumble upon something of importance — who knows? And in such an affair as this I deem it best to leave no stone unturned, no chance untried."

"Quite so, Mr. Narkom, quite so," agreed the captain. "Mr. Headland, I am delighted to meet you, though, of course, I should have preferred to do so under happier circumstances."

"Thanks very much," said Cleek with an inane drawl, but a quick, searching look out of the corner of his eye at the young duke. "Awfully good of you to say so, I'm sure. Your Grace, pleased to meet you. Charmed, Mrs. Glossop. Yes, thanks, I will have a cup of tea. So nice of you to suggest it."

"Must be rather interesting work, this looking into criminal matters on your own initiative, Mr. Headwood — pardon, Headland, is it? Do forgive me, but I have a most abominable memory for names," said the captain. "Believe me, I shall be willing to give you any possible assistance that I can in the present unhappy case."

"Thanks — jolly kind of you, and I very much appreciate it, I assure you," returned Cleek in his best "blithering idiot" fashion. "Should be ever so much obliged if you'd — er — permit me to view the scene of the tragedy and the — er — body of the deceased, don't you know. Of course, Mr. Narkom has said I may, but — er — after all, an Englishman's house is his castle and all that, so it's only polite to ask."

"Oh, certainly, do so by all means, Mr. Headland. You will excuse my saying it, but I doubt if you will find any clues there, however, for the regular officials have already been over the ground."

"Searched the room, have they, in quest of the diamonds? Thieves do funny things sometimes, you know, and it's just possible that they got in a funk and hid the things instead of taking them away."

"Well, of all the blessed id – " began the young duke, looking over at him disgustedly; and then discreetly stopped and left the term unfinished.

"I fancy, my dear Headland," interposed Narkom, "I neglected to tell you that the captain had my men search the place from top to bottom, go through every cupboard, into every nook and corner, turn out the servants' boxes — even his own and Mrs. Glossop's, as well — so that it is certain the jewels could not have been concealed anywhere about the premises either by accident or design. Nothing was found — nothing. The Siva stones have utterly and completely disappeared."

"And no other jewels besides?"

"Not a solitary one, Mr. Headland."

"Rum sort of a thief, wasn't it, to cut off with only half the booty? The duchess must have had lots of other jewels and there were Mrs. Glossop's, too. Those superb rings of yours, for instance, madam, fancy a burglar getting in and not paying his respects to those. Pardon me – " Her hand a-glitter with splendid flashing diamonds was resting on the edge of the tea table. He bent over and looked at them closely. Naturally she resented this under the circumstances, but though her cheeks flushed she let the hand rest where it was until he had studied it to his heart's content.

"May I say, Mr. Headland, that all her Grace's jewels have been identified by her banker, to whose care the police have returned them," she said with just the shadow of an indignant note in her low, sweet voice. "These have been in my possession for years, thank you. A thousand people can testify to that; and the insinuation is not nice."

"My dear madam, I assure you I had not the slightest thought – "

"Very likely not. As a matter of fact, I don't see how you could, Mr. Headland; but under these distressing and extraordinary circumstances it was an unhappy attention and a most suggestive one. Pray say no more about it. You are at liberty, Mr. Narkom, to show Mr. Headland over the house whenever he chooses to investigate it."

And as he chose to investigate it at that moment the superintendent led the way to the death chamber forthwith.

"I say, old chap, that was a bit thick, and no mistake," whispered Narkom as they went up the stairs. "To be talking about the dead woman's jewels and then to stoop and examine Mrs. Glossop's own — a woman worth millions!"

"Clear your mind of the idea that I meant to suggest anything of that sort at all, Mr. Narkom," Cleek replied. "It was the beauty of the rings themselves that appealed to me — that, and the wonder of the circumstances."

"Circumstances? What circumstances?"

"Two very extraordinary ones. First: why a woman of such evident taste, breeding, and position as Mrs. Glossop should choose to load her fingers with diamond rings in the daytime; and, second, why she should choose this particular day of all others to do so."

"Possibly she neglected to take them off when she went to bed last night and, in the excitement of the things which have happened since, has thought no more about them. But here's the room at last. Still on duty, I see, Hammond." This to the plain-clothes officer before the door of the death chamber. "Yes, going in; thanks. Come along, Headland."

Then the improvised door opened, closed again, and Cleek and the superintendent stood in the presence of it — the silent, immutable It which yesterday had been a living woman. Cleek went over and looked at the quiet figure, particularly at the wounds on the arms, both of them close to the shoulder, and immediately below the larger, muscle, then turned and looked round the room. It was richly appointed, indeed, the suite had been especially fitted up for her Grace's occupancy, and was, as might have been expected in such a house, in extremely good taste from the rich, dull-coloured Indian carpet to the French paper on the walls. This was a striped paper in two tones of white, one glazed slightly, the other dull, like two ribbons — a white velvet and a white silk one — drawn straight down over its surface from ceiling to floor at regular distances of half a yard apart. He admired that paper, and it interested him!

"Here, you see, old chap, not a possibility of anybody getting in or out save by the door which we ourselves have just entered," said Narkom, opening one door which led into a dressing-room, another leading to a spacious and richly appointed sitting-room, and a third which gave access to a porcelain bath set in a marble-floored, marble-walled apartment lighted and aired by a window of painted glass. "All windows and all doors locked on the inside when the body was found, and everything as you see it now; no furniture upset, no sign of a struggle. There is the bell-rope that was cut; there the noose that was made from it; and there on the dressing-table the bedroom candles that were found burning just as the maid left them when she went out and met the young duke coming up the stairs."

Cleek walked over and looked at the candles.

"If I remember correctly, Mr. Narkom," he said, "I believe you told me that her Grace retired to this room at half-past eleven, and that something like twelve or fifteen minutes later the young duke came up for the purpose of speaking to her. That would make it somewhere in the close neighbourhood of a quarter to twelve when the maid left her mistress; and it was three o'clock in the morning, was it not, when the murder was discovered? Hum-m-m! Singular, most singular, amazingly so!"

"What?"

"The condition of these two candles. Look at them," said he, taking one out of the silver holder and extending it for Narkom's examination. "One would suppose that candles which had been burning for three hours and a quarter would be fairly well consumed, Mr. Narkom; yet, look at these. They are hardly an inch shorter than the regulation length, so that they cannot have burned for more than a quarter of an hour at most! Now, granting that the duchess herself burnt them for ten minutes in undressing and imbibing her nightly whisky-and-water — and that would just about tally with the young duke's assertion that the door was locked and her Grace in bed when he reached the room — that would leave them to have been burning for just five minutes when the cook, Godwin, says she discovered the light shining under the door and through the keyhole."

"By George, you're right. We must have a word with that cook, Cleek. Either she lied about the time, or else – Great Scott, man! What if she, that cook, that Godwin woman, had a hand in it — was herself in league with the murderer — even let him out of the house before she gave the alarm? Good heaven, Cleek, we mustn't let that woman get away!"

"She won't — if she's guilty. I'll tell you that for certain if you can manage to find out what preparations, if any, have as yet been made for the duchess's funeral."

"But, man alive, what can that have to do with it?"

"Perhaps a great deal; perhaps nothing at all. Just slip down-stairs, will you, and, without giving the subject away, or mention-ing anything about the candles, do a little quiet 'pumping' of the young duke. See if he knows, or has any plans. I seem to fancy that I have heard somewhere of a splendid mausoleum being built by the Dowager Duchess of Heatherlands and the young duke will know if it's so or not. Pump him, I'll stop here until you return."

It was a full twenty minutes before the superintendent got the information he wanted and came back with it.

"Well?" said Cleek, as he came in. "There is a mausoleum be-ing built, is there not?"

"Yes. The murdered woman has been having it built for the past five or six months for the express purpose of having herself and her late husband entombed there, apart from all other Hea-therlands and with all the pomp of dead royalty. The structure will not be completed for quite another half year. In the mean-time, as this tragical affair has disorganised all arrangements and the body cannot be interred in the mausoleum until its comple-tion, and it would be difficult to get an order to disinter it if it were once underground, Captain Glossop has consented to have it placed for a time in the new and as yet unused vault which he had erected last month in Brompton Cemetery."

"'A friend in need is a friend indeed,'" quoted Cleek senten-tiously; then, after a moment, "Mr. Narkom," he said.

"Yes, old chap?"

"Let's go down and have another cup of tea, I want to have a word or two with the young duke."

"My dear fellow! Good heaven, do you think – "

"No; I've got past 'thinking.' I know one thing, however; for I've been poking about while you were away. The cook's room is just over this one, but the cook didn't do it. A five-foot woman can't reach up and cut down eight and a half feet of bell-rope, and

— look, see! She wouldn't be likely to do it with the blade of a safety razor if she could!"

III

The little gathering in the drawing-room had not undergone much in the way of a change since they left it Cleek and the superintendent saw when they returned. The tea things had been removed, for the young duke's peppery temper was still in the ascendant and he was parading his six-feet-one of vigorous young manhood up and down the floor in a manner which wasn't the best thing in the world for the white-and-green Persian carpet. The tall captain sat on a low sofa beside his beautiful wife, who thoughtfully turned her rings on her fingers and followed with grave, sad-looking eyes the constantly pacing figure of the restless duke.

"My dear fellow, of course neither Amy nor I believe," the captain was saying, as Cleek and Narkom made their reappearance; "but the thing is, can you make others as disbelieving when your unhappy condition is so well known and her Grace's maid positively swears that the door was not locked, and – Ah, here you are again, Mr. Narkom, and your good friend the amateur investigator with you."

"Amateur fiddlesticks!" blurted out the young duke, with a short, derisive laugh. "Fellow who doesn't know any better than to look for jewels that are not lost, and look for them on a lady's fingers at that! By Jove, you know, Glossop, if it had been my wife! – But there! you easy-going fellows will swallow anything for the sake of keeping peace. Well, Mr. Crime Investigator, found out who did it yet, eh?"

"Perhaps not exactly," replied Cleek, moving over toward the sofa; "but I've found out who didn't do it, and that's something."

"Oh, yes, decidedly!" flung back the duke, with another sarcastic laugh. "Wonderfully brainy, that! Not more than two or three million people in Great Britain who could tell you that Napoleon didn't do it, and the Black Prince didn't do it, and it's twopence to a teacup that Shakespeare hadn't any hand in it at all. You'll be out-Cleeking Cleek by the time you've sucked the head off that cane. Well, whatever other amazing thing have you 'unearthed'? What's next — eh?"

"Only this," said Cleek quietly, making a feint of dropping his cane and stooping to recover it. Then he moved like a quick-leaping animal. There was a sharp metallic "click-click," a frightened scream from Mrs. Glossop, a half-indignant, wholly excited roar from the captain, and the duke, glancing toward them, saw that they both had got to their feet in a sort of panic and were standing there, white, quaking, and handcuffed together.

"Good Lord!" began the duke. "Look here, Mr. Narkom — I say! This idiot's out of his head."

"More than out of it!" swung in the captain furiously. "To people in our position! Good God! I can stand a fool as far as any man can, Mr. Narkom, but when it comes to this - Look here, you, Mr. Woodhead, or Thickhead, or whatever your infernal name is - "

"Call a spade a spade, my dear captain. The name is Cleek, if you can't remember my other."

"Cleek!" The duke repeated it with a sort of gulp; the captain spat it out as though it were something red-hot, and the captain's wife merely whined it and fainted.

"Yes, Captain — Cleek! Oh, I've got you, my friend, got you foul!" said Cleek in reply. "All but ruined by the failure of the gold reefs and the milling and mining companies last autumn, weren't you, and have been playing a bluff game and living on your credit ever since? A pretty little scheme you two beauties hatched up between you to get the old duchess into your clutches, to rob her of the Siva stones, and to have Mrs. Glossop and your Hindu ally slip over to India with them and claim the reward before the truth of your financial condition leaked out! Oh, yes; I've got you, my friend, got you tight and fast.

"And, Captain, I've got something more as well! I've got the place where the panel slides in the striped wall-paper and leads to the wardrobe with the false back in your own room; I've got your private papers; I've got the safety razor-blade, and I've got the hiding-place of the Siva stones as well! Humph! Fainted like any other human brute when he's pushed to the wall! That's right, Hammond; call the constable in from outside and take the pair of them away. Oh, don't waste any pity on them, your Grace," as the duke moved impulsively toward the stricken and defeated pair. "They wouldn't have hesitated to hang you if they could have turned the evidence your way and saved their own wretched skins — and all for a pair of rose-pink diamonds that are red enough now, God knows. What's that? Where are they? Where you must get a surgeon to abstract them, for I wouldn't touch them for millions, your Grace. They are hidden in the body itself, embedded in the flesh, jammed out of sight through those cuts in the arms and embedded under the muscles!"

"Good heaven, how horrible!"

"Yes, isn't it? Oh, they laid their plans well, those two, and they laid them together. The body would not be put underground for a long, long time, and when it was the Siva stones would not go to earth with it. There was the specially constructed vault at Brompton, their private property. They would get the stones while the body lay there, and nobody would be a whit the wiser.

"Ring for a glass of wine, your Grace, and after you have steadied your nerves I'll take you upstairs and show you something. In the captain's room there's a wardrobe which has a false back, and behind that is a sliding panel, its joining hidden by the stripes of the wall-paper, which leads into the old duchess's bedroom. That is how they got in and got out again and left every door and window locked on the inside. When they had finished their work, they lit the candles, and the rest you know. If there is anything to joy over in this appalling affair, find it in this fact: I am convinced that the dowager duchess died intestate. That being so, and she having no other living relatives, her property will no doubt be divided equally, by order of the Crown, between three persons: yourself, for one, and those two poor, homeless creatures, Tom Spender and his sister, for the others; and as it amounts to several millions sterling, dark days are over for you and for them forever!"

*****

"How did I find it out?" said Cleek, answering Narkom's question, as they drove home through the shadows of evening together. "Well, I think I first got a suspicion of the captain and his wife when you told me about the cut bell-rope, because, you see, it is hardly likely that anybody could get into the room and cut that without disturbing the old lady, and, as she didn't cry out, I came to the conclusion that that somebody must certainly be some one she knew and trusted, and whose presence in the room would not be unusual. That at once suggested Mrs. Glossop, and the possibility of the lady saying that she had heard a noise, and had come up and found the door unlocked. The captain, who would make his entrance unheard while they were talking, would cut the rope, throw the noose round the victim's neck while she was off guard, and the rest would follow easily.

"But I could find no motive and could get no actual clue until I looked at the lady's rings. Clearly the putting of them on was an attempt to accentuate the presumed fact of their great wealth by exhibiting open evidence of how richly the lady was dowered with jewels and how little she need covet those of others. I got upon the trail of the true state of affairs when I examined those rings and found that they were simply paste, close imitations of the splendid originals which she had no doubt long since been obliged either to pawn or sell.

"As for the hiding-place of the Siva stones, the fact of the utterly unnecessary wounds in the arms – unnecessary as helping the assassin to kill her, I mean – gave me the first hint of that. Afterward, when I saw the body, and noticed the position of those wounds, I was sure of it. That is where Glossop bungled. They could not have come about in any struggle or any possible effort of the deceased to protect herself by throwing up her arms, for they were in the wrong position, for one thing, and they were deep, clean-cut punctures, for another, and – My corner at last! The riddle is solved, Mr. Narkom. Good-night."

CHAPTER XI
THE DIVIDED HOUSE

"Superintendent Narkom waitin' upstairs in your room, sir. Come unexpected and sudden like about five minutes ago," said Dollops, as the key was withdrawn from the lock and Cleek stepped into the house. "Told him you'd jist run round the corner, sir, to get a fresh supply of them cigarettes you're so partial to, so he sat down and waited. And, oh, I say, guv'ner?"

"Yes?" said Cleek inquiringly, stopping in his two-steps-at-a-time ascent of the stairs.

"Letter come for you, too, sir, whilst you was out. Envellup wrote in a lady's hand, and directed to 'Captain Burbage.' Took it up and laid it on your table, sir."

"All right," said Cleek, and resumed his journey up the stairs, passing a moment later into his private room and the presence of Maverick Narkom.

The superintendent, who was standing by the window looking out into the brilliant radiance of the morning, turned as he heard the door creak, and immediately set his back to the things that had nothing to do with the conduct of Scotland Yard, and advanced toward his famous ally with that eagerness and enthusiasm which he reserved for matters connected with crime and the law.

"My dear Cleek, such a case; you'll fairly revel in it," he began excitedly. "As I didn't expect to find you out at this hour of the morning, I dispensed with the formality of 'phoning, hopped into the car, and came on at once. Dollops said you'd be back in half a minute, and," looking at his watch, "it's now ten since I arrived."

"Sorry to have kept you waiting, Mr. Narkom," broke in Cleek, "but — look at these," pulling the tissue paper from an oblong parcel he was carrying in his hand and exposing to view a cluster of lilies of the valley and La France roses. "They are what detained me. Budleigh, the florist, had his window full of them, fresh from Covent Garden this morning, and I simply couldn't resist the temptation. If God ever made anything more beautiful than a rose, Mr. Narkom, it is yet to be discovered. Sit down, and while you are talking I'll arrange these in this vase. No; it won't distract my attention from what you are saying, believe me. Somehow, I can always think better and listen better when there are flowers about me, and if – "

He chopped off the sentence suddenly and laid the flowers down upon his table with a briskness born of sudden interest. His eye had fallen upon the letter of which Dollops had spoken. It was lying face upward upon the table, so that he could see the clear, fine, characterful hand in which it was written and could read clearly the Devonshire postmark.

"My dear Cleek," went on Narkom, accepting the invitation to be seated, but noticing nothing in his eagerness to get to business, "my dear Cleek, never have I brought you any case which is so likely to make your fortune as this, and when I tell you that the reward offered runs well into five figures – "

"A moment, please!" interjected Cleek agitatedly. "Don't think me rude, Mr. Narkom, but – your pardon a thousand times. I must read this letter before I give attention to anything else, no matter how important!"

Then, not waiting for Narkom to signify his consent to the interruption, as perforce he was obliged to do in the circumstances, he carried the letter over to the window, broke the seal, and read it, his heart getting into his eyes and his pulses drumming with that kind of happiness which fills a man when the one woman in the world writes him a letter.

Even if he had not recognized her handwriting, he must have known from the postmark that it was from Ailsa Lorne, for he had no correspondent in Devonshire, no correspondent but Narkom anywhere, for the matter of that. His lonely life, the need for secrecy, his plan of self-effacement, prevented that. But he had known for months that Miss Lorne was in Devon, that she had gone there as governess in the family of Sir Jasper Drood, when her determination not to leave England had compelled her to resign her position as guide and preceptress to little Lord Chepstow on the occasion of his mother's wedding with Captain Hawksley. And now to have her write to him — to him! A sort of mist got into his eyes and blurred everything for a moment. When it had passed and he could see clearly, he set his back to Narkom and read these words:

The Priory, Tuesday, June 10th.

Dear Friend:

If you remember, as I so often do, that last day in London, when you put off the demands of your duty to see me safely in the train and on my way to this new home, you will perhaps also remember something that you said to me at parting. You told me that if a time ever came when I should need your friendship or your help, I had but to ask for them. If that is true, and I feel sure that it is, dear Mr. Cleek, I need them now. Not for myself, however, but for one who has proved a kind friend indeed since my coming here, and who, through me, asks your kind aid in solving a deep and distressing mystery and saving a threatened human life. No reward can be offered, I fear, beyond that which comes of the knowledge of having done a good and generous act, Mr. Cleek, for my friend is not in a position to offer one. But I seem to feel that this will weigh little with you, and it emboldens me to make this appeal. So, if no other case prevents, and you really wish to do me a favour, if you can make it convenient to be in the neighbourhood of the lych-gate of Lyntonhurst Church on Wednesday morning at eleven o'clock, you will win the everlasting gratitude of —

Your sincere friend,

Ailsa Lorne.

The superintendent heard the unmistakable sound of the letter being folded and slid back into its envelope, and very properly concluded that the time of grace had expired.

"Now, my dear Cleek, let us get down to business," he began forthwith. "This amazing case which I wish you to undertake and will, as I have already said, bring you a colossal reward - "

"Your pardon, Mr. Narkom," interjected Cleek, screwing round on his heel and beginning to search for a railway guide among the litter of papers and pamphlets jammed into the spaces of a revolving bookcase, "your pardon, but I can undertake no case, sir — at least, for the present. I am called to Devonshire, and must start at once. What's that? No, there is nothing to be won, not a farthing piece. It's a matter of friendship, nothing more."

"But, Cleek! God bless my soul, man, this is madness. You are simply chucking away enough money to keep you for the next three years."

"It wouldn't make any difference if it were enough to keep me for the next twenty, Mr. Narkom. You can't buy entrance to paradise for all the money in the world, my friend, and I'm getting a day in it for nothing! Now then," flirting over the leaves of the guide book, "let's see how the trains run. Dorset — Darsham — Dalby — Devonshire. Good! Here you are. Um-m-m. Too late for that. Can't possibly catch that one, either. Ah, here's the one — 1.56 — that will do." Then he closed the book, almost ran to the door, and, leaning over the banister, shouted down the staircase, "Dollops — Dollops, you snail, where are you? Dol – Oh, there you are at last, eh? Pack my portmanteau. Best clothes, best boots, best everything I've got, and look sharp about it. I'm off to Devonshire by the 1.56."

And, do all that he might, Narkom could not persuade him to alter his determination. The 1.56 he said he would take; the 1.56 he did take; and night coming down over the peaceful paths and the leafy loveliness of Devon found him putting up at the inn of "The Three Desires," hours and hours and hours ahead of the appointed time, to make sure of being at the trysting place at eleven next morning.

He was. On the very tick of the minute he was there at the old moss-grown lych-gate, and there Miss Lorne found him when she drove up in Lady Drood's pony phaeton a little time afterward. She was not alone, however. She had spoken of a friend, and a sharp twitch disturbed Cleek's heart when he saw that a young man sat beside her, a handsome young man of two-or

three-and-twenty, with a fair moustache, a pair of straight-
looking blue eyes, and that squareness of shoulder and uprightness of bearing which tells the tale of a soldier.

In another moment she had alighted, her fingers were lying
in the close grasp of Cleek's, and the colour was coming and going in rosy gusts over her smiling countenance.

"How good of you to come!" she said. "But, there! I knew
that you would, if it were within the range of possibility; I said so
to Mr. Bridewell as we came along. Mr. Cleek, let me have the
pleasure of making you acquainted with Lieutenant Bridewell.
His fiancée, Miss Warrington, is the dear friend of whom I wrote
you. Lieutenant Bridewell is home on leave after three years' service in India, Mr. Cleek; but in those three years strange and horrible things have happened, are still happening, in his family
circle. But now that you have come – We shall get at the bottom
of the mystery now, lieutenant; I feel certain that we shall. Mr.
Cleek will find it out, be sure of that."

"At least, I will endeavour to do so, Mr. Bridewell," said
Cleek himself, as he wrung the young man's hand and decided
that he liked him a great deal better than he had thought he was
going to do. "What is the difficulty? Miss Lorne's letter mentioned
the fact that not only was there a mystery to be probed but a human life in danger. Whose life, may I ask? Yours?"

"No," he made reply, with a sort of groan. "I wish to heaven
it were no more than that. I'd soon clear out from the danger zone
and put an end to the trouble, get rid of that lot at the house and
put miles of sea between them and me, I can tell you. It's my dad
they are killing — my dear old dad, bless his heart — and killing
him in the most mysterious and subtle manner imaginable. I don't
know how, I don't know why, that's the mystery of it, for he has-
n't any money nor any expectations, just the annuity he bought
when he got too old to follow his calling (he used to be a sea captain, Mr. Cleek), and there'd be no sense in getting rid of him for
that, because, of course, the annuity dies with him. But somebody's got some kind of a motive and somebody's doing it, that's
certain, for when I went out to India three years ago he was a hale

and hearty old chap, fit as a fiddle and lively as a cricket, and now, when I come back on leave, I find him a broken wreck, a peevish, wasted old man, hardly able to help himself, and afflicted with some horrible incurable disease which seems to be eating him up alive."

"Eating him?" repeated Cleek. "What do you mean by 'eating' him, Mr. Bridewell? The expression is peculiar."

"Well, it exactly explains the circumstances, Mr. Cleek. If I didn't know better, I should think it a case of leprosy. But it isn't. I've seen cases of leprosy, and this isn't one of them. There's none of the peculiar odour, for one thing; and, for another, it isn't contagious. You can touch the spots without suffering doing so, although he suffers, dear old boy, and suffers horribly. It's just living decay, Mr. Cleek — just that. Fordyce, that's the doctor who's attending him, you know, says that the only way he has found to check the thing is by amputation. Already the dear old chap has lost three fingers from the right hand by that means. Fordyce says that the hand itself will have to go in time if they can't check the thing, and then, if that doesn't stop it, the arm will have to go."

Cleek puckered up his brows and began to rub his thumb and forefinger up and down his chin.

"Fordyce seems to have a pronounced penchant for amputation, Mr. Bridewell," he said after a moment. "Competent surgeon, do you think?"

"Who — Fordyce? Lord bless you, yes! One of the 'big pots' in that line. Harley Street specialist in his day. Fell heir to a ton of money, I believe, and gave up practice because it was too wearing. Couldn't get over the love of it, however, so set up a ripping little place down here, went in for scientific work, honour and glory of the profession and all that sort of thing, you know. God knows what would have become of the dad if he hadn't taken up the case! might be in his grave by this time. Fordyce has been a real friend, Mr. Cleek; I can't be grateful enough to him for the good he has done: taking the dear old dad into his home, so to speak, him and Aunt Ruth and — and that pair, the Cordovas."

"The Cordovas? Who are they? Friends or relatives?"

"Neither, I'm afraid. To tell the truth, they're the people I suspect, though God knows why I should, and God forgive me if I'm wrong. They're two West Indians, brother and sister, Mr. Cleek. Their father was mate of the *Henrietta*, under my dad, years and years ago. Mutinied, too, the beggar, and was shot down, as he ought to have been, as *any* mutineer ought to be. Left the two children, mere kiddies at the time. Dad took 'em in, and has been keeping them and doing for them ever since. I don't like them — never did like them. Fordyce doesn't like them, either. Colonel Goshen does, however. He's sweet on the girl, I fancy."

Cleek's eyebrows twitched upward suddenly, his eyes flashed a sharp glance at the lieutenant, and then dropped again.

"Colonel Goshen, eh?" he said quietly. "Related, by any chance, to that 'Colonel Goshen' who testified on behalf of the claimant in the great Tackbun case?"

"Don't know, I'm sure. Never heard of the case, Mr. Cleek."

"Didn't you? It was quite a sensation some eighteen months ago. But you were in India, then, of course. Fellow turned up who claimed to be the long-lost Sir Aubrey Tackbun who ran away to sea when a boy some thirty odd years ago and was lost track of entirely. Lost his case at that first trial, and got sent to prison for conspiracy Is out again now. Claims to have new and irrefutable refutable evidence, and is going to have a second try for the title and estates. A Colonel Goshen, of the Australian militia, was one of his strongest witnesses. Wonder if there is any connection between the two?"

"Shouldn't think so. This Colonel Goshen's an American or he says he is, and I've no reason to doubt him. Deuced nice fellow, whatever he is, and has been a jolly good friend to the pater. As a matter of fact, it was through him that Fordyce got to know the dad and became interested in his case, and – What's that? Lud, no! No possible means of connecting my old dad with any lost heirs, sir — not a ghost of one. Born here in Devon, married here, lived all his life here, that is, whenever he was on land, and he'll die here, and die soon, too, if you don't get at the bottom of this and save him. And you will, Mr. Cleek, and you will, won't you? Miss Lorne says that you've solved deeper mysteries than this, and that you will get at the bottom of it without fail."

"Miss Lorne has more faith in my ability than most people, I fear, Mr. Bridewell. I will try to live up to it, however. But suppose you give me the facts of the case a little more clearly. When and how did it all begin?"

"I think it was about eight months ago that Aunt Ruth wrote me about it," the lieutenant replied. "Aunt Ruth is my late mother's maiden sister, Mr. Cleek. My mother died at my birth, and Aunt Ruth brought me up. As I told you, my father retired from the sea some years ago, and, having purchased an annuity, lived on that. He managed to scrape enough together to have me schooled properly and put through Sandhurst, and when I got my lieutenancy, and was subsequently appointed to a commission in India, I left him living in the little old cottage where I was born. With him were Aunt Ruth and Paul and Lucretia Cordova. Up to about eight months or so ago he continued to live there, devoting himself to his little garden and enjoying life on land as much as a man who loves the sea ever can do. Then, of a sudden, Lucretia Cordova fell in with Colonel Goshen, and introduced him to the pater. A few days after that my father seems to have eaten something which disagreed with him, for he was suddenly seized with all the symptoms of ptomaine poisoning. He rallied, however, but from that point a strange weakness overcame him, and at the colonel's suggestion he went for a sail round the coast with him. He did not improve. The weakness seemed to grow, but without any sign of the horrible bodily suffering with which he is now afflicted.

"Colonel Goshen is a great friend of Dr. Fordyce's, and through that friendship managed to interest him in the case to such a degree that he made a twenty-mile trip especially to see my father. They struck up a great friendship. Fordyce was certain, he said, that he could cure the dad if he had him within daily reach, and, on the dad saying that he couldn't afford to come over to this part of the country and keep up two establishments, Fordyce came to the rescue, like the jolly brick he is. In other words, his place here being a good deal larger than he requires, he's a bachelor, Mr. Cleek, he put up a sort of partition to separate it into two establishments, so to speak, put one-half at the dad's disposal rent free, and there he is housed now, and Aunt Ruth and the two Cordovas with him. Yes, and even me, now; for as soon as he heard that I was coming home on leave, Fordyce wouldn't listen to my going to 'The Three Desires' for digs, but insisted that I, too, should be taken in, and a clinking suite of rooms in the west wing put at my disposal.

"But in spite of all his hopes for the dear old dad's eventual cure, things in that direction have grown steadily worse. The horrible malady which is now consuming him manifested itself about a fortnight after his arrival, and it has been growing steadily worse every day. But it isn't natural, Mr. Cleek; I know what I am saying, and I say that! Somebody is doing something to him for some diabolical reason of which I know nothing, and he is dying — dying by inches. Not by poison, I am sure of that, for since the hour of my return I have not let him eat or drink a single thing without myself partaking of it before it goes to him and eating more of it after it has gone to him. But there is no effect in my case. Nothing does he touch with his hand that I do not touch after him; but the disease never attacks me, yet all the while he grows worse and worse, and the end keeps creeping on. There! that's the case, Mr. Cleek. For God's sake, get at the bottom of it and save my father, if you can."

Cleek did not reply for a moment. Putting out his hands suddenly, he began to drum a thoughtful tattoo upon the post of the lych-gate, his eyes fixed on the ground and a deep ridge between his puckered brows. But, of a sudden:

"Tell me something," he said. "These Cordovas — what reason have you for suspecting them?"

"None, only that I dislike them. They're half-castes, for one thing, and — well, you can't trust a half-caste at any time."

"Hum-m-m! Nothing more than that, eh? Just a natural dislike? And your Aunt Ruth; what of her?"

"Oh, just the regulation prim old maid: sour as a lemon and as useful. A good sort, though. Fond of the pater, careful as a mother of him, temper like a file, and a heart a good deal bigger than you'd believe at first blush. Do anything in the world for me, bless her."

"Even to the point of putting up a friend of yours for a couple of days?"

"Yes; if I had one in these parts, which I haven't."

"Never count your chickens — you know the rest," said Cleek, with a smile. "A fellow you met out in India, a fellow named George Headland, lieutenant, remember the name, please, has just turned up in these parts. You met him quite unexpectedly, and if you want to get at the bottom of this case, take him along with you and get your Aunt Ruth to put him up for a day or two."

"Oh, Mr. Cleek!"

"George Headland, if you please, Miss Lorne. There's a great deal in a name, Shakespeare or anybody else to the contrary."

II

It was two o'clock in the afternoon when, after lunching with Cleek at the inn of "The Three Desires," Lieutenant Bridewell turned up at the divided house with his friend, "George Headland," and introduced him to the various occupants thereof; and, forthwith, "Mr. George Headland" proceeded to make himself as agreeable to all parties as he knew how to do. He found Aunt Ruth the very duplicate of what young Bridewell had prepared him to find, namely, a veritable Dorcas: the very embodiment of thrift, energy, punctiliousness, with the graceful figure of a ramrod and the martial step of a grenadier; and he decided forthwith that, be she a monument of all the virtues, she was still just the kind of woman he would fly to the ends of the earth rather than have to live with for one short week. In brief, he did not like Miss Ruth Sutcliff, and Miss Ruth Sutcliff did not like him.

Of the two Cordovas, he found the girl Lucretia a mere walking vanity bag: idle, shiftless, eager for compliments, and without two ideas in her vain little head. "Whoever is at the bottom of the affair, she isn't," was his mental comment. "She is just a gadfly, just a gaudy, useless insect, born without a sting, or the spirit to use one if she had it."

Her brother Paul was not much better. "A mere lizard, content to bask in the sunshine and caring not who pays for the privilege so long as he gets it. I can see plainly enough why a fellow like young Bridewell should dislike the pair of them, and even distrust and suspect them, too; but, unless I am woefully mistaken, they can be counted out of the case entirely. Who, then, is in it? Or is there really any case at all? Is the old captain's malady a natural one, in spite of all these suspicions? I'll know that when I see him."

WITH THAT HE STRIPPED DOWN THE COUNTERPANE, LIFTED THE WATER-JUG FROM ITS WASHSTAND AND EMPTIED ITS CONTENTS OVER THE MATTRESSES

When he *did* see him, about an hour after his arrival at the divided house, he did know it, and decided forthwith, whatever the mysterious cause, foul play was there beyond the question of a doubt. Somebody had a secret reason for destroying this old man's life, and that some body was quietly and craftily doing it. But how? By what means? Not by poison, that was certain, for no poison could have this purely local effect and confine itself to the right side of the body, the right hand, the right arm, the right shoulder, spread to no other part and simply corrode the flesh and destroy the bone there as lime or caustic might, and leave the left side wholly unblemished, entirely without attack. Wholly unlike the case of old Mr. Bawdrey, in the affair of the "Nine-fingered Skeleton," this could be no poison that was administered by touch, injected into the blood through the pores of the skin; for whatsoever Captain Bridewell touched, his son touched after him, and no evil came of it to him. Then, too, there was no temptation of wealth to inherit, as in old Bawdrey's case, for the little that Captain Bridewell possessed would die with him. He had no expectations; he stood in no one's way to an inheritance. Why, then, was he being done to death? — and how?

A dear, kindly, lovable old fellow, with a heart as big as an ox's, a hand ever ready to help those in need, as witness his adoption of the mutineering mate's children, a mind as free from guile as any child's, he ought, in the natural order of things, to have not one enemy in the world, one acquaintance who did not wish him well; and yet –

"I must manage to get a look at that maimed hand somehow and to examine that peculiar eruption closely," said Cleek to Bridewell, when they were alone together. "I could get so little impression of its character on account of the bandages and the sling. Do you think I could get to see it some time without either?"

"Yes, certainly you can. Fordyce always dresses it in the evening. We'll make it our business to be about then, and he'll be sure to let you see it if you like."

"I should, indeed," said Cleek. "And by the way, I haven't

seen Dr. Fordyce yet. Isn't he about?"

"Not just at present; be in to tea, though. He's off on his rounds at present. Makes a practice of looking after the poor for the simple humanity of the thing. Never charges for his services. You'll like Fordyce, he's a ripping sort."

And so indeed he seemed to be when, at tea, Cleek met him for the first time and found him a jovial, round-faced, apple-cheeked, rollicking little man of fifty-odd years.

"Pleased to meet you, Mr. Headland — very pleased indeed," he said gaily, when young Bridewell introduced them. "Lon-doner, I can see, by the cut of you, Londoner and soldier, too. No mistaking military training when a man carries himself like that. Londoner myself once upon a time. But no place like the country for health, and no part of the country like Devon. Paradise, sir, Paradise. Well, Captain, and how are we to-day, eh? Better?"

"No, I'm afraid not, doctor," replied the old seaman. "Pain's been a little worse than yesterday. Never was so bad as when I woke up this morning; and, if you'll pardon my saying it, sir, that lotion you gave me doesn't seem to have done a bit of good."

"Oho! there's a lotion, is there?" commented Cleek mentally, when he heard this. "I'll have a look at that lotion before I go to bed to-night." Yet, when he did, he found it a harmless thing that ought to have been beneficial even if it had not.

"I say, Fordyce," put in young Bridewell, remembering Cleek's desire and seeing a chance of gratifying it sooner than he had anticipated, "don't you think it would be a good thing to have a look at the pater's arm now? He says the pain's getting up to the shoulder, and so bad at times he can hardly bear it. Do look at it, will you? I hate to see him suffering like this."

"Oh, certainly, of course I will. Just wait until I've had my tea, old chap," replied the doctor; and, when he had had it, moved over to the deep chair where the captain sat rocking to and fro and squeezing his lips together in silent agony, and pro-ceeded to remove the bandages. He had barely uncovered the maimed hand, however, ere Cleek sauntered over in company with the old seaman's son and stood beside him. He was close enough now to study the character of the eruption, and the sight of it tightened the creases about his lips, twitched one swift gleam of light through the darkness of his former bewilderment.

"Good God!" he said, swept out of himself for the moment by the appalling realization which surged over him; then, remembering himself, caught the doctor's swiftly given upward look and returned it with one of innocent blankness. "Awful, isn't it, doctor? Don't think it's smallpox, or something of that sort, do you?"

"Rubbish!" responded the doctor, with laughing contempt for such a silly fool as this. "Smallpox, indeed! Man alive, it isn't the least thing like it. I should think a child would know that. No, Captain, there isn't any change in its condition, despite the increased pain, unless it may be that it is just a shade better than when I dressed it this morning. There, there, don't worry about its going up to the shoulder, Lieutenant. We'll save the arm, never fear." And then, without examining that arm at all, proceeded to rebandage the maimed hand and replace it in the supporting sling; and, afterward, went over and talked with Aunt Ruth before passing out and going round to his side of the divided house. But so long as he remained in sight, Cleek's narrowed eyes followed him and the tense creases seamed Cleek's indrawn, silent lips. But when he broke that silence it was to speak to the captain and to say some silly, pointless thing about that refuge of the witless — the weather.

"Bridewell," he said ten minutes later, when, upon Aunt Ruth's objecting to it being done indoors, the lieutenant invited him to come outside for a smoke, "Bridewell, tell me something: Where does your father sleep?"

"Dad? Oh, upstairs in the big front room just above us. Why?"

"Nothing, but, I've a whim to see the place, and without anybody's knowledge. Can you take me there?"

"Certainly. Come along," replied the lieutenant, and led the way round to a back staircase and up that to the room in question. It was a pretty room, hung with an artistic pink paper which covered not only the original walls but the wooden partitions which blocked up the door leading to Dr. Fordyce's own part of the house; and close against that partition and so placed that the screening canopy shut out the glare from the big bay window, stood a narrow brass bedstead equipped with the finest of springs, the very acme of luxury and ease in the way of soft mattresses, and so piled with down pillows that a king might have envied it for a resting-place.

Cleek looked at it for a moment in silence, then reached out and laid his hand upon the papered partition.

"What's on the other side of this?" he queried. "Does it lead into a passage or a room?"

"Into Fordyce's laboratory," replied the lieutenant. "As a matter of fact, this used to be Fordyce's own bedroom, the best in the house. But he gave it up especially for the dad's use as the view and the air are better than in any other room in the place, he says, and he's a great believer in that sort of thing for sick people. Ripping of him, wasn't it?"

"Very. Suppose you could get your father not to sleep here to-night for a change?"

"Wouldn't like to try. He fairly dotes on that comfortable soft bed. There's not another to compare with it in the house. I'm sure he wouldn't rest half so well on a harder one, and wouldn't give this one up unless he was compelled to do so by some unforeseen accident."

"Good," said Cleek. "Then there is going to be 'some unforeseen accident' — look!" With that he stripped down the counterpane, lifted the water-jug from the washstand and emptied its contents over the mattresses, and when the pool of water had been absorbed, replaced the covering and arranged the bed as before.

"Great Scot, man," began the lieutenant, amazed by this; but Cleek's hand closed sharply on his arm, and Cleek's whispered "Sh-h-h!" sounded close to his ear. "Keep your father up after everybody else has gone to bed, especially Aunt Ruth," he went on. "If she's not at hand, the damage can't be repaired for this night at least. Give him your room and you come in with me. Bridewell, I know the man; I know the means; and with God's help to-night I'll know the reason as well!"

III

Everything was carried out in accordance with Cleek's plan. The captain, trapped into talking by his son, sat up long after Miss Sutcliff and the one serving maid the house boasted had gone to bed, and when, in time, he, too, retired to his room, the soaked mattress did its work in the most effectual manner. Whimpering like a hurt child over the unexplained and apparently unexplainable accident, the old man suffered his son to lead him off to his own room; and there, unable to rest on the harder mattress, and suffering agonies of pain, he lay for a long time before the door swung open, the glimmer of a bedroom candle tempered the darkness to a sort of golden dusk, and the very double of Dr. Fordyce came softly into the room. It was Cleek, wrapped in a well-padded dressing-gown and carrying in addition to the candle a bottle of lotion and a fresh linen bandage.

"Why, doctor," began the old captain, half rising upon the elbow of his uninjured arm. "Whatever in the world brings you here?"

"Study, my dear old friend, study," returned a voice so like to Dr. Fordyce's own that there was scarcely a shade of difference. "I have been sitting up for hours and hours thinking, reading, studying until now I am sure, very, very sure, Captain, that I have found a lotion that will ease the pain. For a moment after I let myself in by the partition door and found your room empty I didn't know where to turn; but fortunately your moans guided me in the right direction, and here I am. Now then, let us off with that other bandage and on with this new one, and I think we shall soon ease up that constant pain."

"God knows I hope so, doctor, for it is almost unbearable,"

the old man replied, and sat holding his lips tightly shut to keep from crying out while Cleek undid the bandage and stripped bare the injured arm from finger-tips to shoulder. His gorge rose as he saw the thing, and in seeing, knew for certain now that what he had suspected in that first glance was indeed the truth, and in that moment there was something akin to murder in his soul. He saw with satisfaction, however, that, although the upper part of the arm was much swollen, as yet the progress of decay had not gone much beyond the wrist; and having seen this and verified the nature of the complaint, he applied the fresh lotion and was for bandaging the arm up and stealing out and away again when he caught sight of something that made him suck in his breath and set his heart hammering.

The captain, attracted by his movement and the sound of his thick breathing, opened his pain-closed eyes, looked round and met the questioning look of his.

"Oh," he said with a smile of understanding. "You are looking at the tattooing near my shoulder, are you? Haven't you ever noticed it before?"

"No," said Cleek, keeping his voice steady by an effort. "Who did it and why? There's a name there and a queer sort of emblem. They are not yours, surely?"

"Good heaven, no! My name's Samuel Bridewell and always has been. Red Hamish put that thing there — oh, more than five-and-twenty years ago. Him and me was wrecked on a reef in the Indian Ocean when the *Belle Burgoyne* went down from under us and took all but us down with her. It might as well have took Red Hamish, too, poor chap, for he was hurt cruel bad, and he only lived a couple of days afterward. There was just me alone on the reef when the *Kitty Gordon* come sailin' along, see my signal of distress, and took me off near done for after eight days' fastin' and thirstin' on that bare scrap of terry firmer as they calls it. I'd have been as dead as Red Hamish himself, I reckon, in another twenty-four hours."

"Red Hamish? Good heavens, who was Red Hamish?"

"Never heard him called any other name than just that. Must have had one, of course; and it's so blessed long ago now I disremember what it was he put on the back of my shoulder. A great hand at tattooing he was. Fair lived with his injy ink and his prickin' needles. Kept 'em in a belt he wore and had 'em on him when the *Belle Burgoyne* went down and I managed to drag him on to the reef, poor chap.

"'Had your call, Red,' I says to him when I got him up beside me. 'I reckon you're struck for death, old man.' 'I know it,' says he to me. 'But better me than you, cap'n', he says, "cause there ain't nobody waitin' and watchin' for me to come home to her and the kid. Though there is one woman who'd like to know where I'd gone and when and how death found me,' he says, after a moment. 'I'd like to send a word — a message — a sign just to her, cap'n. She'd know — she'd understand and — well, it's only right that she should.'

"'Well, give it to me, Red,' I says. 'I'll take it to her if I live, old man.' But, bless you, there wasn't anything to write the message on, of course; and it wasn't for a long time that Red hit upon a plan.

"'Cap'n,' he says, 'I've got my inks and my needles. Let me put it on your shoulder, will you? Just a name and a sign. But she'll understand, she'll know, and that's all I want.' Of course I agreed — who wouldn't for a mate at a time like that? So I lays down on my face and Red goes at me with the needles and works till he gets it done.

"'There,' he says when he'd reached the end of it. 'If ever anybody wants to know who died on this here reef, cap'n, there's Red Hamish's answer,' he says. 'She'll know, my mother, the only one that cares,' says he, and chucks his belt into the sea and that's all.

"Thanky, doctor, thanky. It does feel better, and I do believe that I shall sleep now. At first I missed the hummin' of that electric fan in your laboratory, I fancy, but bless you, sir, I feel quite drowsy and comfortable now. Remember me to Colonel Goshen when you go back to your rooms, will you? I see him go round

279

the angle of the buildin' and into your side of the house just after you left me to-night, sir, and I thought likely he'd come round and call, but he didn't. Good-night, sir — good-night, and many thanks!"

But even before he had finished speaking Cleek had gone out of the room, and was padding swiftly along the passage to where Lieutenant Bridewell awaited him.

"Well?" exclaimed the young man breathlessly as the fleet-moving figure flashed in and began tearing off the beard, the dressing-gown, and the disguising wig. "You found out? You learned something, then?"

"I have learned everything, everything!" said Cleek, and pouncing upon his portmanteau whisked out a couple of pairs of handcuffs. "Don't stop to ask questions now. Come with me to the partition door and clap those things on the wrists of the man that gets by me. There are two of them in there, your Dr. Fordyce and your Colonel Goshen, and I want them both."

"Good heavens, man, you don't surely mean that they, those two dear friends – "

"Don't ask questions, come!" rapped in Cleek, then whirled out of the room and flew down the passage to the partition door, and pounded heavily upon it. "Doctor Fordyce, Doctor Fordyce, open the door, come quickly. Something has happened to Captain Bridewell," he called. "He's not in his room, not in the house, and it looks as if somebody had spirited him away!"

A clatter of footsteps on the other side of the partition door answered this; then the bolt flashed back, the door whirled open, two figures — one on the very heels of the other — came tumbling into sight, and then there was mischief!

Cleek sprang, and a click of steel sounded. The doctor, caught in a sort of throttle-hold, went down with him upon the floor; the colonel, unable to check himself in time, sprawled head-long over them, and by the time he could pull himself to his knees young Bridewell was upon him, and there were gyves upon his wrists as well as upon the doctor's.

"Got you, you pretty pair!" said Cleek, as he rose to his feet and shut a tight hand upon the collar of the manacled doctor; "got you, you dogs, and your little game is up. Oh, you needn't bluster, doctor; you needn't come the outraged innocence, Colonel. You'll, neither of you, bolster up the rascally claim of your worthy confederate, the Tackbun Claimant; and your game with the X-rays, your devil's trick of rotting away a man's arm to destroy tattooed evidence of a rank imposter's guilt is just so much time wasted and just so many pounds sterling thrown away."

"What's that?" blustered the colonel. "What do you mean? What are you talking about? Tackbun Claimant? Who's the Tackbun Claimant? Do you realize to whom you are speaking? Fordyce, who and what is this infernally impudent puppy?"

"Gently, gently, Colonel. Name's Cleek, if you are anxious to know it."

"Cleek? Cleek?"

"Precisely, doctor. Cleek of Scotland Yard, Cleek of the Forty Faces, if you want complete details. And if there are more that you feel you would like to know, I'll give them to you when I hand you over to the Devonshire police for your part in this rascally conspiracy to cheat the late Lady Tackbun's nephew out of his lawful rights and to rot off the arm of the man who constitutes the living document which will clearly establish them. The lost Sir Aubrey Tackbun is dead, my friend, dead as Julius Cæsar, dead beyond the hopes of you and your confederates to revive even the ghost of him now. He died on a coral reef in the Indian Ocean five-and-twenty years ago, and the proof of it will last as long as Captain Bridewell can keep his arm and lift his voice to tell his story, and I think that will be a good many years, now that your little scheme is exploded. You'll make no X-ray martyr of that dear old man, so the money you spent in the instrument on the other side of that board partition, the thing whose buzzing you made him believe came from an electric fan, represents just so many sovereigns thrown away!"

* * * * *

"Yes, it was a crafty plot, a scheme very well laid indeed," said Cleek, when he went next day to the lych-gate to say good-bye again to Ailsa Lorne. "Undoubtedly a mild poison was used in the beginning, as an excuse, you know, for the 'colonel' to get him away and into the charge of the 'doctor,' and, once there, the rest was easy if subtle. The huge X-ray machine would play always upon the partition whilst the captain was sleeping, and you know how efficacious that would be when there was only a thin board between that powerful influence and the object to be operated upon. Then, too, the head of the bed was so arranged that the captain's right side would always be exposed to the influence, so there was no possibility of evading it.

"How did I suspect it? Well, to tell you the truth, I never did suspect it until I saw the captain's hand. Then I recognized the marks. I saw the hand of a doctor, an X-ray martyr, who sacrificed himself to science last year, Miss Lorne, and the marks were identical. Oh, well, I've solved the riddle, Miss Lorne, that's the main point, and now — now I must emulate 'Poor Joe' and move on again."

"And without any reward, without asking any, without expecting any. How good of you — how generous!"

He stood a moment, twisting his heel into the turf and breathing heavily. Then, quite suddenly:

"Perhaps I did want one," he said, looking into her eyes. "Perhaps I want one still. Perhaps I always hoped that I should get it, and that it would come from you!"

A rush of sudden colour reddened all her face. She let her eyes fall, and said nothing. But what of that? After all, actions speak louder than utterances, and Cleek could see that there was a smile upon her lips. He stretched forth his hand and laid it gently on her arm.

"Miss Lorne," he said very softly, "if, some day when all the wrongs I did in those other times, are righted, and all the atonement a man can make on this earth has been made, if then — in that time — I come to you and ask for that reward, do you think

— ah! do you think that you can find it in your heart to give it?"

She lifted up her eyes, the eyes that had saved him, that had lit the way back, that would light it ever to the end of life and, stretching out her hand, put it into his.

"When that day dawns, come and see," she said, and smiled at him through happy tears.

"I will," he made answer. "Wait and I will. Oh, God, what a good, good thing a real woman is!"

CHAPTER XII
THE RIDDLE OF THE RAINBOW PEARL

"Note for you, sir, messenger just fetched it. Addressed to 'Captain Burbage,' so it'll be from the Yard," said Dollops, coming into the room with a doughnut in one hand and a square envelope in the other.

Cleek, who had been sitting at his writing-table with a litter of folded documents, bits of antique jewellery, and what looked like odds and ends of faded ribbon lying before him, swept the whole collection into the table drawer as Dollops spoke and stretched forth his hand for the letter.

It was one of Narkom's characteristic communications, albeit somewhat shorter than those communications usually were, a fact which told Cleek at once that the matter was one of immense importance. It ran:

My Dear Cleek:

For the love of goodness don't let anything tempt you into going out to-night. I shall call about ten. Foreign government affair — reward simply enormous. Watch out for me.

Yours, in hot haste.

Maverick Narkom.

"Be on the look-out for the red limousine," said Cleek, glancing over at Dollops, who stood waiting for orders. "It will be along at ten. That's all. You may go."

"Right you are, guv'ner. I'll keep my eyes peeled, sir. Lor'! I do hope it's summink to do with a restaurant or a cookshop this time. I could do with a job of that sort, my word, yes! I'm fair famishin'. And, beggin' pardon, but you don't look none too healthy yourself this evening, guv'ner. Ain't et summink wot's disagreed with you, have you, sir?"

"I? What nonsense! I'm as fit as a fiddle. What could make you think otherwise?"

"Oh, I dunno, sir — only - Well, if you don't mind my sayin' of it, sir, whenever you gets to unlocking of that drawer and lookin' at them things you keep in there — wotever they is — you always gets a sort of solemncholy look in the eyes, and you gets white about the gills, and your lips has a pucker to 'em that I don't like to see."

"Tommy rot! Imagination's a splendid thing for a detective to possess, Dollops, but don't let yours run away with you in this fashion, my lad, or you'll never rise above what you are. Toddle along now, and look out for Mr. Narkom's arrival. It's after nine already, so he'll soon be here."

"Anybody a-comin' with him, sir?"

"I don't know, he didn't say. Cut along now; I'm busy!" said Cleek. Nevertheless, when Dollops had gone and the door was shut and he had the room to himself again, and, if he really did have any business on hand, there was no reason in the world why he should not have set about it, he remained sitting at the table and idly drumming upon it with his finger-tips, a deep ridge between his brows and a far-away expression in his fixed, un-winking eyes. And so he was still sitting when, something like twenty minutes later, the sharp "Toot-toot!" of a motor horn sounded.

Narkom's note lay on the table close to his elbow. He took it up, crumpled it into a ball, and threw it into his waste basket. "A foreign government affair," he said with a curious one-sided smile. "A strange coincidence, to be sure!" Then, as if obeying an impulse, he opened the drawer, looked at the litter of things he had swept into it, shut it up again, and locked it securely, putting the key into his pocket and rising to his feet. Two minutes later, when Narkom pushed open the door and entered the room, he found Cleek leaning against the edge of the mantelpiece and smoking a cigarette with the air of one whose feet trod always upon rose petals, and who hadn't a thought beyond the affairs of the moment, nor a care for anything but the flavour of Egyptian tobacco.

"Ah, my dear fellow, you can't think what a relief it was to catch you. I had but a moment in which to dash off the note, and I was on thorns with fear that it would miss you; that on a glorious night like this you'd be off for a pull up the river or something of that sort," said the superintendent as he bustled in and shook hands with him. "You are such a beggar for getting off by your-self and mooning."

"Well, to tell you the truth, Mr. Narkom, I came within an ace of doing the very thing you speak of," replied Cleek. "It's full moon, for one thing, and it's primrose time for another. Happily for your desire to catch me, however, I — er — got interested in the evening paper and that delayed me."

"Very glad, dear chap; very glad indeed," began Narkom. Then, as his eye fell upon the particular evening paper in ques-tion lying on the writing-table, a little crumpled from use, but with a certain "displayed-headed" article of three columns' length in full view, he turned round and stared at Cleek with an air of awe and mystification. "My dear fellow, you must be under the guardianship of some uncanny familiar. You surely must, Cleek!" he went on. "Do you mean to tell me that is what kept you at home? That you have been reading about the preparations for the forthcoming coronation of King Ulric of Mauravania?"

"Yes; why not? I am sure it makes interesting reading, Mr. Narkom. The kingdom of Mauravania has had sufficient ups and downs to inspire a novelist, so its records should certainly inter-est a mere reader. To be frank, I found the account of the amazing preparations for the coronation of his new Majesty distinctly en-tertaining. They are an excitable and spectacular people, those Mauravanians, and this time they seem bent upon outdoing themselves."

"But, my dear Cleek, that you should have chosen to stop at home and read about that particular affair! Bless my soul, man, it's — it's amazing, abnormal, uncanny! Positively uncanny, Cleek!"

"My dear Mr. Narkom, I don't see where the uncanny ele-ment comes in, I must confess," replied Cleek with an indulgent smile. "Surely an Englishman must always feel a certain amount of interest in Mauravanian affairs. Have the goodness to remember that there should be an Englishman upon that particular throne. Aye, and there would be, too, but for one of those moments of weak-backed policy, of a desire upon the part of the 'old-woman' element which sometimes prevails in English politics to keep friendly relations with other powers at any cost.

"Brush up your history, Mr. Narkom, and give your memory a fillip. Eight-and-thirty years ago Queen Karma of Mauravania had an English consort and bore him two daughters and one son. You will perhaps recall the mad rebellion, the idiotic rising which disgraced that reign. That was the time for England to have spoken. But the peace party had it by the throat; they, with their mawkish cry for peace, peace at any price, drowned the voices of men and heroes, and, the end was what it was! Queen Karma was deposed, she and her children fled, God knows how, God knows where, and left a dead husband and father, slain like a hero and an Englishman, fighting for his own and with his face to the foe. Avenge his death? Nonsense! declared the old women. He had no right to defy the will of Heaven, no right to stir up strife with a friendly people and expect his countrymen to embroil themselves because of his lust for power. It would be a lasting disgrace to the nation if England allowed a lot of howling, bloodthirsty meddlers to persuade it to interfere!

"The old women had their way. Queen Karma and her children vanished; her uncle Duke Sforza came to the throne as Alburtus III., and eight months ago his son, the present King Ulric, succeeded him. The father had been a bad king, the son a bad crown prince. Mauravania has paid the price. Let her put up with it! I don't think in the light of these things, Mr. Narkom, there is any wonder that an Englishman finds interest in reading of the affairs of a country over which an Englishman's son might, and ought to, have ruled. As for me, I have no sympathy, my friend, with Mauravania or her justly punished people."

"Still, my dear fellow, that should not count when the reward for taking up this case is so enormous, and I dare say it will not."

"Reward? Case?" repeated Cleek. "What do you mean by

that?"

"That I am here to enlist your services in the cause of King Ulric of Mauravania," replied Narkom impressively. "Something has happened, Cleek, which if not cleared up before the coronation day, now only one month hence, as you must have read, will certainly result in his Majesty's public disgrace, and may result in his overthrow and death! His friend and chief adviser Count Irma has come all the way from Mauravania, and is at this moment downstairs in this house, to put the case in your hands and to implore you to help and to save his royal master!"

"His royal master? The son of the man who drove an Englishman's wife and an Englishman's children into exile — poverty — misery — despair?" said Cleek, pulling himself up. "I won't take it, Mr. Narkom! If he offers me millions, I'll lift no hand to help or to save Mauravania's king!"

The response to this came from an unexpected quarter.

"But to save Mauravania's queen, monsieur? Will you do nothing for her?" said an excited, an imploring voice. And as Cleek, startled by the interruption, switched round and glanced in the direction of the sound, the half-closed door swung inward and a figure, muffled to the very eyes, moved over the threshold into the room. "Have pardon, monsieur, I could not but overhear," went on the newcomer, turning to Narkom. "I should scarcely be worthy of his Majesty's confidence and favour had I remained inactive. I simply had to come up unbidden. *Had* to, monsieur" — turning to Cleek — "and so - " His words dropped off suddenly. A puzzled look first expanded and then contracted his eyes, and his lips tightened curiously under the screen of his white, military moustache. "Monsieur," he said, presently putting into words the sense of baffling familiarity which perplexed him. "Monsieur, you then are the great, the astonishing Cleek? You, monsieur? Pardon, but surely I have had the pleasure of meeting monsieur before? No, not here, for I have never been in England until to-day; but, in my own country, in Mauravania. Surely, monsieur, I have seen you there?"

"To the contrary," said Cleek, speaking the simple truth, "I

288

have never set foot in Mauravania in all my life, sir. And as you have overheard my words you may see that I do not intend to even now. The difficulties of Mauravania's king do not in the least appeal to me."

"Ah, but Mauravania's queen, monsieur, Mauravania's queen."

"The lady interests me no more than does her royal spouse."

"But, monsieur, she must if you are honest in what you say, and your sympathies are all with the deposed and exiled ones, the ex-Queen Karma and her children. Surely, monsieur, you who seem to know so well the history of that sad time cannot be ignorant of what has happened since to her ex-Majesty and her children?"

"I know only that Queen Karma died in France, in extreme poverty, befriended to the last by people of the very humblest birth and of not too much respectability. What became of her son I do not know; but her daughters, the two princesses, mere infants at the time, were sent, one to England, where she subsequently died, and the other to Persia, where, I believe, she remained up to her ninth year, and then went no one seems to know where."

"Then, monsieur, let me tell you what became of her. The late King Alburtus discovered her whereabouts, and, to prevent any possible trouble in the future, imprisoned her in the Fort of Sulberga up to the year before his death. Eleven months ago she became the Crown Prince Ulric's wife. She is now his consort. And by saving her, monsieur, you who feel so warmly upon the subject of the rights of her family's succession, will be saving her, helping Mauravania's queen, and defeating those who are her enemies."

Cleek sucked in his breath and regarded the man silently, steadily, for a long time. Then:

"Is that true, count?" he asked. "On your word of honour as a soldier and a gentleman, is that true?"

"As true as Holy Writ, monsieur. On my word of honour. On my hopes of heaven!"

"Very well, then," said Cleek quietly. "Tell me the case, count. I'll take it."

"Monsieur, my eternal gratitude. Also the reward is - "

"We will talk about that afterward. Sit down, please, and tell me what you want me to do."

"Oh, monsieur, almost the impossible," said the count despairfully. "The outwitting of a woman who must in very truth be the devil's own daughter, so subtle, so appalling are the craft and cunning of her. That, for one thing. For another, the finding of a paper which, if published, as the woman swears it shall be if her terms are not acceded to, will be the signal for his Majesty's overthrow. And, for the third" – emotion mastered him; his voice choked and failed; he deported himself for a moment like one afraid to let even his own ears hear the thing spoken of aloud, then governed his cowardice and went on – "For the third thing, monsieur," he said, lowering his tone until it was almost a whisper, "the recovery – the restoration to its place of honour before the coronation day arrives of that fateful gem, Mauravania's pride and glory, 'the Rainbow Pearl!'"

Cleek clamped his jaws together like a bloodhound snapping, and over his hardened face there came a slow-creeping, unnatural pallor.

"Has that been lost?" he said in a low, bleak voice. "Has he, this precious royal master of yours, this usurper – has he parted with that thing; the wondrous Rainbow Pearl?"

"Monsieur knows of the gem then?"

"Know of it? Who does not? Its fame is world-wide. Wars have been fought for it, lives sacrificed for it. It is more valuable than England's Koh-i-noor, and more important to the country and the crown that possess it. The legend runs, does it not? that Mauravania falls when the Rainbow Pearl passes into alien hands. An absurd belief, to be sure, but who can argue with a

superstitious people or hammer wisdom into the minds of ba-
bies? And *that* has been lost, that gem so dear to Mauravania's
people, so important to Mauravania's crown?"

"Yes, monsieur — ah, the good God help my country! —
yes!" said the count brokenly. "It has passed from his Majesty's
hands; it is no longer among the crown jewels of Mauravania and
a Russian has it."

"A Russian?" Cleek's cry was like to nothing so much as the
snarl of a wild animal. "A Russian to hold it — and Russia the
sworn enemy of Mauravania! God help your wretched king,
Count Irma, if this were known to his subjects."

"Ah, monsieur, it is that we dread; it is that against which we
struggle," replied the count. "If that jewel were missing on the
coronation day, if it were known that a Russian holds it — Dear
God! the populace would rise, monsieur, and tear his Majesty to
pieces."

"He deserves no better!" said Cleek through his close-shut
teeth. "To a Russian — a Russian! As heaven hears me, but for his
queen - Well, let it pass. Tell me how did this Russian get the
jewel, and when?"

"Oh, long ago, monsieur, long ago; many months before
King Alburtus died."

"Was it his hand that gave it up?"

"No, monsieur. He died without knowing of its loss, without
suspecting that the stone in the royal palace is but a sham and an
imitation," replied the count. "It all came of the youth, the reck-
lessness, the folly of the crown prince. Monsieur may have heard
of his — his many wild escapades, his thoughtless acts, his —
his - "

"Call them dissipations, count, and give them their real
name. His acts as crown prince were a scandal and a disgrace. To
whom did he part with this gem, a woman?"

"Monsieur, yes! It was during the time he was stopping in
Paris — incognito to all but a trusted few. He — he met the

woman there, became fascinated with her, bound to her, an abject slave to her."

"A slave to a Russian? Mauravania's heir and a Russian?"

"Monsieur, he did not know that until afterward. In a mad freak — there was to be a masked ball — he yielded to the lady's persuasions to let her wear the famous Rainbow Pearl for that one night. He journeyed back to Mauravania and abstracted it from among the royal jewels, putting a mere imitation in its place so that it should not be missed until he could return the original. Monsieur, he was never able to return it at any time, for once she got it, the Russian made away with it in some secret manner and refused to give it up. Her price for returning it was his royal father's consent to ennoble her, to receive her at the Mauravanian court, and so to alter the constitution that it would be possible for her to become the crown prince's wife."

"The proposition of an idiot. The thing could not possibly be done."

"No, monsieur, it could not. So the crown prince broke from her and bent all his energies upon the recovery of the pearl and the keeping of its loss a secret from the king and his people. Bravos, footpads, burglars, all manner of men, were employed before he left Paris. The woman's house was broken into, the woman herself waylaid and searched, but nothing came of it, no clue to the lost jewel could be found."

"Why, then, did he not appeal to the police?"

"Monsieur, he — he dared not. In one of his moments of madness he — she — that is - Oh, monsieur, remember his youth! It appears that the woman had got him to put into writing something which, if made public, would cause the people of Mauravania to rise as one man and to do with him as wolves do with things that are thrown to them in their fury."

"The dog! Some treaty with a Russian, of course!" said Cleek indignantly. "Oh, fickle Mauravania, how well you are punished for your treasonable choice! Well, go on, count. What next?"

"Of a sudden, monsieur, the woman disappeared. Nothing was heard of her, no clue to her whereabouts discovered for two whole years. She was as one dead and gone until last week."

"Oho! She returned then?"

"Yes, monsieur. Without hint or warning she turned up in Mauravania, accompanied by a disreputable one-eyed man who has the manner and appearance of one bred in the gutters of Paris, albeit he is well clothed, well looked after, and she treats him and his wretched collection of parakeets with the utmost consideration."

"Parakeets?" put in Narkom excitedly. "My dear Cleek, couldn't a parakeet be made to swallow a pearl?"

"Perhaps; but not this one, Mr. Narkom," he made reply. "It is quite the size of a pigeon's egg, I believe; is it not, count?"

"Yes, monsieur, quite. To see it is to remember it always. It has the changing lights of the rainbow and – "

"Never mind that; go on with the story, please. This woman and this one-eyed man appeared last week in Mauravania, you say?"

"Yes, monsieur; and with them a bodyguard of at least ten servants. Her demand now is that his Majesty make her his morganatic wife; that he establish her at the palace, under the same roof with his queen; and that she be allowed to ride with them in the state carriage on the coronation day. Failing that, she swears that she will not only publish the contents of that dreadful letter, but send the original to the chief of the Mauravanian police and appear in public at the coronation with the Rainbow Pearl upon her person."

"The Jezebel! What steps have you taken, count, to prevent this?"

"All that I can imagine, monsieur. To prevent her from getting into close touch with the public, I have thrown open my own house to her and received her and her retinue under my own roof rather than allow them to be quartered at an hotel. Also, this has given me the opportunity to have her effects and those of her followers secretly searched; but no clue to the letter, no clue to the pearl has anywhere been discovered."

"Still, she must have both with her, otherwise she could not carry out her threat. No doubt she suspects what motive you had in taking her into your own house, count. A woman like that is no fool. But tell me, does she show no anxiety, no fear of a search?"

"None, monsieur. She knows that my people search her effects; indeed she has told me so. But it alarms her not a whit. As she told me two days ago, I shall find nothing; but if I did it would be useless, for, on the moment anything of hers was touched, her servants would see that the finder never carried it from the house."

"Oho!" said Cleek with a strong rising inflection. "A little searching party of her own, eh? The lady is clever, at all events. The moment either pearl or letter should be removed from its hiding-place her servants would allow nobody to leave the house without being searched to the very skin?"

"Yes, monsieur. So if by any chance you were to discover either – "

"My friend, set your mind at rest," interposed Cleek. "If I find either, or both, they will leave the house with me, I promise you. Mr. Narkom" — he turned to the superintendent — "keep an eye on Dollops for me, will you? There are reasons why I can't take him, can't take anybody, with me in the working out of this case. I may be a couple of days or I may be a week, I can't say as yet, but I start with Count Irma for Mauravania in the morning. And, Mr. Narkom."

"Yes, old chap?"

"Do me a favour, please. Be at Charing Cross station when the first boat train leaves to-morrow morning, will you, and bring me a small pot of extract of beef, a very small pot, the smallest they make, not bigger than a shilling nor thicker than one if they make them that size. What's that? Hide the pearl in it? What nonsense! I don't want one half big enough for that. Besides, they'd be sure to find it when they searched me if I tried any such fool's trick as that. Dollops isn't the only creature in the world that gets hungry, my friend, and beef extract is very sustaining, very, I assure you, sir."

II

"A Beautiful city, count, an exceedingly beautiful city," said Cleek, as the carriage which had been sent to meet them at the station rolled into the broad Avenue des Arcs, which is at once the widest and most ornate thoroughfare the capital city of Mauravania boasts. "Ah, what a heritage! No wonder King Ulric is so anxious to retain his sovereignty; no wonder this — er — Madame Tcharnovetski, I think you said the name is - "

"Yes, monsieur. It is oddly spelled, but it is pronounced a little broader than you give it, quite as though it were written Sharno-*vet*-skee, in fact, with the accent on the third syllable."

"Ah, yes. Thanks very much. No wonder she is anxious to become a power here. Mauravania is a fairyland in very truth; and this beautiful avenue with its arches, its splendid trees, its sculpture, its - Ah! *cocher*, pull up at once. Stop, if you please, stop!"

"*Oui*, monsieur," replied the driver, reining in his horses and glancing round. "*Dix mille pardons*, m'sieur, there is something amiss?"

"Yes; very much amiss, from the dog's point of view," replied Cleek, indicating by a wave of the hand a mongrel puppy which crouched, forlorn and hungry, in the shadow of an imposing building. "He should be a Socialist among dogs, that little fellow, count. The mere accident of birth has made him what he is, and that poodled monstrosity the lady yonder is leading the pet and pride of a thoughtless mistress. I want that little canine outcast, count, and with your permission I will appropriate him and give him his first carriage ride." With that, he stepped down from the vehicle, whistled the cur to him, and taking it up in his arms, returned with it to his seat.

"Monsieur, you are to me the most astonishing of men," said the count, noticing how he patted the puppy and settled it in his lap as the carriage resumed its even rolling down the broad, beautiful avenue. "One moment upholding the rights of birth, the next rebelling against the injustice of it. Are your sympathies with the unfortunate so keen, monsieur, that even this stray cur may claim them?"

"Perhaps," replied Cleek enigmatically. "You must wait and see, count. Just now I pity him for his forlornity; to-morrow, next day, a week hence, I may hold it a better course to put an end to his hopeless lot by chloroforming him into a painless and peaceful death."

"Monsieur, I cannot follow you, you speak in riddles."

"I deal in riddles, count; you must wait for the solution of them, I'm afraid."

"I wish I could grasp the solution of one which puzzles me a great deal, monsieur. What is it that has happened to your countenance? You have done nothing to put on a disguise; yet, since we left the train and entered the landau, some subtle change has occurred. What is it? How has it come about? The night before last, when I saw you for the first time, your face was one that impressed me with a sense of familiarity, now, monsieur, you are like a different man.'"

"I am a different man, count. Like this puppy here, I am a waif and a stray; yet, at the same time, I have my purpose and am part of a carefully laid scheme."

The count made no reply. He could not comprehend the man at all, and at times, but for the world-wide reputation of him, he would have believed him insane. Not a question as to the great and important case he was on, but merely incomprehensible remarks, trifling fancies, apparently aimless whims! Two nights ago a pot of beef extract; to-day a mongrel puppy; and all the time the hopes of a kingdom, the future of a monarch resting in his hands!

For twenty minutes longer the landau rolled on; then it came to a halt under the broad porte-cochère of the Villa Irma, and two minutes after that Cleek and the count stood in the presence of Madame Tcharnovetski, her purblind associate, and her retinue of servant-guards.

A handsome woman, this madame, a woman of about two-and-thirty, with the tar-black eyes and the twilight-coloured tresses of Northern Russia; bold as brass, flippant as a French cocotte, steel-nerved and calm-blooded as a professional gambler. It had been her whim that all the women of the count's family should be banished from the house during her stay; that the great salon of the villa, a wondrous apartment, hung in blue and silver, and lit by a huge crystal chandelier, should be put at her disposal night and day; that the electric lights should be replaced with dozens of wax candles (after the manner of the ballrooms of her native Russia); that her one-eyed companion, with his wicker cage of screeching parakeets should come and go when and where and how he listed, and that an electric alarm bell be connected with her sleeping apartment and his.

"Your hirelings will tamper with his birds and his effects in the night, I know that, Monsieur le Comte," she had said when she demanded this. "He is a nervous fellow, this poor Clopin; I wish him to be able to ring for help if you and your men go too far."

Clopin was sitting by the window chattering to his birds when Cleek entered, and a glance at him was sufficient to decide two points: first he was not disguised, nor was his partial blindness in any way a sham, for an idiot could have seen that the droop of the left eyelid over the staring, palpably artificial eye which glazed over the empty socket beneath was due to perfectly natural causes; and, second, that the man was indeed what the count had said he resembled, namely, a gutter-bred outcast.

"French," was Cleek's silent comment upon him. "One of those charlatans who infest the streets of Paris with their so-called 'fortune-telling birds,' who, for ten centimes, pick out an envelope with their beaks as a means of telling you what the future is supposed to hold. What has made a woman like this pick up with a fellow of his stamp? Hum-m-m! Puppy, I think you are a good move," stroking the ears of the mongrel dog; "a very much better move than a cage of useless parakeets that are meant to throw suspicion in the wrong direction and have a seed-cup so large and so obviously overfilled that it is safe to say there is nothing hidden in it and never has been. And madame has a fancy for wax lights," his gaze travelling upward to the glittering chandelier. "Hum-m-m! How well they know, these women whose beauty is going off, that wax-lights show less of Time's ravages than gas or electricity. Candles in the chandelier; candles in the sconces; candles on the mantelpiece. This room should be very charming when it is lighted at night."

It was – as he learned later. Just now things not quite so charming filled the bill, for madame was jeering at him in a manner not to be misunderstood.

"A police spy, that is what you are, monsieur!" she said, coming up to him and impudently snapping her fingers under his nose. "Such a fool this white-headed old dotard of a count, to think that he can take me in with a silly yarn about going to visit a nephew and bringing him back here to stay. Monsieur, you are a police spy. Well, good luck to you. Get what the Mauravanian king wants, if – you – can!"

"Madame," replied Cleek, with a deeply deferential bow and with an accent that seemed born of Paris, "Madame, that is what I mean to do, I assure you."

"Ah, do you?" she answered, with a scream of laughter. "You hear that, Clopin? You hear that, my good servitors? This silly French noodle is going to get the things in spite of us. Oho, but you have a fine opinion of yourself, monsieur. You need work fast, too, pretty boaster, I can tell you. For the royal jewellers will require the Rainbow Pearl very soon to fix it in its place in the crown for the coronation ceremony, and if that thing his Majesty holds is offered to them, how long, think you, will it be before all Mauravania knows that it is an imitation? Look you," waxing suddenly vicious, "I'll make it shorter still, the time you have to strive. Monsieur le Comte, take this message to his Majesty from me. If in three days he does not promise to accede to my demands and give me a public proof of it over his royal seal, I leave Mauravania. The pearl and the letter leave with me, and they shall not come back until I return with them for the coronation."

"For the love of God, madame," said the count, "don't make it harder still. Oh, wait, wait, I beseech you!"

"Not an hour longer than I have now said!" she flung back at him. "I have waited until I am tired of it, and my patience is worn out. Three days, count; three days, monsieur with the puppy dog; three days, and not an instant longer, do you hear?"

"Quite enough, madame," replied Cleek, with a courtly bow. "I promise to have them in two!"

She threw back her head and fairly shook with laughter.

"Of a truth, monsieur, you are a candid boaster!" she cried. "Look you, my good fellows, and you too, my poor dumb Clopin, pretty monsieur here will have the letter and the pearl in two days' time. Look to it that he never leaves this house at any minute from this time forth that you do not search him from top to toe. If he resists — ah, well, a pistol may go off accidentally, and things that Mauravania's king would give his life to keep hidden will come to light if any charge of murder is preferred. Monsieur the police spy, I wish you joy of your task."

"Madame, I *shall* take joy in it," Cleek replied. "But why should we talk of unpleasant things when the future looks so bright? Come, may we not give ourselves a pleasant evening? Look, there is a piano, and – Count, hold my puppy for me, and please see that no one feeds him at any time. I am starving him so that he may devour some of Clopin's parakeets, because I hate the sight of the little beasts. Thank you. Madame, do you like music? Listen, then; I'll sing you Mauravania's national anthem: 'God guard the throne; God shield the right!'" and, dropping down upon the seat before the open instrument, he did so.

That night was ever memorable at the Villa Irma, for the detective seemed somehow to have given place to the courtier, and so merry was his mood, so infectious his good nature, that even madame came under the spell of it. She sang with him, she even danced a Russian polka with him; she sat with him at dinner, and flirted with him in the salon afterward; and when the time came for her to retire, it was he who took her bedroom candle from the shelf and put in into her hand.

"Of a truth, you are a charming fellow, monsieur," she said, when he bent and kissed her hand. "What a pity you should be a police spy and upon so hopeless a case."

"Hopeless cases are my delight, madame. Believe me, I shall not fail."

"Only three days, remember, *cher ami* — only three days!"

"Madame is too kind. I have said it: two will do. On the morning of the third madame's passport will be ready and the Rainbow Pearl be in the royal jewellers' hands. A thousand pleasant dreams, *bon soir!*" And bowed her out and kissed his hand to her as she went up the stairs to bed.

III

Thrice during the next twenty-four hours Cleek, who seemed to have become so attached to the mongrel dog that he kept it under his arm continually, had reason to leave the house, and thrice was he seized by madame's henchmen, bundled unceremoniously into a convenient room, and searched to the very skin before he was suffered to pass beyond the threshold. And if so much as a pin had been hidden upon his person, it must have been discovered.

"You see, monsieur, how hopeless it is!" said the count despairfully. "One dare not rebel; one dare not lift a finger, or the woman speaks and his Majesty's ruin falls. Oh, the madness of that boast of yours! Only another twenty-four hours, only another day and then God help his Majesty!"

"God has helped him a great deal better than he deserves, count," replied Cleek. "By to-morrow night at ten o'clock be in the square of the Aquisola, please. Bring with you the passports of madame and her companions, also a detachment of the Royal

Guard, and his Majesty's cheque for the reward I am to receive."

"Monsieur! You really hope to get the things? You really do?"

"Oh, I do more than 'hope,' count, I have succeeded. I knew last night where both pearl and letter were. To-morrow night — ah, well, let to-morrow tell its own tale. Only be in the square at the hour I mention, and when I lift a lighted candle and pass it across the salon window, send the guard here with the passports. Let them remain outside, within sight, but not within range of hearing what is said and done. You alone are to enter, remember that."

"To receive the jewel and the letter?" eagerly. "Or, at least to have you point out the hiding-place of them?"

"No; we should be shot down like dogs if I undertook a mad thing like that."

"Then, monsieur, how are we to seize them? How get them into our possession, his Majesty and I?"

"From my hand, count; this hand which held them both before I went to bed last night."

"Monsieur!" The count fell back from him as if from some supernatural presence. "You found them? You held them? You took possession of them last night? How did you get them out of the house?"

"I have not done so yet."

"But can you? Oh, monsieur, wizard though you are, can you get them past her guards? Can you, monsieur, can you?"

"Watch for the light at the window, count. It will not be waved unless it is safe for you to come and the pearl is already out of the house."

"And the letter, monsieur, the damning letter?"

Cleek smiled one of his strange, inscrutable smiles.

"Ask me that to-morrow, count," he said. "You shall hear

something, you and madame, that will surprise you both," then twisted round on his heel and walked hurriedly away. And all that day and all that night he danced attendance upon madame, and sang to her, and handed her bedroom candle to her as he had done the night before, and gave back jest for jest and returned her merry badinage in kind.

Nor did he change in that when the fateful to-morrow came. From morning till night he was at her side, at her beck and call; doing nothing that was different from the doings of yesterday, save that at evening he locked the mongrel dog up in his room instead of carrying him about. And the dog, feeling its loneliness or, possibly, famishing, for he had given it not a morsel of food since he found it, howled and howled until the din became unbearable.

"Monsieur, I wish you would silence that beast or else feed it," said madame pettishly. "The howling of the wretched thing gets on my nerves. Give it some food for pity's sake."

"Not I," said Cleek. "Do you not remember what I said, madame? I am getting it hungry enough to eat one or perhaps all of Clopin's wretched little parakeets."

"You think they have to do with the hiding of the paper or the pearl, *cher ami*? Eh?"

"I am sure of it. He would not carry the beastly little things about for nothing."

"Ah, you are clever, you are very, very clever, monsieur," she made answer, with a laugh. "But he must begin his bird-eating quickly, that nuisance-dog, or it will be too late. See, it is already half-past nine; I retire to my bed in another hour and a half, as always, and then your last hope he is gone — z-zic! like that; for it will be the end of the second day, monsieur, and your promise not yet kept. Pestilence, monsieur," with a little outburst of temper, "do stop the little beast his howl. It is unbearable! I would you to sing to me like last night, but the noise of the dog is maddening."

"Oh, if it annoys you like that, madame," said Cleek, "I'll take him round to the stable and tie him up there, so we may have the song undisturbed. Your men will not want to search me, of course, when I am merely popping out and popping in again like that, I am sure?"

Nevertheless they did, for although they had heard and did not stir when he left the room and ran up for the dog, when he came down with it under his arm and made to leave the house, he was pounced upon, dragged into an adjoining apartment by half a dozen burly fellows, stripped to the buff, and searched, as the workers in a diamond mine are searched, before they suffered him to leave the house. There was neither a sign of a pearl nor a scrap of a letter to be found upon him, they made sure of that before they let him go.

"An enterprising lot, those lackeys of yours, madame," he said, when he returned from tying the dog up in the stable and rejoined her in the salon. "It will be an added pleasure to get the better of them, I can assure you."

"*Oui*, if you can!" she answered, with a mocking laugh. "Clopin, *cher ami*, your poor little parakeets are safe for the night, unless monsieur grows desperate and eats them for himself."

"Even that, if it were necessary to get the pearl, madame," said Cleek, with the utmost sang-froid. "Faugh!" looking at his watch, "a good twenty minutes wasted by the zealousness of those idiotic searchers of yours. Ten minutes to ten! Just time for one brief song. Let us make hay while the sun lasts, madame, for it goes down suddenly here in Mauravania; and for some of us it never comes up again!" Then, throwing himself upon the piano-seat, he ran his fingers across the keys and broke into the stately measures of the national anthem. And, of a sudden, while the song was yet in progress, the clock in the corridor jingled its musical chimes and struck the first note of the hour.

He jumped to his feet and lifted both hands above his head.

"Mauravania!" he cried. "Oh, Mauravania! For thee! For thee!" Then jumped to the mantelpiece, and, catching up a lighted candle, flashed it twice across the window's width, and broke again into the national hymn.

"Monsieur," cried out madame, "monsieur, what is the mean-ing of that? Have you lost your wits? You give a signal! For what? To whom?"

"To the guards of Mauravania's king, madame, in honour of his safe escape from you!" he made reply; then twitched back the window curtains until the whole expanse of glass was bared. "Look! do you see them, do you, Madame?" he said. "His Majesty of Mauravania sends Madame Tcharnovetski a command to leave his kingdom, since he no longer has cause to fear a wasp whose sting has been plucked out."

Her swift glance flashed to the fireplace, then to the corner where Clopin still sat with his jabbering parakeets, then flashed back to Cleek, and she laughed in his face.

"I think not, monsieur," she said, with a swaggering air. "Truly, I think not, my excellent friend."

"What a pity you only think so, madame! As for me – Ah, welcome, count, welcome a thousand times. The paper, my friend; you have brought the paper? Good! good! Quick, give it to me. Madame, your passport – yours and your people's. You leave Mauravania by the midnight train, and you have but little time to pack your effects. Your passport, madame, and your bed-room candle. Oh, yes, the paper is still round it, see!" slipping off a sheet of white notepaper that was wrapped round the full length of the candle from top to bottom, "but if you will examine it, madame, you will find it is blank. I burned the real letter the night before last when I put this in its place."

"You what?" she snapped; then caught the tube-shaped cov-ering he had stripped from the candle, uncurled it, and screamed.

"Blank, madame, quite blank, you see," said Cleek serenely. "For one so clever in other things, you should have been more careful. A little pinch of powder in the punch at dinner-time – just that – and on the first night, too! It was so easy afterward to get into your room, remove the real paper, and wrap the candle in a blank piece while you slept."

"You, you dog!" she snapped out viciously. "You drugged me?"

"Yes, madame; you and the one-eyed man as well! Oh, don't excite yourself; don't pull at the poor wretch like that. The glass eye will come out quite easily, but — I assure you there is only a small lump of beeswax in the socket now. I removed the Rainbow Pearl from poor Monsieur Clopin's blind eye ten minutes after I burnt the letter, madame, and it passed out of this house to-night! A clever idea to pick up a one-eyed pauper, madame, and hide the pearl in the empty socket of the lost eye, but it was too bad you had to supply a glass eye to keep it in, after the lid and the socket had withered and shrunk from so many years of empti- ness. It worried the poor man, madame; he was always feeling it, always afraid that the lump behind would force it out; and, what is an added misfortune for your plans, the glass shell did not allow you to see the change when the pearl vanished and the bit of beeswax took its place. Madame Tcharnovetski, your passport. I know enough of the King of Mauravania to be sure that your life will not be safe if you are not past the frontier before daybreak!"

* * * * *

"Monsieur le comte — no! I thank you, but I cannot wait to be presented to his Majesty, for I, too, leave Mauravania tonight, and, like madame yonder, return to other and more promising fields," said Cleek, an hour later, as he stood on the terrace of the Villa Irma and watched the slow progress down the moonlit ave- nue of the carriage which was bearing Madame Tcharnovetski and her effects to the railway station. "Give me the cheque, please; I have earned that, and there is good use for it. I thank you, count. Now do an act of charity, my friend: give the little dog in the stable a good meal, and then have a surgeon chloro- form him into a peaceful and a merciful death. They will find the Rainbow Pearl in his intestines when they come to dissect the body. I starved him, count, starved him purposely, poor little wretch, so that he would be hungry enough to snap at anything in the way of food and bolt it instantly. Tonight, when I went up to take him out to the stable, a thick smearing of beef extract over the surface of the pearl was sufficient; he swallowed it in a gulp!

For a double reason, count, there should be a cur quartered on the royal arms of this country after tonight."

His voice dropped off into silence. The carriage containing madame had swung out through the gateway, and its shadow no longer blotted the broad, unbroken space of moonlit avenue. He turned and looked far out, over the square of the Aquisola, along the light-lined esplanade, to the palace gates and the fluttering flag that streamed against the sky above and beyond them.

"Oh, Mauravania!" he said. "An Englishman's heritage! Dear country, how beautiful! My love to your Queen, my prayers for you."

"Monsieur!" exclaimed the count, "monsieur, what juggle is this? Your face is again the face of that other night, the face that stirs memory yet does not rivet it. Monsieur, speak, I beg of you. What are you? Who are you?"

"Cleek," he made answer. "Just Cleek! It will do. Oh, Mauravania, dear land of desolated hopes, dear grave of murdered joys!"

"Monsieur!"

"Hush! Let me alone. There are things too sacred; and this – " His hands reached outward as if in benediction; his face, upturned, was as a face transfigured, and something that shone as silver gleamed in the corner of his eye. "Mauravania!" he said. "Oh, Mauravania! My country – my people – good-bye!"

"Monsieur! Dear Heaven – *Majesty!*"

Then came a rustling sound, and when Cleek had mastered himself and looked down, a figure with head uncovered knelt on one knee at his feet.

"Get up, count," he said, with a little shaky laugh. "I appreciate the honour, but your fancy is playing you a trick. I tell you I never set foot in Mauravania before, my friend."

"I know, I know. How should you, Majesty, when it was as a child at Queen Karma's breast Mauravania last saw – Don't leave like this! Majesty! Majesty! 'God guard the right' — the pearl and the kingdom are here."

"Wrong, my good friend. The kingdom is there, where you found me in England; and so, too, is the pearl. For there is no kingdom like the kingdom of love, count, and no pearl like a good woman."

"But, Majesty – "

"Good-night, count, and many thanks for your hospitality. You are a little upset to-night, but no doubt you will be all right again in the morning. I will walk to the station and alone, if it is all the same to you."

"Majesty!"

"Dreams, count, dreams. The riddle is solved, my friend. Good luck to your country and good-bye!"

And, setting his back to the palace and the lights and the fluttering flag, and his face to the land that held her, turned and went his way — to the West — to England — to those things which are higher than crowns and better than sceptres and more precious than thrones and ermine.